The Farm

Author.HP.Moore@gmail.com

ISBN: 979-8-9928488-1-6 (Paperback)
ISBN: 979-8-9928488-0-9 (eBook)

To the ones I hold close – Henry, Emma, Matt, and Indiana.

And to Atticus. We miss you.

CHAPTER I

Dust billowed into dirty brown clouds as the pickup rambled down the two-lane road. Once a vivid shade of "crimson red," the truck was now so heavily rusted that its brown-tinged paint nearly disappeared into the fog of dirt. It jolted and groaned with each bump along the drive.

Bryan leaned back in the passenger side, staring out of the smudged side window. Outside, during the occasional moments when the dust dispersed, he saw the brilliant white fluff of cotton surrounding the road. Clearly leftover from some forgotten time, the rows of cotton were no longer neat little lines but rather grew wild and tangled throughout the fields.

Bryan was pretty sure his great-grandfather (or maybe it was his great-great-grandfather, or his great uncle perhaps – one of those distant, now barely memorable relatives) had farmed cotton. Mama kept a wisp of cotton on the mantle, and he knew that she had told him why, but come to think of it he could not remember at all. It meant something to her, and that was enough. He and Winnie had knocked it off the mantle more than once while playing, likely too roughly, in the living room. Mama would come through, see it on the floor, pick it up and smile at it, like she and the cotton shared some sort of inside joke, and place it gently back on the dustless, cotton-shaped spot on the mantle where it had lain as long as Bryan could remember.

The cotton disappeared into a billow of dust, and the next time the air cleared Bryan saw open fields. Patches of thick weeds mixed in with straggly grasses. A dandelion or evening primrose pushed its head up from the suffocating weeds from time to time, adding a pop of color amidst the carpet of green.

Houses and barns spotted the fields as infrequently as the flowers. A dilapidated two-story farmhouse stood solemn as the truck passed by. Its white-painted walls were chipping and dropping in little flakes onto the dirt below, like an out-of-place summer snow. The imposing columns mounted onto the expansive wrap-around porch were starting to lean to the left, as the weight from the splitting awning became too much to bear. Shingles were strewn about the yard, leaving tiny holes atop the roof, like so many missing teeth.

A brown and white coonhound lay motionless on the porch. The dog blended in perfectly with the aging house, only alerting the world to his presence when he gingerly lifted his head to gaze at the passing truck. His ears pricked slightly as his clouded eyes turned in the direction of the road. Finding no cause for concern, the hound lowered his head and resumed his slumber.

As Bryan was considering whether the hound was the only soul living in the farmhouse, he suddenly realized that his father was talking to him. From the pitch and pace of his voice, Bryan could tell that Pa had been going for some time and was deep into some or other subject. Bryan took a moment to focus in on Pa's voice, but he found it difficult to make out any words and instead heard only a monotone drone, much like the muted adults in a Charlie Brown cartoon.

Bryan glanced at his father. Pa's thick, leathery hands nearly engulfed the seemingly small steering wheel on the rattling truck. He was tickled by whatever he was saying, as his mouth pulled to one side in a sideways grin as he spoke. Pa had his window slightly cracked, and the incoming wind whipped his thick hair up and backward, making a slightly longer strand on top wiggle back and forth, as if waving. His rust-colored hair almost perfectly matched the truck he was driving, with the veins of gray winding through even matching the sprawling cracks in the truck's rusted paint.

Bryan was tall at around six feet, but Pa towered nearly a foot above him. Bryan wondered if he had always been so large or if he had continued to grow all of his life, and if Bryan, too, would one day be such a giant of a man. Pa's features were all exaggerated ones of Bryan's. Bryan was thick and solid for his age, but Pa was as broad as any doorway and often had to stoop when he went through openings. He tanned easily and was always a solid shade darker than Bryan at any time of the year, even during the peak of winter, when Bryan's own tan started to lighten and fade. A few thick wrinkles ran across his vast forehead, like tracks leading from a trailhead hidden in his hair. Veins protruded from his arms, pushing outward as if there were no room left for them in the man's tree-like limbs.

Pa continued talking, turning to Bryan from time to time with a chuckle. His light blue eyes locked onto Bryan's slightly dimmer blue eyes. He paused his talking.

"You okay?" Pa asked.

Bryan pulled his mouth to one side. He suddenly wished he had driven himself.

Pa took that as answer enough and continued. "Hey I know this isn't what you want, bud. It's just something for now. Who knows what you'll be doing at the end of the summer. You know? This is just a start."

What you'll be doing at the end of the summer. Bryan turned the words over in his head. What he *should* be doing is starting State. Not just starting, but starting on a full ride. He did not know a lot about college, but he knew enough to know that he was missing out on what would have been the time of his life. Damn fucking leg.

Pa turned off onto a side road. The fields surrounding the road had lost most of their green and were becoming more and more covered in shades of brown, as dirt and dried up clumps of weeds carpeted the ground. A row of six sagging trailers were the only homes Bryan noticed. Two had crudely built porches attached to them. A third had a heap of boards in front of it that appeared to be the remains of a porch. A black and white pit bull-type dog was chained behind one of the trailers. He sat in a dry circle of dirt, attached with a logging chain at least double his weight to a plastic igloo-style doghouse. An overturned five-gallon bucket lay near the dog. His short-cropped ears flicked as the truck drove by, but he remained otherwise motionless.

In the distance, Bryan saw the farm. From the outside, the four long metal buildings did not resemble a farm but rather some secret military base where government scientists performed shady experiments – alien autopsies or mind control perhaps. Bryan smiled at the thought.

Pa slowed and turned down the long driveway to the farm. White dust rose from the gravel as the truck bumped along over it. Pa stopped the truck in front of the first metal building.

"Well, here we are," Pa said.

Bryan pressed his lips together and opened the truck's passenger door. As they were pulling in, the farm had looked abandoned. No other cars were present, and not a soul was anywhere to be seen. As soon as he stepped out of the truck, however, a thick bear of a man lumbered over. He seemed to appear out of nowhere, and he moved briskly over to the truck. He wore jeans and a t-shirt that, while perhaps once white, was almost fully coated in a reddish-brown dirt. He was not nearly as tall as Pa, but what he lacked in height, he made up for in breadth.

"Hey Hank," Pa called, raising his hand and giving a slight grin.

"James," Hank responded, nodding and then turning to the side and spitting out a thick black wad of tobacco.

"Hank, this is my son, Bryan." Pa motioned to Bryan.

Hank raised his dark eyes to meet Bryan's and gave him a slight nod. Bryan met Hank's gaze but said nothing.

Pa glanced from Hank to Bryan and, finding that no one seemed willing to speak, he decided it was best to fill the silence. "I really appreciate you taking him on for the summer, Hank. I'm sure he'll be a good hand for you." He said the last part with a chuckle. There was nothing particularly funny about it, but he had the habit of giving a little laugh when he felt uncomfortable.

Bryan decided the least he could do was make an attempt to put Pa at ease. "Thank you for having me, Mr. Brewer," he addressed Hank.

Hank pulled his mouth into a slight smile. He spat again. "No trouble at all. We just lost a man. Mexican. Couldn't speak a word of English but he worked hard. Then one day he was up and gone. That's how those wetbacks are. Here one day; gone the next. Got the urge to swim back across the damn river, I guess."

Bryan furrowed his brow and looked down. An appropriate response to Hank's comment escaped him.

Bryan heard a door slam and looked up to see a younger man approaching. The boy looked to be around Bryan's age. He had a short and slender yet stocky build. He wore jeans with holes in each knee and a black shirt sporting a Mountain Dew logo with the words "Do the Dew." The shoelaces on both of his boots were untied. His dirty blonde hair was sticking to his head, apparently from sweat, and he continually wiped at the overgrown bangs that kept falling into his eyes.

Hank motioned to the boy as he approached. "Justin will show you around."

Justin grinned at Bryan. "You ready?"

Bryan glanced at Pa.

"I'll be back for you at the end of the day," Pa said. "I've got some work to do this side of town today. Hank, while I'm here, you got anything that needs my attention?"

"As a matter of fact, I do." Hank motioned for Pa to follow him, and they walked off toward one of the more distant metal buildings. Bryan heard Hank saying something about a fan as they walked off.

Pa was an electrician by trade, but he had found over the years that he needed to be a Jack of all trades to really make a living in Ashfield. He had worked as an electrician for the paper company for fourteen years, but when the company heads found that Ashfield was no longer a lucrative location for them, they made the quick decision to pull up stakes, quietly lay off 400 employees, and get out of Dodge without either a "thank you" or a "go fuck yourself." Since then, Pa had managed by taking odd jobs as either an electrician or a general handyman. He sometimes had to travel over an hour to get to a job, but, with the help of Mama's income, he had managed to make enough to keep the family going.

Justin slapped a hand on Bryan's shoulder. "Come on, man. Let's take a little tour."

Bryan forced a smile and followed Justin to the first metal building. He watched as Justin used his full weight to pull the heavy metal door open. He stepped back and held the door for Bryan. "Ladies first," he grinned.

Bryan furrowed his brow slightly, eyeing Justin. He stepped through the door. The summer heat outside was intense, but the sweltering wall of heat he felt when he entered the building was like a blow to the face. He felt sweat immediately bead up on his forehead. Accompanying the heat was a thick stench that was almost tangible. The acrid odor crawled up through his nostrils and into his mouth. He felt sick and focused on keeping his composure.

The contrast from the bright sunlight outside to the dim indoor lighting made it nearly impossible for him to see when he entered the building. Bryan squinted around to try to get his bearings. As his eyes adjusted, he was able to make out a small room that appeared to be divided into different sections.

Just a few feet inside the door, he saw a long wooden bench that ran the full width of the room, flanked at one end by a set of six metal lockers. A pair of tattered boots had been left on the floor in front of the bench.

Justin plopped down on the bench. "You can put your wallet or keys or whatever you have in one of the lockers." He paused. "But I'm guessing you don't have any keys, since you're riding with Daddy."

Bryan shot him an annoyed look. Justin was grinning again. *I'd like to slap that stupid grin off his face.*

Bryan realized his face must have betrayed his thoughts.

"Man, I'm just kidding," Justin said. "Just put your stuff over there."

Bryan opened one of the lockers and put his wallet on the metal interior. He glanced at Justin. "Phone, too?"

"Yeah," Justin replied. "Hank's always worried we'll have some fucking PETA spy in here taking photos of the animals." He was grinning again.

"PETA?" Bryan looked at him blankly.

"You know," Justin said. "Like, the animal people. They don't eat meat."

"Oh," Bryan said. He had no idea what Justin was talking about, and he did not really care.

Justin patted the bench beside him. "So plop down here and take your boots off, but don't let your feet touch the floor once your boots are off."

Bryan did as Justin instructed, and Justin did the same. Justin then swung his socked feet over the bench and sat facing away from the door. Bryan copied Justin and found that on the other side of the bench were several pairs of black rubber boots.

"What size are you?" Justin asked.

"Eleven," Bryan replied.

Justin picked up a few of the boots, then he handed a pair to Bryan. "Put these on, then wash your hands." He pointed to a sink on this side of the bench, mounted on the right side of the room.

Bryan looked down at the boots. They had a black substance, likely mud or shit, caked to the outside edges. He put them on and trudged over to the sink. Little flakes of the mud-shit substance fell to the floor as he walked. The brown-tinged sink looked like it could use a washing itself, and the soap in the wall dispenser next to the sink was a thick, slimy pink substance that smelled not at all like soap but rather like a mixture between bleach and bubblegum. Bryan raised his upper lip slightly as he washed his hands in the filthy sink, then he dried them off on an even dirtier towel to his left, seemingly defeating any cleanliness that the washing might have provided.

Bryan turned back around, and Justin handed him a pair of thick brown coveralls. "Okay, last thing. Put these on. They won't really keep your clothes clean, and they sure as shit won't keep you from carrying home the smell, but it's supposed to help keep the animals from getting sick, so you don't carry in germs from outside."

Bryan slid the coveralls on over his clothes, and Justin did the same with another set. About six feet ahead there was a wall with a solid metal door in the middle. Justin waited until Bryan was dressed and then opened the door. "Okay, this way." He stepped through.

Bryan stepped through the doorway and immediately stopped. The smell on entering the first room had been strong, but the wave of putrid stench that filled his nostrils as he crossed the threshold was instantly nauseating. He momentarily felt faint and reached forward for something to hold, struggling to see exactly what was in front of him in the even darker interior room. He stumbled into Justin, who helped him keep his balance, chuckling the entire time.

"It's a lot to take in the first time," Justin tittered, "but you'll definitely get used to it. Won't be no big thing after a day or two."

Bryan was unable to respond. He was intensely focused on not vomiting. He felt his blood rising to his skin. He opened his mouth to breathe, but it seemed that there was no oxygen to be had, only the thick, suffocating air that stuffed itself down his throat. As his body screamed for relief, he stayed focused on maintaining his composure. *I'll be damned if I give this jackass anything else to laugh about.*

He was finally able to pull his head up and look forward. Justin was watching him but, for once, was silent. Bryan initially had trouble making out what was in front of him, as this room was darker than the last, but as his eyes adjusted, and as his body relaxed, the sights and sounds of the room became clearer.

The room was long and narrow, running what appeared to be the length of the building. The floor was slatted concrete, and there was a walkway running directly down the middle of the building. To either side were pens full of pigs. The pens were composed of metal bars spaced three or four inches apart to contain the pigs. Each pen appeared to hold only one pig, which, Bryan thought, was a good thing, as the pens were so narrow that most of the pigs' sides rubbed against the side bars of the pens. Some pigs were lying down at contorted angles, with either their snouts or limbs squished up against one or more sides of the pens. Other pigs were standing, apparently facing the same direction into which the pig had been put in the pen, as there appeared to be no way for any of the pigs to turn around.

On the whole, the room was relatively quiet, with a few grunts or snorts rising up occasionally from the mass of bodies. An ever-present whooshing noise could be heard from several large fans at one end of the building. As Bryan moved forward down the walkway, following Justin, one pig released a blood curdling scream. The sound was so shocking that Bryan jumped and took a quick gasp, bringing in a mouthful of thick acrid air. He spat the air back out, flinging saliva in front of him.

Justin was a couple of steps ahead and had doubled over with laughter. "I guess you've not been around a lot of pigs, huh?" He stopped laughing long enough to grin.

"Not really, no," Bryan replied. "Why the hell did it scream like that?"

"That's just what they do," Justin said, moving down the walkway in the direction of the scream. "It doesn't mean anything. They just do that."

"Jesus." Bryan took a second to scan the pigs. He was not sure which one had let out the offensive noise, as they all appeared more or less the same at the moment, standing or lying listlessly in their stalls.

"It was probably this one," Justin said, apparently reading Bryan's mind. He was pointing at a sow further down the line, in a stall to the right. She was shuffling around as much as the pen allowed. As she lurched back and forth, her sides squished into the metal bars on each side of the pen, leaving red rub marks. She was snorting more than the other pigs and occasionally releasing a slightly louder squeal.

As Justin approached the pig, she started frantically gnawing at the front bars of the pen. The grinding of teeth against the metal made Bryan's skin tingle and crawl, and he shuddered at the sound. He imagined fingernails on a blackboard. *No, not fingernails – more like the finger bones grinding into the blackboard.*

Justin stood in front of the pig. Her squeals increased in volume and frequency, and she released another one of the deafening screams Bryan had heard earlier. Bryan did not jump this time, but he closed his eyes slightly, as the scream cut through his head.

Justin kicked the metal bars at the front of the cage. "Eh, get back. Get back!" The pig, obviously not taking the message, squealed louder and gnawed more frantically. During one of the kicks, Justin's foot collided with the pig's snout, which was sticking through the bars. Blood rushed from her nose and pooled on the floor. Justin ceased his kicking and looked at his boot, which was now covered in crimson droplets. He cast an annoyed glance at the pig and then turned back to Bryan.

"She's probably about ready to move to farrowing," Justin said.

Bryan looked at him blankly.

"Ah geez," Justin said, chuckling and slapping a hand on Bryan's shoulder. "You don't know a damn thing about pigs."

Bryan said nothing. He was right. Bryan knew nothing about pigs and did not care to know anything about pigs.

"Look," Justin said, pointing around the room. "These girls are all pregnant. That's why they're here. This is gestation. When they're almost ready to give birth, we'll move 'em to farrowing. That's where they give birth. Make sense?"

Bryan nodded.

Justin grinned. "I'm guessing there weren't a lot of job options for you, huh?"

Bryan looked down, feeling his face get hot.

"Don't worry," Justin added. "It's better than dealing with the shitheads at Wal-mart. You'll get it. Come on."

Justin continued down the seemingly interminable aisle. Bryan followed. The wave of stench thickened as Bryan moved further down the aisle. Evident on either side of the walkway was the cause of the offending odor, as each pig lay or stood in two to three inches of her own waste. Despite the grated floors, which would likely allow at least some of the waste to fall through the cracks, the pigs wallowed in thick pools of urine and feces, squishing between their toes, or in fact their hooves, and covering their abdomens and even parts of their faces. Bryan imagined the mud-based facial masks his mother sometimes wore at night. *I imagine the sting of ammonia in this dung heap would do wonders for your pores.*

Justin was pointing out and explaining the automatic waterers and feeders as they continued. Bryan attempted to half listen as they went, struggling to draw his eyes from the captive subjects on either side. As dimly lit as the building was, Bryan could make out the beady eyes that rose to look at him as he walked by. Most of the pigs, even those who lay on their sides with their heads on the floor, cast him a suspicious glance as he passed. Bryan dropped his gaze whenever he made eye contact with one of the beasts, feeling slight embarrassment for the pigs, as if he had caught them at a moment when they had not had time to tidy up.

Justin reached the end of the line and turned back to Bryan. "So that's gestation. Now when they are about to give birth, they move to farrowing – this way."

Justin slid a heavy metal door open and stepped through. Bryan had felt sure that they had already traversed the full length of the building, but as he stepped through the doorway, he saw another walkway ahead that seemed to be at least as long as the one he had just traveled, with even more pigs to either side.

The sounds in this room were discernibly louder, with dozens – or hundreds, even thousands perhaps – of small grunts and squeals filling the air. The room appeared similar to what Justin had called "gestation," with metal pens to either side of the walkway. Only here, there were not only sows but also piglets. Bryan observed that most of the adult pigs in this area appeared to be nursing mothers. As he passed down the center aisle, most of the sows were lying on one side in pens no larger than their bodies, with the metal bars on each side of the pen pressing into their bulging sides, similar to the gestation area. Groups of piglets were penned next to each nursing mother and suckled from the mother's teats through openings in the metal bars between them.

The piglets were releasing the small snorts, grunts, and squeals that Bryan had heard upon entering. Some were milling about in their tiny enclosures, while others tugged and sucked at their mother's teats. They were speckled with brownish stains that Bryan suspected to be their own feces, and the smell in this room was as palpable as the last. Even so, Bryan felt a smile rising on his face as he stared at the awkward, wobbly-legged piglets. He felt the urge to pick one up and examine its tiny pink ears, but he refrained, acutely aware that Justin, for all his seemingly idiotic grinning, had kept a sharp eye on him throughout their venture, and he did not care to give him any fodder for further banter.

In any case, the smile slowly slid off of Bryan's face as he noticed a piglet who lay perfectly still in one of the pens. Bryan thought, or perhaps hoped, that the piglet was sleeping, but the slightly flattened posture and blueish hue of the piglet clearly showed that this was not the case. Another one of the piglets walked over to the still one and nudged it with its snout, but the motionless piglet did not respond.

"Hey," Bryan motioned to Justin. "Is that one okay?" He pointed.

Justin looked at the piglet. "Oh, yeah. I mean, it's dead, but that happens. That's part of what we'll do every day. We'll go through and get out all the little dead ones. Here –" Justin reached into the pen, plucked out the dead piglet, and flung it onto the center walkway. "Just pull 'em out and put 'em in the middle here. We'll come back through later and throw 'em away."

Justin looked at Bryan's blank face, and his grin returned. He chuckled. "It ain't no big thing. You have a dozen or more little piggies in a litter. You gotta expect to lose a few of 'em."

As Bryan continued down the aisle, he noticed more of the motionless piglets. One such piglet had its abdomen torn open, and another piglet, evidently a sibling, appeared to be eating the contents. Bryan again felt his stomach turning and reached out for the top railing on a pen to steady himself.

"Yeah, they'll eat just about anything," Justin said, eyeing Bryan. "They're not wasteful animals, I'll tell you that." He grinned.

Justin completed his tour of the barn. "We move the piglets to the other barns once they're weaned. We can check those out later. You'll mostly be in this barn to start. I'll be in here with you, and we have one more guy, Jeffrey. He'll be in soon."

Justin said they might as well get started. "So the first thing you'll want to do every day is check and make sure the feeders and waterers are working. The feed ain't such a big deal. They'll let you know if they're not getting fed, but you gotta check the water." He leaned over one pen and touched the automatic water nipple inside the front gate. "Sometimes these things get jammed up. That dumbass you're replacing wasn't any good at checking things like that. Came in one day and half the piglets were dead in three pens – one sow, too. Turned out the waterers were all jammed up, so the sows hadn't been getting any water, and the piglets weren't getting any milk. I said, 'What the hell, amigo?' He just looked at me and shrugged, like, 'Oops.'" Justin scoffed and added an extra "dumbass."

Justin and Bryan went through and checked the feed and water. Bryan found two water nipples that were not working. He showed them to Justin, who fiddled with them momentarily, then cleaned them with something from a spray bottle.

"Vinegar," he said. "It helps with the hard water buildup that can jam 'em up."

After that, they went through and performed what Justin ingeniously called the "dead collection," pulling out the dead piglets from each pen and plopping them down on the center walkway. Bryan was initially hesitant about picking up the small and still pink piglets. He could not recall ever having touched something dead. As he tentatively picked up the first one, his fingers felt the cold, stiff nature of the body, and he could not suppress a shudder. The frigid skin offered a sharp contrast to the light pink coloring of the piglet. He laid the piglet in the center aisle and looked up to see Justin watching him. Justin gave a wry smile and flung another dead piglet into the walkway next to the one Bryan had set down.

He moved down one side of the aisle, as Justin moved down the other. Justin moved quickly and with the movements of one who had completed this routine many times before. Bryan picked along slowly, looking into each pen with dread and hoping, most often in vain, that there would be no still little bodies in the oncoming pen.

As Bryan was pausing to gaze at the collection of piglet bodies littering the walkway, he saw the barn's end doorway open and a man enter. The man was tall and lean and wearing the same coveralls as Justin and Bryan. He had dark, short-cropped hair speckled with flecks of gray, and he wore a five o'clock shadow that looked like it had been growing for several days. Most prominent about this man was his manner of walking. He seemed to not have the energy or perhaps the inclination to fully raise his feet, so with each step he lumbered along, dragging his feet and making a distinctive shuffling sound.

As the man made his slow trudge down the walkway, he wore a grin that rivaled even Justin's. The dense stench and mounds of small piglet bodies apparently brought out quite a jovial nature in the farm workers.

"Big J," Justin called. The so-called "Big J" grinned to the point where the grin threatened to overtake his head and slash his face in two.

"Bryan, this is Jeffrey." Justin pointed to the man as he shuffled closer. "Jeffrey, this is our new guy, Bryan. He's James' kid."

Jeffrey grinned with wide, bright eyes and bobbed his head up and down. "Nice to meet you," he said in a thick, slightly slurred manner of speaking. "We all like James. He's right much help around here."

Bryan gave a polite smile. "Nice to meet you."

"Jeffrey'll work with us in this barn about half the time and then in the nursery barn, with the weaners, the rest of the time." Justin explained.

Jeffrey bobbed his head again in lively agreement. Bryan wondered if something was just slightly off with the man. His manner of grinning and nodding, along with the wide-eyed gaze he wore, seemed a bit child-like.

Justin caught Jeffrey up on the current status of the "dead collection," and Jeffrey joined in to help. As he went down the line, flinging out the little dead bodies like rotten potatoes, he whistled the tune to a song Bryan had never heard. Unlike Justin, who would lean far over the pen railings and contort his body every possible way to avoid having to enter the pen, Jeffrey frequently unlatched a pen's front gate and entered the side with the piglets, moving slowly as he went. Despite his shuffling, he occasionally must have stepped on a piglet's toe or tail, as a scream would rise from the pen in which he was present. "Oh excuse me, little pig," he would say to the offended piglet, grinning and shuffling along, more often than not landing on another piglet and starting the painful interaction all over again.

At one point, Jeffrey paused as he was bending down in a pen, and Bryan heard him say, "Oh poor baby, you're still hanging on." Bryan looked up to see Jeffrey gently carrying a limp piglet out of a pen. He would have thought the piglet dead, if not for a slight kicking motion made by its back left leg. Jeffrey gave the piglet a little pat on the head, then he grabbed the piglet's two hind legs with his right hand, swung the piglet by its legs behind his shoulder, and thrust the piglet forward and down, apparently with all his might, slamming the piglet's head into the concrete walkway and sending blood splattering up.

Bryan took in a quick gasp of air in reaction, feeling his mouth fall open. Jeffrey picked the piglet up, gave it a quick once over, and then let it fall to the walkway with the other dead bodies.

Bryan looked wildly at Justin, who was carefully watching Bryan's reaction to the scene. "You'll find 'em like that sometimes," he said. "Best thing to do is just what Big J did – give 'em a good knock on the head. That'll usually do it. Can't let 'em suffer."

Bryan forced himself to close his mouth and give a slight nod. Justin smiled and went back to work.

The day continued on in much the same manner. They took a short break for lunch, during which Justin, Bryan, and Jeffrey – the "three amigos," as Justin had already taken to calling them – sat at a covered picnic table outside. As they were eating, Hank walked by in the distance with another man who appeared to be in his mid-fifties and nearly as hardy and leathered as Bryan's own Pa. The man cast a mildly interested glance in their direction, as Hank said something to him and motioned their way.

"Who's that?" Bryan asked Justin.

"That's Wayne," he said. "He works mostly in the barns with the weaners and feeders." Justin sneered in Wayne's direction, adding, "Which is good because he's a son of a bitch."

At that, Jeffrey laughed a big, goofy laugh. Bryan looked at Justin, but Justin said nothing further on the subject.

They spent the latter half of the day checking the pigs again and weighing most of the piglets. Justin said they used the weights to see when the pigs could be weaned and moved to the nursery barn. He wrote the weights on a sheet of paper attached to a clipboard on each pen, and he marked a star next to the piglets with lower weights than the others.

Justin then showed Bryan how to dispose of the dead piglets that were still lying in the center walkway of the barn. They went through and collected them in a wheelbarrow, and then they took the wheelbarrow out a back door, which could only be exited and not entered. Justin wheeled the little bodies behind the barn and dumped them out next to a bin that was already overflowing with what Bryan initially thought was trash. On closer examination, however, he found that the bin was full of the dead and rotting corpses of other pigs and piglets. Necrotic pig skin was rotting in the heat of the sun and sluffing off in the bin, revealing a colorful array of muscle, ligaments, tendons, and bones.

"Trash man comes and empties this twice a week, so it gets pretty full sometimes," Justin said, in apparent explanation of the mound of pig pieces and bodies surrounding the bin.

Jeffrey brought out another load of piglets, along with what appeared to be a dead sow, and heaved them out beside the bin. One of the piglets, apparently having passed somewhat earlier than the rest, was so hardened with rigor mortis that its right front leg stuck straight up in the air where it fell on the ground. Jeffrey, noticing the little leg pointing up at the sky, was overcome with a chuckle that he seemed unable to control.

"He's pointing at something!" Jeffrey cried. He looked at Justin, who returned a wide grin. Encouraged, Jeffrey added, addressing the corpse, "Hey buddy, what do you see? What's that? I can't quite hear you!" Jeffrey shook with laughter until tears rolled down his face. "Ah," he said, wiping his face. Then he turned, still laughing, and shuffled back to the barn.

Justin noted Bryan's frown. "Hey, the first day can be rough. Why don't we grab a drink? Take a little break from pig shit. Day's about done anyway." He grinned.

Bryan flushed slightly. "I, I don't think I can get served anywhere. I'm eighteen."

Justin grinned wider than ever. "Now that's where you're wrong. I know just the place. I'm only twenty myself. Just let your daddy know that I'll get you home."

Bryan hesitated. He did not relish the thought of spending any more time with Justin, but the idea of seeing Pa and answering a hundred and one questions about how the day went did not sound appealing either. "Okay," he said.

"Alright," Justin exclaimed, slapping him on the back. "Let's go."

CHAPTER II

The interior of Justin's pickup truck had more than one empty beer can lying on the floor, and Bryan hesitated on opening the door to get in.

"Oh, you can just step on those," Justin said, mistaking the reason for Bryan's hesitation. Bryan pushed the cans aside and climbed in.

The buckle on the passenger side seat belt was so rusted that it would not properly fasten. Bryan worked at it for a moment and then let it go, resigning himself to whatever lay ahead. Justin did not attempt to fasten his own seat belt. He slid into the driver's seat carelessly, flashed a grin at Bryan, and pushed the gas with enough force to make the truck hop forward with a jerk.

Justin took the road out from the farm at a much faster speed than Pa had, causing the little Ford Ranger to buck and bounce on each encounter with a pothole. He shifted the manual transmission roughly, which Bryan thought perhaps he was doing on purpose, leading to more jerks and jolts as they careened down the road.

"So how was your first day slinging pig shit?" Justin asked with a grin.

Bryan, who was beginning to wonder if going with Justin was a mistake, muttered a garbled answer, which most closely resembled "fine."

Justin laughed. "Well, you did better than some I've seen. We had a guy last summer – he lasted about an hour. Came in and started puking all over the floor, holding his stomach and gagging so much he couldn't talk. He just kept on puking until he turned around and ran back out the door. That was it. Shortest work day I've ever seen." He chuckled again.

"How long have you been there?" Bryan asked.

"Well about four years officially," Justin answered. "But I've been helping since I was a kid. School wasn't my thing, so the day I turned sixteen I went in, dropped my books on the desk, gave my teacher a little salute, and walked out the door. Best decision I ever made."

Justin turned down a narrow dirt road, which, to Bryan, did not at all seem like one that would lead to any sort of business establishment. Even so, they were not on it long when Bryan saw a neon sign illuminating the outline of a fist grasping a beer mug. Under the image were the words "Rancher's Respite." The bar was a small metal building that, if not for the neon sign, could have been mistaken for a storage building. There were a handful of cars out front. Justin pulled in.

Justin led the way with notable familiarity, raising his hand to give a slight wave to the bartender – a broad, middle-aged man with a ruddy complexion – as he entered. The bartender returned Justin's wave with a slight nod.

They seated themselves in a corner booth. The inside lighting, in sharp contrast to the overpoweringly bright neon sign outside, was low and dim, making it hard to get a good view of any patron's face more than two or three feet away.

Justin slouched back in the booth and gave a slight wave, apparently to a waiter. Bryan heard a shuffling sound and looked up to see Jeffrey. He had changed shirts but was wearing the same pants and boots from earlier.

Bryan stared. He and Justin had come straight to the bar from the farm. How Jeffrey – who, from what Bryan had seen, did not move as if he were in any particular hurry – had possibly had time to change shirts and beat them to the bar was beyond Bryan's comprehension. He felt his mouth fall slightly open.

Justin and Jeffrey grinned. "Hey Big J," Justin said as Jeffrey approached. "Can you start us with a couple of Coronas and two shots of the house whiskey?" He raised his eyebrows at Bryan. "Sound good?"

Bryan looked back and forth between Jeffrey and Justin. He gave a slight nod. Jeffrey left to get the order.

"He won't get in trouble for serving us?" Bryan asked.

"No way," Justin said. "I mean, it's handy that Jeffrey works here, but if you work a farm you get served pretty much wherever you go in town. People know these are shit jobs but the farms bring in some money, so the least they can do is serve you a drink."

Jeffrey returned with the drinks and took their food order. Justin raised his glass of whiskey. "Here's to your first day," he said. Bryan returned the toast, and they both drank. Justin immediately followed the toast by an order of tequila shots.

"So what are you doing at the farm, little B?" Justin asked, leaning forward. "Are you that hard up for a job?"

Bryan furrowed his brow and glanced down, rolling his empty shot glass between his fingers. "Well, I had other plans," he paused. "But they didn't work out."

"Ah," said Justin. "Other plans, eh?" He finished his beer and ordered another.

"Yeah, I, I had a scholarship to State. A football scholarship. I should have started this fall. But I blew out my damn knee and" – Bryan raised one hand whimsically in the air – "that was that."

Justin gave him a blank look. "Well shit, man. That sucks."

"Yeah," Bryan gave a light laugh. "Yeah it does."

"Well damn." Justin took another shot, and, in the apparent need to commiserate Bryan's misfortune, ordered two more.

"Yeah," Bryan continued. "I have no fucking idea what I'm gonna do, but I can tell you it's not this shit." He glanced at Justin quickly. "I mean, no offense. It's just not for me I think."

Justin gave an overly loud laugh and slapped the table. "Ha! It's not for anyone! But, you know, sometimes you just start something and, before you know it, it's just what you do." He gave Bryan a direct stare. "But I got plans, too. I'm getting out. I won't be doing that shit forever." He leaned back and glanced off, apparently distracted.

"Yeah?" Bryan was starting to feel the liquor.

"Yeah," Justin replied, returning to the conversation. "Yeah, I've been saving up. I won't be there another year. I'm just waiting for the right time."

Bryan eyed Justin, wondering how realistic that statement was. He had lost count of the shots and was starting to struggle to follow the conversation. Justin was at least three drinks ahead of him but did not seem to be slowed in the least by the alcohol.

At some point, Jeffrey shuffled over with the food, threw them a grin, and then went on to other tables.

Bryan's eyes followed Jeffrey as he went. He shuffled along, from table to table, grinning and taking orders. At times he would stop and release an ear-piercing chuckle at something that someone had said. A patron or two started at the sound, but others, possibly regulars, simply smiled at one another.

Bryan turned back to Justin. "Is he," Bryan started, nodding in Jeffrey's direction. "Is he, you know?"

Justin laughed. "Is he all there? Ha! I mean he's not gonna be flying rockets into space any time soon, but he gets along okay." Justin watched Jeffrey as he shuffled through the bar. "He also delivers pizzas when he's not working here. He has to take care of his mama, so he's always working. She's a hot mess, his mama, but he loves her."

"He seems pretty decent," Bryan offered. He took a few bites of his grease-soaked fried chicken, then he asked, "What about Hank? I just met him this morning, but he didn't come off as overly friendly, and Pa has never had much good to say about him."

"Oh yeah?" Justin said, raising his eyes. "What's your Pa say?"

Bryan hesitated, silently cursing the liquor for making him overly loquacious. "Well, he's said that he can be a bit cheap. You know, like that he cuts corners sometimes." Bryan looked down and added, "Pa wasn't sure about me working on the farm, but there weren't really a lot of options."

Justin looked down and gave a dry smile. "Well, your Pa's right. He's a real son of a bitch." He looked back at Bryan and grinned, adding, "And I should know, since he's my daddy."

Bryan flushed, nearly spitting out his swallow of beer. "Oh shit, I'm sorry. I didn't realize."

Justin gave a short laugh. "Oh it's no big thing. I know he's an asshole." Justin added, less audibly, "In fact I probably know better than anyone else."

Justin paused a moment, took a deep swallow of his drink, then continued. "I've seen him beat a sow with a metal pipe until her eyes popped out of her head, all because she didn't get out of his way fast enough." Justin took another large swallow, looking past Bryan as he appeared to recall the event. "I mean we've all done some shitty stuff in there. It's part of the job. But Hank – I think he likes it. Or, maybe, he gets off on it. I don't know."

Justin sat his drink down clumsily. It wobbled momentarily then toppled over and spilled onto the floor. A female waitress of maybe sixteen or seventeen immediately came over with a dishrag and cleaned up the spilt beer. She had coal black hair pulled up into a ponytail that bobbed as she moved. Her bright blue eyes stayed focused on Justin, and she kept a small pleasant smile on her face.

"You doing okay tonight, Justin?" she asked.

Justin, swaying slightly in his seat, grinned at her. "Doing just great now, Mandy."

Mandy flushed and looked down. "You want another drink?"

Justin's grin widened. "Why yes, that would be just the thing."

Mandy smiled brightly and whisked away for the drink. Justin looked at Bryan, who was eyeing him.

"Oh I know," Justin said, slurring. "She's way too young, but it don't hurt to flirt a bit."

Mandy returned with the drink and gave it awkwardly to Justin, spilling a bit onto the table, which she immediately wiped up with the rag she was carrying. She gave another little smile and then turned away quickly and went back to tending other tables.

"You got a sister?" Justin asked.

Bryan looked slightly surprised. "Yeah," he said slowly. "A younger sister, Winnie. She's fifteen."

Justin nodded. "Yeah I got one, too. Older, though. Amanda. She's mean as a snake. We get along alright, but she'd cut your throat if it suited her." Justin laughed.

They passed a few minutes without conversation. Justin was watching Mandy as she made her way in and out of tables and occasionally threw him a sideways glance. He always caught it and returned it with a smile.

Justin, still watching Mandy, added, "She's got a kid, you know."

Bryan looked back at him. "The waitress?"

Justin laughed. "No, my sister. She's just a year older than me, but her boy, Conner, is three. Got pregnant by some football player the summer before her senior year. So," he laughed, "don't ever mention to Hank that you're a football man." He took a drink, still watching Mandy. "Yeah, Hank nearly lost his mind when he found out. Went raging through the house, throwing shit and yelling. Said he was gonna kill the guy. Well

Amanda started crying and fussing and said he shouldn't be causing her so much stress, since she was pregnant and all. She said she was in love and was gonna marry the baby's daddy."

Justin shrugged. "Maybe she thought she would. I don't know. Anyway, the day she went into labor, she went to the hospital and called the guy. He said he'd be there shortly, but he never came. She had Conner, and by the time she got home, the guy had left town. His mama and daddy didn't even know where he was. Said he just up and left. Took some clothes and all the money he'd saved."

Justin continued, "Amanda kept saying that maybe this guy would come back. Maybe he had gone to find a better job or whatnot. Stupid shit. When Conner was about six months old, Hank told Amanda it was time to stop with that nonsense, and that he knew for a fact that this guy wasn't ever coming back."

Justin paused for a while and looked at his drink. A few droplets of beer had spilled onto the table, and he pushed the beer bottle into them, spreading them out along the table top. After a few minutes, he looked at Bryan and continued. "I got to talking to Hank late one night after he'd had a few too many beers. He told me he knew where this guy had gone. That he had gone down to Greystone Landing and was working at a paper plant down there. He told me that apparently the guy was coming out of a bar one night and was run down by a car. The car plowed him over and then took off. He lived, but just barely. Can't walk, can't hardly talk, can't do nothing on his own now. He's in some facility down there, where he has to have somebody spoon feed him and wipe his ass."

Justin flagged down Jeffrey, who came around with another beer. Justin smiled and gave him a little salute. Jeffrey grinned and shuffled off.

Justin turned back to Bryan, who was staring at him intently with a furrowed brow. Justin gave a faint smile. "Of course, he could have been lying as far as I know, but I haven't seen the guy since."

Their table fell silent after that. Justin sat slumped back against the seat, alternatively looking from his beer to Mandy and back again. Bryan was turning Justin's story over in his head, not sure what to make of it. He had not had words to respond when

Justin had stopped talking, so they simply sat at the table, nursing their beers.

Bryan looked out over the rest of the bar. The crowd was growing thinner. A few hardy young men were sitting at the bar and raising their voices over a baseball game on the television mounted to the ceiling. He could not see who was playing from his vantage point, but the men's team appeared to be losing, as they were spouting out bursts of profanity.

At a table beyond were two middle-aged women who appeared to be in deep conversation. They occasionally cast annoyed looks at the boisterous men, but their looks fell on uncaring backs, and they in return crowded closer to one another to share their captivating gossip. One woman, with a bit too much makeup covering her face and with fingernails painted a bright crimson, spoke quickly and expressively to the other, who, in a look of awe, raised her slightly chubby hands to cover her mouth, which had apparently fallen open beyond her control from the sordid nature of the information being conveyed.

In a far corner, an elderly gentleman sat holding an empty pipe between his teeth. Bryan saw that his eyes were on the two gossiping women. He wore an overcoat that had thinned around one elbow to the point where the faded green flannel shirt beneath the coat was visible. He bobbed the pipe up and down in his teeth, as he cradled a glass of wine in his right hand. From time to time he removed the pipe momentarily to drink the wine, then he refilled his glass from the bottle, which sat on his table. The pipe seemed to bob up and down with some sort of rhythm, and the man rhythmically tapped his toe along with the bobbing.

Bryan looked at Justin and realized he was dozing. "Hey," he said. Justin opened an eye and twisted his face at Bryan. "You ready to get out of here?" Justin pulled himself up and looked around.

"Yeah, I guess it's about that time," he said. He stood up and wobbled a bit. He threw a wad of cash on the table, saying, "I got this one." Bryan started to protest, but Justin held up a clumsy hand and waved him off, saying, "You get the next one."

Bryan hesitated, considering, but Justin was already at the door. Bryan followed as Justin opened the door and staggered into the parking lot. He went to his truck and pulled out his keys.

"Hey, whoa, whoa." Bryan caught up with Justin. "You better let me drive."

Bryan reached for the truck keys. Justin pulled away, shrugging him off.

"I'm fine," Justin said, drawing out the words. He stumbled to the driver's side of his truck and fumbled with the keys, dropping them. They clattered onto the ground, and Bryan scooped them up before Justin even realized he had dropped them. Bryan frowned at him.

Justin grinned. "Well, hell, I guess you can drive then."

Bryan got in the driver's side and started the truck. Justin made his way around to the passenger side, attempted to climb into the truck, and fell backward onto the ground. Sighing, halfway in frustration and halfway in amusement, Bryan got out and helped Justin into the truck.

"Where do you live?" Bryan asked. "I'll drop you off and then take your truck home. I can pick you up in the morning."

Justin, with his eyes closed, shook his head. "No, just go home, and I'll sleep it off here. It's better I don't go home when I'm jacked up like this. Hank would kill me – literally." He laughed as he said the last word.

Bryan paused. "What? You can't sleep in the truck."

Justin muttered something, possibly, "Done it many times before," and waved Bryan off again.

Bryan looked at him. *What a fucking mess this guy was.* He headed toward home, accepting that he was stuck with his inebriated partner for the night.

As he bumped over the uneven road, Justin's head bobbed, but otherwise he did not stir. Bryan took several moments to get his bearings. He had virtually no cell phone service, so he was unable to map his route, and he started the wrong way twice. Eventually, he found himself in familiar territory and driving in the right direction.

He texted Winnie, *Pa up?*

She returned, *Nope! Good for you he's not!*

Bryan winced. Whether he was up or not now, he would be up in the morning, and he would want to know where Bryan had been all night. Bryan was not worried about any repercussion as a result of his night. His parents gave him a fair bit of freedom and seemed to trust his judgment, more or less, but Pa would be disappointed, he thought, to know that he had spent the night getting wasted with someone he barely knew. He could picture Pa, looking down at his morning coffee, stirring it restlessly, and raising heavy eyes to look at Bryan. That look was enough to make him shrink up and wish he had gone straight home after work. Too late now, though.

Mama up? Bryan texted Winnie.

Nope. No one but me! Bryan could picture her batting her eyes and giving him a "just little ol' me" look.

Can you keep Boomer quiet? I'm 5 min out. Bryan wrote.

I'll do my best! Winnie replied.

Bryan pulled in not long after that. Winnie was sitting on the front porch, rocking in one of the big white rocking chairs Pa had built for Mama and rubbing Boomer behind the ears. The big hound had his head arched backward, enjoying the attention, and barely glanced at the approaching truck.

Not much of a guard dog, Bryan thought. Of course, Boomer was not a guard dog. Back in his day, some twelve or fifteen years ago – no one seemed to remember anymore how old the dog was – he had been quite a hunter. Pa had an endless supply of stories of the great Boomer and how he could tree any raccoon in the county. At one point, Pa said there were no raccoons left, as Boomer had done away with them all.

Now Bryan quietly closed the door to the pickup and went to the passenger side to retrieve Justin. Justin was more or less passed out. Bryan jostled him to wake him enough so that he could lean heavily on Bryan and make his way, stumbling, toward the house.

Upon seeing this newcomer, both Winnie and Boomer expressed some interest, with Boomer slowly standing up, stretching, and walking, stiffly, toward the edge of the porch. Winnie, raising one eyebrow at Bryan, silently opened and held the door for him, as he struggled to get Justin over the threshold without him toppling over.

Bryan managed to get Justin over to the couch and dropped him onto it with more than a little annoyance.

Winnie fetched a blanket and laid it over Justin.

"Well now," she said, giving a teasing smile, "this is going to be fun to explain in the morning."

Bryan frowned at her. "Well he was gonna sleep in his truck, and that seemed crazy."

Winnie stepped closer to Bryan. She raised both eyebrows. "You been drinking tonight, big brother?"

Bryan frowned harder, and she laughed.

"Well," she said, "you better get it off of you before you see Pa in the morning. I don't think he was thrilled that you were going out with – what's his name?"

"Justin," Bryan replied.

She continued. "Yeah, he's Hank's kid, right? That's what Pa was saying, and you know Pa doesn't care much for Hank."

Bryan looked down and pulled his mouth to one side. He said nothing for a moment or two, until Winnie shrugged and smiled, adding, "Oh don't worry. It's fine. You know Pa. You want a snack?"

The two sat up for a while, talking about Bryan's first day at the farm. Although, for the sake of Winnie, Bryan entirely left out any mention of piglets.

CHAPTER III

Getting up before Mama and Pa was nearly impossible, but Bryan made a point to do it the morning after bringing Justin home. He woke Justin, who, as an apparent result of a throbbing headache, was in a less than friendly mood. He gave him some clothes and told him to get ready, which Justin did reluctantly, showering Bryan with annoyed and sullen looks, and he tidied up the couch.

By the time his parents came downstairs, Bryan and Justin were chatting over a breakfast of eggs, bacon, and biscuits that Bryan had prepared.

Pa, as much surprised to see the elaborate breakfast as he was to see Justin, let his mouth fall open for a moment. Mama simply gave Bryan the same knowing smile that Winnie often wore, which gave Bryan the impression that he never did anything of which she was unaware.

"Morning, Pa. Morning, Mama," Bryan said. "Y'all know Justin?"

Justin looked up and grinned somewhat, adding awkwardly, "Nice home you have."

Pa looked at him for a moment, tilting his head slightly to one side with confusion.

"Thank you, Justin," Mama said, smiling. "You're welcome here anytime."

Justin grinned at her and then Bryan. Bryan saw Justin's gaze shift as Winnie came down the stairs, dressed for school.

She grinned at Justin. "Morning," she said.

He beamed back at her. "Good morning to you," he grinned widely. Bryan gave him his deepest frown, and he chuckled.

"Well we better get going," Bryan said, standing up. Justin was still in the middle of eating and had just shoveled down a mouthful of eggs. He glanced up at Bryan, who raised his eyebrows in slight impatience. Justin swallowed and grinned.

"I guess we better be going then," he said as he stood, grinning at Bryan.

"You don't need a ride, Bryan?" Pa asked.

Bryan glanced at Justin. "No, sir, I don't. I'll go on with Justin today."

Confusion remained on Pa's face, even as he nodded and sat down at the table. Mama and Winnie glanced at each other, smiling, and Bryan shuffled Justin out of the house, as he gave a final nod and wave to Winnie.

"Nice family you got," Justin said as they neared his truck. "Cute little sister," he grinned.

Bryan frowned at Justin. "Yeah, she is," he said as he climbed into the truck. He looked over at Justin. "Don't even think about messing with her."

Justin burst out laughing and slapped Bryan on the back. "Well, as long as we're clear," he said, continuing to laugh as they drove away.

* * *

Amanda pulled back the eggshell curtains when she heard the rumble of the pickup coming up the drive. She watched the truck bump along the dusty driveway toward the house. She took a half step in an instinctive urge to run to Daddy and alert him that his wayward son had just returned home after being out all night, but she paused when she saw that the passenger side of the pickup was not empty.

She lingered a moment, tugging at a loose strand of fabric on the fraying lace curtains. She saw the truck come to a lurching stop in front of the house. Justin made some gestures to the passenger before departing from the truck and jogging toward the house. Amanda saw the passenger run a hand through his hair before looking out the side window and, after a brief pause, climbing out of the pickup.

Amanda's pale green eyes widened slightly as she recognized the tall, stocky figure emerging from her brother's truck – Bryan Bradford, wide receiver for the Ashfield Anglers. She had been a senior when he first came on the team, and she had watched him, along with every other football player of the Caucasian persuasion, every Friday night during football season. She remembered how his muscles had tensed and hardened with every move he made on the field, rippling under his tight uniform. She remembered how the players had hooted and bumped chests whenever they scored, and how they had held their heads and cursed when the other team was ahead.

Amanda had loved going to those football games. She had started going her freshman year, and the feeling she got when she sat in those cool metal bleachers was electric. For the first time, she had space to be herself. She was not in school, doing her best to keep just slightly above average grades. She was not at home, trying to fill in the roll of Mommy for her younger brother, since her own mother had decided she had more important things to do with her life. She was not playing housekeeper, tidying up, packing Daddy's lunch, cleaning up his beer cans, or covering him with a blanket as he lay passed out in his armchair in front of the television. Instead, she was just herself. She would huddle up in the crisp autumn air with Amber and Nicole, whispering and giggling. Amber would make her big hand gestures as she spoke, clutching Amanda's hands in excitement, her dark eyes flickering in the bright stadium lights. Nicole would be leaning back in her seat, rolling her eyes and sneaking sips from a small flask in her backpack.

Amanda watched as Bryan slowly walked around the pickup, stretching first one arm across his chest, then the other, as he ran his eyes over her home. She tucked back into her room, away from the window, when he was just about to raise his eyes to her level.

When Amanda's baby bump had started to push through her shirts senior year, Amber and Nicole had suddenly become too busy to go to the games. Amber, after failing to respond to Amanda's texts, had given Amanda a quick apology when she passed her in the hallway at school. "Oh geez, Amanda, my parents are riding me to get these college apps in. I'm pretty much on house arrest until that happens. I'm sorry." She glanced down as she fumbled with her books and backed down the hallway. She gave a sweet smile before turning briskly and heading into a classroom. That was Amber – always sweet, always smiling, and always avoiding conflict.

Nicole was more direct. "My parents say I can't hang out with you anymore," she said one day after school. She sat on the bleachers, swinging her legs and looking down at the dirt below. Amanda had cast her a questioning look. "'Cause you're knocked up," Nicole said, still looking down. She lit a cigarette and inhaled deeply. It was fairly rich coming from Nicole, or rather from her parents, since they owned the sole ABC store in town.

Nicole was a bit of a pariah herself. Amanda remembered wondering if Nicole's parents thought the pregnancy was contagious. Amanda laughed a little. She could do that now. The pain of the initial break was over.

Amanda had gone to a few more games on her own. She sat alone, cheering on the team at the appropriate times. When the team scored, she would give a small shout and look around smiling, trying to catch the other fans' eyes. She rarely did. Most of the other kids turned to look at their own friends. Once, when she was nearly due with Conner, she did lock eyes with a girl nearby. She smiled, clapping her hands and giving a small hoot. She vaguely recognized the other girl from class – Rebecca or Becca maybe. She was a curly-haired redhead with a fair complexion and hazelnut-colored freckles. The girl smiled back, widening her eyes slightly. She turned back to her group of friends, cupped her hands to the ear of the girl nearest to her, and whispered something. The other girl immediately snapped her head around to where she was facing Amanda. She eyed Amanda, not smiling, not frowning, just looking, then she grinned at the first girl.

Amanda had felt a cold chill at that moment. A lump formed in her throat. She looked down, trying to get a grasp on her feelings before the tears came. She realized that, try as she might, there was nothing left for her here. She waited a few minutes and then gathered her things to leave. As she was getting up to leave, she glanced around and saw Amber and Nicole. They were sitting a few rows behind her. She looked at them, starting to smile a bit and naturally wanting to go to them. Nicole held her gaze, furrowing her brow slightly, and Amber looked away. Amanda hesitated, then she left. That was the last game she attended.

"Mama?" A small voice startled Amanda. She turned around to see the short, slight figure standing in the doorway to her bedroom. The boy, still in his pajamas, made a few short, quick shuffled steps toward her, getting close enough to read her face, but remaining several feet away.

"Mama?" he repeated, eyeing her cautiously.

Amanda felt a frown forming on her face. She tried to force down the feeling of annoyance, but it spread through her body like a toxin.

The boy, apparently seeing the darkness come over his mother's face, remained in place, waiting.

"What are you doing up so early, Conner?" Amanda asked.

Conner took a small, quick step toward her. "I'm not tired anymore. I'm ready to get up." He held a ragged teddy bear, and he rotated it in his hands as he spoke.

Amanda sighed. "Go back in your room, Conner. I'll be there in a minute."

"But mama –"

"Conner!" Amanda raised her voice. "What did I say?"

Conner looked down. "Okay," he said quietly. He turned, keeping his eyes on the ground, and retreated out of the room.

A pang of guilt shot through Amanda. She instantly brushed it aside then hurried to her bathroom. She eyed herself in the mirror, frowned, then quickly brushed her hair and threw it up in an intentionally messy ponytail. She brushed her teeth, smiled to ensure that they were as lovely as she imagined, then threw on a quick layer of makeup. She smiled at herself before turning to leave.

She hurried down the stairs but then slowed her pace to a more leisurely speed as she approached the front door. She let the screen door slam behind her as she glided onto the front porch. Bryan turned around to look at her, furrowing his brow slightly.

"So you must be the one who kept my brother out all night, huh?" She grinned at him.

A look of understanding came over Bryan. He glanced down and shuffled slightly, rubbing the back of his neck with one hand. "Yeah, yeah I guess that's me."

"Well you must be some saint to have taken him in last night. He's a mess when he's drunk, and I'm sure he was drunk." She gave a short hard laugh as she approached. "I'd 'a let him sleep it off in the barn if it were me." She smiled and extended a hand. "I'm Amanda."

"Bryan," he replied, giving her hand a quick shake and then taking a step back.

"You played for the Anglers, right?" She eyed him.

His expression brightened for a moment, before returning to the sullen look that he had carried the last few months. "Yeah, yeah I did."

"Yeah you were really something, right? I heard you were going to school for football or something like that."

Bryan sighed the heavy sigh that had become his primary form of communication lately. "Yeah, well that didn't work out." He looked toward the house, into which Justin has disappeared a good ten minutes earlier.

"Oh well that's okay," Amanda smiled. "So now you're working at the farm?" She made a face as if smelling a foul odor. "Ugh, well that must be a change of pace." She tilted her head at him slightly, as if waiting for a response.

Bryan looked down and kicked the toe of his boot against the dirt a couple of times. He heard the screen door slam again and looked up to see Justin coming out.

Justin grinned at Bryan as he approached. He moved to his side so he was facing Amanda and put a hand on Bryan's shoulder. "She bothering you?" he asked with a grin.

Amanda narrowed her eyes at Justin, then she turned toward Bryan, smiling. "Well shoot if you're gonna be staying out all night I at least better find out who you're staying with."

Justin rolled his eyes. "Alright, Amanda, well we gotta hit it." He moved to get in the truck, and Bryan did the same.

Amanda took a step closer. "Hey Justin, don't you think you should invite your friend to dinner, to pay him back for his hospitality?" She shot Justin a dry smile.

Justin snorted. "You're ridiculous, Amanda."

She jerked back as if offended. "What? It only seems the right thing to do."

Justin glanced at Bryan, who had climbed into the truck and was looking out the side window, as if he did not hear the conversation, which would have been impossible if he could hear at all.

Justin shook his head. "Okay, we'll see." He started the truck, raised an eyebrow at Amanda, and backed out of the driveway.

Amanda watched the truck go down the road for a moment, then her face fell as she headed back inside.

CHAPTER IV

"She's something else," Justin said, grinning.

Justin's words brought Bryan out of his daydream. "Who?" he asked, looking over at him.

"Amanda," Justin said, laughing. "She's a real piece of work."

Bryan paused. "She seems nice," he said, finally.

"Ha!" Justin lurched forward with the laugh. "Well don't believe it for a second. That one's a snake." He chuckled as they drove on.

When they arrived at the farm, they followed the same routine as the day before, checking each pen and fiddling with the waterers. As with the day before, they spent most of the morning picking out the dead piglets from the pens. Bryan uncomfortably watched as Justin made a sort of game of the task.

"There's one!" Justin yelled upon finding a dead piglet. He would lean over the railing into the pen, wrap his finger around the piglet's tail, and sling the body onto the middle walkway. "That's one for me and none for you," he would chuckle to Bryan.

Bryan trudged along, looking into the pens as he went. He leaned into each pen as he passed, checking the automatic waterers and glancing at the feeders to ensure each was working correctly. The stench from the pigs forced him to move slowly. He felt sure that if he moved too quickly, he would lose the contents of his stomach in one of the pig pens.

About halfway down the aisle, he came to a pen with a mostly motionless piglet lying on its side. He felt a sick feeling rising in his stomach. He poked gingerly at the piglet, which appeared to flinch and kick a hind leg when he touched it. Bryan looked up and saw that Justin was watching him.

"Do you want help with that one or can you take care of it?" Justin asked, coming closer. Bryan hesitated. *Take care of it? Meaning, bash its head into the concrete?* He was not sure if he was ready for that, but of course he could not leave the piglet to suffer either. He opened his mouth, then, unable to find a response, he closed it again.

Justin, watching him, took this as his cue to move in. In a matter of seconds, he pushed past Bryan, grabbed the piglet by the hind legs, swung it over his shoulders, and slammed it forward and down onto the concrete walkway, causing a loud cracking sound to echo through the building. The piglet convulsed momentarily, then lay motionless. Justin looked at Bryan, raised his eyebrows, and shrugged. Then he quickly turned and went back to his side of the aisle.

Bryan found two more piglets in similar condition. Each time, he removed the piglets from their pens, took them to Justin, and asked what he wanted to do. Each time, Justin gave a short laugh, grinned at Bryan, and flung the piglet against the concrete walkway, bashing its head.

"I mean it really is the most humane thing, you know?" Justin said. "Leaving 'em to lay there and die is way worse. Think about it. If it were you, wouldn't you wanna go quick?"

Bryan didn't have a response to this. Instead, he shrugged and went back to checking the pens.

Jeffrey was in and out of the barn during the day. His gait could be recognized easily from the shuffling sound he made as he trudged through the building. When he first saw Bryan, he gave a wide grin and raised a stiff hand in a wave.

"You came back!" he said, chuckling as he shuffled along, stopping at first one pig pen and then another.

Toward the end of the aisle in the farrowing section, Bryan came to a pen confining a sow and seven piglets. Like the other sows, this pig was forced to lie on her side, unable to make any significant movements in the pen. Her teats protruded through the bars of her pen into the adjoining pen, where her piglets were confined. Unlike the other sows Bryan had observed, this one was vocalizing, making low, long groans as she lay there. Bryan watched her for a moment. Her dark eyes flicked toward him, watching his movements.

Bryan found Justin, who was working on a clogged waterer, and returned with him to the sow. Justin watched her a minute, giving his head a thorough scratch as he did so. He then turned back to Bryan.

"We need to move the little ones over with another sow," he said. Bryan looked at him blankly. Justin grinned and laid a hand on Bryan's shoulder. "She ain't doing real great," he said. "She can stay there, but the piglets need to move to another mama."

Bryan nodded slowly, still trying to understand what he was supposed to do. Justin leaned into the pen, plucked up three of the piglets, then looked into several neighboring pens. Finding a sow with only three piglets herself, he added the newest three to her litter. The sow, lying on her side, grunted and raised her head. She watched the new additions to her litter as they crawled toward her and attached themselves to her nipples. She snorted and laid her head back down. Justin then repeated the process with the remaining four piglets, giving them to a different sow.

The sow remained alone in her pen. When the piglets were removed, she grunted loudly for a moment, raising her head as if to look for them, then she sank back into her resting position. Justin started to head back down the walkway.

"Wait," Bryan said, taking a step after Justin. "What do we do with her?"

Justin paused and turned, sighing audibly. He walked slowly back to Bryan. "Well, we just have to wait on her," he said. "She's still alive, so we can't put her in the dead pile yet. Maybe a day or two more."

Bryan stared at him. Justin chuckled and gave Bryan a light hit on the back. "Come on, man, it's gonna happen. Nothing you can do."

Bryan held his mouth slightly open and continued staring at Justin, as if Justin might suddenly change his mind and tell Bryan something totally different. Justin waited a moment, then he pulled his mouth to one side, shrugged at Bryan, and continued down the aisle.

Bryan watched the sow as she lay on her side, her piglets all removed to other pens. She gave a fairly consistent low moan as she lay there, occasionally kicking her feet in little spurts, but otherwise remaining motionless. At one point Bryan saw her attempt to rise, struggling to pull herself up. She groaned and grunted, huffing and puffing, then fell back down onto her side.

Bryan furrowed his brow. He looked up and saw Justin, who was several pens away, fiddling with an automatic waterer. Justin glanced up at Bryan and gave his eyebrows a slight lift as he flashed a half grin. He chuckled at Bryan's frown.

"Oh come on, man. You've got to loosen up. Nature will take care of things. Just give her a little peace." He finished working on the waterer, tested it, then got of the pen.

35

Bryan looked back at the sow, frowned, and then continued down the aisle.

At lunch, the "three amigos" ate outside again. Jeffrey chuckled as he told them about a particular piglet he had struggled to dispatch that morning.

"Little man just wouldn't die," he grinned. "Every time I tried to pop him, he'd just bounce right back! Craziest thing I've ever seen," he chuckled.

Justin grinned at Bryan, who simply looked down at his ham and cheese sandwich. Justin moved closer to Bryan and slapped him on the shoulder.

"Don't let it bring you down too much," he said. "It'll get easier. And you're only here for the summer anyway, right?" He grinned especially wide at that.

Bryan looked at him steadily. *I sure as shit hope I'm only here for the summer.* But really, he thought, what's after that?

Bryan noticed that Jeffrey, who was eating some sort of meat and cheese sandwich, was tearing away little bits of his bread, meat, and cheese and setting them aside. Justin saw Bryan eyeing the little sandwich pieces. He shook his head and rolled his eyes, grinning as he did.

When they finished eating, Justin went to talk to Hank about some of the pigs. Bryan started back inside, but then he hesitated when he noticed that Jeffrey was headed to a small storage shed a short distance away from the pig buildings. He sighed, thought what the hell, and followed. The shed, unlike the pig buildings, was made of wood and seemed to be from some earlier time period, perhaps when the farm was smaller and not filled with thousands of squealing pigs. White flecks of paint dusted the ground around the shed like fallen cherry blossoms. Jeffrey opened the door of the shed, looked cautiously inside, and then made a clicking sound with his tongue.

The clicking continued until Bryan heard a "oh there you are" come from inside the shed. Bryan moved forward until he could just see inside the door. It was small and dimly lit, with an uncovered lightbulb hanging from the ceiling. There were a few standard tools in the shed – a rake, a shovel, a posthole digger. Items that might be found on any farm and woefully inadequate to maintain the massive expanse of land covered by the metal pig buildings. There were built-in wooden shelves toward the back of the shed, and Jeffrey was facing the shelves, with his back turned to the door.

"Look what I gotcha," Jeffrey said, reaching into his pocket and pulling out the bits of sandwich. He laid them down on the shelf, and Bryan saw a cat move forward to take them. The cat was a gray tabby and clearly female, as her belly bulged with apparent pregnancy. Jeffrey reached down to stroke her, and she accepted the petting, continuing to eat the food. Then, he poured some water from a thermos he carried into a dull metal bowl resting on one of the shelves.

Bryan heard the gentle vibrations from the cat's purring as she finished the food and brushed back and forth against Jeffrey. She rubbed against him, then she turned quickly away, then back again, as if she could not quite decide if she wanted to stay or go. Jeffrey held his rough hand out, and she pushed her head into it, closing her eyes and purring, sounding like a small engine in the quiet building.

Bryan took a step forward, putting one foot onto the threshold of the shed. A small creak escaped the wooden flooring, and Jeffrey and the cat both jerked their heads in his direction. Jeffrey met him with a grin, and the cat, shooting a skeptical look in Bryan's direction, skittered back into the shelving and out of sight.

"She's a pretty one, huh?" Jeffrey grinned at him.

Bryan gave him a half smile and a nod. "Looks like there will be more of them soon," he said.

Jeffrey looked at Bryan, tilting his head to one side.

"Oh, I mean, she looks pregnant," Bryan said in answer to Jeffrey's stare.

Jeffrey furrowed his brow for a moment, looked back in the direction of the cat, then smiled. "Oh yeah?"

Bryan frowned. *How the hell had he not noticed?* "Yeah," he said. "She looks like she's due any time now."

Jeffrey, smiling more now, continued looking at Bryan.

"Uh, my mom works in a vet's office," Bryan said in response to Jeffrey's apparent questioning.

Jeffrey grinned and nodded vigorously. "Huh," he exhaled a pleased utterance and looked back around for the cat, who was nowhere to be seen. "Who knew."

Well, pretty much anyone with eyes should have known, Bryan thought, thinking of the cat's bulging belly. He scanned the shelves again, but the cat was gone.

Bryan turned at the sound of heavy steps behind him and saw Justin trudging their way.

"What are you ladies doing?" he called, grinning at them. He saw Jeffrey inside of the shed. "Oh," he chuckled, "playing with that damn cat." He shook his head, smiling.

"Bryan says she's gonna have kittens," Jeffrey blurted out happily.

Justin raised his eyebrows at Jeffrey, then he glanced at Bryan, his expression darkening slightly. "Really?" he asked Bryan.

"I think so," Bryan replied.

Justin looked down, and Bryan felt a somewhat sick feeling of foreboding, although he had no idea why. It lasted only momentarily, as, when Justin looked back up, he was grinning again.

"Well, Jeffrey, I guess you're gonna be a daddy," he chuckled, slapping a hand on Jeffrey's back. Jeffrey gave a burst of laughter and nodded vigorously. He left the shed and headed back toward the pig buildings, still laughing.

"He's so crazy," Justin grinned at Bryan.

They returned to the pig buildings and finished out the afternoon weighing each of the piglets. Justin made notes of the weights, adding a meaningful "oh" or "hmm" to a few of the notations. As they went through the pens, they found another handful of dead piglets. Justin slung each into the center walkway, and they collected them all for the dead pile at the end of the day.

Bryan walked past the pen containing the listless sow. She was still on her side, apparently unmoved, and she vocalized when he stopped at her pen. He frowned at the sow and looked to Justin, who gave a heavy sigh and said, "She'll be gone when we get in tomorrow. Don't worry."

But, despite Justin's confidence in his abilities to project a time of death, the pig lay in the same manner the following morning. Bryan grimaced upon seeing her, lying on her side, vocalizing and writhing at frequent intervals. He caught Justin's attention and motioned him over. Justin frowned.

"Well, I mean, she's not really suffering. She's just going slow." Justin said, eyeing the pig. "It really can't be much longer."

Bryan frowned at Justin, who, catching the look, shrugged and said, "I still think putting her on the dead pile would be worse. Just give her time. Don't rush her into dying."

Bryan bristled at the insinuation that he was rushing the sow to her death. He gave the sow another long stare, then he went back to helping Justin check the automatic feeders and waterers, pulling dead piglets from the pens as he did so.

For the next two days, Bryan dreaded passing the pen with the dying sow. Twice he attempted to give her water from a bowl, but as soon as he entered her pen, she began screaming, and the sound sent a shiver down his spine that seemed to physically thrust him from the pen. Each time he entered the pen, he noticed a putrid smell coming from the sow. His stomach turned, and he felt the need to vomit, but he steadied himself and quickly retreated from the smell, so as not to lose control in front of Justin.

The following week, Bryan came in to find Justin standing in front of the sow's pen. Justin looked up. "Well, she's gone," he said, giving a half smile. "Must've happened last night."

Bryan looked into the pen and saw that the sow was still. Her side was sunken in, and her color had a grayish hue.

"Well, let's get her outta here," Justin said, climbing into the pen. Bryan hesitated. He looked around for another possible option, but there was none. Jeffrey was nowhere in sight, and there was no way that Justin could lift the sow on his own.

Bryan lingered a moment longer, and Justin frowned at him, raising an eyebrow. "Come on," he said. "It's not that bad. You've been pushing to get her out of here all week. Come on now."

Bryan sighed heavily and climbed into the pen after Justin. The stench hit him hard, pushing him back and taking his breath. He staggered slightly, feeling lightheaded, and reached out for support. Justin, chuckling, caught him, only adding to his embarrassment. He felt himself getting hot, and he was sure his face was reddening. Justin's gleaming grin did not help matters.

Justin steadied Bryan and then reached down for the sow. He got a solid grasp around her front legs and directed Bryan to grab her back legs. Bryan did so, clumsily grabbing the stiff, cold legs, which stuck straight out and had no bend or flexibility when he touched them.

"Okay, one, two, three, lift," Justin said, heaving the sow up by her legs. Bryan lifted as well, but as soon as the sow was raised off of the ground, the smell amplified, completely surrounding Bryan. He gagged, his eyes watering, as he stumbled forward and out of the pen with the sow. He and Justin heaved her onto the center walkway. She landed on the side that, for the last five days, had been facing upward, exposing her opposing side, which had been on the ground the last several days. This side was the apparent reason for the smell, as it was a bloody mess of open sores that oozed dark red, coagulated blood and thick yellowish pus. Although the sow's body was stiff, the sores still appeared wet and viscous.

The sight mixed with the smell was too much for Bryan. He eyed the sow for a moment, then, feeling a wave of nausea overwhelm him, he turned back to the pen and vomited. As he grasped the pen's railing and tried to raise himself, his eyes fell on the spot where the sow had laid. The area was wet concrete, giving a damp, mildewy smell to the pen. Splotches of crusted, dried discharge, which had apparently leaked from the sow, were stuck to the concrete. As he realized what he was seeing, Bryan was again overcome with nausea, and he continued retching over the side of the pen, unable to calm his body.

He heard Justin move closer to him from behind, and he turned quickly, raising a hand to motion him to stop. Justin's face was half comical, half concern, but he stopped and waited. They both turned when they heard the door open at the end of the walkway. A shuffling immediately followed as Jeffrey came in, nodding and grinning at them and giving a stiff-handed wave.

Justin brightened. "Big J, give me a hand over here." He met Jeffrey on the walkway, slapped a hand on his shoulder, and led him back to the sow. Bryan heard Jeffrey ask Justin something, and Justin responded, "Oh man, he's feeling rough. Some bad tacos, amigo. Know what I mean?" Justin chuckled as he and Jeffrey hoisted the sow and carried her out of the building.

CHAPTER V

The image of the sow stayed with Bryan through the day and into the evening. At dinner, he pushed his ribs around with his fork. As he poked at the slightly pink meat, he momentarily thought he saw yellow pus oozing out from the edges. He tilted his head and studied the ribs until Winnie elbowed him in the side, furrowing her brow at him.

Bryan looked up and saw Mama and Pa watching him. Pa coughed, fiddled with his napkin, and asked, "Everything going okay at the farm?"

Bryan glanced at Winnie and, seeing that she was nearly at eye level, he realized how slumped he was in his seat. He sat up a bit and answered, "Oh it's fine – as good as can be expected, I guess." He saw Winnie and Mama meet each other's eyes for a moment.

Pa looked down at his napkin, folding it in half and using his fork to push down on the crease. "I know it can be a little rough sometimes. It's good to see where your dinner comes from, though, don't you think?" He lifted his eyebrows at Bryan. "You know most people have no idea. They just know they pick up their ribs at the meat counter and that's it." He chuckled. "Really everybody should work on a farm at some point, at least for a little bit."

Winnie flashed a smile at Pa. "Oh yeah? So when should I start? Tomorrow?" Her smile broadened.

Pa squinted at her. "Okay now, you know what I mean."

"What do you mean?" Winnie asked with false innocence. "Surely you don't mean that only the *boys* should work on a farm? That seems a bit sexist. You're not sexist, right, Pa?" She beamed.

Pa looked at Mama for help, but she was smiling at Winnie. He raised his hands and shook his head. "You girls," he said, smiling and continuing to shake his head.

Bryan excused himself and took his uneaten meal to the kitchen. Boomer, who had been perched under the table in the case of any falling crumbs, lifted his head when Bryan stood up, then he followed him into the kitchen. Bryan cut the meat off of the ribs on his plate, then he scraped the meat into Boomer's bowl. The old dog lumbered over, gave his bowl a sniff, then devoured the meat in a single gulp, licking his lips and looking up at Bryan when he finished.

"That's it, old man," Bryan said.

Winnie came into the kitchen. "You okay?" she asked.

"Oh yeah," Bryan said. "I'm good."

She raised an eyebrow skeptically. "Yeah? You look it." She put her hands on her hips.

Bryan rolled his eyes. "Yeah, yeah, I just don't think I'll be eating many ribs while I'm working this job." He paused and then looked at Winnie. "It's ugly, you know? It's just, ugly."

Winnie watched him for a minute, then she reached out and squeezed his arm. "Well, just do what you can to make it pretty – or, at least, not so ugly." She smiled.

CHAPTER VI

When Bryan pulled into the farm the following Monday, Jeffrey met him with an eager wave. He was at the side of the truck before Bryan could even get out, pushing so closely that Bryan struggled to have room to open the door.

"It's happened. They're here!" Jeffrey spurted, grinning wider than ever.

Bryan slid out of his truck and faced Jeffrey. He tilted his head, furrowing his brow slightly.

"The babies!" Jeffrey said, insistently. "The kittens! Come and see!"

"Oh," Bryan said. He smiled a little and followed Jeffrey as he moved at a faster pace than Bryan had thought possible for him. Jeffrey made it to the washed-out shed and then paused, gently opening the door. "Look," he whispered.

Bryan looked inside, his eyes taking a moment to adjust to the dimness of the room. In a back corner, in a heap of towels that Jeffrey had likely provided, Bryan slowly made out the shape of the mother cat. She lay on her side, methodically licking one of her kittens, which was so tiny it looked more like a mouse than a feline. It was difficult to see inside of the shed, but Bryan thought he saw at least four small bundles squirming at the mother's side.

Bryan's gaze shifted from the kittens to Jeffrey, who was staring intensely at the little family. After a moment, Jeffrey reached into his pocket and took out a handkerchief filled with what looked like bits of meat. Jeffrey moved slowly forward, put the morsels in front of the cat, gave her a light pat on the head, and then moved back. He grinned at Bryan when she started eating the meat, and he quietly made his way out of the shed.

Outside of the shed, he spoke a bit louder. "Did you see that?" His eyes were wide.

Bryan gave a soft laugh. "Yeah, that's great. Looks like she's taking good care of them."

Jeffrey smiled even more. "Yeah, you think so?" He looked away, apparently not really waiting for an answer.

Bryan smiled. "When did she have them?"

"Must have been last night," Jeffrey said.

Bryan and Jeffrey started walking back toward the pig buildings. "Did you show Justin yet?"

Jeffrey shook his head. "No, he's not here yet. I'm not sure if he's working today."

Bryan stopped. He furrowed his brow at Jeffrey. "Oh, really?"

Jeffrey turned his focus to Bryan. "Oh yeah, but don't worry. I'll just be one building over this morning, and I'll check in on you this afternoon."

Bryan hesitated, but Jeffrey had already split with him and was heading toward a different building than the one he was entering. He sighed and continued on.

As he heaved open the heavy metal door, Bryan was prepared for the thick wave of stench that accosted him. What he was not prepared for was the silence. Even in the entryway, he could hear the faint murmuring of the pigs and the whir of the fans, but that was all. Normally Justin would be talking about something or another that had happened to him overnight or else his future plans for leaving the farm. Justin was almost always talking about something. Normally, Bryan found this tedious, but now, when there was no sound other than the low, ever-present grumble of the building's occupants, he wished for Justin's incessant talking.

Bryan put his wallet and phone in his locker, then he put on a pair of mud and shit-smeared boots and coveralls. He cautiously opened the door that would take him into the pig area.

A low drone came from the pigs inside. Occasionally a pig would give a sudden squeal or cry, which startled Bryan to the point that he cursed each time it happened. He went slowly down the aisle, looking into each pen and checking the automatic feeders and waterers. He found two waterers that had apparently stopped. He cleaned and adjusted them and was able to get the water flowing again.

He moved into the farrowing area. In doing so, the quiet din of the pigs increased in volume to a low roar. After making his initial walk down the aisle, checking the feeders and waterers, he slowly and cautiously made his way back up. This time, he looked into each pen for dead piglets. His eyes felt heavy in his head, reluctant to look at the pigs, in case he spotted one who was not moving. He paused when he approached each pen, looking down until the last possible moment, when he would then lift his eyes to the contents of the pen.

In the first several, he found nothing out of order. The mother sows lay on their sides, letting their young piglets suckle them through the metal bars separating the mothers from their babies. In a pen midway down the line, Bryan found his first dead piglets. Two of the seven piglets in the pen lay motionless. Bryan hesitated, then he moved into the pen, stepping gently so as not to excite the mother. He touched the still piglets, and they were cold. A wave of relief rushed through Bryan. Dead was fine, he thought. Dead he could handle. What he did not want to find was a piglet on the edge of life and death. He had always had Justin to handle those piglets, and he did not want to find one on his own now.

Bryan continued down the aisle, removing a few more dead piglets from the pens and lining them up on the center walkway. When he had nearly reached the end, he saw another motionless piglet. The sow nursing this piglet only had two other piglets, and both were nursing vigorously. The third piglet lay still near her side.

Bryan reached down and grasped the piglet around the abdomen. When the piglet gave a hard gasp and jerked, Bryan emitted a startled cry and jumped back. "Shit," he cursed. The piglet arched its back and gave a low, gurgled cry. Bryan looked at the sow. She lay motionless, allowing the two remaining piglets to nurse. Her eyes followed Bryan, but she otherwise did not move.

Bryan ran his hands through his hair, which was becoming wet not only from his own sweat but from the thick humidity of the building, as well. He glanced around, in hopes that perhaps Jeffrey would be coming by, but the building was quiet, other than the low sounds of the pigs. Bryan considered the piglet for a moment. It would not be the worst thing in the world for it to die by its mother's side, would it? It did not really seem to be suffering. It did not really seem to be conscious at all – it was listless, other than the occasional moan and spasmodic movement. Bryan hesitated, then he gently moved the piglet closer to its siblings. He watched it for a moment, saw its slow, labored breathing, then quietly climbed out of the pen, as if trying not to wake the pig from its nearly unconscious state.

45

Bryan made his way down the rest of the aisle, glancing a bit more quickly into each pen, hoping to avoid any further situations. He found several more dead piglets and moved them to the center walkway. He then gathered the dead piglets in the wheelbarrow and took them out to the dead pile behind the building. The hum of flies around the pile was almost deafening as he approached, and he swatted uselessly at them as they flew up to and even landed on his face. He quickly dumped out the piglets and retreated from the pile.

Jeffrey shuffled over as Bryan was headed back toward the building. He grinned, giving his stilted, over-enthusiastic wave. "You ready for lunch, friend?" he asked. Bryan nodded, wiping the sweat off his forehead, and followed Jeffrey to the picnic table.

Jeffrey spent most of the lunch break talking, and Bryan spent the time trying to focus on what Jeffrey was saying, forcibly pushing the image of the listless piglet out of his mind. He struggled to follow the conversation, hearing Jeffrey saying something about his mother and how she was starting to collect "a few too many things" and needed a little help "tidying up." As he talked, Jeffrey picked off pieces of his sandwich and laid them aside, undoubtedly for his feline friend.

"She wants a dog, but she ain't got time or room for a dog. I'm thinking maybe she can take one of these kitties, you know? Once they get bigger." Jeffrey beamed at Bryan and raised his eyebrows.

Bryan, realizing that Jeffrey was waiting for some sort of response, tried to pull himself back to the conversation. He nodded. "Yeah, yeah, a cat would probably be good. Are the kittens doing okay?"

At Bryan's mention of the kittens, sheer delight overcame Jeffrey's face. He nodded eagerly. "Oh yeah, they're great. They're the most eatin' little babies I've ever seen. Always nursin' on mama, and she's so good to 'em. She just lets 'em go, keeps 'em clean, does a real good job." He smiled and pulled a little more of his sandwich to the side. "Speaking of, I better go out and check on 'em." Jeffrey got up to leave, then he glanced back at Bryan. "You all good in there? Do you need any help?"

Bryan wavered, thinking of the piglet. He considered, then he shook his head. "No, I'm all good." Jeffrey grinned and headed off toward the shed.

Inside the building, Bryan completed his afternoon tasks more slowly than normal, doing nearly anything he could think of to avoid the pen with the dying piglet. He worked on several waterers that had become clogged, made sure the sows had access to their food, and even started weighing the piglets, although he did not have a great sense of which piglets needed to be weighed and why. He found a few more dead piglets and pulled those out of the pens. When the afternoon was nearly finished, he returned to the pen with the three piglets, hoping to be able to remove the third piglet, now dead, from the pen.

When he peered into the pen, the third piglet lay where he had left it, motionless and stretched out on its side near its siblings. The other two were now resting and breathing easily. Bryan watched the third piglet for a few moments, but he saw no movement. He had just decided that the piglet must be dead when he saw it give a slight flick of its leg and take in a deep, heavy breath. *Shit. Shit, shit, shit.* Bryan sighed. Leave it, and let nature run its course? Or put it out of its misery? He thought the second option was probably more humane.

Wincing, Bryan lifted the piglet out of the pen. He held it for a moment. In his hands, he was able to see more easily that it was in fact breathing, and he heard that it made a thick, wet, congested-type noise with each breath. It probably does not have much longer, he thought. Bryan looked at the concrete walkway. He shifted the piglet fully into his right hand and started to raise it. He hesitated. God damn you, he thought, mentally cursing Justin. Where the hell are you? He heaved a sigh and raised the piglet higher, aimed at a spot on the concrete, and closed his eyes. As he stood there, waiting, he felt a faint thumping against his palm. A sick feeling started to spread over him as he realized that he was feeling the piglet's heartbeat. He lowered his hand, opened his eyes, and looked at the piglet. It was still motionless. Still unsure of what to do, but knowing at least what he could *not* do, he shoved the piglet into his pocket and headed for the door. Most likely, he thought, it will be dead when I get home.

* * *

"Oh my God," Winnie said, eyes widening. She stared at the piglet, then she raised her eyes to Bryan's. "What's wrong with it?"

"I don't know," Bryan said. "I mean, a lot of them don't make it." He saw Winnie's forehead crease. "I guess it's just hard with so many or something."

Winnie took the motionless piglet from Bryan and raised it to her face. The piglet's eyes were closed, but it was still emitting slow, labored breaths that sounded thick and congested. "Well we gotta show Mama."

Bryan pulled his mouth to one side and sighed. "I mean, I don't know that there's much she can do."

Winnie narrowed her eyes at him. "Then why did you bring it home?"

He shrugged. "I don't know. I mean, normally Justin takes care of these things, and he wasn't there today."

Winnie tilted her head slightly. "What do you mean he takes care of these things?" She stared at Bryan.

Bryan sighed, closed his eyes, and scratched the back of his head. "It doesn't matter," he said, shaking his head with his eyes still closed. "The thing is, he wasn't there, so I didn't know what to do with this one."

Winnie continued staring at him. After a moment, she flipped around, her ponytail flying up and nearly slapping him in the face. She cradled the piglet to her chest and left the room, already yelling, "Mama!" as she left.

Bryan felt suddenly sick as a heavy feeling of regret washed over him. He followed Winnie out of his room, where he had gone to show her the piglet, and went into the kitchen where Winnie was already showing the piglet to their mother.

When Bryan entered the kitchen, he saw Mama and Winnie standing close together, looking down at the piglet in Winnie's arms. He hesitated at the doorway as the two women spoke in low tones. The heat from the oven reached Bryan where he stood and carried with it the smell of grease and salt and something else, likely chicken, that was baking in the oven.

Bryan moved closer, and his mother looked up. Mama was almost always smiling when he saw her. She had wrinkles at the edges of her eyes and mouth where the smiles and laughter had creased her skin over the years. He always thought these marks made her even more beautiful. Now, however, her face was solemn, and her brow was lightly furrowed.

"Bryan, honey, take the chicken out when the timer goes off, and keep stirring the potatoes. Winnie, bring that baby over here." She moved to one corner of the kitchen, and Bryan, almost mechanically, moved forward to the oven. He saw a pan full of mostly browned potatoes on one eye of the oven, and he used the wooden spoon on the counter to stir them, as he watched Mama reach into the pantry and pull out a jar of Karo syrup. She put a line of syrup on one finger, and then she put her finger into the piglet's mouth, rubbing along its gums.

"Winnie, go ahead and start rubbing him to try to get his temperature up." She gave Winnie a brief demonstration by quickly rubbing the piglet's visible side, then she briskly left the kitchen. She returned momentarily with a couple of her long wool socks. As a rule, she hated wool. The itchy, scratchy material rarely seemed worth the aggravation. Now, however, it seemed to be just what she needed. She took a bag of white rice from the pantry, poured some into each sock, tied off the top of each sock so that the rice would not spill, then put the socks into the microwave. After about half a minute, she removed the socks and placed them in Winnie's arms, on either side of the piglet. She assisted Winnie, who was now weighed down with rice and piglet, with continuing to rub the piglet's side.

Winnie alternated between looking down at the piglet and staring at her mother. Her face was slightly tensed, and her lips were pursed. "So it's a boy?" she asked, lifting her eyes to Mama's.

Mama continued rubbing for a moment, then she met Winnie's gaze with a light smile. "Yeah, a little boy." The two held each other's gaze for a moment, then both looked back to the piglet.

Bryan watched but said nothing. He felt awkward, unsure of what to do in his own home. He had brought the piglet home, and he was not even sure if that had been the right thing to do. Now, his mother and sister were doing their best to save a pig that likely could not be saved. He knew that they would hurt when the piglet died. The thought of their pain at the piglet's passing tore through Bryan and left a feeling of sudden and sick dread. *God damn it. Why didn't I just handle it back at the farm?*

49

Looking down at the perfectly browned potatoes, Bryan realized that Mama had just given him busy work to do, as the potatoes were as good as they could ever be, and she had already turned the eye to low. The timer went off for the chicken, and Bryan removed the Pyrex baking dish from the oven. He hesitated, then he mumbled something about Boomer and left the kitchen, even though Boomer lay sprawled out on a flattened dog bed in the corner. The dog had lazily opened one eye when the commotion in the kitchen began, but he had since closed it again.

Bryan went into his room and sat heavily on his bed. He put his head in his hands and sighed. His eyes rose to his wall, which was still littered with football memorabilia from his senior year. In the center of the wall was an oversized portrait Mama had gotten him. It was focused in on a football resting on a dew-covered football field. The rich brown of the football contrasted against the nearly lime green of the grass. He had not liked it at all when Mama gave it to him. He had pulled the brown paper off of the frame and looked at it for a moment, feeling his brow furrow and his mouth pull to one side. Mama's eager face had fallen for a moment, but she quickly brushed the look away, smiled, and said, "It's okay if you don't like it. You don't have to put it up." He had set it aside in his room and left it for a few weeks. The longer it sat there, however, the more he longed to see it. He would get home from school and immediately look at it. He found the colors and the quiet of the field pleasing. He often imagined himself in that field, grabbing that football and running – no fans, no teammates, just the ball and the sound of his breathing and light steps on the wet grass. He had finally hung it, to Mama's great pleasure, and he often found himself just staring at it.

To the left of the portrait was one of his old jerseys. The crisp contrast between black and gold had faded, and the cloth was dingy and tattered. A quarter-sized hole was in one of the sleeves, and a few threads hung down from the fraying edges of the jersey. Bryan stared at the jersey for a moment. He had been so proud when he wore it – so confident, so self-assured. He knew he was right where he was supposed to be. Now, he felt a feeling of bitter resentment rising in him. The lost opportunity and the unfairness of it all made him angry in a way that he had rarely, if ever, previously felt.

Bryan was so distracted by his thoughts that he did not notice Winnie standing in his doorway. Finally noticing her, Bryan turned, half started to rise, then remained where he was on the bed, trying to read her face. She looked at him questioningly for a moment, wanting to know what he was thinking, but she soon let that pass in place of more pressing matters. Her right hand was cradling something, apparently the piglet, close to her body, and her left hand moved over the bundle in a caressing manner.

Bryan could not see the piglet, only the blanket wrapping the piglet in Winnie's arms. He watched the motionless bundle, deciding that if the piglet had not already passed, Winnie must be waiting for him to do so. His eyes widened and his mouth fell slightly ajar when he heard a faint grunting noise and saw a small pink nose push out from under the blanket. Winnie smiled as Mama came up behind her.

"He's okay?" Bryan asked in amazement.

Mama, whose face was still strained, stroked the piglet's nose and answered. "He's not out of the woods yet, but he's better than he was." She gave a light smile as she stroked the piglet. The smile quickly faded when she heard gravel crunching outside, indicating that Pa had just pulled in.

Mama turned quickly, brushing a strand of hair out of her eyes, and headed toward the front door. "Kids, give me just a minute with your Pa."

Bryan frowned, but Winnie rolled her eyes. Winnie was fearless when it came to Pa. Bryan had always been a little jealous of Winnie's relationship with Pa. There was a wall between Bryan and Pa that simply was not there with Winnie. Bryan was always careful and respectful around Pa. He did as he asked and did not question him. Winnie, on the other hand, did as she liked. She would laugh when he would frown at her disapprovingly, sometimes wrapping her arms around him and giving him a small peck on the cheek. Pa would melt, apparently under some spell of hers. He was never able to be angry with her, not really, and she was well aware of that.

Bryan and Winnie heard the low voices of Mama and Pa outside. At first they were warm and playful, but, after Mama spoke for a few moments, there was a minute of silence, followed by Pa's slightly raised voice. Bryan could not hear exactly what he was saying, but he could hear worry and frustration in his voice. Mama's voice was calm but firm. Bryan could imagine her, patiently allowing Pa to talk, letting him feel like he was being heard, but ultimately knowing that he would be giving in by the end of the conversation.

That was how it always went. Mama would play the domestic role as much as she could, making the meals, cleaning the house, and handling the children. She would defer to Pa's decisions in most situations, backing him up when needed, and allowing him to reside as head of the household. Both Bryan and Winnie knew, though, that if Mama wanted something, it was going to happen. She allowed Pa to run the family, but she steered him in whatever direction she thought was best, just as a captain might steer a ship. She loved him, Bryan thought, but not in the way that he had seen in some of his friends' parents. She was not blinded by love to the point that she had no mind of her own. She was not so under the influence of romance that she would let Pa control any aspect of her life.

Bryan had no doubt that Pa would do anything for Mama, but he was not always sure that the reverse was true. When he had first realized this, it had bothered him deeply. Winnie had laughed at him, flicking her hand at him to wave him off.

"Don't be silly," she had said. "Mama loves Pa, but that doesn't mean she's going to let him rule her. Is that what you want?" She had raised an eyebrow at him. "You want us weak little women to be barefoot and pregnant in the kitchen?" She winked, and Bryan had frowned at her. Things came so easily for Winnie. She never second guessed herself like he did. She never questioned whether something was right or wrong; she always knew exactly where she stood on any issue. Given that she was three years younger than him, Bryan was always a bit jealous of this.

The voices outside became hushed, and Bryan heard heavy footsteps coming up and onto the porch. Winnie raised her eyebrows at him and turned around to leave the room. He followed her, and they both watched as Pa came in through the front door, followed by Mama.

Pa's face was creased with tension. He eyed the piglet in Winnie's hands. He met Bryan's gaze, pressing his lips together tightly as he did. Bryan immediately knew that he was displeased with him, and he knew why. He was kicking himself already for dragging Mama and Winnie into this, making them try to save a piglet that likely could not be saved. Or, if they could save it, then what? What the hell were they going to do with it? Send it back to the farm? He closed his eyes momentarily and shook his head at the thought. That would not work. Keep it? Where would they put it? He thought of the sows at the farm. They were huge – maybe 300, 400 pounds at least. Where could they keep an animal that large?

Bryan opened his eyes again and saw that Pa was now looking at Winnie. Mama stepped past Pa and approached Winnie. She pulled back the blanket just a bit to see the piglet underneath. She smiled.

"He looks good," she said. "We have a fighter here."

"What do you think, Pa?" Winnie smiled. "Have you ever seen anything so cute?"

Pa used the back of his right arm to wipe sweat off his forehead. He sighed heavily, before giving a small smile. "I guess you've already picked out a name for him, huh?"

Winnie beamed. "Of course I have. Wilbur."

* * *

Winnie fell asleep that night with Wilbur tucked in beside her. His breathing was still labored, but it was noticeably stronger, and he was now warm to the touch. Mama checked in on them but left him where he was next to Winnie.

Bryan was sitting on his bed, listening to Bob Marley and staring at his wall, when Pa gave a light knock on the door and entered. His look was softer than earlier, although still strained, making Bryan once again feel deep regret for his decision to bring the piglet home.

"You doing okay?" Pa asked, standing just inside the doorway.

Bryan nodded. "Yeah."

Pa sighed. "Look, I know the farm can be a lot. We can try to find you something else. There's just not a lot of jobs right now." Pa scratched the back of his head. "But you can't be bringing pigs home, you know? Really. I mean does Hank even know you brought this pig home?"

Bryan looked down and shook his head. "No, I was alone today. I, I didn't know what to do with it."

Pa gave a few short nods, a look of understanding starting to spread over his face. "I got you. I get it. Just find another way next time, okay? I don't even know what we're gonna do with this one, but I know we can't have a whole herd of pigs here."

Bryan looked up and nodded. "Yeah, I will."

Pa smiled and moved closer to pat Bryan's shoulder. "Well, I'll tell you what, there's no luckier pig than that one, tucked up in there with Winnie. You are some crazy children." He grinned. "I'll see you tomorrow," he said, leaving the room and pulling the door closed behind him.

Bryan sat for a moment, thinking about the piglet. He thought about the other piglets on the farm. He thought that most of them were probably huddled up right now in their putrid pens, suckling on their mothers. He figured there was probably at least one or two who were currently in the process of dying. The thought made him shudder. He thought of the ones who he had seen bashed against the concrete to ease their suffering. He thought of all these, as he drifted off into a heavy sleep.

CHAPTER VII

Justin was not at the farm the rest of the week. Luckily for Bryan, all of the piglets he found were either alive or already dead, with none in that gray zone in which he had found Wilbur. He ate lunch with Jeffrey and watched as Jeffrey trotted off to feed his feline family.

Justin finally returned the following week, and Bryan found, surprisingly, that he was glad to see him. He approached him quickly when he saw him. As he neared, he saw that Justin walked stiffly and with apparent discomfort. His face was tight, with his lips pinched together. Bryan slowed as he neared him, taken a bit back by his change in demeanor. He saw that the left side of his face was a slightly darker hue than his right. Bryan stopped a few feet before reaching Justin.

Justin, who seemed distracted by his own thoughts, finally looked up just before running into Bryan. He smiled, with the smile turning into his normal grin. "You miss me?"

Bryan shrugged but returned a smile. "What happened to you, man? You look like shit."

Justin laughed. "Well damn, you just tell it like it is, huh?" He ignored the question and motioned for Bryan to follow him. "Come on, let's get going."

Bryan followed Justin into the gestation building, feeling sweat immediately sprout on his brow as he pushed against the wave of humidity behind the door. Bryan watched Justin out of the corner of his eyes as he pulled on his boots and coveralls. Justin moved with noticeably stiff movements, and he was quieter than normal, with no teasing or friendly hassling.

Once inside the pig area, Bryan and Justin moved along the center walkway, observing the sows in each pen. There was generally nothing remarkable in this building. Small snorts and grunts would emanate from the sea of pigs and echo through the building in a rhythmic lull.

Bryan eyed Justin as he moved from pen to pen, observing the sows in each and checking the waterers and automatic feeders. About halfway down the aisle, Justin apparently found a waterer that was not working. He leaned over the pen and jostled the tip of the waterer. He then left momentarily and returned with the spray bottle of vinegar. He hoisted himself into the pen to view the waterer at a better angle.

As Justin fiddled with the waterer, the sow in the pen pushed into him, snorting and grunting. He flapped his hand at her to wave her off. "Go on," he said, continuing to tinker with the waterer. The sow, not understanding or not caring, continued pushing into him, adding light squeals each time she did. Justin, focusing his eyes on the waterer, pushed her away from him without turning. She squealed but immediately came back, continuing to nudge him with her head.

Bryan, who was a few pens down, turned when he heard Justin curse. "God damn pig," he said. "Get the fuck away from me." Justin turned toward the pig. Grasping the bars behind him to support his weight, he leaned back against the bars of the pen, jerked back one leg, and kicked forward with all his apparent strength. His boot made audible contact with the sow's face. She screamed and pulled away from him, shaking her head. As she shook, blood splattered onto the neighboring pens and the center walkway.

"Fuck it," Justin said and climbed out of the enclosure. He faced Bryan, and Bryan saw that Justin's face was also coated in blood. The pig was still screaming. Justin saw Bryan eyeing his face and used the back of his arm to wipe his brow. He looked at his arm, which was now smeared with blood. He sighed and frowned.

Bryan narrowed his eyes at him. "What the fuck, man?"

Justin gave a short laugh and then frowned again. "I'm just not in the mood today. Here, you work on the water for that pen. I'll check the rest of the row."

Justin handed the spray bottle filled with vinegar to Bryan, who reluctantly took it. Justin moved down the line with his back to Bryan. Bryan looked at the pig, who was still squealing and shaking her head. He waited a few minutes for her to settle, feeling a touch of fear at getting into the pen with the bloodied pig.

When the sow's cries had quieted, Bryan pulled himself into the pen and turned to work on the waterer. The sow moved somewhat cautiously toward him, then, as she had done with Justin, she pushed her snout into him. Bryan looked down at the blood stains on his shirt where her nose had touched him. He frowned and kept working. The sow continued nudging him, emitting soft grunts and squeals as she did. He finally got the water working and moved out of the way. The sow immediately moved to the water and drank, pushing frantically at the nipple to obtain the water. Bryan watched the sow drink for several minutes, until he climbed out of the pen. Her eyes followed him as he left, but she continued pushing on the nipple for more water.

Justin remained quieter than normal throughout the rest of the day. Bryan felt annoyance toward him for kicking the sow, and he had little to say. When it was time to leave, Bryan moved hastily toward his truck, but Justin called out and ran after him.

"Hey, man," Justin said, looking down and scratching his head. "I'm sorry about the pig. That was stupid."

Bryan frowned at him but said nothing.

"Look," Justin continued. "Let's go get a drink. First round's on me." He grinned.

Bryan shook his head slightly, looking down, and moved toward his truck. "I really gotta get home."

Justin jumped in front of him, grinning again. "Oh come on, I know you're pissed. Let me buy you a drink. We'll both feel better afterward. If you go home you'll just come back still pissed off tomorrow."

Bryan hesitated. He knew Justin was right, which made him all the more annoyed. He sighed, "Fine."

They made their way to the Rancher's Respite, with Bryan driving behind Justin. Once they were in and seated, Jeffrey shuffled over, just like last time, to take their order.

"Big J's in the house!" Justin laughed, giving Jeffrey an exaggerated high five.

Jeffrey grinned, then he shuffled off to get their order.

Bryan watched him. "God, is he ever not working?"

Justin looked toward Jeffrey. "Yeah, he's always doing something. His mama needs a lot, and, as you know, the farm don't pay great." Justin winked at Bryan.

As Justin had his head turned toward Jeffrey, Bryan caught a better view of the deep bruise creeping up the side of Justin's face.

"What the hell happened to you?" Bryan asked.

Justin looked back at Bryan. He rolled his eyes. "It's no big thing, man. I just got into it with Hank."

Bryan's eyes widened. "Hank did that?" He thought about Pa. Pa had spanked him when he was younger, and a few times those spankings had stung more than a little, but he had never hit him. Bryan shook his head as he thought about it. Even the idea of it seemed impossible.

"Yeah, you know, just over some stupid shit. Hank's got a pretty bad temper, you know, and he's a piece of shit when he's drunk." Justin chuckled, but the laugh fell flat.

"That's messed up," Bryan said.

Justin smiled and took a drink. "Yeah, maybe, but it is what it is."

"Why don't you just move out?" Bryan asked.

Justin raised his eyebrows, looked around the room, and shrugged. "I mean, I will, but I gotta save up some money, you know? I'll get outta here. I'm not gonna die in this shithole of a town. The timing just ain't right right now."

Bryan frowned and took a drink. He waved at Jeffrey and ordered a couple of tequila shots. Justin grinned at this and downed the shot when it came, wiping the salt from his mouth. They ordered two more each and felt the tension release as the alcohol took hold.

The room buzzed around Bryan. As the tequila made its way through his body, he felt himself losing focus on Justin, who he could see was saying something. He looked around and saw a few people moving about. A couple of girls sat in a booth across the room from him. Both were wearing skirts, one of which was so short that he was sure the girl's bare bottom had to be resting on the booth seat. His eyes wandered up the girl's legs, past her skirt, until he reached her face, and he saw that she was looking at him. She smiled, then she leaned across the table to whisper something to the other girl, who turned to look at Bryan, smiling as well.

Bryan flushed and immediately thought of Winnie, who was not much younger than these girls. The idea that some guy in a bar might be watching Winnie, scanning her body with his eyes, and thinking of doing, well, things he did not want to think about with her made him feel sick. He looked down at his empty glass, which he was still holding. Luckily for him, Winnie did not, at least at this point in time, have a lot of interest in guys. She was fairly dedicated to school and focused on getting out of this small town. She had had a crush here and there, but each time she got close to a guy, she was never willing to give any serious time or thought to him, which did not make for a lasting relationship.

"I'm not looking for a boy to keep me tied down," Winnie would say when Pa occasionally tried to gently nudge her toward dating. Pa would sigh and look at Mama, who would smile and raise an eyebrow at him. "That's my girl," she would sometimes say, leaving Pa to throw up his hands and give up.

Bryan looked up again at Justin, who was grinning and looking at him.

"Shit, man," Justin said. "You didn't hear a God damn thing I said, did you?" He laughed, then he motioned Jeffrey over. "Hey, Big J, wrap those burgers up to go. We're getting out of here." Jeffrey grinned and obliged.

Justin leaned closer to Bryan. "Let's go. You can ride with me, as you're clearly shit faced. I'm gonna show you something."

* * *

After numerous assurances that his truck would not be towed if left at the Rancher's Respite, Bryan found himself bouncing along in the passenger side of Justin's pickup. He still had not eaten, and between the alcohol in his system and the lurching of the truck, he felt that at any second he was going to have to hold his head out the window and spew vomit into the humid evening air.

Justin had the radio up and was singing along to Tim McGraw's *Something Like That*, calling out incorrect lyrics with absolute confidence. He had followed the main highway for a few miles but was now on an unpaved and apparently poorly maintained dirt road. To the left of the road was an open field, and into this field Justin took a sharp turn, slinging Bryan forward and, since he had failed to fasten his seatbelt, smashing his face against the dash. Bryan cursed and pulled back to see Justin laughing as he rubbed his face.

"Shit, man. What the hell?" Bryan said angrily as he wiped away a small trickle of blood that was exiting his nose.

Justin laughed again but quelled it, raising a hand and saying, "Sorry, sorry, just buckle your damn seatbelt, man. You'll be fine." He grinned.

Bryan looked ahead and strained his eyes. He thought he saw the slight hint at a path before them. Not a road, to be sure, but the faint indentations in the short grass where tire tracks had previously left their mark.

About a quarter mile from the road, Justin slowed as he approached a fence. The fence was three strains of barbed wire held between wooden fence posts spaced a few yards apart. He turned to drive parallel to the fence for a moment, until they reached a livestock gate made of metal railing. Justin stopped the truck without speaking, got out and swung the gate open, pulled the truck inside, and got out again to close the gate behind them.

Bryan gave Justin a slightly worried look. Justin waved him off. "It's our property. Well, it's Hank's. It's fine."

"Are there animals in here?" Bryan asked, straining to see in the waning light of dusk.

"Cattle," Justin said, "but at this point in the day I'd expect they'd be headed toward the shed for the night."

Justin drove along, and Bryan was no longer able to tell whether he was on a path or not. Bryan wondered how exactly he had gotten here, in the middle of a field, teetering on the verge of vomiting with each bounce of the truck, with a guy he hardly knew and only half liked. *Good life choices.*

After a few minutes, Bryan saw another fence line come into view. Justin pulled close and then turned the truck around and backed up to it before parking. "Come on," he said, getting out.

Bryan hesitated, but at this point, really, what were the options? He slid out of the truck and followed Justin to the back.

Justin pulled down the tailgate and put the food on it. He opened the toolbox and, after rifling around for a moment, he pulled out a bottle of Jack Daniel's and grinned, apparently pleased with himself. He hopped up on the tailgate. "Come on. Let's eat."

Bryan reluctantly joined him and, less reluctantly, accepted a drink of the whiskey. They ate in silence for a few moments, until Bryan finally said, "So why are we out here?"

Justin pointed straight ahead. "Out there," he said.

Ahead of them, on the other side of the fence, Bryan saw that the field extended for about a dozen more yards. Where the field ended, loblolly pines stood tall, their outlines visible against the darkening sky. Their tall trunks were fairly naked at the bottom, with sprigs of green shooting out along the upper portions and filling out in thick clumps at the top. Beyond that, Bryan saw nothing but more trees. He shot a glance at Justin, who was staring straight ahead.

"So," Bryan said slowly, drawing out the o, "what am I looking for?"

Justin responded, without looking at him, "You'll see."

Bryan felt some slight annoyance rising, but at the same time he was wondering if Justin might not be entirely sane. How could he be, he thought, with a father like Hank.

In the silence of the early evening, the hum of the cicadas grew loud. Their noise was as thick as the heat around them and nearly tangible. At irregular intervals, a frog would croak and momentarily break through the buzz of the cicadas, but their humming quickly returned and engulfed all other sounds, taking over the evening air.

Justin sat looking straight ahead, eating his burger and taking frequent drinks from the whiskey. He noticed Bryan watching him, grinned, and handed him the drink. Bryan briefly hesitated and then took several swallows before handing it back.
Bryan suddenly noticed that the buzzing of the cicadas was turning into almost a roar. It took him a moment to realize that the noise was no longer the insects but rather some other sound, a steady rumble that was getting louder every second. A whistle blew, and there was no mistaking the sound – a train.

"Here it comes," Justin said excitedly. Bryan strained to see in the dim light, but soon he made out the outline of a train, running down a track that apparently ran parallel to the Brewer property. The whistle sounded again, almost deafening at this point, as the train was less than half a football field away from them. Justin whooped as the train went by in a flash. Each car was a blur, but some of the cars appeared to have lights on inside, and Bryan could just make out what looked to be passengers in the cars.

Just as quickly as it had come, the train was gone. Justin turned to Bryan and grinned. "That's it, my friend. Pretty cool, right?" He took another swig of whiskey and sighed.

Bryan watched him. "Where does it go?" he asked.

Justin shrugged. "Beats me, but anywhere has to be better than here, right?" He grinned wider. "All those people are going somewhere – going somewhere and leaving somewhere else behind." He swallowed another mouthful of whiskey and added, staring in the direction of the now-distant train, "That's where I wanna be."

Bryan said nothing, only continued to look at the empty space in the woods where the train had been. As crazy as he generally found Justin to be, he thought about what Justin had said. What would it be like to just hop on that train, head down the track, and not have a worry about where you were going? He had had a plan for his life, and look where that had gotten him. He was no better off than Justin, and as of now he had no plan for his future.

Bryan took the whiskey back from Justin and had a few more drinks. They sat drinking and eating and talking about the endless possibilities of life for a while longer, until Bryan got a text from Winnie showing Wilbur in the bathtub, surrounded by bubbles and a yellow rubber duck. Bryan laughed, then he quickly put the phone away when Justin glanced over to see what was funny. "Oh nothing," he said, "just Winnie being stupid."

"You're lucky you got a good one," Justin said. Bryan tilted his head at him, and Justin added, "A good sister, I mean."

When all signs of light were gone and the humidity of the day was being replaced by the cool evening air, the two loaded up in the truck to head back. Justin stumbled to the driver's side. This time, Bryan, who was also unsteady on his feet, was in no place to replace him as driver. He mumbled a slurred "be careful," as he climbed into his seat.

Justin grinned and revved up the truck. They started back through the field. The thick darkness of night had settled in, and the moon provided only dim light. The truck bounced over the uneven ground, which had previously been planted in rows of crops and which had left low hills and shallow trenches long after the crops dried up and ceased to grow. Justin sped up and grinned at Bryan as the truck bumped along. Bryan grinned and laughed, but, on catching a glimpse of movement out of the corner of his right eye, he snapped his head forward. He momentarily strained to see but then jerked back as he saw a large moving mass directly in front of the truck.

"Look out!" Bryan yelled. Justin slammed on the brakes, and he and Bryan both narrowed their eyes to see what lay ahead in the dimly lit field.

"Ah, it's a damn cow," Justin said with a half smile as he made out the shape of the cow. "Well, a calf really," he added. The calf stood directly in front of the truck. It stuck its head out and mooed in their direction. Justin chuckled. "Get out of the way, cow!" He grinned at Bryan.

Bryan watched the calf as it twitched its tail back and forth. Its head was low to the ground, but its round eyes stared up in the direction of the truck. Justin tapped the gas, and the truck lurched forward. The calf mooed and bounded a few feet away, still in the path of the truck.

Justin sighed. "Come on, cow," he said. He revved the truck up and took his foot off the brake, letting the truck jump forward again. The calf mooed, a bit louder this time, and again moved away, although still remaining in the way of the truck.

Justin let the truck start rolling forward at a slow pace. The calf plodded along, mooing and staying just a few feet ahead of the truck. No matter which way Justin tried to turn the truck, the calf seemed to stay in the way, stumbling along just a few feet ahead. Justin gave another frustrated sigh and increased his speed. The calf picked up its speed as well, and Justin, a grin creeping across his face, kept his speed up with the calf, increasing it little by little.

"What the fuck are you doing?" Bryan asked. "You're gonna hit it."

"No, man, I'm just having some fun. Teachin' it to stay out of the way," Justin responded with a chuckle.

Bryan felt himself sobering as he watched the calf. He dug his fingers into the armrest as he watched the calf awkwardly attempting to run away from the truck. "You need to fucking stop," Bryan said, raising his voice.

Justin grinned and turned to look at him. At that exact moment, the calf fell.

Bryan's cry of Justin's name emerged just as the truck thudded against the calf. Justin slammed on the brakes. His grin was gone, and he looked pale as he turned to Bryan. They both sat still momentarily, then Bryan slowly opened his door, with Justin doing the same.

As soon as the doors were open, they heard the low moaning. A sickening fear creeped up Bryan's back, making his hair stand on end. The wails sounded like a person in the throes of extreme pain and distress. Bryan slowly moved around the truck, scanning the dark grass for any signs of life.

"Shit," Bryan heard Justin curse. "God damn it."

Bryan went to Justin's side of the truck and saw him bending down to look at the calf where it lay on the ground. Bryan hesitated, then he slowly approached. The calf arched its head backward, lowing mournfully where it lay. As Bryan approached, he saw the calf's round eyes roll to look at him momentarily, before rolling upward again as the lowing continued. The moon provided little light, but Bryan could see a dark liquid running out of the calf's nose and pooling around its head.

"What the fuck is wrong with you?" Bryan said angrily. "I mean what the fuck. What were you doing?"

Justin had both of his hands on his head and was clutching strands of his hair. He shook his head slowly but did not respond.

"Is it one of yours?" Bryan asked.

Justin continued staring at the calf, as if frozen.

"Justin?" Bryan neared him, but Justin remained as he was, apparently unaware of Bryan. Bryan pushed his arm lightly, and Justin startled, turning to face him.

"What?" Justin asked. "What did you say?"

Bryan motioned to the calf. "Is it one of yours?"

Justin nodded. "One of Hank's."

Justin stood still for a moment, then, as if he had just woken up, he quickly turned back toward the truck and said, "We have to go."

Bryan remained where he was but scrunched up his face. "What?"

Justin turned, now with some annoyance, and repeated, more deliberately, "We have to go."

Bryan shook his head. "We can't go. What the hell? We can't leave it suffering like that."

Justin had reached the truck, but he came back hastily. "There's nothing we can do. It's going to die. The best thing we can do is get the fuck out of here."

Bryan hesitated, looking back at the calf. It was still in the same position, still lowing as strongly and painfully as before. "No way." He reached out and grabbed Justin, who had started to walk away again. "If you're sure it's going to die, you need to shoot it. You can't just run it over with the truck and then leave like nothing happened. That's insane."

Justin narrowed his eyes and shook his head. "No, man. All I have is a rifle on the truck. If I shoot it, Hank will definitely hear, and I'm not trying to end up like the fucking cow." He tried to jerk away but Bryan had tightened his hold.

"We're not leaving it like this," Bryan said.

Justin's mouth fell open slightly. He threw his hands up and ran his free hand through his hair, cursing again. He mumbled something to himself, shaking his head. With a deliberate thrust, he jerked away from Bryan. He glared at him for a moment, then he made his way back to the truck. He opened the toolbox in the bed of the truck and retrieved a .22-gauge rifle. He came back over to Bryan and the calf, stumbling as he came.

Justin held the rifle by his side and frowned at the calf. Her large eyes watched him as she continued to low. Her body had not moved since they arrived, but she continued to arch her neck, and the blood continued to pool around her.

Justin sighed and raised the gun, cocked it, and aimed it at the calf's head, stepping closer as he did so. Bryan did not see him pull the trigger in the darkness, but standing just a couple of feet away, he jumped when the deafening sound of the gun rang through his ears.

Like any boy – and for that matter any girl – in Ashfield, Bryan grew up knowing how to shoot. Unlike a lot of other kids his age, though, he did not do it frequently. Pa liked to fish, but he was never much for hunting. Bryan had gone hunting with Pa once, when he was just entering middle school, but they had ended up just sitting around, eating pimento cheese sandwiches and playing cards for most of the day. They had at one point seen a doe go by, but Pa had said that shooting a doe was not a kind thing to do, since she might be leaving a fawn behind, so they had continued on with their eating and card playing until the sun began to set.

Now, the sound reverberated in his head, making him instinctively put his hands to his ears. He looked down at the calf, who was no longer moving. Her head was no longer a head to be spoken of, but rather it was a bloody pile of pulp.

Justin held the gun where he had fired it, and only after Bryan came over and lightly touched him did he lower it. Justin gave him a hard look and said, "Now we really need to go."

They sat in silence in the truck, headed toward Bryan's home. Although the lighting was dim, Bryan thought Justin looked pale and drawn in the moonlight. "You might as well stay at our place tonight," Bryan said.

Justin looked at him briefly and nodded.

Bryan then texted Winnie, *Justin's coming over. Put Wilbur away.*

Little dots appeared on Bryan's screen, followed by, *Gotcha.*

Winnie was waiting for them on the porch when they arrived. Boomer sat beside her but, as he was too greatly absorbed in the ear scratching Winnie was giving him, he declined to offer so much as a growl when the truck pulled in. Justin smiled when he saw Winnie, and Bryan, noticing this, narrowed his eyes at him.

"Good evening, ma'am," Justin said, tipping an imaginary hat to Winnie.

Winnie gave a slight grin and glanced at Bryan, rolling her eyes when she saw his concerned face. "You boys sure do like staying out late and coming home drunk," she said, flicking her ponytail.

Justin grinned at her. "It's what I do best."

Bryan and Justin sat in the rocking chairs on the porch, and Winnie brought out some coffee and leftover blackberry pie. They said little, listening to the slow creak of the rocking chairs as they rocked back and forth. The calls of frogs filled the air with their high-pitched chirps.

Winnie chatted with Justin about their high school and the various changes it had undergone since Justin left. She told him how the student population had grown so much that two trailers had to be hauled in, and some of the extracurriculars that were generally considered somewhat less important, like theatre and French, were held in these trailers. Winnie had taken a course in creative writing, which was held in one of these trailers. She told Justin that the air conditioning unit for the trailer worked about as well as spitting in the wind, and that she sat there and sweated the entire semester. She was embarrassed to get up at the end of each class period, as there was always a little puddle of sweat that had dripped down her body and pooled on the seat under her.

Justin laughed and cast a glance at Bryan, who was slowly rocking in his chair with a sullen look on his face. Winnie, on seeing Bryan's face, cleared her throat, stood up, and said it was about time for her to head to bed. She told Justin she had laid out some blankets on the couch, and he nodded and thanked her. Winnie threw her arms loosely around Bryan and planted a quick kiss on his cheek. She grinned at Justin and then disappeared inside, with Boomer slowly following behind.

Justin watched Winnie leave and then locked eyes with Bryan, who was frowning at him. Justin cocked his head and pulled his mouth to one side.

"Hey man, don't be pissed. I'm sorry about the cow. That was stupid. I had too much to drink and was driving like a fucking idiot." He gave a small grin.

Bryan sighed. "I'm going to bed," he said. Still frowning, he got up and went inside.

Justin remained on the porch a while longer, listening to the chirps and buzzes filling the otherwise quiet evening air, until the temperature cooled to the point where cold pushed him to leave the rocking chair and head in for the night.

CHAPTER VIII

In the morning, Bryan and Justin were up, as usual, before anyone else. Bryan had made sure of that. He made a somewhat elaborate breakfast of French toast and fresh strawberries, which he and Winnie had picked from Mara Greene's strawberry patch a week earlier. Mama smiled pleasantly when she came downstairs.

"Justin, honey," she said, giving him a light squeeze on the arm, "as much as I enjoy seeing you in the early morning hours, I would rather get to know you when we're not all in a rush to get to work. Why don't you come over for dinner this week? Any night will work, and if you tell me what you want to eat, we'll have it."

Justin slowed his rather hasty gobbling of food and gave a hesitant grin, glancing at Bryan. Bryan was still frowning at him, but his frown lessened when he saw Mama looking at him. Justin nodded and said, "For sure, I'd love to, Mrs. Bradford."

Mama smiled at him. "Oh please call me Maggie. How's tomorrow then?"

* * *

Bryan remained annoyed with Justin for most of the day. He said little, and he ignored most of Justin's attempts at joviality, only mumbling incoherent grunts in response to his lighthearted taunts. His coldness only seemed to make Justin try harder, and he had finally relented somewhat by lunchtime, allowing a half grin whenever Justin teased him about what he called his "perfect family."

He was finishing up lunch with Justin when Hank came over. Hank nodded to Bryan and asked Justin to come with him. Justin momentarily hesitated but then followed Hank, telling Bryan he would meet him back in the pig buildings. Bryan watched as Hank put his hand on Justin's shoulder, causing him to visibly wince. Hank said something low into Justin's ear, and Justin shook his head, raising his hands slightly. Bryan saw Hank's arm tense as he apparently gripped Justin's shoulder harder, but the two went behind one of the buildings and out of Bryan's sight.

Bryan stared down at what was left of his sandwich, then he gathered up his lunch and went to the small shed where the cat, whom Bryan thought of as Jeffrey's cat, lived. The shed was quiet and dim when he entered, and only after a few moments did his eyes adjust. He saw the cat resting on a shelf in the shed, lying on the makeshift bed of old towels and blankets. Her small kittens were nursing vigorously, and her wide green eyes watched Bryan carefully. Bryan laid the remains of his sandwich on the shelf near the cat, then he quietly backed out of the shed.

Bryan found Justin back in the farrowing building. He was weighing a litter of piglets and noting the weights on a clipboard. He wiped his nose with the back of his hand several times, and Bryan saw that he was wiping at a trickle of blood that was slowing running from his nose.

"You good?" Bryan asked, watching Justin carefully.

Justin stayed focused on his task, hoisting each piglet up onto the scale, glancing at the weight and noting it on the clipboard, and then plopping the confused piglets back into their pens. He would reach down and clutch whatever part of the piglet he could grab, sometimes lifting them up by the abdomen, sometimes by a leg, and sometimes by their short tails. When he grabbed a tail, the ensnared piglet would scream and writhe, attempting to get away. Justin would swing the piglet absentmindedly onto the scale, entirely ignoring the high-pitched squeals.

"Hey, man, are you good?" Bryan repeated.

Justin continued working but nodded, glancing up at Bryan and flashing a grin. "Yeah, man. Here, help me weigh 'em."

Bryan did not question Justin further, and they made it through the rest of the day with much less conversation than normally passed between them. At the end of the day, Justin asked if Bryan wanted to get a drink, but Bryan shook his head and said he needed to get home. Justin gave a half grin, teased Bryan for being a "homebody," then slapped him on the arm and said he would see him tomorrow.

Justin was more talkative the following day, and he made several mentions of dinner throughout the day. At the end of the day, after he had hastily discarded all of the dead piglet bodies, along with one sow, he changed into a new shirt and told Bryan

69

they should get going so as not to be late. Bryan wondered if all of Justin's excitement was over the food, but he had a sinking feeling that Winnie might have something to do with it, as well.

When they arrived, Winnie and Mama were in the kitchen with the windows open. Old country music – Patsy Cline from the sound of it – rolled out of an old style radio that Mama kept on the counter, and Winnie swayed slightly to the beat as she chopped spinach for a salad. The boys approached from behind, and Justin paused in the doorway, watching Winnie for a moment, until Bryan jabbed him in ribs with his elbow.

Justin grinned and put his hands up. "Okay, okay," he chuckled.

Mama sat Justin at the kitchen table, saying that he was a guest and that "guests sit," while she put Bryan to work dicing onions. Bryan frowned, and Justin winked at him. Mama offered Justin either lemonade or sweet tea, and he went with the tea. She poured him a glass and handed it to him, smiling as the ice clinked inside.

"Now Justin," she said, her back to him as she turned back to her work in the kitchen, "my son's been spending a lot of time with you." Justin had the glass raised halfway to his mouth, but he paused expectantly, clearly unsure of where the question was leading. Mama, focusing back on the cooking, also paused, quickly throwing on a blue checkered oven mitt and removing a pan of golden bread from the oven. Justin glanced at Bryan, who shrugged.

Mama pushed a fallen strand of coal black hair out of her eyes. "Sorry," she said, smiling. "What I was saying was, Bryan spends nearly all his time with you now, between work and whatever you two do in the evenings, so we've got to get to know you better. You can't just be sleeping on the couch and sneaking out in the morning." She gave Justin a half grin. "So tell us everything we need to know about you."

Justin had noticeably relaxed at Mama's playful nature, and he grinned as he gulped down a few sips of the sweet tea. He caught Winnie's eye, and she smiled at him, causing him to shed any remaining tension.

"Oh," he started, "there's not a whole lot to tell about me." He stopped talking momentarily, but Mama looked at him with her eyebrows slightly raised, with an expression that clearly told him to go on. "I spend most of my time working on the farm. Hank, my daddy, owns it, so I've been there since I was a kid."

Mama was focused on stirring a panful of some sort of vegetables. She glanced up when Justin stopped talking. "And do you want to keep working there?"

Justin gave a short, hard chuckle. "No, ma'am. No way."

Mama raised an eyebrow and looked at him. "So what would you like to do?"

"Oh," Justin raised his hands and gave a slight shrug. "Maybe go to the coast. Maybe work on a fishing boat a little ways up north. Really anywhere other than the farm would suit me." He nodded toward Bryan. "I'm not sure how much he's told you, but it's not really the kind of work you want to be doing all your life."

"Well," Mama said, glancing at Winnie, "I can imagine that's true." She said nothing more for a few moments as she checked the oven, adjusted the temperature, and added the onions Bryan had been chopping to some potatoes and greens in a pan on the stove. She turned back to Justin and said, "Are you much of a fisherman, then?"

Justin grinned. "Oh yeah. Yes, ma'am, I am. Aside from handling hogs, hunting and fishing is what I do best."

"Oh you'll have to take me sometime then," Winnie said cheerfully. Bryan quickly raised his head and shot her an annoyed look, which she intentionally ignored.

Justin nodded eagerly. "Sure thing," he said grinning. He glanced at Bryan, who was frowning at him, which made him grin all the more.

Mama, focused on moving around various dishes and ingredients in the kitchen, wiped a bit of sweat off her brow. "Well," she said to Justin, "I hope you aren't tired of fish. Winnie just stopped eating pork and beef, so we're a little heavy on the fish and chicken lately."

Justin raised an eyebrow. "Oh yeah?"

Winnie beamed and raised her head a bit. "That's right. I haven't had any red meat in a week." She smiled proudly, and Bryan rolled his eyes.

The gravel crunched outside as Pa's oversized diesel truck rolled in. A few moments later, Pa appeared at the door. His features were warm as he saw Mama and moved in to give her a light kiss on the forehead. He did the same to Winnie, who popped up to meet him. He then glanced around and noticed Justin. Justin smiled, and Pa hesitated, as if confused. He started to frown, but then, perhaps realizing that his face was clearly in Justin's view, he paused, pulled his frown back in, and pursed his lips together in his best attempt at a smile.

Justin nodded at Pa awkwardly, giving a slight out-of-place wave, and Pa returned it no less awkwardly. Pa emitted a muffled grunt and then went off to change out of his work clothes.

When dinner was ready, they ate on the back porch, as was their usual habit during the warmer months. A cool breeze gently rocked the bright green leaves on the maple and sassafras trees surrounding the house. The rapid drumming of a woodpecker occasionally sounded in the distance, and as the evening came on, the calls of frogs filled the air.

Mama asked Justin a bit about his family during the meal, and he answered her questions, although in a more guarded manner than Bryan was used to him speaking. His mother, he said while pushing his fried potatoes around with his fork, had left when he was younger. He gave no explanation as to why, and Mama, seeing that the subject was clearly a sensitive one, did not press. Justin sighed heavily, and Bryan saw a look of pity on Mama's and Winnie's faces. Changing the subject, Justin lit up when he told them about Amanda's son, Conner, and what a "funny little devil" he was.

Bryan caught Winnie and Justin sharing a few more glances than he would have liked, and he half wondered if she was doing it just to annoy him. He made a mental note to address it later, but before he had the chance, she and Justin had already set a day to go fishing.

"That day good for you?" Justin asked Bryan, obviously assuming that he would be coming as well. Bryan started to say he had to check his calendar, immediately realized how ridiculous that sounded, and simply nodded.

As soon as Justin had left for the evening, after extolling numerous thanks and praises on Mama, Bryan went to Winnie's room. She was on her bed, lying on her stomach with headphones in her ears. She was kicking her legs back and forth behind her back as she listened to something with an upbeat tempo. Wilbur lay on the bed beside her. She was gently rubbing his belly with one hand, and he was stretching and kicking his short hind legs, making soft grunting noises. Beside her bed, she had erected a playpen and filled it with blankets and some of Boomer's old toys. Bryan had seen Wilbur in the playpen once since he had arrived. Every other time, he was either in Winnie's arms or right beside her.

Winnie pulled one earbud out when she saw Bryan watching her. "What?" she asked.

"What are you doing, Winnie?" Bryan asked, sighing.

Winnie narrowed her eyes. "What do you mean, 'What am I doing?'"

Bryan looked at the floor and shuffled. "You know Justin isn't the kind of guy you want to get involved with."

Winnie raised her eyebrows. "Oh, is that right?" She narrowed her eyes and pointed at him. "You know he's like your best friend, right?"

Bryan's eyes widened and his brow furrowed as he looked at Winnie. "What? What are you talking about?"

Winnie rolled her eyes. "Seriously? You spend all of your time with him."

Bryan shook his head. "I work with him."

Winnie stood up and put a hand on her hip. "Oh really? Is that what you're doing at midnight, when y'all both come in totally trashed? Working? Come on. You can't hang out with him, bring him to dinner, and then act like he's not worth the time of day." She closed her eyes and shook her head, as if just thinking of Bryan's actions was too much for her to bear. Wilbur, possibly sensing Winnie's agitation, was emitting short, high-pitched noises as he watched her.

"Anyway," Winnie continued, "we're just going fishing. It's not even a date. You're coming, too. And I don't know if I even like him like that, but I think he's funny, and it's nice to be around someone funny, rather than a dark gloomy cloud all the time."

Bryan winced slightly at the last sentence, as he knew it was directed at him. He also knew that it was true.

"Whatever," Bryan said, shaking his head slightly. "I can't tell you what to do, but I don't think you should date him. He's way older than you, and he's . . . ." Bryan hesitated.

Winnie looked up. "He's what?"

Bryan looked at her. "He's not always nice. I mean, he's not mean really, but he's done some stupid things."

Winnie held his gaze. "What does that even mean?"

Bryan ran his hands through his hair, leaving his hair looking disheveled and slightly greasy. "It doesn't matter," he said, defeated.

Winnie watched him for a moment. She tilted her head slightly, then she came closer and gave him a quick hug around the neck. "Don't worry, big brother. It'll all be fine." She smiled, then she lay back down on her bed and returned her earbud to her ear.

Bryan lingered a moment longer, then he left, feeling more confused than ever.

* * *

Amanda saw the lights from Justin's truck shine through her bedroom window and slowly creep up her wall as he made his way up the driveway. It was late, but she was still up, thinking of what her brother might be doing at his dinner with Bryan Bradford. She was lying on her back on her bed and holding her phone over her, swiping through Facebook. Facebook, as she thought of it, was the place where everyone showed off the most wonderful and beautiful moments in their lives. Ninety-eight percent of your life might be shitty, but if you posted a photo of yourself sipping a four-dollar coffee at Starbucks, you suddenly seemed happy and carefree and confident. You were now the kind of person who has time to enjoy the precious moments in life, like a grossly overpriced cup of coffee. You were certainly not the kind of person who works part-time at the Shell gas station and part-time at the worst diner in town, only to make just enough money to keep yourself and a three-year-old fed and clothed in thrift store clothing.

She got up from the bed and went to the window, where she watched Justin quietly shut the driver's side door on his truck. She lost sight of him as he headed up onto the porch. She heard the screen door creak downstairs, and she heard Justin's booted feet on the stairs.

Justin was about to pass her room when she stuck her head into the hallway. "Hey, you," she said. Justin halted and gave a hesitant smile. She hated that smile. Conner looked at her the same way, as if he were never sure if he should smile, cry, or simply turn and run.

"Hey, sis," he returned, scratching his head. "What are you doing up?"

"Oh," she said, shrugging a bit, "just hanging out. How was your dinner?"

Justin smiled a bit more. "Oh, pretty good really. Their mama is real nice – and not a bad cook either." Justin paused and thought for a second. "I don't really think his daddy likes me very much, but I guess that don't matter."

Amanda tried to appear nonchalant, but she was burning to know everything about the football star now turned farm worker. Since she had seen him with Justin the morning after their first night of drinking together, he continually lingered in her mind. She thought of his rigid body and tight muscles, his relaxed demeanor with his friends, and his intense focus on the field. She wanted him to think about her as much as she was thinking about him.

"You should invite him to our place, to return the favor," she said, raising an eyebrow and smiling.

Justin looked at the floor. "Yeah, I mean, I can ask."

Amanda tilted her head at him.

"You know, he's just busy I think, with his family and sister and all." Justin said. He started to move around Amanda and on to his room, but she took a step further into the hall, blocking him.

"Hey Justin," she started, moving a bit closer to him. "What happened to your truck?"

Justin looked up blankly. "What?"

Amanda smiled. "Yeah, you've got a pretty good dent on the bumper. You hit something?" She stared at him.

Justin looked at her with his brow furrowed.

Amanda continued, sighing and picking at an imperceptible spot on her arm. "You want me to see if Daddy can help you get that dent out? Maybe by the weekend. He's not in the best mood right now, what with one of his calves getting killed and all. Did he tell you about that?"

Justin stood silent. He opened his mouth to say something, but then he closed it again. Amanda smiled at him, then she gave him a light hug. "Oh don't worry, little brother," she said, close to his ear. "I'm sure Daddy will never notice that little dent."

Justin's face had reddened. Amanda released him, smiling, and headed back into her room. She paused in the doorway and looked back. "Let me know when Bryan can come over for dinner. I'll make him something nice." She gave him one more smile, ignoring the strained look on his face, and went into her room, shutting the door behind her.

CHAPTER IX

When Bryan pulled down the dusty road to the farm the following Monday, he found Hank with Justin in front of the pig building. Hank was talking, and Justin was looking at the ground but nodding occasionally. As Bryan pulled closer, he saw Hank glance his way and nod in his direction to Justin, who also looked his way. Justin grinned and waved, and then he said something to Hank, who, after looking toward Bryan once more, left to go to the buildings containing the older, weaned pigs.

Bryan got out of his truck, and Justin came to meet him. Justin grinned and slapped Bryan on the shoulder. He turned to walk with him into the building and said, "Hey man, we got some work to do today."

Bryan tilted his head, prompting Justin to add, "We need to process some of the pigs today."

"What do you mean?" Bryan asked.

Justin laughed. "Man, it'd sure be a lot easier if you knew something about pigs." He shook his head. "Look, there are three things you gotta do with pigs once they're a few days old. You gotta cut their tails, cut their teeth, and take away their manhood." He grinned at Bryan, who looked at him blankly. "I mean, you gotta castrate 'em."

Bryan furrowed his brow. "Why?"

"Well you gotta cut their tails and teeth so they don't hurt each other. Pigs can be real assholes to each other. They'll bite each other's tails or chew 'em clean off. It's better to take 'em off, then they can't do that. And they have these razor sharp little teeth. We cut those off, so if they do bite, they can't do as much damage. Plus, if you leave 'em, they can tear their mama up real bad biting on her."

Bryan gave the idea some thought and winced, causing Justin to chuckle.

"But why do you castrate them?" Bryan asked. "I mean, what's it matter?"

Justin shook his head. "It's about the taste. If you don't castrate the boys, then the meat will taste like shit, 'cause of the testosterone I think."

Bryan frowned, not really understanding most of what Justin was telling him.

"Hank and Wayne have been handling most of it, since you're new, but Hank was telling me he's ready for you to start helping. We got a litter that needs to be processed today, so you can help me with that."

Justin went over the process in more detail as they went inside the building and dressed for the day. He told Bryan to get started checking the pigs and the waterers and feeders while he gathered supplies. Bryan did as he asked, anxious, as always, as he checked each pen. After a few minutes, Justin returned with a metal tray, like a lunch tray, on which he had several tools. Justin set the tray down and helped Bryan finish checking the pens in the gestation area. Then, he picked up the tray, and they made their way into the farrowing section.

They went from pen to pen, checking the waterers and feeders and removing any dead piglets. As he neared each pen, Bryan felt his heart start to race a bit. It was not so much the dead piglets that he feared but rather the ones who were still alive and in the process of dying. He found two such piglets. Each one was lying on its side, apparently unable to move. Each time he brought the piglet to Justin, who simply looked at Bryan, sighed, and dispatched the piglet by slamming its head into the concrete walkway. The second piglet was still writhing after the initial bashing, so Justin, frowning, picked up the piglet and tried again, seeming to put more effort into slamming down the piglet's head this time. After the second blow, the piglet did not move.

After they finished, Justin motioned to Bryan, and they moved to a pen with a sow and seven piglets. The piglets, apparently done nursing for the moment, were piled into a heap on the concrete floor. The floor looked damp, and the piglets on the outer layer of the pile shivered as they slept.

"Okay," Justin said. "So I'm gonna need you to hold each one, and I'll do the processing, okay?"

Bryan nodded hesitantly.

Justin grinned. "It's fine. They're only a few days old, so they really can't feel pain like you would think. They're gonna scream, 'cause that's what pigs do, but it don't mean nothing."

Bryan said nothing but watched as Justin stooped down and scooped up one of the piglets. He handed the piglet to Bryan. The piglet, just waking up, was still fairly calm but starting to make a series of rapid grunts, with an occasional high-pitched squeal mixed in.

Justin showed Bryan how to hold the piglet by grabbing the top legs and keeping a hand around its neck to hold the piglet still. Justin took a syringe from the tray with a dark colored liquid inside. He took the cap off of a needle on the end.

"It's iron," he said. "They all need it right after they're born. Hold her real still."

Bryan tightened his grip, and the piglet, in apparent response, started to squirm and emit a few sharp squeals.

Justin held the piglet's bottom, which was dangling down, with his left hand and inserted the needle into the upper thigh area on the piglet's right leg. The piglet emitted a high-pitched scream that seemed to touch every nerve in Bryan's body. He winced and instinctively loosened his grip on the piglet, who fell free from Bryan's grasp, thudding onto the floor. The syringe fell with the piglet and stuck out of her upper right leg.

"Damn it," Justin cursed. He ran after the piglet, who was running blindly along the concrete walkway. He grabbed her fairly easily and returned to Bryan.

He laughed as he caught his breath. "God damn it, Bryan. You can't drop 'em."

Bryan apologized, and Justin waved it off, saying, "Just hold on this time."

Justin handed the squealing piglet back to Bryan, raising his eyebrows at him with a slight grin on his face. "Hold on," he said. Justin took hold of the syringe, which was still poking out of the piglet and waggling around each time the piglet moved. He injected the liquid in the syringe into the piglet and then removed the needle from the piglet's side.

Justin put the syringe down and picked up a tool that looked like the nail clippers Mama had for Boomer. He had a cup filled with a clear liquid, which he told Bryan was alcohol, and he dipped the end of the tool into the liquid.

"Okay, hold her tight," Justin said. He grabbed the piglet's tail and pulled it down, then, taking the tool out of the alcohol, he put the cutting end around the tail, near the base, and squeezed the handle.

The scream was nearly deafening in Bryan's mind. He felt the piglet jerk and try to pull away. He tightened his grip, but as he saw blood trickling out of the tail at a steady rate, he felt nausea start to overwhelm him. He closed his eyes and tried to steady himself, feeling the piglet jerk and writhe in his hands. He opened his eyes and saw Justin staring at him.

"You okay?" Justin asked with a hesitant smile. "You got this?"

Bryan felt too ill to speak, but he nodded quickly.

"Okay then, one more thing for her."

Justin jabbed the cutting tool into the alcohol, and he picked up a different tool. This one looked similar to the first but more like pliers than nail clippers. The end of the tool differed from the blunt points of pliers in that it consisted of two blades that appeared capable of cutting.

Justin shifted himself in front of the piglet and wedged his left hand between her teeth, at the back of the mouth, so she was unable to close her mouth. He glanced up at Bryan, who was watching him, took in a breath, and then moved the plier-like tool to the piglet's mouth. Bryan watched as Justin positioned the blades around one of the piglet's teeth and squeezed the handle. There was an audible crunching sound, and Bryan saw the top half of the tooth fly into the air. At the same time, he felt the piglet lurch in his hands, and he struggled to keep a hold on her. Justin looked at him briefly and then turned back to the piglet. He moved quickly from tooth to tooth, repeating the process. The piglet continued her bloodcurdling scream, and she continued thrusting in Bryan's hands. Bryan felt the muscles in his arm becoming sore as he struggled to keep the piglet still.

After Justin had repeated the tooth cutting more times than Bryan could keep up with, Justin dropped the cutting tool into the alcohol and said, "She's done," taking the piglet out of Bryan's hands and dropping her back in her pen. The piglet ran around the pen squealing for several minutes. Then she curled into a pile on the floor near her siblings and lay shivering and squealing, with each squeal seeming more defeated than the last.

"So that was one," Justin said. "There's six more in this litter. You good, or do you need a break?"

Bryan wondered what good a break would do, if he knew he would have to come back and finish the process. He shook his head and said, "Let's just get it done."

Justin grinned. "Okay, let's do the girls first."

Four of the litter turned out to be girls. They repeated the process three more times, and each time it went more or less the same. The one exception was the third girl they did. When Justin clipped one of her teeth, blood started spewing upward, speckling Justin's face. He blinked and spit out the blood that had made its way into his mouth.

"Shit," he said. "I guess I clipped her tongue on that one."

After finishing the girls, there were three boys that needed to be done. With the first boy, Justin repeated the process – iron injection, then tail cutting, then teeth cutting. After that, Justin asked Bryan to hold the pig upside down. Bryan did, and the piglet, who was already apparently upset and squealing, increased his protestations. Justin took what looked like a scalpel off of the tray. He held the piglet's testicles in his hand, and he pushed them upward in their sacs until the skin was tight around them. Glancing briefly at Bryan, he made a slight cut in each of the sacs. He then pushed the left testicle harder, popping it from the sac. He grabbed the testicle with his right hand and gave it a fast and quick jerk.

Bryan heard a clear tearing sound as the testicle pulled away in Justin's hand. Strings of some bodily tissue trailed behind it, and the piglet immediately screamed louder than ever. Between the sound and the sight of the trailing, bloody strings, Bryan lost his composure. He felt hot and weak, and nausea overcame him. He let go of the piglet and doubled over, vomiting. Justin was still holding the piglet's remaining testicle, but the weight of the falling piglet pulled his hand down. Justin stumbled forward as the piglet fell, and his right hand, which was still holding the scalpel, jerked upward as he attempted to catch his balance. The blade of the scalpel slashed into his left hand, and he let out a short cry of pain. Blood gushed from his left hand, and he clamped his right hand over the cut, cursing as he did.

"Jesus Christ, Bryan," he yelled angrily. "What the fuck are you doing?"

Bryan was doubled over and vomiting, and he lifted his head to look at Justin. "I'm sorry, man," he mumbled.

Justin's face relaxed somewhat as he realized that Bryan was struggling. He winced with the pain and was dripping blood on the floor in quantities that Bryan thought were really too much to be insubstantial. He shook his head and said, "Okay, I have to do something with this. Just try to get up and then get the pig if you can." Justin quickly left, leaving Bryan to try to regain enough strength to stand.

Bryan took a couple of minutes to steady himself, watching the piglet run around the concrete walkway, squealing as it did. The piglet seemed to have no direction and was simply running and squealing. Bryan stood slowly, then he followed the piglet to the end of the walkway, cornering it against a pen. He reached down for the piglet, who was pressing away from him against the metal bars of the pen. Bryan put one hand under the piglet and scooped him up, cupping his other hand behind the squealing piglet. The piglet screamed and writhed, but Bryan held him firmly. He attempted to soothe the piglet with a hushing sound, and he gently patted his back with each soft "shhh" sound he made. The piglet finally settled, ceased his screaming, and tucked his head between Bryan's arm and body.

Bryan thought of Wilbur. Winnie was still bottle feeding him, and she often tucked him into her arms while she gave him the warm bottle. He clearly thought of her as his mother, as he followed her around constantly. Wherever she was, he sat either in her lap or by her side. Even when she showered, he sat on the bathroom mat outside of the shower, looking up at the closed curtain with his head cocked to one side. Pa had initially tried to insist that he stay in the barn, but after Winnie rolled her eyes and Mama simply laughed, he had realized he should cut his losses and at least push to get him out of the house before he reached his full size. He assumed, incorrectly, that this was something they could all agree on.

The piglet shivered as Bryan held him, but his shivers decreased in intensity the longer he stayed wrapped in Bryan's arms. After a few minutes, Justin returned. He had gauze wrapped around his left hand, but Bryan saw a few trickles of bright red blood seeping through. Justin approached, looking a shade too white, Bryan thought, and commented that Bryan had nearly put the piglet to sleep.

Bryan smiled looking down at the piglet. Justin lifted his eyebrows slightly, asking, "You ready to finish with this one?"

Bryan hesitated, looking down at the piglet. No, he did not want to finish. He wanted to be done with this whole wretched business. He wanted to be done with this farm, where you cut off pigs' tails with fingernail clippers and crush their teeth with pliers. He did not want to hear the ripping sound again as Justin pulled a testicle from its sac. But, he thought, that was why he was there, and that was what was expected. Unsure of how to respond, he simply looked at the piglet, resting comfortably in his arms.

Justin sighed. "Look, we can call it a day with this one, but let's do the other two. Sound good?"

Bryan nodded, knowing that this was the best he would get. He put the piglet back in its pen, and Justin handed him another male. Justin finished off the last two piglets in the same manner as the first, cutting the tails and teeth, and then pulling the testicles out of their respective sacs. Each time Justin prepared to pull the testicles, Bryan closed his eyes and gritted his teeth. The ripping sound that each testicle made as it was violently torn away was nearly unbearable. It was always immediately followed by a nerve-wracking shriek from the piglet, who then struggled and writhed to remove itself from Bryan's grasp. Justin moved quickly, and the last two piglets were finished and put back into their pen, shivering and whimpering, in no time.

Bryan said he needed some fresh air, and he went outside while Justin put away the supplies he had needed to process the piglets. Justin joined him a moment later, cocking his head to one side as he approached.

"That was a bit much for you, huh?" He grinned.

Bryan looked at him, and, still feeling queasy, he simply nodded.

Justin chuckled. "Okay, well, I can try to get Jeffrey to help me sometimes, but it'd be good if you could help, too, if I need you." He slapped Bryan on the back, and Bryan struggled to fight off another wave of nausea.

Justin asked Bryan to get a drink after work, and, after some convincing, he agreed. As they drove to the bar, Justin texted Amanda, *We'll be at Rancher's Respite, if you want to meet us. That's the best I can do.*

After they had each had their first drink, and the sickening feeling from the day was slowly fading, Bryan said, "You know, I have no idea how you do that every day. That was awful."

Justin, who had been watching Mandy run drinks from the bar to a table of guys, turned to Bryan. He shrugged. "I mean, I've been doing it since I was a kid, so I'm pretty good at it at this point."

He let his eyes fall back on Mandy, in her crisp blue polo and dark blue denim skirt, as she leaned over the table to get the boys' orders. The boys appeared to be around Justin's age, and they had already had a few drinks. One was watching Mandy closely as she took their order, and he leaned over to his friend and whispered something in his ear. The friend grinned and nodded.

Justin looked back at Bryan. "But anyway, I don't think they feel pain like we do, so really it's not that bad. You just gotta get your head around that."

Bryan pulled his mouth to one side, not sure he agreed with this sentiment, but not really thinking it mattered enough to dispute. He was about to say more when he saw Justin's eyes flick to someone behind him. Justin's eyes narrowed, and his face tightened. He got up quickly and walked past Bryan. Bryan turned to see a girl he recognized as Justin's sister, with a small boy tailing along beside her.

Justin grabbed Amanda's arm and said in a low tone, "Amanda, what the fuck? You brought Conner? To a fucking bar?"

Amanda rolled her eyes and pulled away. "Oh he's fine," she said. "I mean I couldn't leave him at home."

Justin looked at her, exasperated, then, apparently deciding it was not worth the fight, he bent down to Conner and grinned. "Hey, little buddy, what are you up to?"

Conner, who was hiding behind Amanda's legs, came out at the sound of Justin's voice. He was beaming, and he quickly left Amanda and rushed into Justin's arms.

"Hey, Uncle Jus," he said in the slow, stilted speech of a three-year-old. "Mama said I could get a hamburger."

Justin raised an eyebrow. "Oh, is that right? Hm, let me see if I can help with that. Come over here and meet my friend Bryan." Justin led Conner by the hand over to the booth where he and Bryan were sitting. Amanda had already made her way there and was talking with Bryan.

When Justin pulled Conner into the seat beside him, Amanda asked Bryan, "Do you mind if I sit on your side?"

Bryan glanced at Justin, who shrugged and rolled his eyes. Bryan gave a forced smile to Amanda and slid over in the seat to make room for her.

Justin flagged down Jeffrey and ordered a hamburger with fries and a Coke for Conner.

"I'll have a glass of cabernet," Amanda said.

"Amanda," Justin said, glaring at her. He did not think it would be appropriate to chastise her in front of Conner, so he just raised his eyebrows at her in a "what the fuck" manner.

Amanda smiled, "Yes, little brother?" She smiled at Justin's frustration in being unable to say what he was thinking while sitting next to Conner. Justin glared at her until she turned away and started talking to Bryan.

Bryan was wedged uncomfortably back in the booth, attempting to give Amanda as much room as possible. She asked how his day had gone and, after being unable to say anything that he felt was appropriate for a toddler, he simply put up his hands and said, "Oh, you know."

Amanda pursed her lips. This was going to be harder than she thought. *This might be easier if I hadn't had to bring the little brat.* She scowled at Conner, who was focused on Justin.

Amanda tried again. "I heard you had Justin over for dinner."

Bryan nodded.

"That was nice of you," Amanda said sweetly. She looked at Justin, who was leaning in close to Conner and showing him something on his phone. Conner was laughing deep belly laughs, and Justin was grinning at him.

Amanda leaned a little closer to Bryan. "He doesn't have a lot of friends," she said in a low voice, "so it meant a lot to him." Bryan stared at his drink, which he no longer felt like drinking.

"You should come over one night," Amanda said brightly. "Let us treat you. I'm a pretty good cook." She grinned at him. Bryan continued staring at his drink, with both hands wrapped tightly around it. He wondered if he could make the glass burst by focusing all his energy on it.

"What do you say?" Amanda asked, jabbing him lightly in the ribs with her elbow.

Bryan continued looking down. *What did she say?* He was not sure. He did not want to say anything. He wanted her to leave, but it seemed like that was not going to happen. He looked up and met her eyes. "That would be nice," he said, smiling awkwardly.

Amanda beamed. "Perfect. How about next Friday?"

Bryan returned to staring at his drink, but he nodded. Justin was shooting them glances, but he was clearly unable to follow the conversation, as Conner was nearly in his lap and shaking with laughter over whatever Justin was showing him on the phone.

Amanda quickly finished off her glass of wine and ordered another. Justin glared at her but said nothing. Jeffrey came by and asked if he wanted another beer, but he shook his head "no," looking at Conner. Conner's hamburger had arrived, and he was looking it over, picking up the bread to examine the meat inside then cautiously picking a pickle off the top and laying it flatly on his tongue. He looked at Justin and grinned wildly. Justin returned an even crazier grin, causing Conner to laugh so hard he spit out the pickle.

Amanda narrowed her eyes at Conner and said in a stern tone, "Hey, don't spit at the table. What's wrong with you?" Conner dropped his eyes, and the smile fell from his face. He looked down at his burger and started poking at it with his fork.

Justin frowned at Amanda, but she ignored the look and turned back to Bryan. Bryan was stuck in the booth between Amanda and the wall, and he pressed back against the wall, as if it might move and allow him to escape. Amanda, not noticing, talked incessantly. She told Bryan how much work it was to try to keep up with Conner and all that he needed. She said that his daddy had run out on them when she was having Conner, and she had not seen him since. She said that she worked two jobs to support him and that she never had enough time. She had not been out with her friends in ages, and the last time she had gone out, she was so tired that she had one drink and fell asleep in her seat.

Amanda told Bryan how she was a waitress at Pickett's Grill, commonly considered the worst diner in town, with grilled cheese sandwiches that dripped thick yellow grease and left shimmering pools of oil on whatever plate they were placed. She said that she did a fantastic job and that she would have been promoted to a manager position by now, except that her asshole supervisor was one of the "good ol' boys" and did not care to see a woman rising in the workplace. Bryan's eyes flicked to Conner on hearing the word "asshole," but if Conner heard, he did not acknowledge it. He was still intently focused on his burger, now picking small chucks off, evaluating them, and plopping them into his mouth.

Amanda continued chatting, apparently not noticing that Bryan had not spoken a word. As she spoke, she drank, and she quickly made her way through four glasses of wine. The alcohol appeared to have little effect on her, as she continued her long discourse with hardly even a pause for breath.

Conner began to lean heavily against Justin, and Justin, looking at Amanda, said, "I'm going to take him home."

Amanda smiled her sweetest smile. "Aw, thank you, little brother." She looked at Conner. "Good night, buddy," she said. "Uncle Jus is gonna take you home, okay?"

Conner nodded sleepily and leaned more heavily into Justin. Justin hoisted him up into his arms and slid out of the booth with him. He saw a look of panic cross Bryan's face as he stood up, but, unable to do anything else, he gave an apologetic shrug and said, "Sorry, man, he needs to get to bed."

Bryan could not argue with that, but he did not want to be left alone with Amanda. He ran several excuses through his head for why he needed to leave, and he was just about to let the winning excuse escape his mouth when Justin, hesitating, said, "Amanda, do you want me to take you home now, too?"

Amanda narrowed her eyes at Justin in a "what the fuck are you doing" manner. She quickly pushed the annoyance off her face and smiled at Bryan. "No, no, I'm good. I'll hang out here until I'm good to drive."

Justin looked from her to Bryan, hesitated, then left with Conner.

Once they were gone, Bryan waited for Amanda to move to the other side of the booth, which was now empty. When she failed to do so, he cleared his throat and asked if she could let him out to go to the restroom. She smiled, of course she could, and she scooted out and moved to the other side of the booth.

Bryan thought about simply leaving, making a break for it once he was out of her sight. He reached the restroom and turned back to look at Amanda. He felt just a hint of pity as he looked at her, sitting alone in the booth, looking around the room and occasionally checking her phone. He guessed it was flattering that she liked him, as it seemed that she did, and she was attractive enough, but there was something about her that he did not like. He did not know exactly what it was, but she made him want to get away, quickly. Maybe he was leading her on, he thought. He needed to be clear and set things straight.

He returned to the table and stood without sitting. "Hey, Amanda," Bryan began, "I really have to go. I, I didn't realize how late it was."

Amanda smiled. "Oh sure, no problem. I know you're a working man and need your sleep." She grinned widely in the similarly startling way that Justin tended to grin, and Bryan wondered if he and Winnie shared such resemblances.

Amanda stood, leaning heavily on the table and wobbling as she did so. She made her way out of the booth and headed toward the door, patting Bryan on the shoulder clumsily as she passed him.

Bryan sighed and shook his head slightly. He briefly wondered how horrible it would be if he just let her drive herself home. She was an adult, right? She could make her own choices. Then he thought about how he would feel if it were Winnie, and he quickly pulled out some cash to leave on the table and hurried out after her.

Amanda was stumbling toward her car, and Bryan intercepted her. "Let me drive you home," he said. She smiled and nodded.

On the way home, Amanda grilled Bryan about his football days, asking if he was still friends with any of his teammates, if he missed playing, if he could teach Conner how to play, and innumerable other random questions. Bryan gave mostly short, sometimes mumbled answers, having no interest in reliving his former glory days.

When they were nearly to her house, Amanda slid into the middle seat and leaned her head on Bryan's shoulder. He felt hot and tried to move nearer to the door, but Amanda just scooted in closer. Bryan pulled into their driveway and parked, and Amanda kept her head on him for a moment longer.

"Do you need help getting in?" Bryan asked, immediately regretting the question, as he thought she might take it to mean that he was asking to come in.

Amanda lifted her head and smiled sweetly. "I think I can make it," she said. She paused, then she leaned in and kissed him. Bryan instinctively jerked his head back, but he slammed it into the driver's side window. When Amanda pulled back, Bryan was rubbing the back of his head. She chuckled, then she got out of the truck.

"I'll see you next Friday," she said, then she gave a small wave, closed the door, and turned to go into the house. There was a light on the front porch, and Bryan watched just long enough to make sure she made it inside, then he quickly pulled the truck around and headed toward home.

When Amanda got upstairs, she walked past Conner's room and peeked inside. There was a dim nightlight on, and she saw Conner's head poking out from under a layer of sheets and blankets. His eyes were closed, and he was breathing audibly. Beside him, Justin was lying on top of the sheets, with one arm wrapped around Conner. He was slumped down, also asleep, and Amanda felt a jolt of annoyance run through her. She started to go into the room and jostle Justin awake, but she imagined Conner waking up, too, and her having to deal with getting him back to sleep, so she simply shut the door and retreated to her own room.

CHAPTER X

The following morning was cloudy as Bryan drove into the farm. The air was thick and humid, and the sun mostly hid in the gray sky, occasionally peeking out and casting a bit of sunlight onto the ground in patches.

Bryan found Justin already at work inside the pig building. Justin looked up and cocked an eyebrow, "Everything go well last night?" He grinned.

"Man, what the hell," Bryan said, throwing his hands up. "Your sister needs to back off."

Justin laughed. "Yeah, she tends to go after what she wants, and, right now, that seems to be you." He chuckled.

Bryan shook his head. "I'm really not interested right now," he said.

"I know," said Justin, "but you have to make that clear to her."

Bryan sighed. "Yeah, I guess. It was just hard last night. I mean, she was a little pushy."

Justin laughed loudly at that, slapped Bryan on the back and said, "Welcome to my world."

The morning was mostly uneventful, with the boys only finding a handful of dead piglets and none on the verge of death. At lunchtime, they went outside and looked for Jeffrey, but they were unsuccessful in locating him.

"He's probably with the damn cats," Justin said, grinning.

Bryan and Justin made their way to the shed. As they neared, they heard a low moaning noise that made the hair rise on Bryan's arms. He froze and looked at Justin. Justin had slowed. His forehead was creased, and he was looking around for the source of the wailing. He glanced at Bryan and held up a hand for him to wait, which Bryan gladly did, and Justin made his way to the back of the shed.

Bryan saw Justin stop when he came within view of the area behind the shed. He could not see his face, but he saw him raise his hands and run them slowly through his hair. His hands stopped midway on his head, and he stood there motionlessly.

After a moment or two, Bryan took a step and started moving closer to the shed. He saw Justin finally unfreeze and step forward and behind the shed, out of Bryan's view. Bryan hurried to catch up.

When he turned the corner around the shed, Bryan saw Justin, kneeling down and looking forward. He was crouched beside Jeffrey, who also had his back turned to Bryan. Justin's hand was on Jeffrey's back, patting it softly, as Jeffrey rocked back and forth and emitted the painful moan that Bryan had first heard in passing. He heard Justin murmuring a soft, "I'm sorry, man. It'll be okay," as he continued to pat Jeffrey's back.

Bryan approached cautiously. When he was within a few feet of Justin and Jeffrey, he was able to see over them, and he could see a blue five-gallon bucket in front of them, with "Lowe's" written on it in white lettering. He moved closer and saw that the bucket was filled with water. Several small objects were floating on the surface of the water. Bryan froze. He felt his heart skip a beat, and he felt a strong urge to vomit. It was the kittens.

The kittens' dead bodies bobbed along the surface of the water in the bucket. Their small forms were bloated from the water and had distended, clown-like features. One was on its back, and its still blue eyes were frozen looking upward. The mother cat was on the ground, moving somewhat frantically back and forth in front of the bucket, rubbing against it and meowing loudly.

The bucket was several feet away from the shed, with nothing around it, so there was no possibility that the kittens had fallen into the bucket. Bryan shook his head, not understanding. He stepped closer, and Justin looked up slightly but did not make eye contact. Bryan saw that Jeffrey, still wailing, had his hands covering his face and was sobbing. His moaning rose and fell as he rocked forward and back.

Bryan stood, unable to move, feeling sick and weak. Justin glanced up again, saw his face, and, after giving Jeffrey's shoulder a squeeze, stood up. He leaned in to Bryan and in a low voice asked him to head back in, if he did not mind, and start the afternoon work. He said he would stay with Jeffrey a bit and help "take care of" the kittens. Bryan nodded and went inside.

Bryan checked the sows and piglets, and he paused at the pen containing the piglets that he had helped Justin "process." Six of the piglets were nursing, but one stayed in the corner, lying on its side and taking slow, deep breaths. Bryan could see the piglet's chest rise and fall with each breath. He went into the pen, and the piglet squealed and attempted to right itself as he approached. Bryan hesitated, the scream of the piglet causing him to pause and close his eyes to maintain his strength, then he reached and picked up the piglet.

The piglet cried when he picked it up and continued screaming until Bryan was able to soothe it through a hushing sound and constant rubbing of its sides. He saw that this was a boy, and he looked at the empty sac where Justin had pulled out the testicles. The sac had a foul, sickening odor, like rotting fish, and there was a thick yellow mucous oozing out of it. Bryan winced, knowing that the piglet would likely not have a good outcome, and he moved it over to the sow, where its siblings were nursing, so that it could at least be near the others. The piglet looked at its siblings but did not attempt to nurse. It lay its head down and fell motionless again.

Bryan sighed and climbed out of the pen, just as Justin came into the building.

Bryan went to meet him. "What the hell happened?"

Justin continued looking down for a moment, and Bryan was not sure if he had heard him. He started to repeat himself, when Justin looked up, made eye contact, and said, "The kittens, they drowned. They're all dead."

"But how did they drown?" Bryan asked.

Justin looked down, furrowing his brow. He scratched his head and looked up. He started to say something but then stopped, letting his eyes fall again.

Justin looked so guilty that Bryan suddenly asked, "Did you . . . ?"

Justin jerked his head up and narrowed his eyes at Bryan. "What? No. Why the hell would you think that? Of course not." He shook his head and started to walk off.

"Sorry, man," Bryan said, "I just, I mean, you're just acting like you know more than you're saying."

Justin stopped and turned back. He squeezed his eyes shut tight and shook his head. He finally opened his eyes and looked at Bryan. "Yeah, I mean, this isn't the first time. I'm sure," he closed his eyes again, "I'm sure it was Hank. He fucking hates cats. I just thought maybe this time would be different, since they were so far away from the pig buildings."

Bryan felt his mouth fall slightly open with this information. "Jesus," he whispered.

They stood there for a moment not talking.

"Are you gonna say anything to him? To Hank?" Bryan asked.

Justin looked at Bryan, a slightly pained expression on his face. He shook his head. "It wouldn't matter."

Bryan stared after Justin, but he had already turned away. He felt annoyance rising into anger. He hurried after Justin and reached out to put a hand on his shoulder, slowing him down.

"What do you mean it wouldn't matter? You're his kid; he'll listen to you. It's crazy that you're saying this isn't the first time this has happened. Why can't you tell him to stop? That drowning kittens is insane?" Bryan shook his head and felt his anger rising. "I mean you need to try."

Justin pressed his lips together and looked at Bryan, frowning. He took a few moments to respond. He finally relaxed his face a bit, shook his head slowly and said, "Like I said, it wouldn't matter. He doesn't give a damn what I think or say."

Justin started to walk away again, then he turned back and said, "Jeffrey's lucky he didn't kill the mama cat. He probably couldn't get her."

Bryan stared at Justin. Then, suddenly seeming to realize something, he quickly turned and left the building. He nearly ran to the shed, with Justin following after several minutes. He arrived at the shed breathless, and he found Jeffrey still sitting behind it, only now he was no longer sobbing uncontrollably. He was sitting on the ground with his back against the shed. He was looking down, and Bryan saw that his face was still wet with tear stains. The mother cat was weaving in and out of his legs, rubbing against him and meowing loudly, although less frantically than before.

"Jeffrey, man, I'm so sorry," Bryan started. Justin had caught up and was eyeing Bryan. "Listen, why don't we take the mama cat to your house, then you won't have to worry about her. Can you get her in a box?"

Jeffrey, who had been staring at the ground, now looked up hesitantly. He looked to Justin, who raised an eyebrow and looked back at Bryan.

Bryan saw that they were unsure. "My mama," he said, "she works in a vet's office. I'm sure she could help get her fixed, if you want, and you can just take her home. You won't have to worry about this again."

Jeffrey furrowed his brow and looked at Justin again, who was now nodding to Jeffrey that he was in agreement with this idea. Jeffrey turned back to Bryan and nodded. "I can get her in a box."

Toward the end of the day, Justin found an empty box near the trash and brought it to Jeffrey. Jeffrey went into the shed, letting the mama cat follow. She was still meowing loudly and moving in somewhat manic motions, but she followed Jeffrey closely. Jeffrey closed the shed door behind them, while Bryan and Justin waited outside.

There was momentary silence, followed by a low yowling sound, which increased in volume until it was a scream. The screaming alternated with hissing and growling sounds, along with the occasional curse from Jeffrey. Bryan and Justin looked at each other. Bryan's eyes were widening, but Justin just shrugged.

"He'll be fine," he said. "Not much we can do to help anyway."

Bryan nodded but winced as the screeches and curses continued to pour out of the shed. Finally, when Bryan was on the verge of giving in and entering the shed, Jeffrey emerged, holding the box, which seemed to shake and move all on its own. Jeffrey gave half a grin as blood dripped from deep scratches and bite marks on his arms and neck and down his left cheek.

"Jesus," Bryan whispered, causing Jeffrey to grin wider.

At home, Bryan presented the growling box to Mama, telling her the story – albeit without the mention of any kittens – and asking if she could get the cat fixed.

Mama's puzzled look softened after Bryan's explanation, and she gave a half smile as she took the box, nodding. "Well, yes, I'm sure I can. Although she can't stay in here until tomorrow." Mama raised her eyebrows at Bryan. "Seems like she's pretty wild?"

Bryan nodded.

They set the cat up in an old dog crate they had from when Boomer was a puppy. Bryan did not remember it, but Mama said Boomer chewed up everything when they got him – socks, shoes, power cords, pillows, books, picture frames – really anything he could sink his teeth into. Mama laughed as she remembered how Pa, who was already fit to be tied at having a dog living inside the house, had nearly lost his mind when Boomer chewed several holes in his brand new Carhartt work boots. He had grabbed Boomer's collar and was starting to throw him outside when the collar slipped off. Boomer ran back to the bedroom and jumped into Mama's arms, and Mama had dared Pa to even try to take the dog. Pa had left the house with hole-ridden shoes and his head hanging. Mama had bought the crate for Boomer, along with a new pair of boots for Pa, and, with age, the chewing habit had passed.

A day later Mama brought Jeffrey's cat back home, spayed and no less wild. She suggested they keep her confined for a few days, to keep a check on her, and Bryan made arrangements with Justin for them to return the cat to Jeffrey's home the following week.

CHAPTER XI

When the day of Amanda's anticipated dinner came, Justin spent the day grinning at Bryan.

"She's so excited that you're coming over," Justin said chuckling. He suddenly became serious. "Now listen, Amanda is a horrible cook, but she's gonna try real hard. Just act like you like it, okay? It would mean a lot to her."

Bryan, frowning, nodded. It had escaped him how exactly he had been tricked into this dinner, but he was sure that he had been tricked, as this was not something he wanted to do. He wondered for a moment why he had not just said that no, he did not want to go to dinner, but thank you for asking. That would have been easy. That is something people say every day, right? Why did he not say that? It did not matter. What was done was done, and what was done was that he said yes.

At the end of the day, Bryan told Justin he was going home to shower and that he would be over shortly. Justin grinned, winked, and turned and left, leaving a billowing cloud of dust behind his truck.

When Bryan arrived home, Winnie was sitting on the porch in a white wooden rocking chair, gently rocking Wilbur and bottle feeding him. He was suckling quietly and apparently trying to fall asleep. Winnie looked up and smiled.

"Hey, big brother, you getting ready for your fancy date tonight?" She grinned when she saw Bryan wince at the statement. She laughed lightly. "You know, if you didn't want to go, you could've just said no."

Bryan rolled his eyes and stepped onto the wooden porch steps that creaked and sagged under his weight. "Whatever," he said. "She's just trying to be nice."

Winnie raised her eyebrows. "Oh yeah? I bet she'll be real nice to you." She laughed, and Bryan huffed and went inside.

Bryan got ready and struggled with what to wear. His inclination was to wear something decent, given that he was a guest for dinner, but he did not want Amanda to get the wrong idea. He settled for jeans – not his best, but not his worst – and a faded blue polo.

As he passed through the kitchen on his way out, he saw Winnie and Mama working on dinner. Wilbur and Boomer were both positioned near the counter, waiting for any tidbits of food to fall to the floor. The smell of garlic and onions was tempting, and Bryan paused, half considering texting Justin that he was sick and could not make it.

Winnie, eyeing him, said, "Nope, get on out of here. I'm sure what you're having is just as good." She grinned.

He frowned at her, told Mama goodbye, and headed out.

* * *

Amanda was in the kitchen when Bryan arrived. She saw his truck lumbering up the long driveway, and she darted to the bathroom mirror to make sure she looked just as she hoped. After having spent an hour and a half getting herself ready, and not even half that time preparing the food, she did not want a stray hair or disconcerting piece of food in her teeth to ruin the night.

Justin heard the crunch of gravel and came into the kitchen. He grinned at Amanda, who was hurriedly drinking her second glass of wine. "You need help with something?" he asked.

She shook her head. "No, just take him out back. I'll be out in a minute."

Justin grabbed a couple of beers and went out to meet Bryan. He took him around to the back of the house, where Amanda had set a table in the back yard. Behind the house were open fields that ran for several hundred yards, until they met with a distant tree line.

"Is that all y'all's?" Bryan asked.

Justin gulped his beer and nodded. "Yep, well, Hank's. It's mostly for cattle" – he paused momentarily and glanced at Bryan – "and a few goats. There's some chickens around the house, but they're not kept up."

To the side of the house, Bryan saw several small wooden box-like structures that he assumed were chicken coops. Each had a small door leading inside, and he saw two or three chickens lingering around them.

Behind the chicken coops, a row of dog kennels caught his eye. He counted eight kennels, with each kennel being maybe six feet long and four feet wide and elevated on what looked like wooden pallets. There was a blue plastic barrel in each kennel, with a hole cut in the end, which was apparently meant to be a makeshift shelter for each dog. He saw several hound dogs in the kennels. A couple were lying down on the pallets, while several more were pacing back and forth excitedly, going quickly from one side of the kennel to the other. Most of the hounds were the larger, Walker hound types, but there were at least two beagles in the kennel on the end.

Justin saw Bryan's gaze and said, "Those are Hank's hunting dogs."

"That's a lot of dogs," Bryan said. "Does he hunt a lot?"

Justin shrugged. "Maybe once a month or so. The girl on the end is for breeding. He's got three litters out of her. And the male next to her is Diesel. That's his stud dog. The others come and go, depending on the season."

Bryan was a little confused by the last statement, but before he had a chance to ask, Amanda came outside. She wore a short denim skirt and a yellow and black checkered shirt that she had tied up in the front, showing off the lower half of her stomach. Bryan flushed and took a drink of beer, causing Justin to chuckle.

"Hey, stranger, how are you?" Amanda asked as she neared Bryan. She sat down a plate of hushpuppies on the table. The little round balls were glistening with grease that was pooling in the middle of the plate.

"I'm good," Bryan responded. "Thanks for having me for dinner."

Amanda beamed. "It's our pleasure." She looked at Justin and added, "Jus, you wanna grab the rest of the food?" She smiled at Bryan, adding, "Since I made it and all, the least you can do is carry it out."

Justin rolled his eyes and went inside. Amanda handed Bryan a small glass filled with a brown liquid. "I thought you might want something stronger," she said, taking up a glass of her own. Bryan raised the glass and smelled the thick scent of whiskey. He hesitated, then, seeing Justin coming back with food, he quickly gulped it down. Amanda smiled and refilled the drink.

In addition to the hushpuppies, Amanda had prepared fried chicken, a green bean casserole, dinner rolls, and corn on the cob. The food was fine, but not amazing, and each item left a pool of either grease, oil, or butter on Bryan's plate. He naturally compared the meal to Mama's cooking and thought that, while Mama never thought herself a great cook, he loved just about everything she made. She would try new dishes at least once a week, with Pa often frowning when she would tell him that he was having some sort of vegetable medley or fish tacos. Pa was a meat and potatoes man, and as much as he loved Mama, Bryan thought that he had never really come to love her cooking quite as much as he loved her. When she had served him a new dish one night made with "quinoa," he had shaken his head and said, "Maggie, if I can't say it, then I don't need to be eating it." Mama had laughed and replied, "Well, you better start practicing how to say it."

Amanda kept Bryan's glass filled with whiskey, and Justin took the liberty of keeping his own filled. He stayed a few drinks ahead of Bryan, but he did not seem at all affected. As Bryan had his fourth glass, he felt his head becoming heavy and his coordination unsteady. He set the glass down and tried to focus on the food.

"So Bryan," Amanda was saying, "how long you planning to be at the farm?"

Bryan looked up but seemed unable to respond.

"Till the end of the summer, Amanda," Justin said. "I already told you. He's not in it for the long haul."

Amanda frowned at him. "Well, you've been saying you're leaving for years now, but there you are, same as always."

Justin waved her off then swallowed another mouthful of whiskey.

Bryan, finally finding his words, said, "Yeah, I mean, I'd like to be gone by the end of the summer." He looked at Justin, watching him pour another glass of whiskey. "But I don't really have any set plans right now."

Amanda nodded. "Well, you have plenty of time to figure it out. Just be careful that you don't end up like this one," she nodded toward Justin. "He acts like he's too good for the farm, but it's the only thing he's ever been halfway good at." She looked at Justin, who was frowning at her. "I mean, really, I don't think you'd know what to do if you weren't playing with those stinky pigs every day."

Amanda suddenly looked brighter and turned back to Bryan. "Justin says you have a sister. What's her name? Willow?"

"Winnie," Bryan responded, thinking of what Winnie would think if she were here. She would frown and ask to be excused, he thought, causing him to smile.

"Oh *Winnie*, that's right." Amanda looked at Justin, who was looking down at his food, swirling his glass of whiskey. "What's she like? Are y'all close?"

Bryan lightened. "Yeah, I guess we are," he said. "Oh she's good. Stubborn, but kind. She's way smarter than me. Wants to be a writer."

Amanda raised her eyebrows. "Oh yeah? A writer? That's pretty cool. What would she write about?"

Bryan shrugged. "I have no idea. She writes a little now, but she never really tells me what it's about."

Amanda tilted her head and seemed about to ask another question when they heard a screen door slam shut, and Amanda's gaze shifted behind Bryan. She frowned and narrowed her eyes.

"Conner, what are you doing out here?" Amanda asked sharply, a tinge of annoyance audible in her voice.

Bryan turned to see the small boy standing on the back porch, looking down and holding the top of the stair railing, squeezing slightly behind it. He was swaying a little and had on a pair of gray cotton shorts and a pale yellow t-shirt with frayed edges. He mumbled something inaudible, and Amanda asked, "What? Don't mumble, Conner. Why aren't you in bed?"

Conner swayed and mumbled that it was "too early." Bryan thought to himself that it was in fact quite early, as it was not yet past seven o'clock. Bryan did not feel that he was any expert on children, but he could imagine that it would be hard to sleep when it was still daylight. He personally had to have the room pitch black to be able to sleep.

Bryan glanced at Amanda and saw that Conner's response had apparently annoyed her. Her lips were pressed together tightly, and her eyes were narrowed. "Conner, you need to get back in your room. Now."

Conner hesitated, swaying on the railing. "But I can't sleep," he said in a whining tone, still looking down.

Amanda huffed and suddenly stood up. Bryan saw the boy stop swaying and look up, wide eyed. Amanda started toward him, but Justin stood and put up a hand. "I got it, Amanda. You stay here."

Amanda eyed him for a moment, until Justin added, "You already spent all this time on dinner. You enjoy it. We'll go read some stories."

This seemed to satisfy Amanda, and she visibly relaxed. "Okay, little brother." She smiled. Then, remembering Conner, she looked back toward the porch and narrowed her eyes again. "Uncle Jus is gonna put you to bed, Conner. Do what he asks."

The boy brightened, smiling at Justin. Justin grinned back. He glanced at Bryan, who was looking agitated, and he nodded toward Conner, shrugging slightly as if to say, "What can I do?" Bryan opened his mouth as if to say something, and Justin paused, but Bryan could think of nothing to say, so he simply closed his mouth and shook his head slightly. Justin took this as his cue to leave, and he bounded onto the porch, scooped up a giggling Conner, and whisked him off to bed.

Bryan could hear the little boy chuckling as Justin carried him away. Amanda had her mouth pulled to one side and her eyes narrowed, but she instantly relaxed her face into a smile when she saw that Bryan was looking at her.

"Kids," she said, giving a terse laugh and shaking her head slightly. "That boy wears me down. Always needing something." She looked back at the empty porch. "And it's just me, you know? That's a lot. I mean Justin helps a fair bit, but at the end of the day, he gets to come and go as he pleases, and I'm always stuck here, making sure Conner is fed and clean and whatnot. It's exhausting." She audibly sighed and seemed to slump down in her seat with this last statement.

Bryan did not say anything, but his first thought was to wonder why Amanda had Conner to begin with. He knew the answer to that of course. It was the same reason that any high school girl has a baby – she did not intend to. He thought back to health class freshman year. The only form of birth control discussed was abstinence. That sounds great to parents who do not want their children actually learning how to have sex safely. To think that a high school kid is going to practice abstinence, when emotions and hormones are running high, is a bit childish, for lack of a better word, but that was the way of it. If the parents and teachers pretended that sex did not happen, then maybe it really would not happen. The odd pregnant teen, like Amanda, was just some fluke of nature. Girls like that were treated as pariahs and pushed out of sight and out of mind. If you did not *see* a pregnant high school girl, then she must not exist.

Bryan glanced up at Amanda. She looked like she had been pretty at some point. Her eyes were sea foam green and stormy, and her figure was rather slight and thin. Her complexion was fair and clear. Even so, Bryan thought as he looked at her, she was not really attractive. He could not tell if it was the lines of stress that creased her face, or if it was actually the expressions on her face. While she tended to smile at Bryan, he had noticed the looks she gave Justin and Conner – looks of annoyance or bitterness, he was not sure which. The smiles she flashed at him seemed false, and he felt a bit of distrust toward her, although he was not exactly sure why.

He noticed that Amanda was staring at him as he stared at her, and he quickly looked away. When he looked back, she was smiling at him, which made him feel all the more uncomfortable. He shifted in his seat and asked, "Where's Hank?"

"Oh," Amanda said, rolling her eyes and looking back at the house, "I'm sure he's out with Wayne. He'll be back late tonight, drunk as a skunk." She shook her head, then she laughed. "On Saturday mornings, Conner always asks why Paw Paw is sleeping on the couch, and I can't say, 'Well, buddy, because he was too damn drunk to make it to his room.' So I just say, 'He thought he heard a bear, so he came downstairs to make sure it didn't get in.'" She laughed again, apparently pleased with her cleverness.

Bryan gave an awkward half grin and worked on his whiskey. He looked away from the house at the fields behind it. There was a barbed wire fence around the fields as far as he could see, and there appeared to be a leaning, dilapidated structure – some cross between a barn and a shed – midway in the field between the house and the distant tree line.

Amanda, following Bryan's gaze, said, "Hey, one of our cows just gave birth. Do you wanna see the calf?" She stood up before Bryan could answer and started walking toward the field. Bryan, not seeing a lot of options, stood and fell in behind her.

Amanda leaned down and squeezed horizontally through two rows of barbed wire on the fence to enter the pasture. Bryan did the same, although somewhat slower. He was a lot bigger than Amanda, and getting through the fence without touching the barbs proved to be harder than he had expected. He caught the collar of his shirt on a barb and pulled back, scraping the barb against his face as he did and bringing a small line of blood to the surface. He cursed, and Amanda turned back.

"Oh shit," she said, laughing. "Here." She approached him and unstuck his collar from the barb, guiding him through the fencing without further incident.

"Thanks," he said gruffly, putting his hand to his face and wiping away the trickle of blood.

"It doesn't look bad," Amanda said. She paused, then she chuckled and said, "Although I hope you have your tetanus shot."

Bryan frowned, thinking that in fact he had no such shot, as far as he knew.

He followed Amanda through the field. The ground was uneven and consisted of long bumpy rows where crops had apparently been planted at some point in the past. There was no sign of anything having grown in a long time, but the ground still held the old formation, as if it were ready at any point to resume its former usage.

Bryan stumbled on the uneven terrain a few times, and each time Amanda turned and chuckled. The ground would have been difficult enough to navigate if he were fully sober, but he felt the blurring effect of alcohol starting to take hold, and he struggled to maintain his footing as he followed.

After what seemed like an interminable amount of time, they reached the barn. The barn had an open front and three walls, with a roof and what looked to be an area for storage above. It was made of wood, and several boards on each side of the structure had apparently rotted and fallen to the ground, leaving long open gaps in the siding. The structure had clearly been painted red at some point, but that paint had mostly chipped away, and the brown wood underneath was prominent on each side.

Amanda slowly peered into the dark interior of the barn, and Bryan did the same. He saw pale yellow straw covering the dusty dirt floor, and in the back corner, he saw what appeared to be a cow lying down. The cow lifted her head at seeing Bryan and Amanda and made a mild lowing sound. Bryan was surprised that the cow was black and not black and white, as he tended to think of most cows. She was hard to make out in the darkness, and at first he thought she was lying alone. Finally, as Amanda moved further into the barn, he saw a bit of movement at the cow's side. A miniature version of the mother was lying by her side, and she raised her head and stared at the newcomers with dark, blank eyes.

Bryan instantly pictured the calf that Justin had hit with his truck. That calf had had the same wide eyes and had looked at him just as intently. He closed his eyes momentarily, and when he opened them he saw Amanda watching him.

"What do y'all do with them?" Bryan asked.

"They're meat cows," she replied. "Hank keeps a few for breeding, but most of them go for slaughter when they're old enough."

Bryan watched the calf, who had finally taken its eyes off of him and returned to nuzzling against its mother. The mother kept her head lifted, watching him and Amanda carefully, occasionally snorting and flicking the buzzing flies with her tail.

Bryan started to feel sick and quickly went back out of the barn. He went behind it and fell over, vomiting. Amanda followed and started rubbing his back.

"You okay?" she asked with a half smile. "Can't handle your whiskey, huh?" She grinned.

Bryan wiped his mouth, embarrassed, and started to stand. He stumbled and Amanda caught him, helping him lean back against the barn to steady himself.

"Jesus," he said. "I need to go."

Amanda laughed. "I mean, you probably need to wait this off a bit."

Bryan shook his head. "I'll see if Justin can drive me home." He started to push off the barn, but Amanda gave him a light push back. She stood in front of him, and he raised his eyes to meet hers, confused.

"Why don't you just take it easy a minute," she smiled. She leaned in a bit closer and ran her hand down his side. "Justin's still putting Conner down, so you might as well relax a few minutes." Before he could respond, her hand moved down to his belt.

Shit, he thought, as he head spun. He squeezed his eyes shut and shook his head. "Amanda," he said, opening his eyes, "I can't."

Amanda laughed. "Well, I'm pretty sure you can." She leaned her body into his, and he felt himself harden. She laughed again. "Yep, I am pretty positive you can."

Bryan flushed and pulled away from Amanda. He stumbled away, holding a hand up slightly as if to hold her at arm's length. He shook his head a few times to try to clear the fog that was settling in. "I'm, I'm sorry, Amanda. I really need to go." He heard her laugh but did not look to see her face.

He made his way through the uneven field toward the fence, stumbling repeatedly on the furrowed ground and falling more than once. Each time he fell, he scrambled to get up quickly, worried that if he lingered too long Amanda would catch up with him.

When he got to the fence, he hesitated. He was swaying slightly and felt unsteady on his feet. He glanced along the fence line. *Where the fuck is the gate?* He suddenly wondered if this was how Hank got in and out of the pasture, squeezing his tall body through the barbed wire. He doubted it, but he could see no opening in the fence, and he did not really want to ask Amanda for anything. He took a breath, steadied himself as best he could, and leaned down to go through the barbed wire. He ducked down and put one leg over the lowest line of barbed wire. He started to move through the fencing but, in doing so, raised his body a bit too high and felt the jab of the barbs on the wire above him. He jerked downward, losing his balance and falling forward on top of the lower wire. The wire, put in place some years ago, had rusted and weakened with age, and Bryan's full weight was more than it could bear. The wire snapped and coiled back, slashing his face and wrapping around his arm.

Bryan's fall pulled the wire tight, and the barbs embedded themselves in his arm. The jolt of pain and flash of blood sent a moment of panic through him, and he instinctively tried to pull away, further tightening the wire around his arm and burying the barbs deeper into his flesh.

"God damn it," he cursed. He reached with his right hand to grab the wire and pulled his hand back instantly, dripping blood from the barbs. He felt the panic in him rising as he sat slumped on the ground next to the fence, unsure of what to do. No matter how he moved, he felt the wire tighten, and the haze imposed by the whiskey made it impossible for him to think clearly. He was struggling to get a deep breath and made an intentional effort to slow his breathing. Nearby, he thought he heard a soft laugh. *Amanda?* He shook his head. *Where was she?*

As he slowed his breathing, he felt exhaustion creeping over him. He saw a star out early in the evening sky, and he tried to focus on it. It was bright, so maybe it was not a star. A planet, then? He had no idea, except that he thought planets were brighter than stars for some reason. He was staring at the star-planet when he heard hurried footsteps, followed by, "Holy shit – Amanda, what the hell happened?"

Bryan saw Justin come into view as he knelt down beside him. "Shit, man, are you okay?" Justin's brow was creased, and there was tension in his voice. Bryan nodded slowly, feeling his eyes starting to close. He felt Justin give him a light push, and he forced his eyes open. He saw Justin look at him, frown, and then look up. He followed his gaze to Amanda, who was a few feet away.

"Amanda," Justin said, "hey go get some wire cutters out of the shed, will you?"

Amanda laughed distinctly, and Bryan saw Justin narrow his eyes at her. Amanda chuckled again, then she walked away, saying, "Yeah, I'll get them."

Justin watched her for a moment, frowning, then he looked back at Bryan. "What the hell, man? You really did a number on the fence." Justin gave a half smile and waited for a response, but Bryan just closed his eyes. Embarrassment and pain sent his blood to his face, and Justin pushed him again.

"Listen," he said. "I'm gonna cut the wire off, but then we gotta get it cleaned up, okay? It's in pretty good . . . I mean, do you want me to take you to a hospital?"

That statement made Bryan more alert. No, he did not want to go to a hospital. He did not want to drag out this moment of pain and humiliation any longer than he had to. He shook his head.

"Winnie can fix it," he said. "Just take me home."

Justin hesitated, started to say something, then seemed to decide against it. He nodded.

Amanda returned with wire cutters, and Justin cut the wire where it was still attached to the post, immediately relieving some of the tension around Bryan's arm. Bryan winced as the wire shifted, and Justin drew in a breath and held it as he moved to cut the rest of the wire. He cut as quickly as possible, and then he pulled the wire off. Bryan saw Justin's eyes widen slightly, and he decided not to look at his arm, which was throbbing with each beat of his heart.

Justin helped him to his feet, and they went toward Justin's truck. As they were walking, Justin turned back and yelled to Amanda, "Hey, if Hank sees the fence, tell him I'll fix it tomorrow." Bryan kept looking forward but heard Amanda laugh again.

Once they began the drive, Bryan drifted in and out of sleep. At one point, he pulled out his phone to text Winnie. He fumbled with the text, sending her a jumble of letters that made no sense. She texted back, and when he returned another anagram of letters, she called him.

She laughed gently when he answered. "Well, I think someone has had a bit too much tonight, huh, big brother?"

Bryan stammered for a moment, but he finally got out that they were headed her way.

Winnie, sounding a bit more serious, asked if everything was okay.

"Yeah, yeah," Bryan said slowly, "all good. Just, I don't really want to see Mama or Pa right now – are they gone to bed?"

"No," Winnie said, "it's not that late, but come in through the back if you don't want to see them. They're watching a movie."

"Okay," Bryan said, then added, "Winnie, Justin's coming, so put Wilbur up."

Justin glanced at Bryan, then he heard Winnie say quietly, "Bryan, isn't he in the car with you?"

Bryan nodded and repeated, "Yeah, yeah, so put him up. He's coming over."

Winnie assented and ended the call.

Justin turned off his lights as he pulled into the driveway, and Winnie met them at the truck. She gave Justin a hesitant look when he got out of the truck, but when he smiled at her, she returned it.

Justin explained briefly what had happened, then he helped Bryan get out of the truck and into the house. In the darkness, Winnie could not see much, but when they had made it to Bryan's room and she saw him in the light, she gasped and put her hands to her mouth. Her eyes were immediately glossy, and she stood motionless for a moment. Then, releasing a breath, she turned and left the room.

She returned after a moment with a couple of damp washcloths, hydrogen peroxide, Neosporin, and gauze, as well as bottles of water for both Bryan and Justin. She set to work cleaning the cuts with the washcloths and hydrogen peroxide. Bryan had not realized that the wire had cut his face until Winnie moved to clean it, and he saw her troubled expression as she looked at him. After she cleaned the cuts, she slathered them with Neosporin and wrapped the gauze around them. For the cuts on his face, she went back and then returned with Band-Aids, which she applied. She got Bryan to drink some water, gave him an ibuprofen, and then pushed him to lie down, where he immediately fell asleep.

She remained in Bryan's room for a few minutes, sitting on the floor with Justin.

"You're pretty good at the nurse stuff," Justin said, grinning at her.

Winnie smiled. "Our mom's a vet tech, so she's basically a nurse for animals. I've spent a fair amount of time at work with her."

Justin nodded. They were both silent for a moment while, outside the room, the stairs creaked as Mama and Pa made their way to their bedroom. Winnie heard Pa saying that the movie had made no sense at all, after which she heard Mama respond that it would have made a whole lot more sense to Pa if he had stayed awake during it. Winnie looked at Justin and grinned.

After the stairs had become quiet, Justin told Winnie that he should probably go. She thanked him for bringing Bryan home and said he could sleep on the couch if he was too tired to drive home. Justin considered this, then he accepted the offer. Winnie went out quietly into the hallway, got him blankets, and took Justin downstairs to the couch. She told him goodnight and started to head back upstairs when he asked, "Hey, Winnie, who's Wilbur?"

Winnie turned and looked at Justin blankly. "What?"

Justin eyed her. "Yeah, I heard Bryan tell you to put Wilbur up when we were on the way over. But who's Wilbur?"

Winnie reddened slightly. "Oh, I think he meant Boomer. He seemed really out of it."

Justin watched her for a moment, then he nodded and told her goodnight.

CHAPTER XII

Justin awoke to delicious smells wafting in from the kitchen. After a moment of tidying up, he went in to find Winnie in the kitchen, making French toast, eggs, and bacon. She smiled when she saw him, and he returned it, asking if he could help. She gave him a few nominal tasks and continued with the cooking.

Mama and Pa came down next. Mama laughed when she saw Justin. "You might as well keep a toothbrush here," she said, winking at Justin. Justin suddenly realized that he in fact did not have a toothbrush there, and he gave a little more distance between himself and Winnie.

Pa gave his usual awkward nod, accompanied by a somewhat gruff "hello," and he sat down to breakfast. When Pa inquired about Bryan, Winnie quickly said that he was not feeling well and might sleep in a bit. She glanced at Justin, who briefly held her gaze and then looked down.

Pa filled his plate full of eggs and toast, but he paused when he got to the plate of bacon. He picked up a piece with his fork and tilted his head at it. Justin saw Winnie and Mama exchange a smile.

"Winnie," Pa said slowly, "what's going on with this bacon?"

Winnie stifled a laugh and said sweetly, "What do you mean, Pa? Does it not taste good?"

"Well," he continued, "to be honest, I hadn't tried it yet. It looks a little odd, though. Did you cook it different?"

Winnie smiled. "A little," she said, "but try it first, then tell me what you think."

Pa cautiously lifted a piece of the suspect bacon with a fork and plopped it down on his plate. He studied it for a moment, trying to form an opinion about it, then he picked it up and took the smallest possible bite off the end. He chewed slowly, raising his eyes to Winnie as he did so. He narrowed them a bit and said, "Winnie girl, this ain't bacon, is it?"

Winnie and Mama cracked up at the same time. Mama used a white cloth napkin with bright yellow flowers on it to wipe at her eyes, which had started leaking tears during her laughter.

Winnie went over and wrapped her arms around Pa's neck. She pulled back and grinned.

"Pa, this is what you might call 'fakon.'" She grinned, and Pa raised an eyebrow. "It's bacon of sorts, but just not what you're used to. It's made out of beans, rather than pigs."

Pa nodded. "Oh, I see. There it is. Winnie, I love you, and I love your cooking, but this" – he lifted a piece of the not-so-bacony-bacon on his fork and nodded to it – "this just ain't the stuff for me. I know you got this thing with pigs right now –" He paused when he said that, glancing over at Justin with a slight frown. Justin noticed that Mama and Winnie momentarily did the same. He looked back with slight confusion, until they each turned back to Pa.

Pa stammered a moment then continued, "Give me turkey sausage or chicken fritters or something else, but please don't give me some dried out strips of beans and call it bacon." He gave Winnie a smile and a nod, and she grinned back at him.

"Oh Pa, you're so crazy," she said, laughing.

Mama and Pa finished breakfast and, after a bit, went out to run some errands. Justin waited on Bryan to get up, so they could take the newly spayed mama cat to Jeffrey's. While he was waiting, he helped Winnie clean the breakfast dishes and wipe down the table, and then he sat with her on the porch and had a second cup of coffee. Any shyness she had initially had with him seemed to have worn away, and she talked easily with him now. She told him that she was thinking about going to State, due to the lower cost, but she had some interest in a couple of out-of-state schools as well.

"But," she said, looking down and furrowing her brow slightly, "honestly I don't bring up college much at all right now, after Bryan's scholarship didn't work out. I don't think he's really up for hearing it just yet." She raised her eyes to Justin's. "I mean, hopefully he'll be past it soon, but I think he's a little lost at the moment, not sure about what to do next." She held her steaming mug with both hands and moved it in small circles to swirl the coffee inside.

Justin nodded, not really sure of what to say. He looked down at his own coffee, a rich chestnut color, with warm ribbons of steam rising from it. He studied it for a moment, then he glanced up to see Winnie looking at him. She smiled, and her cheeks reddened slightly. She opened her mouth to say something, but, at the sound of creaking steps coming from inside, she immediately rose and went to the door. She looked through the screen door to see Bryan moving gingerly down the stairs.

"How you feeling?" Winnie asked, tilting her head at Bryan.

Bryan sighed heavily and shook his head. "Like shit," he said. "And like an idiot for ever going over there for dinner. I don't know what I was thinking. It's the freakin' loony bin over there. No wonder Justin's –"

"Bryan," Winnie said, cutting him off shortly.

Bryan caught her tone and looked up. For the first time, he noticed that Justin was standing behind Winnie, looking at him with a half grin.

Bryan reddened and shook his head. "Shit, I'm sorry. I'm just – the whole thing was just fucking embarrassing. And really your sister, she was just too much."

Justin's grin widened, and he chuckled. "You're telling me. I've lived with her my whole life. Although I'm not sure you can entirely blame her for the fence ordeal. It's still beyond me how that even happened." He chuckled again, then added, "Anyway, you wanna get ready so we can take this cat?"
Bryan nodded and slowly lumbered away to get ready.

Once they had the cat loaded and were on the way to Jeffrey's, Bryan apologized again for what he said. Justin waved him off carelessly, saying, "It's no big thing." After a moment he said, "The bigger thing is the dang fence. I'm gonna have to get that straight before Hank notices."

Bryan looked at Justin. "You want help?"

He shrugged. "Meh. It won't take long. Hank should have replaced the wire a long time ago anyway. I bet if you put pressure on any part of the fence it would snap just like that piece did." After a few moments, Justin chuckled again, apparently still at Bryan's expense.

They drove toward the outskirts of town. The road was two lane and filled with a good number of potholes, making it impossible for Justin to go even the speed limit of 35 mph. Bryan looked out of the passenger side window and saw railroad tracks paralleling the road. Beyond the tracks, there were a few shanty houses, built with small frames and sagging roofs with missing shingles. He saw a few figures sitting on the porches here and there, so motionless that they seemed to be part of the scenery, growing on their porches like moss on a tree.

Bryan realized that although he had lived in Ashfield all of his life, he had never seen a fair bit of it. He had never come to the side of town where the farm was located, and he had no idea where they were headed now, as they drove down the barely maintained road toward open farmland.

After a few miles had passed, Justin turned off onto a dirt road, passing over rusted railroad tracks and stirring up dust as he sped through the dirt and gravel. To their right, Bryan saw a trailer park filled with dozens of trailers, lined along small grassy drives, just a few short feet from one another. A Dumpster sat at one end of the park, and several cats crowded around it, swishing their tails and watching the truck pass.

Just beyond the park were a few small trailers situated on their own lots. Justin pulled into one such lot. There was a long driveway leading back to the trailer, which was an eggshell color with orange trim around the windows and door. What looked like water stains ran down the sides of the trailer and met with the rusted metal underpinning. The underpinning was pulled away from the trailer in a couple of places, and Bryan saw a cat emerge from one such hole.

The cat, a large orange tabby Tom, perched on top of the small porch attached to the trailer. He whisked his tail back and forth and flicked his whiskers as he watched the truck pull down his driveway.

At a neighboring trailer, Bryan saw a burly man come out on his porch. He was shirtless and wearing tan overalls. His giant belly exploded through the suspender straps and hung down in jello-like flaps. His grizzled salt and pepper hair clung to his face and head and stuck out in prickly stubble on his chin. Despite the early hour, he held a Budweiser can in his right hand.

As the truck came to a stop, the man made no effort to conceal his interest. He situated himself leaning over the edge of the porch, took a gulp of beer, spat on the ground, and watched the truck intently.

Bryan frowned as he climbed out of the truck. He watched the man, who made eye contact with him and lifted his left hand in a good-natured wave. The man grinned and spat.

Bryan heard Justin laugh. "That's crazy ol' Larry," he said with a chuckle. He lifted his hand to Larry and nodded, and Larry gave an even wider grin and waved back. "He's Jeffrey's uncle or cousin or something," Justin said. "I can't ever keep up with it. I swear it changes every time I talk to him. I don't even know if his name's really Larry. I think once he said it was Al. Anyway, he's related somehow."

Justin waited for Bryan to grab the cat carrier, then they went up on the porch. The steps creaked and cracked under them. The boards on the porch had dark veins of rot running through them, and a damp, dank smell rose up as Bryan made his way up the steps. There were bowls of cat food on the porch, and a recent rain had left the kibble inside soft and bloated and crumbling into piles of mush. Flies were buzzing the bowls and serenading the home with a soft hum.

Justin reached the screen door, opened it, and knocked heartily on the solid door behind it. Bryan heard shuffling inside, followed by a loud, "Be right there!" Justin grinned at Bryan and raised his eyebrows. Bryan felt the cat shifting inside of the carrier, and he put both hands on it to try to steady it for the animal.

There was more murmuring inside, and then the door flung open, revealing a huge woman in a short pink nightgown. She was wearing fuzzy pink bedroom slippers that never seemed to rise from the floor as she walked, but rather just slid along the way a slug slides along the concrete, leaving a silvery trail of moisture behind. Her short, heavy legs were bare, and layers of fat rippled along them, hanging down in crusty white flaps. Spiderwebs of purple veins covered the legs, looking like a roadmap drawn by Harold and his purple crayon. Her nightgown barely covered what Bryan felt was appropriate, causing him to blush. The flush deepened as his eyes rose to her chest, which clearly showed the form of dark brown nipples poking out from beneath the thin gown.

Her face was broad and round, and she appeared to have a faint shadow of hair around her chin and upper lip. The wrinkled lips pulled back into a wide grin when she saw Justin, revealing a set of yellowish, crooked teeth beneath.

"Ah," she said, drawing out the sound in a husky smoker's voice. "Justin, you're here." Justin tilted his head at her and grinned.

"Hey, Mama J," he said, reaching out and wrapping his arms around her, sinking into her fluff as he hugged her.

She pulled back from him and studied his face for a moment. "You look tired, Justin, and thin. That sister of yours don't feed you enough."

Justin chuckled. "Well, you know Amanda wasn't ever much of a cook." He looked at Bryan and winked.

Mama J finally noticed the taller boy standing behind Justin, and she eyed him skeptically for a moment. Justin, noticing, said, "Mama J, this is Bryan. He's working with us at the farm now."

Mama J nodded and smiled. "I know who you are," she said, smiling more. "Jeffrey said you took care of his mama cat, so she won't have no more babies."

Bryan nodded.

Mama J suddenly frowned for a moment and added, "I don't think it's too good to take away a mama's ability to have babies." She eyed Bryan, who looked to Justin for help. Justin shrugged, and Mama J continued, "But, I guess in this case, it was the best thing. A mama shouldn't have to lose her babies like that."

She turned to Justin. "Your daddy is a real son of a bitch," she said.

Justin pulled his mouth to one side, scratched his head, and looked down. "Yeah, I know," he said.

Mama J watched him for a minute, frowning, then she shook her head slightly and said, "Well, in any case, it is what it is. I'm glad we have this little mama here now. Jeffrey's in the back. Let's take her back there. Here, come on in. You want something to drink?"

With what seemed like great difficulty, as when Moses parted the Red Sea, the massive woman turned in the small doorway, moving slowly and with small scoots of the feet, until she was facing the other way and headed back inside.

Justin started inside and then turned to flash a grin at Bryan, giving his head a quick jerk to signal for Bryan to follow him.

As soon as Bryan stepped across the threshold and into the home, he was enveloped in a thick humidity filled with a number of smells, none of which he found appealing. Predominantly was the smell of ammonia, and when he looked down, he saw several litter boxes scattered throughout the living room.

The room was dark, but as his eyes adjusted, he made out a sofa backed up against the front window and an armchair on the other side of the room. The sofa looked to have once been a cream color, but a myriad of stains covered it now, adding spots of reds, browns, and yellows, like a painting of a dirty sunset. A few holes were visible in the cushions, and on one, greenish fuzzy fluff poked through.

The armchair was in a similar state, and its arms were worn down and threadbare, exposing the wooden frame underneath. On the back of the armchair was a yellow hand towel, with a dark, greasy spot in the middle of it, apparently where one's head would rest back on the chair. Beside the chair was a wooden stand covered in a jumble of newspapers, pencils, tissues – both used and unused, emery boards, medicine bottles, lotions, and other items that were likely considered necessities by the chair's occupant.

Bryan made his way slowly through the living room, following behind Justin and Mama J. The floor was carpeted, but he occasionally felt something crunch under his feet. He stepped carefully, as there were boxes full of books, newspapers, and sheets of paper strewn about in no particular order. As he was passing by one such box, a sleek black cat emerged from the box, hissed, and darted across the room, causing Bryan to start and emit a small cry. Justin turned, gave Bryan a quizzical look, and laughed.

Mama J made it to a sliding glass door at the opposite side of the trailer from the front door. She heaved it open with a throaty moan and waddled onto a small back deck. Behind the deck was a small yard filled with yellowish green grass. A growth of woods lay at the far end of the yard, and neighboring trailers were visible to either side.

The yard, small as it was, contained a surprisingly large assortment of lawn ornaments. Bryan guessed that there were at least forty such ornaments. There were the standard gnomes, along with fairies, cats, chickens and a clutch of chicks, and several other odd and end statues, including, Bryan thought somewhat oddly, a couple of black children holding fishing poles. The statues were scattered throughout the small yard in no particular order, taking root here and there with perhaps some importance and meaning to Mama J.

At the back of the yard, Bryan saw Jeffrey, pushing a rumbling little push mower through the maze of yard décor. He was mowing in a slow circle around a statue of a red mushroom with a yellow frog on top, but he left several tall weeds around the statue, as it seemed had been the case with most of the ornaments in the yard. Bryan watched as Jeffrey pushed the tired mower up to the stoic mushroom, pulled it back, studied the still standing weeds for a moment, and then tried again, repeating the same motion a couple more times before giving up and moving on to another area of the yard.

Mama J stood on the porch and yelled out in a husky voice, "Jeffrey! Jeffrey!"

Jeffrey ambled along, unable to hear his mother over the mower. Mama J kept yelling, becoming hoarser and hoarser, until Bryan wondered if the neighbors might at some point call the police, thinking she had a true emergency. He started to leave the porch and get Jeffrey's attention, but at that moment Jeffrey looked up. He stared for a moment, and then understanding spread across his face in a wide grin. He waved enthusiastically and cut off the mower.

As if in slow motion, Jeffrey shuffled through the yard and over to the porch, grinning the entire time. Bryan wondered, given his pace, how long it would take Jeffrey to mow the small yard. *Half the day? The whole day? Maybe.*

"Big J," Justin said, as Jeffrey approached. He grinned at him. "Bryan's got your mama kitty all ready to go. You want her?"

Jeffrey, reaching the porch, nodded quickly and looked at the carrier Bryan was carrying. Bryan handed it over to him, and he raised it to look inside at the cat. The cat, who had been emitting a low growl while Bryan held her, stopped making noise and stared back at Jeffrey. He sat the carrier down, opened the door, and watched as the cat slowly poked her head out and looked around cautiously.

"Come on, girl," Jeffrey said, making a clicking noise at the cat.

The cat turned to look at Jeffrey, flicked her ears, and slowly came out of the carrier. She looked around, taking in her new home, and then rubbed her body against Jeffrey's legs. Jeffrey had a goofy grin on his face like a kid in a candy store. He stroked the mother cat's back, and she arched her body to lean into his hand.

"Looks like she's happy to be here," Justin said, grinning at Jeffrey.

Mama J cut in, waving her hands a bit. "Yes, yes, I'm so glad we have another cat here. Now, Justin, while you're here, why don't you be helpful and give Jeffrey a hand. Will you? He's been a meaning to move that old chicken coop over here to the back, near the brush pile, but he's been putting it off, saying he ain't got no help. Well, the help is here."

Justin raised his eyebrows at Jeffrey. "You want a hand, Big J?"

"Yes, yes, like I said, he needs a hand," Mama J continued, seeming slightly exasperated. "We have too many dang cats to ever have chickens again so we might as well get that thing moved. We'll put it in the back, and the cats can use it at night. Go on now."

Jeffrey and Justin grinned at each other as she shooed them off the porch.

Bryan started to follow, but Mama J held up a hand right in front of him, making him stop short.

"Woah now, son. It don't take three people to move one chicken coop. You come on in here with me; help me make some tea."

Bryan hesitated, looking toward Justin, but Justin was already halfway through the yard with Jeffrey.

"Come on now," Mama J said. "You can be more help to me right now than them. Come on in here," and she shuffled back into the house, with Bryan following reluctantly.

She led him back through the maze inside the house, over to a small kitchen with dark green laminate counters. The countertops were littered with odds and ends, leaving little to no usable space. Styrofoam food containers, wrinkled magazines, salt and pepper packets, chip bags, cat treats, and a half eaten piece of toast covered the countertop closest to Bryan. He recoiled slightly as he looked over the mess, wondering what bugs were likely to make this nest their home.

Mama J ignored Bryan and pulled out an empty plastic pitcher, along with a box of Lipton tea bags. She took a dull chrome teapot off the stovetop and filled it with dingy looking water from the tap. She slapped the teapot back on the stovetop and turned the heat to high to get the water boiling.

Bryan shuffled at the end of the kitchen, unsure of what to do.

"Son, if you're gonna be in my house, go ahead and pull those clodhoppers off. You're messing up my floor," Mama J said firmly.

Bryan looked up, not entirely clear on what had just been asked of him. "I'm sorry?" he stammered.

Mama J looked irritated. "Your Brogans, boy. Your shoes! You're trailing dirt all over my floor."

Bryan looked at her blankly for a moment, then understanding slowly washed over his face. "Oh," he said. Then, hesitating as Mama J shot him sideways glances, he untied his boots. He reluctantly pulled them off, not wanting his socked feet to touch the floor, which was spotted with dirt, a few dead and dried up bugs, and trash – candy wrappers, pieces of paper towels, and at least a couple of Band-Aids, that Bryan could see. His stomach turned as his feet sank into the soft and somewhat damp carpet on the floor.

He looked up to see Mama J watching him, and he realized that his face might be betraying his thoughts. He cleared his throat and stood, moving closer to her to see how he might help. As much as he did not want to be inside helping at all, he was ready to do pretty much anything to keep his mind off of the grime beneath his feet.

"So," Mama J started, flicking some small pieces of food off of her rotund abdomen, "how are you liking the farm?" She got something stuck on her fingers, looked at them intently, rubbed them together, and tried to fling away whatever was on them. Then she raised her eyebrows at Bryan, waiting somewhat impatiently for a response.

Bryan fumbled his words. "Oh, it's, it's fine," he said. "I mean, I don't plan to be there past the summer, but it's alright for now." Then, as an afterthought, he added, "Justin and Jeffrey are great to work with."

Mama J gave a short laugh, almost like a cough, and turned back to her tea kettle, which was starting to quiver back and forth. She opened up a cabinet to reveal stacks of food products – layers on layers of canned goods, bags of potato chips with clothes pins holding the ends closed, enough cereal boxes to support at least half a dozen people for a month, and other odds and ends. A bag of Fritos teetered on top of several others when she opened the cabinet, momentarily swaying until it finally tipped over, sprinkling small yellow chips onto the linoleum. Mama J frowned, picked up the bag and closed it, then returned it to the cabinet, leaving the dusting of Frito crumbs on the floor.

She finally found what she was apparently looking for – a package of Oreo cookies. She removed the cookies from the pantry and handed them to Bryan.

"Here," she said, breathing heavily as she moved. "Make some room on that table for you and the boys. Put these there." She pointed to a small wooden table between the kitchen and the back door.

Bryan nodded, took the Oreos, and went to set them down on the table. He immediately found this to be a significant task. There was no space on the table that was not covered with something. There were several newspapers, all a few days old, on one side of the table. Sales flyers had been removed from the papers and were stacked in a pile toward the middle of the table. A mountain of pill bottles, most with prescription labels on them, was kept at the other end of the table. They were piled in such a mound that it would have been impossible to easily grab one bottle or another, but rather one would have to sift through the whole heap to find anything.

Bryan felt an inclination to remove everything from the table, but, as soon as the thought arose, he realized that this would not work. The rest of the small house was just as crowded. There was no empty space that could support the quantity of items on the table. Instead, he simply pushed all the clutter to one corner, opening up a little space for three of the chairs, and he put the Oreos in the center of this newly created space.

Mama J was bumping around the kitchen. She saw that Bryan had succeeded in his task, and she smiled, asking, "So what do you plan to do at the end of the summer?"

Bryan shrugged. He hated this question. It reminded him that he still had no plans for the end of the summer, other than the plan to be doing anything other than what he was currently doing. He shook his head slightly. "I don't really know yet," he said without looking up. Then he added, "So how long has Jeffrey worked at the farm?"

"Oh," Mama J brightened. "He's been there longer than you – longer than Justin, too. He's been there since that boy's mother was around, and that was ages ago."

Bryan raised his eyes at this, and Mama J, seeing his interest, continued.

"Yeah, my boy Jeffrey's been at that farm at least twelve years, since Justin was maybe eight or so. His mama was always carrying him around everywhere, even though he was plenty big to get around on his own, and she was a tiny little thing herself, but he liked to be carried." Mama J smiled, seeing something in her head that Bryan could not access.

"What happened with Justin's mom?" Bryan asked.

Mama J frowned. "Well really," she began, "that's for Justin to say." She narrowed her eyes at Bryan for a moment. She shrugged a little and shook her head. "But I guess he won't mind." She looked out the kitchen window and saw Justin and Jeffrey working on relocating the chicken coop.

"She left," Mama J said. "She just couldn't take Hank anymore." Mama J looked at Bryan. "You've met him, I'm sure?"

Bryan nodded.

Mama J continued. "Then you know he's a real son of a bitch." She spat the words. "He used to beat her something awful when he was drinking. She came over here a fair bit, dragging Justin and Amanda along with her. She'd be dripping blood and snot and crying and carrying on. I'd say 'Honey, why don't you get away from that man? Take your young'uns and go.' She would just look at me like I was crazy – or like she couldn't hear me maybe."

Mama J sighed. "One time she came over, and both of her front teeth were busted out. She was holding them in her hand, and she had a big ol' hole gaping in her mouth where they were missing. She had the dentist put 'em back in, or maybe some fake ones or something, but they never looked right, and she had to be real careful about bitin' into things after that."

Mama J returned to the overcrowded cabinet, studied it a moment, and then pulled out a Mason jar full of a white powdery substance, which Bryan assumed was sugar. Mama J rotated the jar in her hands, watching the sugar shift and slide inside.

"One day," she continued, "something happened at the farm. I can't remember exactly what it was, and it really don't concern me, but a whole mess of pigs died. Jeffrey came home smellin' to high heaven after dragging them all to the trash out back. Well I guess Hank was pretty fired up, so when he got home, he tore that woman up. Put her in the hospital. I went to see her, and she was just a-layin' there in the bed. Wouldn't look at me or nothing. Just lay there, face all mashed up and purple like a squished prune. When she got out, she went home, made Justin and Amanda a batch of chocolate chip cookies, and then was gone in the morning. That was it – no goodbye, no note, nothing. Don't know how a mother can just turn her back on her young'uns like that."

Mama J looked out the window again momentarily, her face showing no expression one way or another. "That was hard on Justin. Amanda, well, she's always been good at takin' care of herself, and she did a little for Justin, but Hank started comin' down hard on him, and Amanda wasn't no help in protecting him."

Bryan was frowning. "So why does Justin stay? Why doesn't he just leave now?" he asked after a moment.

Mama J tilted her head at Bryan. "Well, I guess he's got a reason to stay." She looked at Bryan, but he was not sure what she meant. "Anyway," she said, raising her hands and wiping them on each other, as if wiping something off, "that's enough talk about that."

Her kettle was finally boiling, and the little teapot was screaming its high-pitched scream. She picked up the kettle and lifted the top off. She put a handful of teabags into the little pot and left them to steep in the boiling water. She occasionally bobbed them up and down, and Bryan had a vivid memory of the little kitten bodies bobbing up and down in the bucket of water. He pressed his eyelids together to push the image out of his mind. When he opened his eyes again, he saw Mama J adding what looked to be at least three cups of sugar to the little pot.

While the tea was steeping, she took a plastic pitcher and filled it with ice cubes. A moment later, having decided that the tea had done just about enough steeping, she poured the contents of the teapot over the ice and into the pitcher.

"Here," she said, handing Bryan the pitcher. "Put this on the table. Those boys should be coming on in in a minute." She set a stack of red Solo cups on the table, then she shuffled to the armchair. She let her body flop onto it, and she seemed to sink down into the cushions, as if she might never rise again. She folded her arms over her mountain of a belly and closed her eyes.

Bryan shifted uncomfortably. He started to speak, decided against it, and made his way to the door. He slipped on his boots and had his hand on the door to go outside, when Justin threw the door open wide with a big grin. He had sweat running down his forehead.

"Whacha doing in here, man?" Justin asked good naturedly. He eyed the tea and Oreos. "Oh, I see," he said, nodding toward the table. "You're in here eatin' all the sweets." He laughed and elbowed Bryan, who frowned at him. He poured some tea for himself and Jeffrey, shoved a handful of Oreos in his mouth, and called out with a full mouth, "Mama J, you sleeping?"

Mama J kept her eyes closed but smiled. "Not me, Justin. I can see you even with my eyes closed." A grin spread across her face.

Justin laughed. "It's true," he said to Bryan.

They stayed a while, eating too many Oreos and drinking too much sweet tea, until Bryan said that he really needed to get back.

When they were driving back, Justin asked, "So what'd you think?"

Bryan, who had been texting Winnie, looked up. "What?"

"What did you think," Justin repeated, "of Jeffrey's mama?"

"Oh," Bryan said, drawing the word out. "She was nice."

Justin laughed. "I know, I know. She's a little odd, but she's always been good to me."

Bryan looked at Justin for a minute, taking in what he had said. He started to say something, but then he hesitated, changed his mind, and just nodded in agreement. He suddenly felt embarrassed that he had such personal knowledge of Justin's life. He felt himself reddening, and he felt some anger toward Mama J for putting him in this position.

"You okay?" Justin asked, casting a sideways glance his way.

"Yeah, yeah," Bryan said, nodding. "I just got some things on my mind."

Justin nodded in acknowledgement. "I got you. Well we're headed back to my place so you can grab your truck. I'm sure Conner's waiting on me. I told him we'd go four wheelin' today." He grinned. "That boy's gonna be the death of me," he said with a chuckle.

Bryan looked up and said nothing.

CHAPTER XIII

The weekend ended and another week began. Justin would occasionally start chuckling and make a joke about the fence incident. "Run into any fences lately?" he would say, grinning. "Hey be careful," he said one time, looking around wide eyed. "There's a fence at the back of the farm – I don't want you running into it. I can't be fixin' every fence around here." He laughed so much at one point that he keeled over and smacked his head into the metal bars of one of the pig pens. He continued laughing, but he stood up rubbing his head, a small scrape down his forehead spotting up with tiny specks of blood.

Bryan initially ignored him, then he started glaring at him or rolling his eyes. Justin was not even a little affected. He kept up the jokes throughout the week, until finally, exhausting all other options, Bryan grinned a little himself, thinking the entire event was fairly stupid on his part.

Midway through the following week, while Bryan and Justin were doing their routine checks of the pens, Hank and Wayne came into the building. Justin was in the middle of recounting to Bryan some of the times he had spent at Mama J and Jeffrey's home.

"Mama J's a shit cook," Justin said, laughing. "I mean, she can eat. She sure as hell can eat, but she can't cook worth a damn. Those Oreos are about the best she can do for dessert. She tried to make some brownies when I was there one time. How the hell you can mess up a brownie is beyond me. You just follow the instructions on the package. But something messed up, and those brownies came out like hard little pieces of shit." He doubled over with laughter.

"Jeffrey, Jeffrey," he struggled to speak through the laughter, "Jeffrey ate a few just to make her happy. You could hear him crunching on 'em, but he just kept on smiling and telling her how good they were." Justin wiped away a few small tears that had formed at the sides of his eyes from the laughter. A few involuntary chuckles escaped him even as the story ended, as he pictured Jeffrey in his mind, chomping down on the rock-hard brownies.

Hank entered the building first, flinging the door back with such force that it slammed into the wall immediately inside the room, sending a loud bang echoing through the building. Hank's broad shoulders and thick stature seemed to fill the entire doorway, and Bryan wondered how he could even fit through the opening. Justin curtailed his laughter but kept a half grin, going over to meet Hank. As he approached Hank, he saw Wayne fall in behind him. Justin gave him a quick glance and pulled his mouth to one side, releasing the grin. He spoke in low tones with Hank for a moment, then he came back to Bryan.

"They're just moving some of the weaned pigs over to the nursery. It shouldn't take long. I'm gonna help, but you can keep on checkin' the pens." Justin waited for Bryan to nod in acknowledgment, then he returned to the pen where Hank and Wayne had stopped.

The pen, like every other in this building, contained a litter of piglets separated from a mother sow, lying on her side. The piglets were a good size and milling about the pen, snorting and sniffing one another. Occasionally one would issue a sharp squeal to another, and now and again one might mouth the other, unable to cause any damage, since its teeth had been cut, but wrapping its little mouth around its littermate as if it were suckling its mother.

Bryan continued making his way through each pen, watching as Hank and Wayne surveyed the pen, asking Justin a few questions, and checking a notepad on which he had previously written the weights of the pigs. After a few moments, Hank nodded, at which Wayne opened the gate to the pen. A couple of the piglets immediately emerged from the pen. Wayne blocked one side of the central walkway, forcing them to walk the other way, which they did. He guided them to the end of the row and opened the door at the end, shuffling them through. He was gone for a few moments, apparently getting the piglets to where they needed to be, then he returned to help with the others.

Justin had entered the pen and was shuffling the piglets along toward the opening in the pen. Three more came out, and Wayne guided them down the aisle, as he had done with the first two. Four piglets remained. Two of them were huddled in one corner, and two others were bolting around the pen madly, snorting and squealing. Justin approached the two in the corner and immediately saw that they appeared ill. Their skin was splotched with shades of red and purple, and both had thick yellow discharge dripping from their snouts. Justin frowned at them. He gave each a firm push. Neither piglet got up but rather only swayed against Justin's touch, making Justin think of a Weeble toy. The catchphrase "Weebles wobble, but they don't fall down" ran through his head, causing him to grin.

He reached down and scooped up one of the piglets. Wayne had returned, so he offered to hand him the pig. Wayne did not move to take the pig, but rather only shot Justin a look of annoyance. He looked to Hank, but Hank, who had somehow managed to squeeze into the pen himself, was intent on chasing down the two wild piglets and never looked up. Wayne sighed and reluctantly accepted the piglet. Justin shot him a dry smile and went to retrieve the last piglet huddled in the corner. When Wayne returned, he handed this one off, as well, then he turned to help Hank with the two he was chasing.

Hank was undoubtedly strong. Years of work on the farm had hardened his body into one solid muscle that could meet any challenge the farm threw his way. However, cardiac endurance was not one of his strengths. He had been chasing the piglets around the small pen, trying to block their path, but each time he attempted to corner them, they slithered by with a shriek and kept running. He was sweating and breathing hard.

Justin tried to help Hank head them off, but he was equally unsuccessful. He moved quickly to try to cut off each pig's path, but more than once he ended up sliding on the slippery shit-covered concrete and falling to the floor. He frowned, but he got up with a half grin and continued the chase.

Wayne had returned and was watching them now with that same look of annoyance on his face, as if he had somewhere much more important to be just at this moment, and as if the pigs' ignorance of this engagement was personally offensive. He disappeared again for a moment, then Bryan saw him return with a piece of metal rebar in his right hand and a longer wand-like device in his left. Bryan initially did not know what the wand was, until he saw a flash of light and heard the crackle of electricity come from the wand – an electric prod.

Wayne handed the rebar to Hank and then moved around the outside of the pen with the prod. He leaned over the pen and touched the prod to one of the piglets. Bryan heard the electric shock only an instant before the excruciating scream of the piglet.

The smell of singed skin and hair floated through the air to Bryan.

The shock apparently did little to entice the piglet to leave. After the initial scream, the piglet continued screaming and snorting, running as fast as it could around the perimeter of the small pen. Its sibling, seeing the first piglet's terror, started screaming as well and followed suit, running blindly after the first, screaming as if it had been the one shocked.

Hank watched the scene for a moment. Then, as the first piglet turned a corner during its mad dash, he swung the rebar at the piglet, making contact between the metal and the piglet's soft head. The piglet ceased its screaming and fell over, shaking in steady tremors as it lay on its side. Its short legs shot out rigidly and vibrated with each tremor. Hank looked at Wayne and gave a slight shrug, then he hoisted the pig up by a hind leg and handed it to Wayne, who carried it down the aisle in a similar manner.

The second pig continued running as furiously as the first, and perhaps even more wildly after having seen its sibling leveled with the rebar. Hank raised the rebar in preparation for another blow, but Justin, having grabbed the electric prod from Wayne when he took the piglet, delivered a shock to the piglet from the prod. The piglet screamed and started to retreat, but Justin moved in front of it, shocked it again, and forced it into a corner. The piglet screamed and quivered, but it had slowed enough for Justin to get his hands around the pig's legs. He grabbed the piglet by the legs and carried it down the aisle himself, pushing past Wayne when he reached for the pig. Justin caught Bryan's glare as he passed with the piglet, and he hesitated, but he could do nothing while holding the squirming pig, so he continued on, taking the piglet to its new destination.

When Justin returned, Hank and Wayne had left, and Justin found Bryan tending to the sow whose piglets had been taken, as she was emitting a number of high-pitched squeals and grunts. Justin was not entirely sure, but he thought that Bryan was talking to her to soothe her. As he approached, he gave Bryan a half grin, but his face fell a bit when Bryan returned a somewhat angered look.

"We'll move her later today or tomorrow," Justin said, sensing some tension with Bryan.

Bryan looked at him coldly then said, "I'm gonna get some fresh air." He turned and quickly walked down the aisle, leaving Justin behind. Justin waited a minute, then he picked up a few odds and ends, including the electric prod, and made his way toward the door.

He caught up with Bryan outside, having to jog a few paces to catch him. "Hey," he said, grinning. "What's the hurry?"

Bryan ignored him for a moment and kept walking, then he quickly stopped, causing Justin to nearly run into him. He turned to Justin and said, with more than a touch of anger in his voice, "That was pretty sick, you know? I mean what the hell is that thing?" He pointed to the prod, which Justin was still holding. "I could smell it burning them."

Justin looked down and scratched his head. "I mean, come on, man. How else are you supposed to move 'em when they won't move?" When Bryan said nothing, he continued, "I think it was better than letting Hank knock the shit out of 'em with that rebar, you know? And, I don't think it really hurts 'em. It just scares 'em."

At this, Bryan narrowed his eyes at Justin. "Seriously?" he said. As Justin was shrugging, Bryan reached down and grabbed the prod from him. He fiddled with it for a moment until he figured out how to turn it on. Then, in conjunction with the loud crackling sound of electricity, he moved it closer to Justin and said, "Okay, then, if it doesn't hurt, you touch it."

Justin looked at him blankly. "What?" he said. He laughed, but there was a touch of discomfort in his laugh.

Bryan suddenly felt amused. Justin always had an answer for everything, but for once, he was quiet. He smiled. "Go on, if it's no big deal. Just touch it and show me."

Justin had visibly paled. He took an unsteady step backward and shook his head slightly. "Come on, man," he said, trying to force a grin. "I mean I think it's different for pigs. They don't feel pain like we do."

Bryan gave him an incredulous look. "Really? You know that doesn't make any sense at all." Still slightly amused, he took a step forward. Justin immediately moved back. He looked down and ran his right hand through his hair. Bryan started to take another step forward when he saw that Justin's hand was shaking slightly. He hesitated, and Justin looked up long enough for

Bryan to notice that not only was he pale but that his eyes were also reddening. Justin quickly dropped his gaze.

Bryan stopped moving, and the amusement washed from his face. "Shit," he said. "Are you okay? I was just kidding. I wouldn't have," he trailed off, shaking his head. He turned the prod off and handed it back to Justin.

Justin, still looking down, gave a weak smile and took the prod. He took in a deep breath before responding. "Yeah, yeah, I'm good. It's just hot as hell out here. I'm gonna, I'm gonna go back in and finish up."

Without making eye contact, Justin moved past Bryan and returned to the pig building. Confused, Bryan waited a few minutes before he followed.

At the end of the day, Bryan asked Justin to get a drink. Justin, who was more or less back to his normal good humor, grinned widely. "That's what I'm talking about," he said, slapping Bryan on the shoulder.

CHAPTER XIV

Bryan waited until they had their first round of drinks at the Rancher's Respite, then he leaned in toward Justin. "Okay, so you gotta tell me what was up with you today. I mean, with the prod. You looked scared shitless, and I was just messing around."

Justin grinned and swirled his drink. "Oh yeah, it's no big thing. I just wasn't trying to get shocked," he laughed.

Bryan tilted his head at him and narrowed his eyes a bit. "Okay," he said slowly. "I mean, I'm not buying that. But," he said, as Justin looked down, "I guess you don't have to tell me."

Justin stared at his short glass of golden whiskey for a moment, watching it spin in a tiny whirlpool as he sloshed it around. "Oh," he said slowly, "it's just that I do know how much those fucking things hurt." He looked back at Bryan, but only briefly, before looking down again. "Don't get me wrong. I do think it's different for pigs. I don't mind using 'em, especially if it keeps Hank and Wayne from splitting their heads open with rebar."

Justin paused and looked around for a minute. He glanced up briefly at Bryan and saw that Bryan was watching him intently. He swallowed, then he sighed heavily and continued. "A few years ago I had to go to the farm late one night. One of the damn alarms went off for the fans. It was fine. Nothing wrong. I think a sensor was just out in the alarm or something. Anyway, Hank also got an automated text about the fans, so he showed up."

Justin paused again and took in a deep breath. "He showed up with Wayne. They'd been out somewhere, and they were both totally wasted. They were fucking hee hawing when they came in the building, and somehow or another one of 'em got the prod, and they started shocking each other. Fucking crazy." He shook his head. "And of course it hurt like hell, so they didn't do that long, but then" – he squeezed his eyes shut as he spoke – "then I guess they thought it would be fucking funny to try it on me."

Justin opened his eyes and saw that Bryan's eyes were wide and that his mouth had fallen slightly open. He laughed a little, but his laugh was cut short by the memory of what he was describing.

Bryan furrowed his brow. "How much did they do it?"

Justin raised his eyebrows and gave a half grin, "Well, I couldn't really tell you. Twenty minutes? Maybe thirty? It probably felt longer than it was. Wayne held me down, and Hank did it. They thought it was just fucking hilarious." He gritted his teeth. "And yeah," he nodded, "you're right. It does fucking burn. I could smell it burning as much as I could feel it. I finally passed out. When I woke up, they were gone."

Justin had started sweating, and Bryan just stared in disbelief. *How the hell could that even happen?* He felt a sickening regret for having teased Justin, and nausea started to rise in his throat as he thought of the fear on Justin's face. A waiter passed, and he ordered two more shots each, which caused Justin to eye him and grin.

"How old were you?" Bryan asked.

Justin waved a hand. "Oh, I don't know, sixteen or seventeen. It wasn't long after I quit school to start working on the farm full time."

Justin stared at Bryan. "Look man, I don't need your sympathy. I wouldn't have ever even told you, but yeah, you did scare me a little today." He grinned. "Those prods just aren't something I wanna play around with."

Bryan nodded, watching Justin.

"Hey," Justin said, suddenly looking up. "Don't tell your sister, okay?"

Bryan cocked his head at him and narrowed his eyes a bit.

Justin shook his head. "It's not that, man." He grinned. "It's just that I don't need a bunch of pity coming from her whenever we're all hanging out, okay? It'll make things weird. Okay?" He looked at Bryan expectantly.

Bryan nodded. "Yeah, sure, no problem."

Justin grinned, then he proceeded to drink enough whiskey to at least momentarily drown the memory of what he had just described.

CHAPTER XV

Justin moved the remaining sow the following day. He initially struggled to get her up. She seemed unwilling to move, and Bryan thought that perhaps she was depressed over the loss of her piglets. Once Justin went into the pen and rolled her over onto her belly, he saw that there might be another reason for her inactivity. Where the sow had been lying, her side was encased in thick, jelly-like discharge that was dark yellow in color, the color that Bryan imagined mustard might turn when it had set in the cabinet for too many years.

In this case, though, the mustard was dribbling out from open sores in the sow's side. Bryan tried to help Justin move the sow, but when his hand slipped in the jelly-like secretion, he had to run to the center aisle to vomit, forcefully expelling the contents of his stomach on the center walkway.

Justin, watching him, started chuckling and soon laughed so hard that he lost his grip on the sow. She slipped from his hands, toppling back over onto her decaying side. "You sure as shit don't have a stomach for this kind of work," Justin said grinning, wiping tears from his eyes.

Bryan frowned at him but then shrugged, smiling a little himself.

"Can you help? Or are you still sick?" Justin asked, starting to chuckle again.

Bryan pressed his eyelids firmly together for a moment, focusing on suppressing the overwhelming urge to retch again. He opened his eyes and saw Justin looking at him, stifled laughter causing him to shake silently.

"I'm good," he said, nodding to Justin. "Let's get this done."

Bryan got into the pen with Justin, and the two of them heaved the dripping sow out of the pen and into a wheelbarrow that Justin had brought into the building. As the cold, rough metal of the wheelbarrow touched her skin, she grunted, but she did not attempt to move, allowing Justin to wheel her out of the building, with Bryan standing at the front of the wheelbarrow to ensure that it did not topple over.

"Where are we taking her?" Bryan asking, looking at the miserable sow. Her eyes appeared fixed, and if not for the occasional rise and fall of her chest as she sucked in deep breaths, Bryan would have thought her dead.

"Back to gestation," Justin said. "She's probably got at least two or three more litters in her."

Bryan looked at the sow. "Already?" he asked. "Doesn't she need a break or something?"

Justin shrugged. "I mean, it's what they do. Anyway, it'll be a few months until she actually has another litter, so I guess that's a break."

Bryan frowned, then he asked hesitantly, "But do they ever, like, go outside or something? Are they always in the pen?"

Justin stopped moving the wheelbarrow for a moment and caught his breath. "Well, I mean, no, not really. They go outside when they're loading up the trucks, but that's, you know, they're going to slaughter, so it's not really like outdoor play time." Justin shrugged.

Bryan continued frowning but said nothing. He helped Justin make it the rest of the way until they entered the gestation area. They wheeled the sow to an empty pen, and then they heaved her into the pen. She made a few low grunts and a couple of short squeals as they moved her, then she lay on her side where they placed her, unmoving. Her eyes watched them as they stepped away; her breathing was hoarse and shallow.

"Do you think she needs a vet?" Bryan asked.

Justin pulled his mouth to one side. "No," he said slowly. "She might perk up. If not . . . ." He trailed off without looking at Bryan. "Anyway, that's all we can do for now. Let's go eat lunch."

He slapped Bryan on the shoulder as he walked past him and made his way out of the building. Bryan lingered in front of the sow for a moment, watching her, as her big dark eyes tracked his movements. Finally, sighing, he looked away and followed Justin outside.

* * *

The sow was in a slightly different spot within the pen the following Monday, but she was still lying on her side, apparently unable to rise. When Bryan came to check on her, she gave a series of short, low grunts, and her nostrils flared inward and outward with each breath. Her dark eyes fixed on his face as he stood nearby, watching her.

Bryan got Justin, feeling a strong sense of déjà vu, and asked him to do something. Justin, after watching the sow for a few moments, said, "Well, there's really not much to do, man. She'll either make it or not. At least we can give her a chance."

Bryan narrowed his eyes at Justin, who gave an apologetic half shrug. "I'm sorry, Bryan, but really there's only so much you can do."

"What about a vet?" Bryan asked, with more than a touch of agitation.

Justin gave a short, harsh laugh. "I mean, they're not my pigs, man, but I can tell you that Hank ain't sending no vet out here to look at a damn pig." He chuckled a little at the idea. He started to walk off, but he saw that Bryan was still lingering near the sow, his brow furrowed.

Justin sighed. "Look, Hank and Wayne will be out here in the next few days to start her insemination. If she needs something, they'll get it. It's just –" he trailed off a bit. "It's just that you may not like it." He looked at Bryan for a moment, then he gave a half grin, turned, and headed to another part of the building.

Hank and Wayne did not show up until the following Tuesday. The pig was lying against the inside corner of her pen. She had been able to get up long enough to drink some water and sniff at her food, but she mainly lay and emitted soft, muffled grunts.

Hank asked Justin a few questions about her, and Bryan saw Justin answer with a shrug. Hank looked irritated, and Justin moved slightly away from him. Hank motioned to Wayne, and the two men entered the pen with the sow.

The sow's breathing became more rapid as the men approached her, and she kicked her hooves against the concrete floor in a futile attempt to move backward. Short, high-pitched squeals erupted from her every few seconds, with the squeals increasing both in frequency and volume as the men came closer.

The sow lay on her left side, and, when the men were close, Hank grabbed her left hind leg and jerked it upward, pulling her body off the ground. The sow's squeals became all-out shrieks, and she kicked her legs frantically as Hank held her, as if she were trying to swim.

Hank apparently observed the sow's rotting underside, as he grimaced and looked at Wayne, nodding to the sow. Wayne nodded and said something inaudible to Hank. Hank dropped the sow abruptly and stood up – as he did so, one of the sow's still flailing legs made direct contact with Hank's right shin. Hank cried out sharply in pain, cursed, and then kicked the sow with what looked to be all of his strength. The sow, still kicking in a panic, screamed abruptly and then fell silent. Her kicking stopped, and she lay still.

Bryan, watching the interaction, felt a surge of anger. Hank was still looking down at the trembling sow, and Bryan started toward him without any particular plan in mind. Justin, who had been fiddling with a waterer in a nearby pen, quickly scrambled out of the pen and grabbed Bryan's arm. Bryan paused and shot him an angry look. Justin shook his head slightly, mumbling under his breath, "Not right now," and then said more loudly, "Come help me with this, man."

Bryan hesitated. He felt Justin give him a slight push, and he glared at him. Justin grinned apologetically, but he looked anxiously at Bryan, clearly wanting to move him along.

Hank was suddenly out of the pen and moving past Bryan, with Wayne following behind. Hank gave a half nod in Bryan's direction, then he pulled Justin aside and said something low to him. Justin listened, then nodded, at which point Hank and Wayne departed from the building.

"They're not gonna try to get another litter out of her," Justin said to Bryan, who had squatted down next to the immobile sow. "There's a truck coming Friday to pick up pigs for –" Justin paused, scratching his head and glancing at Bryan. "For processing," Justin continued, grinning slightly at his clever use of the word "processing," but he saw that Bryan was still frowning. "If she's still, if she's still here on Friday, then we'll add her to the truck."

Bryan thought for a moment about what Justin had said. "So wait, she's going to a slaughterhouse? I mean, even with all the shit that's coming out of her?"

Justin gave a mild shrug. "I mean, it should be fine," he said. "They have, like, inspectors there, so they can say something if they don't think she's good enough for meat. I mean, maybe they can use her for dog food or something." Justin grinned.

Bryan looked at Justin blankly, initially unsure if he had been joking. He saw that he was serious, and he narrowed his eyes at him.

"That's insane," Bryan finally said, unable to think of anything more meaningful to say.

Justin shrugged, slapped Bryan on the back, and went back to work.

Friday morning when Bryan arrived at the farm, he saw a tractor trailer parked next to one of the pig buildings. It was the sort of truck he had seen before and recognized as one for carrying livestock. The metal sides were slated, with openings between the slates. As Bryan approached the truck, he saw that there was a ramp lowered at the back of it, and that the ramp ran directly to the door of the pig building containing the already weaned pigs.

As he approached the truck, he heard squeals and grunts coming from inside of the building. Before he reached the door, Justin came out. He looked dirty and was visibly sweating. His face was tensed, but as he came out of the building and saw Bryan, he quickly relaxed and grinned. He sighed heavily and wiped his arm across his forehead in a somewhat futile attempt to keep the dripping sweat out of his eyes.

"Hey, man, thought you'd never get here," Justin grinned.

Bryan, confused, glanced at his watch.

Justin chuckled. "I'm just messing with you, man. You're fine. We just started early 'cause we gotta get these pigs loaded. So listen, you can help."

A barred metal panel, similar to a livestock gate, was leaning against the pig building near the truck. Justin grabbed it and handed it to Bryan.

"Here," he said. "Just hang onto this, and if any of the pigs try to run out the door and past the ramp, just herd 'em back in and up the ramp. Easy peasy." Justin grinned.

Bryan hesitantly took the panel and mumbled an "okay." He saw that he was meant to stand on one side of the ramp, blocking the path if a pig attempted to come out of the building and turn left. The door to the building itself was open and wedged against the ramp, blocking the way to the right, and, with Bryan holding the panel on the left, a chute was created for pigs to move forward, up the ramp, and onto the truck.

Justin, on hearing his name sharply called, jerked his head toward the interior of the building. "Alright, man," he said, still grinning. "You got this. We'll be done in a jiffy." Justin ran back inside the building, leaving Bryan holding the panel.

Bryan waited, listening to the sound of a blue jay as he stood there. He heard the bird's calls, and he scanned the scant trees around the buildings for signs of life, finally spotting the bird, hopping along under a nearby maple tree, making short flitting jumps and picking at the ground.

The bird kept calling, but the chirps were suddenly overtaken by a wave of increasingly loud squeals. Bryan looked at the open door to the pig building and waited nervously, his knuckles growing white as he gripped the metal panel.

Two screaming pigs suddenly burst through the door and ran up the ramp, not pausing to even glance Bryan's way. They shot into the truck and ran to the back, squeezing themselves into a front corner, as far away from the entrance as they could get.

Bryan relaxed slightly. *Okay, if that's how this goes, then I can do this.* He waited, and the next pig who emerged took a sharp left and tried to get past Bryan. He held the panel but felt the pig's weight slam against it. He groaned and stood his ground, and after a second slam into the panel, the pig changed its course and ran up the ramp, onto the truck.

Justin came out a second later, quickly asked if Bryan was good, and then disappeared back into the building. Several more pigs passed by. The majority ran directly up the ramp and onto the truck, but a few ran into the panel, jostling Bryan. Most only tried once or twice – four times at most – and then they continued on their way, up the ramp and into the truck. A few times, Hank or Wayne had emerged at the heels of the pigs, driving them forward with shouts and slaps. Bryan saw Hank carrying the electric prod, but he was not sure if he was actually using it. In any case, most of the pigs seemed to be going in the direction they were directed.

After the truck was about half full, a large pig shot out of the building and slammed itself hard into the panel. Bryan felt his teeth snap together with the force of the blow, and he stumbled backward slightly. The slight movement of the panel was enough for the pig to squeeze beside it, and he ran past Bryan at full speed, knocking the panel again as he ran by and causing Bryan to fall down under the panel. Bryan lay on the ground for a moment, watching the pig speed past.

"Shit," Bryan cursed. Then, louder, he yelled, "Hey!"

Justin appeared a second later, as Bryan was struggling to get out from under the panel. Hank appeared closely behind him. Justin laughed and pulled Bryan up, asking if he was okay. Then he told him to hold the panel so no more pigs got loose. Hank surveyed the scene for a moment, cast an irritated look at Bryan, then made his way toward the loose pig, jerking Justin along by the arm.

As they moved away and after the pig, Bryan heard Hank rumbling in a low voice. "God damn it," he spat. "I thought you said he could handle this."

Justin mumbled something and shrugged. Hank, still clutching Justin's arm, gave him a visible shake. Justin stumbled and would have fallen, but Hank jerked him forcefully forward.

The pig, rather than running directly toward the edge of the farm, had skittered around the pig buildings in sporadic, panicky movements. Bryan was trying to watch while still holding the panel for a few straggling pigs that Wayne was continuing to push forward. He saw the pig dart between two buildings, and Justin grabbed another panel to try to block him in. Hank came around the opposite side of the building in an attempt to cut the pig off, but the pig, perhaps sensing the entrapment or perhaps simply due to its random, spurting movements, shot past Hank and raced back around the building.

Justin laughed, and Hank shot him a hot glare. Justin stifled his laughter and moved after the pig again, grinning as he went.

Wayne finally emerged from the building. He glanced at Bryan, then he turned to watch Hank and Justin for a moment. A smile slowly spread over his face, but Bryan thought it had much less of the mirth that Justin's grins carried and instead sent a cold chill creeping over him. Wayne looked back at Bryan.

"That's all for now," he said, apparently referencing the pigs he had been driving onto the truck. "We can help them. Bring the panel and try to corner it."

Wayne waited for Bryan to nod, then he walked briskly toward the general vicinity of the pig. Bryan followed.

Bryan went to where Justin was. Justin was looking around, still with a grin on his face. His grin widened when Bryan approached.

"Shit, I'm sorry, man," Bryan said.

Justin shook his head. "It's no big thing. Hank's losing his shit, but it's one pig. And we're not gonna catch it." He laughed. "This is all a big waste of time. We'll just chase it until Hank gets tired and decides to give it up." He raised an eyebrow at Bryan and shrugged.

Bryan suddenly caught a glimpse of movement, and he turned just in time to see the pig scurrying past them. Justin laughed and shook his head.

"Let's go," he said, still shaking his head.

The pig darted from one building to another for cover, dodging the panels when Justin and Bryan approached and moving with so much speed that neither Hank or Wayne was able to get anywhere near the pig. Bryan saw that Hank's face was reddening, and he did not think it was from the heat. Hank was clearly livid. He continuously cursed in low tones, and when Bryan happened to come into his view, the disgust on his face was palpable. Justin seemed to either not notice Hank's irritation or to not care, as he meandered about after the pig, occasionally chuckling, and grinning from time to time at Bryan.

Justin's grin only faded when Hank, clearly exhausted and still fuming, went to his truck. Hank reached into the back and pulled out a rifle. Bryan was not sure what gauge the rifle was, but he could tell that it was larger than what Justin had used to shoot the injured calf so many nights before.

Justin pulled his mouth to one side, ran his hand through his hair, and said, "Well, that's it. He'll shoot it now."

Bryan looked at him, surprised. "But you can't send it to slaughter like that, right? With a bullet in it?"

Justin laughed. "Ah shit, well if there was any chance we could, I'm sure Hank would try. But no, you can't."

"Then why is he gonna shoot it?" Bryan asked.

Justin considered a moment, shrugged, and said, "I guess because it's his."

Bryan frowned and furrowed his brow. He saw Hank come back briskly with the rifle. The pig was attempting to dig under the white shed where Jeffrey's cat had birthed her kittens. As Hank approached, the pig lifted its head, glanced at Hank, and then shot off toward the fields behind the farm.

Hank watched the pig for a moment, then in what seemed to be one swift motion, he raised the gun, aimed it, and fired.

The deafening sound of the rifle reverberated through Bryan's head. Ahead, he saw the pig stagger and fall.

Hank lowered his rifle, then he turned and walked toward Bryan and Justin.

"Y'all can go find that pig and throw it in the trash out back," Hank said to Justin.

He then turned to Bryan and said, "Son, that was a $400 pig, and now he ain't worth shit. That'll have to come out of your pay."

Bryan looked at him but said nothing.

"Oh come on, Hank," Justin said grinning. "There's no way in hell you were gonna get $400 for that pig."

Hank narrowed his eyes at Justin and moved toward him. Justin stepped back quickly, but he bumped into the side of the pig building that was immediately behind him. He grinned, although nervously now, and tensed and dropped his eyes as Hank approached.

"Justin," Hank said slowly when he was close, "you might should stay out of things that don't concern you."

Justin breathed heavily but kept looking down as Hank stayed within inches of his face. Bryan, who had been watching the scene, suddenly seemed to wake from a stupor and moved next to Justin. He edged beside him and, looking at Hank, gave Justin a light push.

"Let's go," he said, still staring at Hank.

Justin looked at Bryan and reddened slightly. He nodded, cast a half grin at Hank, and led Bryan toward the field and the shot pig.

For a while, neither Justin or Bryan said anything. The only sound was the swishing of the tall grass as they moved through it.

After a few moments, Justin, still looking down, said, "You know, he's mostly talk." He cast a quick glance at Bryan. "Hank, I mean."

Bryan narrowed his eyes in return. "Yeah? Yeah, I remember the last time he talked to you. You were out for like a week, and you looked like shit when you did come back. That was a good talk, right?"

Justin winced and reddened again but said nothing. They kept walking, and in a short time, they found the pig.

The pig was lying on its side and at first appeared motionless. As they approached, however, they saw the faint rising and falling of its chest, and they heard the low gargled grunts coming from deep in its throat. The bullet had hit the pig's core, and it lay in a pool of blood, unable to rise.

"Shit," Bryan said. "It's still alive."

Justin sighed heavily and pulled his mouth to one side. "Yeah," he said. "I was afraid it might be. Hank is generally a shit shot."

Justin pulled out a silver pocketknife, flicked it open, and leaned over the pig.

"Wait, wait," Bryan said, eyes widening. "What the hell are you doing?"

"I mean, we need to put it out of its misery," Justin said, looking up at Bryan.

"But," Bryan said, trailing off. He did not have anything to go after that "but," so he simply raised his hands in an exasperated manner.

Justin eyed him for a moment, then he said, "You wanna step away maybe?"

Bryan hesitated, but then he slowly shook his head.

Justin sighed, looked back at the pig, and then sank the knife into the pig's throat. Blood spurted up and covered Justin's face and right hand. The pig convulsed for a moment, with all four legs stiffening and shaking uncontrollably. A deep, wet gurgle came from the pig's now open throat.

Justin wiped the blood from his face, shook it off of his hand, and stood up. He looked at Bryan, who was getting that pallid, sickly look he tended to get in these sorts of situations.

"You good, man?" Justin asked.

Bryan nodded, then he helped Justin half drag, half carry the dead pig to the trash pile.

When the boys returned to the front of the farm, they saw Hank and Wayne carrying a pig up the ramp to the truck. After an initial glance, Bryan realized that it was the sick sow. She grunted in low tones but did not move or squeal as she was carried. Her body jostled with each step the men took, and her eyes stayed half open and glazed over.

When they reached the top of the ramp, the pigs inside the truck skittered back, emitting a roar of high-pitched squeals and boisterous grunts. Hank and Wayne swung the sow and dropped her onto the truck floor. The sow grunted again but did not move. After that, the men returned into the pig building.

Bryan looked at Justin, who was watching him.

Justin scratched his head and said, "Hey, let's go finish up and get out of here."

Bryan frowned and was about to follow when he saw the men emerging from the building with another pig. This one was flailing wildly and screaming in piercing shrieks as it went. Bryan saw that one of the pig's legs was bent sharply at an unnatural angle. He looked closer and saw the brilliant white of bone sticking through the bend in the leg. As the men hoisted this pig onto the truck in the same manner as the sow, Bryan was overcome with nausea. He turned away quickly and reached out for the side of the building to keep from tumbling over.

Bryan saw that Justin was grinning at him hesitantly, with his brow slightly furrowed.

"You know what, why don't you go check on Jeffrey. Make sure he's all good. I'll finish up here, then we can go grab a drink." His grin widened.

Bryan nodded, focusing on not vomiting, then he moved slowly toward the building where Jeffrey was working.

When Bryan reached the building, Jeffrey was emerging with a wheelbarrow full of dead pigs. These were young pigs, although clearly old enough to be weaned and separated from the nursing sows. One of the pigs had a gaping hole in its lower abdomen, and a tangle of intestines was starting to spill out.

Bryan was finally unable to control his nausea. He grasped the side of the building just as the vomit started to surge up and out of him. He retched for a few moments, all the time aware that Jeffrey was staring at him with a slightly confused expression. He finished, wiped the sweat from his forehead, and looked at Jeffrey.

Jeffrey grinned. "Got a little tummy trouble? Lunch not sitting right?"

Bryan said nothing and only looked at Jeffrey blankly.

"Do you need some help?" Bryan finally managed.

Jeffrey shrugged. "Sure," he said smiling. "I'm pretty much done. You can help me unload these and then clean up."

Bryan grimaced but followed Jeffrey. He waited until Jeffrey had unloaded the pig that was bursting at the abdomen, then he helped with the others.

When they closed the building for the evening, Bryan headed back to the farrowing and gestation buildings to find Justin. Justin was just emerging. He grinned, gave Bryan a light slap on the shoulder, and said, "You wanna get out of here?"

Bryan nodded. They started toward their trucks, when Hank yelled out after Justin.

Justin paused, swallowed, and told Bryan to hold up a minute. He went back over to Hank, where they were out of earshot of Bryan. Bryan saw Hank say something to Justin, pointing back toward the pig building. Justin responded, shrugging slightly, and Hank leaned in closer to him. Justin looked down and nodded, then he came back over to Bryan.

"Listen, man," he said. "I guess Hank still needs some help here, so I'll have to pass on tonight."

Bryan eyed him for a minute. "You need me to stay?"

Justin smiled and raised an eyebrow. "Man, I don't think your stomach can handle any more." He laughed, and Bryan flushed slightly.

"But hey," Justin continued, "we still good for fishing tomorrow?"

Bryan nodded, and they settled on a time.

As Bryan pulled out, Justin watched him for a moment. Then he turned and headed back to where Hank and Wayne were waiting for him.

* * *

When Bryan arrived home, he saw Winnie and Wilbur swinging in the white wooden porch swing. Winnie had a book in her right hand, and her left arm was wrapped around Wilbur to keep him secured on the swing. He was lying nestled next to her, and his tail flipped around every few seconds.

Winnie looked up as Bryan came up the stairs to the porch. She smiled.

"Well, I'm surprised to see you home on a Friday night," she said teasingly.

Bryan shrugged. "Justin had to work late."

"But you didn't?"

Bryan pulled his mouth to one side. "Well, I don't think Hank really likes me all that much." He hesitated then added, "Honestly, I'm not sure Justin really needed to work. I just think maybe Hank –" Bryan stopped, looking up at Winnie. He decided that he did not want her to know what he thought.

Winnie looked at him. "You think Hank what?"

Bryan shook his head. "It doesn't matter. Hey, you still wanting to go fishing tomorrow?"

Winnie frowned and narrowed her eyes at him. "Yes to the fishing, but don't you dare start telling me something and then stop. What were you gonna say?"

Bryan sighed, once again cursing his big mouth. "Oh I don't know, Winnie. It's just that, Justin's relationship with Hank isn't like ours with Pa. He's, I mean, I think Hank is pissed at him 'cause of some shit I did today, and I just, I think –" He trailed off again.

Winnie's eyes were narrowed, and her face showed concern. Looking at her, Bryan thought he could see what she was going to look like when she was older, and that thought suddenly filled him with what seemed like an unreasonable amount of sadness.

Bryan shook his head. "Anyway, he'll be fine, and he's coming over tomorrow."

Winnie continued staring for a moment with her worried look, then her face relaxed a bit in apparent acceptance.

Bryan grinned a little. "Does Wilbur actually like swinging with you?"

Winnie smiled. "He seems to. He hasn't tried to get down." She stroked the coarse hair on Wilbur's back. He

145

twitched his nose and looked up at Winnie, emitting apparently pleased grunts.

Bryan sat down in a rocking chair next to them, and they listened as the sound of cicadas grew louder with the coming evening.

CHAPTER XVI

In the morning, Winnie was up early. She went to Bryan's room, knocked on the door, and, getting no response, she knocked louder. Still having no response, she swung the door open and let Wilbur run in. The pig's hooves click clacked on the hardwood floor, and, nearing the bed, he leapt up and landed on top of the quilted bedspread. Bryan grumbled and swatted at Wilbur with his eyes closed, but the pig nuzzled his snout into Bryan's face.

"You better get up," Winnie said from the doorway. "We gotta be ready in an hour."

She called Wilbur, and the pig jumped down and followed her onto the back porch. He was well housed trained by now – in fact, he had learned a good bit faster than Boomer, who had always been a little obstinate about having to go outside to use the bathroom when he could just lift his leg on the chairs.

Wilbur jumped off the back porch and ran into the yard, where Boomer was rambling around and sniffing the new smells of the morning, having already been let out by Mama earlier. Boomer kept his nose low to the ground, making low chuffing sounds as he moved along, smelling leftover scents from raccoons, opossums, and all the other creatures who had traveled through the yard the night before.

Wilbur shot past Boomer with a burst of energy. He bumped into the old dog as he passed. Boomer cast a half irritated glance his way and then kept on sniffing. Wilbur put his nose to the ground in the manner of Boomer, but, in contrast to Boomer's lazy speed, Wilbur zoomed around in fast little patterns, hardly having time to catch one scent before he moved onto the next.

Winnie watched them for a moment, taking in the touch of warm sunlight that was creeping up her arms as she moved out into the yard. The sound of chirping birds was overpowering, and a rich scent of grass filled her nose. Winnie laughed at Wilbur's goofy zigzagging through the yard, and she heard the screen door on the back porch slam as Bryan came out, dressed but with his uncombed hair shooting up in all directions.

Winnie smiled at Bryan, then she heard Boomer give a soft, lazy bark. She looked back at him and saw that he was

147

looking toward the side of the house. She turned in the direction that Boomer was looking, and she felt her heart jump. Justin was just feet away, intently watching Wilbur with a puzzled look.

Justin, hearing Winnie make a quick intake of breath, raised his eyes from Wilbur for a moment to look at her. He saw her smile fading into what looked to him like worry or fear. He waved awkwardly, trying to alleviate her concern, but her face remained the same.

"I knocked," he said, gesturing toward the front of the house, "but no one –" He trailed off and grinned apologetically.

Bryan, having heard Justin's voice, quickly came off the porch. His mouth dropped a little when he saw Justin, and he quickly moved toward him, stopping when he reached Winnie.

"I thought you were coming later," Bryan said with a touch of frustration.

Justin furrowed his brow. "I guess, I thought, I –," but he added no more and simply shrugged. Unsure of what to say, but feeling more and more uncomfortable with the slightly hostile look he was getting from Bryan, he added, "I guess that's Wilbur?"

Winnie had called Wilbur over to her and was rubbing him. She looked at Bryan, who was sighing heavily, and then she nodded at Justin. "Yeah," she said softly. "This is Wilbur."

"Is that," Justin started, eyeing Bryan, "did he come from the farm?"

Bryan started to shake his head, but, realizing that he had put absolutely no thought into a convincing back story for the pig, he stopped.

"I mean, I don't give a shit," Justin said, looking at Bryan. "It's, it's kind of strange," he laughed, "but I don't care."

Winnie, still eyeing Justin, seemed to relax somewhat and gave him a half smile.

Bryan was looking at the ground and shaking his head. "Yeah, but what about Hank?"

Justin grinned widely at that. "What about Hank? Don't even worry about Hank. He'll never know." Justin saw Bryan lose some of his tension and added, "I mean, I'm not gonna tell him, if that's what you're worried about."

Bryan looked at Winnie. She pressed her lips together and raised her eyebrows slightly at him in a look that said *I'll follow your lead.*

Bryan nodded. "Okay," he said, nodding again. "Yeah, I mean, that's what I'm worried about. I mean, especially after yesterday."

Winnie glanced at Bryan, unsure of what he meant, then she turned back to Justin.

Justin grinned. "I got you, man. You're all good. But, you seriously got to tell me why the hell you took a pig home." He laughed, and both Winnie and Bryan visibly relaxed.

The three sat on the porch, drinking coffee and eating grits, while Bryan told Justin how Wilbur had come to the Bradford home. Justin seemed to think it was all fairly hilarious, saying, "I guess if I'm out too many days, you'll have a whole herd of pigs here." He chuckled, and Winnie smiled at him.

Winnie showed Justin some of Wilbur's tricks. Like Boomer, he could "sit" and "lie down," but his talents went a little beyond Boomer's in that he seemed to have a slightly greater understanding of human speech. He could retrieve things that Winnie requested.

"Wilbur, can you go get my jacket?" Winnie asked, emphasizing the word *jacket.*

Wilbur cocked his head and then trotted down to the end of the porch, where Winnie's jacket lay thrown over the railing. Wilbur grasped the jacket with his teeth and pulled it down, dragging it back to Winnie.

Justin watched in obvious surprise, never having seen a pig perform in such a manner. He had also never seen a pig that seemed to enjoy human companionship, and he watched with curiosity as Wilbur snuggled into Winnie's side for attention.

After breakfast, Winnie put Wilbur and Boomer back in the house, and the three packed into Justin's truck, which was loaded with fishing supplies, and headed off.

* * *

When they reached the river and had settled on a good place to fish, they laid down their gear on a blanket Winnie had brought. Bryan started to help Winnie get set up, but he saw that Justin was already helping her.

"Alright," Justin said, grinning at Winnie, "you may not know this, but the key to fishing is the bait."

Winnie smiled in an *Oh wow, who knew?* expression.

Justin opened a Styrofoam container he had brought, and Winnie leaned over to see about a dozen fat earthworms wiggling inside. She shuddered.

"Um," she said, pulling back, "I think I'm good with just the fish bait."

Justin grinned and shook his head. "No way, that won't do it. You wanna catch a puny little fish you're just gonna have to throw back? You gotta use a worm if you want something worth eatin'."

Winnie looked at Bryan, who was already fishing, using the fish bait he had brought. He shrugged.

Winnie turned back to Justin and grimaced. He laughed, then he took her fishing pole, plucked out a wiggling worm, and speared the worm through the middle with the fishhook.

Winnie put her hand to her mouth as her eyes widened. Justin suddenly realized that perhaps the worm was a mistake.

"I'm sorry," he said, quickly reddening. "Do you want me to take it off?"

Winnie's eyes were wide as she watched the worm writhing on the hook. She thought that, if the worm could scream, the piercing scream would likely be deafening right now.

She shook her head and gave Justin a weak smile. "No, you just use my pole for now, that way you can leave it on."

Justin nodded and handed her his fishing pole. Winnie took the pole over to Bryan to get some of the fish bait he had brought.

Justin sighed and threw the line, worm and hook attached, into the river.

They fished for about an hour. Winnie was the first to catch a fish. She grinned at Justin triumphantly and pulled the small bass out of the water. The fish flopped on the riverbank for a moment, but Winnie quickly picked up the fish, pulled out the hook in a quick motion, and threw it back into the water.

A few minutes later, Justin had a strong pull on his fishing line. He pulled back and brought up a largemouth bass. The fish thrashed between the water and the air as Justin tried to reel it in. He finally gave the line a hard jerk and brought the fish out of the water. He quickly reeled in the line, bringing the flailing fish closer. He then dropped the fish onto the grass beside him, where it flopped in a panic as it slowly asphyxiated.

"Now that's a fish," Justin said, winking at Winnie.

She rolled her eyes and smiled. "You keeping it or throwing it back?"

Justin looked at the fish as it lurched on the grass. "I'll keep this one," he said. "It's a pretty good size." He knelt over the fish and jerked the line out of its throat. Blood bubbled up after the hook came out, and Justin dropped the fish onto the ground, where the flops became less prominent as the blood pooled around it.

Winnie glanced up at Justin.

"I guess it was hooked on the gills," he said. "It'll bleed out soon."

Winnie frowned, watching the fish until its movements became imperceptible.

"I think I'm ready for a swim," she said, looking away from the fish.

Bryan, who had been silently holding his fishing pole in a slumped position with his eyes half closed, sat up quickly. "You wearing a swim suit?" he asked somewhat anxiously, glancing at Justin.

Winnie laughed. "Of course! Did you think I was really gonna fish all day?" She patted him teasingly on the head and moved over to the blanket, where she started taking off her shirt and shorts.

Bryan furrowed his brow and sighed in frustration, casting an agitated look at Justin. Justin grinned.

"Well," Winnie said with a note of amusement in her voice, "if you two don't want to stare at me, you could come in, too."

Bryan looked at Justin, who shrugged.

"Fine with me," Justin said. "It's getting hot anyway." Justin stood up, put down his fishing pole, and started taking his shirt off.

Bryan, more frustrated than ever and feeling helplessly stuck, glanced back and forth between Winnie and Justin, who both seemed amused with his expression.

Justin laughed as he pulled off his shoes. "Bryan, man," he said, shaking his head and tugging at his shoes, "you're a good brother. I promise you we're all good, though."

Bryan hesitated, sighed in defeat, then put down his fishing pole and started to undress down to his boxers.

Winnie, now in her swim suit, eased off the riverbank and into the water. She was able to stand waist deep at the edge of the river, then she ducked into the water and swam out to the deeper section in the middle. She came up, hair drenched and falling over her face, and motioned for the two boys to join her.

Justin neared Bryan and waited for him. When he got closer, Bryan saw a large, bluish bruise covering the lower portion of his back. He saw a second, smaller bruise higher up, on his shoulder blade, which was darker and yellowish in the center.

"What the hell happened to your back?" Bryan asked.

Justin, who had been watching Winnie, glanced back, started to say something, but, realizing that Bryan already knew the answer and that lying was pointless, he shrugged. When Bryan frowned, he grinned and said, "Come on, let's go."

The water was cool and refreshing in the heat of the summer day. While the water at the edges moved fast in small rapids, the center seemed slow and calm, hardly moving at all. The middle of the river was well over their heads, and they took turns diving down to touch the bottom.

At one point, a black snake slithered through the water. Winnie was the first to catch a glimpse of the dark form gliding through the water. She shrieked out a scream and jumped on Bryan, who toppled over backward in the water. "Snake!" she cried, pointing at the snake.

Justin fell over laughing. "It's just a rat snake," he laughed out, but Bryan and Winnie were already nearing the shore. He kept laughing and swam after them.

They sat dripping in the grass, drying in the hot sun. Winnie had brought along chicken salad sandwiches and Cokes in glass bottles, which Bryan loved. They ate, feeling sleepy in the afternoon heat, until they heard voices nearing them.

Four boys around Bryan's age appeared further up along the riverbank. They were wearing swim trunks, and a couple of them were shirtless. They walked along the river, laughing and talking loudly as they neared.

Winnie, mostly dry, quickly put her shirt and shorts back on, and Bryan and Justin did the same. Then Winnie, watching the approaching boys, said, "Hey, Bryan, isn't that Luke?"

Bryan looked toward the boys and realized that Winnie was right. The tallest boy, who was lean and blonde and laughing fairly consistently at what seemed to be his own jokes, was none other than Luke Peterson.

"Bryan and Luke played football together," Winnie said to Justin, as Bryan, smiling, made his way toward Luke.

Luke, seeing Bryan approach, looked up, stared a moment, then recognized him and smiled. "Bryan, man, look at you! Good to see you."

"Good to see you, man." Bryan said as he reached Luke. "It's been a while."

"No joke," Luke said. "It's hard to keep up with everyone during the summer, you know?" The other three boys with Luke dropped what few items they had on the riverbank and splashed into the water.

Luke nodded toward the other boys. "I met these guys during orientation at State. They're starting in the fall, too. Those two" – he pointed at two of the boys, who were taking turns pushing one another under the water – "they're starting on the team with me."

Bryan looked down and shuffled slightly.

Luke frowned and said, "Sucks about your knee, man."

Bryan nodded without making eye contact.

"So what are you up to? Are you still gonna try to go to State?" Luke asked.

Bryan sighed and shook his head. "No, I mean, I can't go without the scholarship. I'm just working right now." He glanced back and saw that Winnie and Justin had packed up and were making their way toward him.

"That sucks, man," Luke said. "Where are you working?"

Bryan reddened slightly. "On a farm," he said, giving a half grin.

Luke looked at him, unsure of whether he was joking, then he laughed. "On a farm? Really? What the hell kind of farm would hire you?"

"It's a pig farm," Bryan said, quickly adding, "I mean, it's just for the summer, until I get my shit figured out. I'm not staying there long term or anything."

Luke laughed. "God, I hope not. A fucking pig farm? That's crazy, man." Luke shook his head, still in apparent disbelief. "Oh man, that's gotta be a shit job. You better get your crap together soon and get outta there."

Bryan laughed awkwardly. "Yeah, I will," he said, rubbing the back of his neck. "I mean, I'm not planning to spend all my life shoveling pig shit." He grinned at Luke, who laughed loudly.

Bryan heard movement and glanced around to see Winnie and Justin standing immediately behind him, holding their gear. Winnie's eyes were slightly narrowed at Bryan, and Justin was looking down.

Bryan felt himself grow hot. Luke, noticing Winnie, smiled.

"Hey, Winnie girl," he said.

Winnie withdrew her eyes from Bryan and smiled at Luke. "Hey, Luke," she said. She moved in closer and hugged him lightly.

Bryan noticed that Luke was looking at Justin. "Oh, this is Justin," Bryan said. "Justin, this is Luke."

Justin looked up and nodded a hello, and Luke asked, "How do y'all know each other?"

"We," Bryan started, hesitating, "we work together."

Luke grinned. "On the farm. Gotcha." He chuckled.

Bryan saw Justin look away at nothing in particular, and Winnie shot Bryan a quick glare. She looked back at Luke and smiled.

"It was good to see you, Luke. I hope everything goes well for you this fall. Bryan," she said, turning to him, "we're gonna load up the truck. We'll meet you back there." Winnie tugged on Justin's arm, and Justin followed her back toward his truck.

Bryan lingered with Luke a bit longer, sharing some of their football stories for about the millionth time. Finally, Luke said he should get some swimming in, and he gave Bryan a strong slap on the shoulder.

"Let's get together sometime, man," Luke said. "I'm here until the last week in August."

Bryan agreed, then he said goodbye and headed back to the truck.

When he got to the truck, Winnie and Justin were sitting on the tailgate, with Winnie swinging her legs and Justin grinning at something she was saying.

"Sorry about that," Bryan said when he neared them. "I haven't seen Luke in a while."

"No worries," Justin said, hopping down from the tailgate. "We should probably head back, though. I'm watching Conner tonight."

Bryan nodded, and they loaded up the truck and drove home in relative quiet.

When they got home and Winnie had gone inside, Bryan waited with Justin for a minute.

"Hey, man," he said. "I'm sorry about today. I didn't mean to –" He hesitated, looking for the right words. "I didn't mean to hurt your feelings."

Justin laughed. "It's all good, man. Don't worry about it. I had a good time. I'll see you Monday."

Bryan hesitated, not entirely believing Justin, then he sighed and headed toward the house. Justin's truck rattled out of the driveway, kicking up small clouds of dust that lingered in the air after it had gone.

CHAPTER XVII

During the first couple of days back at work, Bryan thought Justin was a little cooler to him than normal. He was not sure if he really was, or if he was simply imagining it, as Justin still spent most of his day grinning about something or another. He did, however, turn Bryan down two days in a row when he asked him to get drinks after work.

"I gotta watch Conner tonight," Justin said both times.

Bryan was not sure if that was true or not, but he simply nodded and went home.

When he told Winnie, she eyed him sharply and said, "Do you even care if he likes you? If so, maybe you should have thought about that when you were talking with Luke." She raised an eyebrow, and Bryan winced at the truth of what she said.

The following week, Justin teased Bryan a little more, and Bryan felt a bit of relief. Midway through the week, Jeffrey was out, helping Mama J get to and from a doctor's visit, so Justin was scrambling between several different pig buildings.

"Jesus," Justin said at lunch. "We could seriously use some more help here."

Bryan looked up. "Why doesn't Hank hire somebody?"

Justin laughed. "Well, he's cheap as shit for one. Also, there's not a lot of people who wanna work here." Justin eyed Bryan when he said this, and Bryan, feeling his face warming, looked down.

"I mean," Justin continued, "we could probably get some Mexicans, but Hank really don't like 'em, so that makes that kinda hard."

Bryan raised an eyebrow at Justin. He was not at all surprised that Hank did not want to work with Mexicans. He thought Hank would probably be happiest if he and Wayne could just manage the farm by themselves.

"Anyway," Justin said, hesitating, "we do have another litter of pigs we need to process today. I would get Jeffrey but –" He trailed off, then he shrugged.

Bryan stopped eating. He had not helped Justin with this task since the first time, and just the thought made him weak with nausea.

"Okay," Bryan said, frowning and putting away the rest of his sandwich. What was the point, if it was just going to come right back up?

Justin grinned and slapped him on the back. "It'll be fine," he said.

When they went back into the farrowing building, they were hit with a wall of heat and ammonia that had more intensity than normal. Bryan's eyes and nostrils burned, and after a few seconds he doubled over and vomited.

Justin stopped a few feet inside the building. "Shit," he said, coughing a bit himself.

"Bryan, go get Hank, okay? Tell him the fans stopped." Justin started to move toward the end of the building, where the large fans that were normally whirring loudly were sitting motionlessly. He looked back and saw Bryan still hunched and vomiting. He could not help but laugh, and he quickly went back, got Bryan up, and pushed him rather roughly back out the door through which they had entered.

"You good?" Justin said, obviously anxious for Bryan to get moving, but attempting some semblance of patience.

Bryan nodded, feeling anything but good, but he turned and left the building to find Hank. Justin returned to the farrowing side of the building to work on the fans.

Once Bryan was through the gestation side of the building and out into the open air, he doubled over again and coughed heavily. He took in the fresh air, which was like drinking the cleanest, crispest water he could imagine. Then, feeling the sense of urgency that he had seen on Justin's face, he looked around for Hank or Wayne. He saw no one, but, figuring they had to be in one of the other pig buildings, he set off to find them.

Bryan entered first one building, then a second, but both were empty, other than the grunting and snorting pigs who milled about in their pens. He went to another building, but it was empty of men as well. Bryan felt a bit of panic starting to rise, and he looked at his watch and realized he had been gone around twenty minutes.

He went back to the front of the farm but saw no movement anywhere. Unsure of what to do, he returned to the farrowing building.

As he neared the door to the farrowing area, he could hear the amplified murmuring and squealing of the pigs. Even after spending what he felt like was a considerable amount of time working on the farm, he still knew very little about pigs. He could tell, though, that the sounds they were making indicated distress. He slowly opened the door leading into the farrowing section, but he immediately stumbled backward as the thick, putrid heat rushed against him.

"Shit," he said, fighting nausea. Inside the room felt like an oven, and the increasing ammonia burned his face. He wrinkled his nose and blinked frequently.

"Justin?" he called, but no response came.

He peered further down the aisle, tears streaming from his burning eyes, but he saw no one. He started to turn and leave, but he hesitated. *No, he has to be in here somewhere.*

He stepped back into gestation for a moment, heaved a deep breath of the not-quite-so-putrid air, and then fully entered the farrowing area. He pushed quickly down the aisle, knowing he would likely vomit at any moment, moving toward the end of the building and the immobile fans. After he was about halfway down the aisle, he saw Justin, slumped on the floor and not moving.

"Shit," Bryan cursed, increasing his speed.

He reached Justin, who was clearly breathing, but unconscious, and shook him. Justin said something groggily but did not open his eyes.

"God damn it," Bryan cursed, and another round of nausea suddenly overcame him. He lurched forward and spewed out vomit next to Justin. He felt his head getting light and dizziness sinking in.

Shit, we have to go. He stood up, and his head spun so much that he knelt down again.

He gave Justin a rough shake, but he got no response at all this time. Gritting his teeth, he grabbed Justin's arms and started dragging him backward toward the door. Midway down the aisle, his knees buckled, and he collapsed. He felt a strong urge to simply lie down and sleep. Surely someone would come, right? Had Justin not said there was an alarm that went off when the fans stopped? Yes, it had alerted his phone. Hank should have gotten that alarm. He should be coming.

Of course, Bryan thought, looking at Justin, if there were an alarm, it should have gone off some thirty or forty minutes ago, so Hank should have arrived by now. Bryan sighed, heaved himself back up, and continued pulling Justin toward the door. He finally reached the door to the gestation area, pushed it open, and pulled Justin through it, closing the door behind him.

Bryan slumped down next to Justin on the landing in front of the door. The gestation area was filled with its own thick, ammonia-filled air, but it was noticeably fresher than the air on the other side of the door. Bryan, feeling his eyelids growing heavy, leaned back and gave in to the pull of sleep.

* * *

Bryan awoke to rough shaking. He opened his eyes slowly, but his vision was blurred for a moment. Then, after blinking a few times, he saw Pa staring down at him anxiously.

"There you are, bud," Pa said, smiling a bit. "You okay?"

Bryan furrowed his brow, confused, and sat up. A splitting headache caused him to wince as he moved. He rubbed his head. He looked around and saw that he was outside now, on the grass in front of the pig building. Justin was beside him, breathing heavily but still asleep.

"Pa?" Bryan looked up at him. "What are you doing here?"

Some of the lines of worry in Pa's forehead relaxed a bit, and he breathed out slowly. He pointed at the pig building.

"Hank called me when he saw the fans weren't working. I got 'em up and running, but it's still pretty thick in there. It'll take a bit before the air is right again." Pa furrowed his brow. "Probably gonna lose quite a few pigs, though."

Bryan looked back toward the building. He saw Hank and Wayne standing nearby, with Hank occasionally casting an expressionless glance in his direction.

"So what happened with you two? Hank found y'all passed out in the gestation area." Pa raised his eyebrows at him.

Bryan shook his head. "I guess the heat or the air was too much," he said, rubbing his head.

Bryan looked at Justin. "Has he been awake at all?"

Pa shook his head. "Not since I've been here. Hank," he hesitated, "Hank just said to let him sleep it off. He's got a little more experience with this than I do." Pa scratched the back of his head.

Hank motioned to Pa, and Pa, after another assurance that Bryan was okay, made his way over to Hank.

Bryan looked incredulously toward Hank, then he started shaking Justin.

"Hey, man, wake up," he said, shaking him harder.

Justin murmured something but did not stir otherwise.

Bryan frowned. He looked around but saw nothing helpful. He got up slowly, falling back a couple of times, then he clumsily walked to a nearby water spigot with a five-gallon bucket underneath it. He filled up the bucket, returned to Justin, and, with a quick apology, he poured the ice cold water over him, drenching him.

Justin's eyes shot open, and he started coughing uncontrollably. He looked around wildly, sat up, and immediately groaned and put both hands against his head. Bryan knew that his head had to be throbbing even worse than his own.

"Hey, hey, man, it's okay," Bryan said, squatting down in front of Justin.

Justin looked at him in confusion. "What the hell?"

Bryan laughed. "The fans, man, remember? The fans went out? I think you were in there too long and passed out."

Justin's expression relaxed a bit as his memory came back. He nodded. "Right, right, okay."

Justin pushed his hands against his throbbing head and closed his eyes. He opened them again and looked at Bryan.

"So wait, how did I get out?" he asked. "Did Hank?" He looked over at Hank, who appeared to be going over something in detail to James.

Bryan shook his head, then he grinned. "Actually, believe it or not, I got us out."

Justin raised his eyebrows and started to grin. "You? No way, man. You did? How in the world did you manage to do anything other than vomit?" He grinned widely.

Bryan frowned. "I mean, yeah, I vomited, too, but I still got the job done."

Justin started laughing, which intensified the pain in his head. He stifled the laughter but kept grinning at Bryan.

"Well, thanks, man. Much appreciated." He grinned.

Bryan looked back at the building. "So what now? What about the pigs?"

Justin was struggling to stand up. He made a couple of attempts, falling backward each time and quickly bringing his hands to his head. Bryan reached down on the third attempt and pulled him up, where he swayed unsteadily.

"Well," Justin said, "I mean, there will probably be a bunch that don't make it. I mean, they're tougher than us, but it was pretty hot in there." He frowned at Bryan. "We'll have to handle that tomorrow, when we can actually go in without passing out."

Bryan nodded, and he felt himself growing sick at the thought of the likely carnage that he would find tomorrow.

CHAPTER XVIII

The following day, Justin met Bryan in front of the pig building.

"Have you been inside?" Bryan asked.

"Yeah," Justin responded, looking down. "It's not great. There's at least a couple hundred dead." He looked up at Bryan.

Bryan thought perhaps he was joking, but, seeing the seriousness on Justin's face, he realized that he was telling the truth.

"Jesus," Bryan said.

"Yeah," Justin nodded, "we should probably get to it."

Bryan nodded and followed Justin, and they spent the majority of the day getting to it. They went pen to pen pulling out the dead piglets and, occasionally, dead sows. They carried or dragged them into the center aisle, and Jeffrey, back at work, came along and loaded them into the wheelbarrow, taking each full load out to the trash heap behind the buildings.

Many of the pigs were simply stone cold and rigid, but some had their interiors falling out from where the other pigs had started gnawing on them. Bryan's stomach turned when he saw these, and Justin tried to get them out of the pens before Bryan got to them, but the number of dead was too great for him to be able to accomplish this consistently.

At lunchtime, they were only about two-thirds finished, and Bryan was too sick to eat anyway, so they kept at it. Finally, toward the end of the day, they had gotten all of the dead pigs out of the pens. The dead heap behind the buildings was piled nearly as high as the building itself, and the pile sprawled out over an area at least the size of a car.

With the dead pigs removed, Bryan saw that there was a new problem. Some of the sows had died, leaving litters of piglets with no mother. When he pointed this out to Justin, Justin nodded and said, "Yeah, we'll have to move the little ones around."

Bryan and Justin made another round through the pens. They went to each pen that was missing a mother, removed the squealing piglets, and added them to another pen with piglets of around the same age.

"Do the mothers always take them on?" Bryan asked.

Justin considered. "Well, not always, but most of the time." He shrugged. "It's about the best option we have, unless" – he grinned at Bryan – "unless you wanna take 'em home and bottle feed 'em." He chuckled.

Bryan narrowed his eyes and frowned. He followed along after Justin, picking up and moving piglets, until there were no piglets left alone in any of the pens.

When they came out of the building, the sun was low in the sky. Bryan looked at his watch and saw that it was nearly eight o'clock. He looked around and saw that Hank, Wayne, and Jeffrey had apparently already left.

Justin, nearing Bryan, said, "Well, tonight is a night I could use a drink. You?"

He grinned, and Bryan nodded.

* * *

The Rancher's Respite was fairly busy, but Bryan and Justin found an empty booth near the back of the room. Bryan saw Jeffrey carrying orders back and forth from the kitchen in his leisurely, shuffling manner. He caught his eye, and Jeffrey nodded and grinned.

"Today was rough," Bryan said, downing his first beer.

Justin laughed, "Yeah, no joke. It's not the first time it's happened, though. I can think of at least four other times. One time, it happened overnight, and the damn alarm didn't go off. We came in in the morning, and nearly every pig in the building was dead. Hank really lost his shit then." Justin looked down and swirled his drink.

Bryan looked at him. "Honestly, Justin," he started, slowly, "it seems like Hank loses his shit a lot."

Justin gave a short laugh and nodded. "Yeah, yeah, that's true." He looked away, toward the direction of the bar. His eyes landed on Mandy, who was grabbing orders and running them out to one of her tables. She cast a quick glance at Justin, and he grinned back at her. She blushed lightly and smiled back before turning away.

"Have you ever actually hung out with her?" Bryan asked, following Justin's gaze.

Justin looked up and shook his head. "No, she can't be more than sixteen." He looked back at his drink as it swirled in the glass. "But," he said, tilting his head, "maybe in a year or two." He grinned at Bryan.

Bryan watched him a minute, then, on impulse, asked, "Do you like Winnie?"

Justin looked up quickly. He saw that Bryan was staring hard at him, and his face reddened. He shook his head quickly, furrowing his brow. "No, man," he started, then, shaking his head further, he said, "I mean, yes, of course, but not like you're asking."

Bryan tilted his head, considering him.

Justin grinned, although slightly uncomfortably. "I promise, man. I like hanging out with her, but I get that she's your sister. I'm not trying to mess with that."

Bryan finally nodded and gave a half grin. "Okay, just asking." He saw Justin relax in response.

They chatted a while longer, taking a few more shots between beers, until their food came, which Mandy brought. Bryan got up to go to the restroom when Mandy came, in part because he truly did need to go but in part because he wanted to give Justin a minute alone with her. Justin grinned at him as he got up.

A few minutes later, Bryan returned to the table, unsteady on his feet. Mandy had left, but as he approached, he saw another girl moving toward the table. This girl was older, closer to his age, dressed in a pinstripe miniskirt and a light blue blouse that billowed over her petite frame. Her skin was dark, and her jet black hair was pulled into a tight braid that fell like a cord down her back. She moved quickly, and her sharp stilettos cracked against the hard floor of the bar.

Hearing the approaching clicking of heels, Justin looked up, apparently recognized the girl, and frowned, sliding out of his seat to meet her.

The girl, not slowing, nearly plowed into him, but instead she stopped short at the last second and threw the golden-colored contents of her glass on him, covering his face and upper body with the drink.

"God damn it, Jenna," Justin cursed, wiping the liquor off his face. "What is your problem?" He glared at her as the liquor dripped down the side of his face.

"My problem? My problem, Justin? Really? Are you seriously asking me that?" She got closer to him, and he pushed back against the table to keep from touching her. Bryan saw that his right hand was clenched so tightly around the edge of the table that his knuckles were turning white. Bryan edged closer.

The girl, apparently Jenna, flicked her head to look at Bryan.

"You okay, man?" Bryan asked, hesitantly.

Justin nodded. "Oh yeah, just great. Always great to see an old friend." He looked sarcastically at Jenna as he spoke.

"Who the fuck is this?" Jenna asked, pointing to Bryan.

Justin grinned. "Jenna, this may surprise you, but I do have friends other than you."

Jenna gritted her teeth and slapped Justin. He flinched and bit his jaw, apparently suppressing his anger, but he did not make a move toward her.

"Jesus," Bryan said. "You need to back off."

Jenna turned and moved toward Bryan.

"Really, what business is this of yours? Do you even know him? Do you know what a piece of shit he is?" She glared back at Justin, who was running his hands through his wet hair.

"Stop, Jenna," Justin said in a low voice.

Jenna looked at him for a moment, then she turned back to Bryan. "He and his piece of shit daddy run the farm next to my parents' house. They have these giant sprayers that spray pig shit all over my parents' property." She snapped back to Justin. "Isn't that right?"

"Jenna," he said, looking down.

"Yeah, that's right," she continued. "My parents can't even sit on their own front porch because the smell is so bad. They are sick all the time. They used to have a farm themselves, but the Brewers and their pig shit ruined their farm."

The girl, fuming at this point, went back to Justin. He looked up at her with exhaustion.

"Jenna," he started, "there's no point in having this out here. Y'all have already sued. Just wait and see what the court says. Are you even supposed to be talking to me?"

Jenna took a step back, possibly knowing there was some truth in his last statement. "Fine," she said. "We'll see what the court says. We plan to do everything we can to shut your whole farm down."

"Fine," Justin said, raising his hands.

Jenna looked between Justin and Bryan. She opened her mouth, apparently to say more, but at that moment a large hand fell on her shoulder, causing her to flip around.

A tall, broad young man stood beside her, eyeing her. He appeared to be close to seven feet tall and was nearly as wide as the table. His hand looked like a giant's on Jenna's small frame. He looked just slightly older than Jenna, but his face had several lines creased over it, giving him a generally concerned look. He wore a plaid button-up shirt that seemed about to burst off of his stout torso.

"Jenna," the young man said, his voice a low rumble.

Jenna narrowed her eyes at him, and he frowned back.

"Jenna, you need to leave him alone." The man looked toward Justin, who was watching the interaction carefully.

"Hey, Justin," the man said, neither frowning nor smiling.

Justin furrowed his brow and gave a slight nod. "Hey, Darren."

Darren eyed Justin a moment, until Justin dropped his gaze, then Darren turned back to Jenna.

"Jenna, I think that's enough. We need to go." He still had his hand on her shoulder.

Jenna frowned and brushed Darren's hand away. She turned back to Justin, glaring, but, unable to catch Justin's eye, she sighed, relaxed her expression, and turned back to Darren.

"Fine, let's go," she said. "There's nothing worth seeing here."

Justin glanced up at her, and Jenna gave him a final frown, then she turned on her heel and headed toward the door.

Darren stepped closer to Justin, and Justin, still backed against the table, tensed slightly as he approached.

"Justin," Darren said, "I'm sorry about Jenna. It's been rough for her lately. Our mama isn't doing great, and Jenna's not taking it well." Darren glanced at Bryan for a moment, then he turned back to Justin. "She didn't mean all she said. She's just going through a lot."

166

Justin frowned and nodded. He gave a half smile. "It's all good, Darren. No big thing."

Darren looked at Justin for a minute, his face not giving any clues as to his thoughts. Then he nodded, as if to himself, and said, "It's good to see you, Justin." He waited for Justin to give a brief, mumbled response, then he turned and headed toward the entrance to the bar, through which Jenna had exited a moment earlier.

Justin sank back down into the booth and ran his hands through his hair again. He wiped roughly at the liquor that was still trickling down his face.

"What was that about?" Bryan asked.

Justin sighed. He looked in the direction of the door. "That was Darren," he sighed, "and the girl was his sister, Jenna, but I guess you got that." He grinned halfheartedly at Bryan, who just looked back blankly. "Jenna and Darren used to live beside the farm – their parents still do – but now Darren's in the military I think, and Jenna's off at some fancy college up north now. She don't come back here much, but when she does, she's like a fucking tornado." He laughed.

"We actually used to be pretty close when we were younger," Justin said suddenly, almost painfully. "She and her parents are suing us – something about the enjoyment of their property, some shit like that. Basically they are saying they can't enjoy their property 'cause of the sprayers."

Bryan, somewhat confused, asked, "Is that true?"

Justin shrugged. "I mean, maybe? I don't know. The sprayers don't really spray on their property, but they do get close, and you know that smell is pretty rough." Justin paused, then he added, "I mean, I wouldn't want to live next to it."

Bryan furrowed his brow and considered what he had said. "I don't think I've ever seen any sprayers."

Justin shook his head. "No, you wouldn't. They're further out in the fields behind the buildings. They go off on timers and pull shit from the lagoon and spray it over the fields. I mean, it's good fertilizer, but it's pig shit so it smells like pig shit."

Bryan frowned. "Do you think they'll win?"

Justin shrugged. "I don't know. Hank has some hot shot lawyer, so he feels pretty confident about it. I just –" He hesitated and looked up at Bryan. "I just wish Jenna weren't so damn angry at me. I mean, it's not my fault. I don't want her parents to be miserable." He sighed and motioned to the waiter for another round of shots.

Bryan watched him for a moment. "Were y'all, like, really close when you were younger?"

Justin grinned. "I mean, we were pretty close. We had a few moments, but –" He flushed heavily and looked down. "She's, she's black. You know? She light, but she's still black, and Hank had a meltdown when he realized how much time we were spending together." He leaned back in the booth and sighed heavily.

Justin suddenly laughed. "What's really funny is, I'm pretty sure Hank had no idea she was black until her parents gave me a ride home one day. I think" – Justin struggled to speak through the laughter – "I think he just thought she had a really good tan." He continued to crack up, with tears squeezing out the sides of his eyes. Finally, he leaned back in the booth and said, "I guess that could be part of why she's so pissed at me all the time."

The shots arrived, and Justin downed his quickly. Bryan, watching him, did the same.

They stayed another hour or so, until Justin started falling asleep.

"Alright, let's go," Bryan said, jostling Justin awake. "I'll drive – you wanna just stay with us tonight?"

Justin grinned and nodded.

CHAPTER XIX

Winnie was not surprised to see Justin at breakfast the following morning. The boys were up early, getting ready to head to work, and Winnie caught them just before they left.

"Justin, you might as well get a key to the place," she grinned at him. "It seems like you basically live here now."

Justin grinned back, and Bryan rolled his eyes.

Winnie let Wilbur run freely through the kitchen, and Justin watched him as he followed Winnie around and sat for bits of food.

Winnie looked up at Justin. "So, Justin, just how big is Wilbur gonna get, do you think?"

Justin tilted his head and raised his eyebrows at her. "Big," he laughed, "like, really big. I mean, I don't know if you'll be able to keep him in the house when he's close to 300 lbs."

Winnie sighed and looked at Wilbur. "Wow, that is big." She stroked his coarse hair, and he gave his lower back a little wiggle in response. "Well, I guess we'll have to get a bigger house," she said, smiling.

Justin grinned at Bryan, who said nothing but who was in fact wondering exactly how they would manage when the pig was that large. He tried to imagine some of the larger sows he had seen on the farm and how they might fit within the house. Not well, he thought.

Justin, seeing a bit of distress on Bryan's face, shrugged and said, "But maybe he won't get that big. What do I know?"

Before they left, Winnie asked if they would come back for the evening, rather than going "out drinking," as she put it. Mama, who was now in the kitchen on her way to work, seconded that idea. Bryan looked at Justin, and he easily agreed.

The day was more or less uneventful. Several of the piglets that Justin and Bryan had moved around to new mothers did not appear to be nursing from the new sows, so the boys rearranged them again, hoping a different sow might be a better match.

"What if they won't nurse off the new sow?" Bryan asked.

Justin shrugged. "I mean, they're gonna need to nurse if they wanna live."

Justin saw that Bryan was frowning. He added, "But most of 'em will be just fine. They take a minute to settle down and relax after a lot of commotion, but most of 'em will probably be just fine." He tried to smile reassuringly at Bryan, but Bryan just pulled his mouth to one side and looked down.

At the end of the day, after they finished up, they headed back to Bryan's house. As they pulled out, Bryan saw Hank watching them with an expressionless look on his face.

* * *

When the boys arrived home, Mama and Winnie were starting dinner. Pa, who managed all things involving the grill, was preparing to grill some sliced vegetables Winnie had just handed him. He looked skeptically over the makeshift bowl made out of aluminum foil that was filled with cut carrots, zucchini, squash, and onions. He sniffed absentmindedly, then he scratched his head.

"Winnie?" Pa called.

Winnie stuck her head out of the door, and Wilbur bounded past her and onto the porch.

"Winnie," Pa went on, "there is gonna be some kind of meat to grill, right? I mean, your vegetables look just fine, but you got something a little heavier too – right, Winnie girl?"

Winnie smiled and nodded. "Oh yeah, Pa, don't worry. I got some tofu. I'll go grab it."

Winnie disappeared, putting her hand over her mouth to quell the laughter. Pa, looking confused and helpless, continued scratching his head.

As Bryan and Justin came up on the porch, Pa said, "Bryan, will you please go find something that I can grill? I mean, something that is not made out of a plant?" Perhaps unconsciously, Pa let his eyes fall on Wilbur, who was rolling on his back in the grass.

Bryan laughed and went inside, while Justin and Pa exchanged their usual awkward waves and hellos.

When Justin went inside, Winnie pulled him over and set him to work cutting up avocados and scooping out the meat for guacamole.

Justin grinned at her, flushing slightly when she had to correct him twice on how to handle the avocado.

"You've seen an avocado before, right?" she asked, raising an eyebrow.

Justin grinned awkwardly. "I mean, yeah, I've *seen* one I guess."

"Wait," Winnie said, eyes widening in a teasing manner, "you're saying you've never actually had an avocado before?"

"Maybe he doesn't like avocado, Winnie," Mama yelled from the kitchen, her tone suggesting that she was smiling.

Justin shrugged. "I mean, I've had guacamole I think. That counts, right?" He grinned.

Winnie laughed and gave him a light slap on the shoulder. "Justin," she said, "we have so much to show you." She grinned up at him, smiling playfully, and he returned the smile.

After dinner, they played charades for a while, until Mama and Pa decided to call it a night and went to their room to watch the evening news.

Winnie sat on the porch with Bryan and Justin, who drank from a newly opened bottle of Jack Daniel's. She told Justin about some colleges she was considering, more than one of which were out of state. She spoke in low tones about school, shooting darting glances at Bryan as she did, until at one point he stood up and went into the yard on the pretense of helping Boomer find his way back to the porch.

"I think he's still a little sensitive about the whole college thing," Winnie said in a hushed voice to Justin.

Justin nodded, watching Bryan guide the old dog to the porch, as Wilbur ran in fast zig zags around them.

"I've told him at the very least he could start at the community college, but," Winnie paused, considering. "I think, I really think he just has no idea what he wants to do. He was planning to play football, and when that didn't work out, he got sort of stuck." She looked at Justin, who was still nodding.

"You have any interest in going to school?" Winnie suddenly asked.

Justin shook his head quickly and grinned. "No, no not me. I was never any good at school." He looked down, then he added, "I mean, I've never been real good at much except for farmin' and fishin'." He looked up and shrugged.

Winnie smiled, and Bryan returned to the porch.

"Poor old dog can't have much time left," Bryan said, stroking Boomer's thinning coat.

Winnie narrowed her eyes at him. "Don't say that," she said.

Bryan shrugged. "I mean, I think it's the truth."

Winnie went over and hugged Boomer. She sat with him a few minutes, then she got up, called Wilbur and Boomer to her, and told the boys goodnight.

Bryan and Justin sat a few minutes longer, listening to the hum of the cicadas. The cool evening air washed over them, and Justin felt himself starting to doze.

"I should get out of here," he said.

Bryan looked at him sleepily. "You're welcome to stay."

Justin shook his head. "I mean, I would, but I'm watching Conner in the morning, so I better get home." He grinned and added, "Plus, I told him I'd make him some crazy French toast, like with whipped cream and strawberries and little bits of candy bars, but I got no idea how to even make French toast, so I better figure that out." He laughed. "What are y'all up to tomorrow?"

Bryan shook his head. "Well, Winnie's hassling me to teach her how to shoot. She says everybody else at school already knows how." Bryan scratched his head and looked off into the evening darkness. "And she's probably right," he said. "I know I learned when I was about half her age, but I think Pa held off with her 'cause she's the youngest – and a girl."

Bryan looked at Justin and shrugged. "Anyway, I may take her down for some target practice tomorrow afternoon, so you're welcome to join if you're free."

Justin grinned. "I should be – and I'm one hell of a shot." He raised an eyebrow, finished his drink, and headed home.

* * *

When Justin arrived home, only slightly wobbly, he found Amanda waiting on the front porch.

"Hey, you," she said, smiling.

Justin hesitated, giving an awkward half grin. "Hey, Amanda. Were you waiting on me?" He looked at her somewhat uncomfortably.

Amanda frowned. "Yeah, Justin," she said. "You know, sometimes I just want to hang out with my little brother." She smiled, and Justin returned it cautiously.

Amanda was nursing a glass of wine. She leaned back behind her and picked up a beer, extending it to Justin.

Justin, with a little less reluctance, came closer, took the beer, and sat down on the steps beside Amanda.

"So what have you been up to, little brother?" Amanda asked.

Justin told her, and she frowned, pressing her lips together as he spoke. Justin noticed the look on her face and trailed off.

"You okay, Amanda?"

Amanda nodded. "Oh, yeah, for sure." She looked down at her wine, which was nearly gone, and she reached back, further up on the porch, and clutched the bottle. She brought the bottle closer, started to pour more into her glass, and then simply turned the bottle up and drank from it.

She then offered it to Justin, who was grinning at her, and he did the same.

Amanda looked down, picked at a hair on her arm, then said, "Justin, why are you always hanging out over there?" She raised her eyes to his, and he looked at her, confused.

"What?" he asked, looking a bit uncomfortable. His voice was slightly slurred, and, as if in an attempt to remove himself from the question, he stood up and awkwardly moved a few feet into the yard, stumbling as he did. He scratched his head and looked back at Amanda.

Amanda rolled her eyes. "Oh come on, you heard me. You're always over there with them. You never seem like you wanna be here anymore." Amanda looked up at Justin, and he thought she looked slightly hurt.

He looked down and frowned. "Oh, I don't know, Amanda. I like it here, too, but, you know, you gotta have your own friends."

Amanda looked at him, still frowning. She shrugged. "I dunno, little brother. You just seem to think they're the sun and the moon." She looked up at him, anticipating an answer.

Justin frowned. "Well, I mean, I do like 'em. I know you haven't met his sister, but she's pretty cool." He laughed. "I mean, shit, she even taught the damn pig to fetch things around the house."

As soon as the words came out of his mouth, Justin mentally kicked himself. He looked up at Amanda quickly, who was looking at him with a furrowed brow.

"What pig?" Amanda asked.

Justin shook his head quickly. "Nothing, nothing," he said. "I've had too much to drink, Amanda. I need to get some sleep."

Justin made a move to go around Amanda and up the stairs, but as he passed, she reached out and grabbed his arm.

"Justin," she said, "what the hell pig are you talking about?"

Justin again shook his head and tried to move past, but Amanda blocked him.

"I mean," Amanda said, raising an eyebrow, "you can tell me, or I can bring this up in front of Daddy and see if he can tell me what you're talking about."

Justin furrowed his brow in a pained expression. "Amanda, it's really nothing."

"Okay," Amanda said, smiling. She moved to let him pass.

Justin looked at her, distrustful. "Come on, Amanda," he said.

Amanda's smile broadened. "Sure, it's fine. Have a good night," Amanda said, then she got up to go inside herself.

Justin ran his hands over his face, then he quickly reached out and grabbed her. "Wait, Amanda," he said. He was reddening from frustration and the effects of the alcohol.

Amanda smiled, and Justin's frown deepened. He hesitated, then he said, "Look, you can't tell, okay?"

Amanda's smile widened as she nodded. Then, she sat back down on the porch steps, waiting. Justin, sighing heavily, sat down next to her, and he told her the story of Wilbur and how he came to be at the Bradford home. Amanda listened, saying very little, and watching Justin as he spoke. When he had finished, she raised her eyebrows and simply said, "Wow."

Justin looked hard at her. "Please don't say anything, Amanda. This is really important."

Amanda smiled, put a hand on Justin's back, and said, "Don't worry, little brother. I got better things to talk about than pigs."

Justin gave her a cautious look, then he told her goodnight, stood, and made his way unsteadily to bed.

Amanda remained on the porch, listening to the hooting of a nearby barred owl, and running this new information through her head in tight little circles.

CHAPTER XX

The following afternoon, Justin met Bryan on the porch with his 0.22-gauge rifle.

When Bryan opened the door, Justin grinned.

"I have some others in the truck," he said, "but this is the one I learned on. It's pretty easy and don't kick bad."

Bryan nodded. "Okay, let's just be careful and make sure she doesn't shoot the dog – or the pig." He laughed.

Winnie was out of her mind with excitement and was rushing the boys to get set up.

"Okay, Winnie, we got it," Bryan said, slightly annoyed, as he gathered a few items he thought might make good targets.

The boys and Winnie made their way into the field behind the Bradford home. A couple hundred yards from the house, a large maple tree lay on the ground where it had fallen after a particularly harsh ice storm the previous winter. The tree trunk, now rotting, had a grayish hue as it lay in the field with no particular purpose. Its bark had started to split and fall to the ground, and armies of ants crawled over it in neat little rows.

"This'll do," Bryan said. He set up several empty tin cans along the top of the tree trunk. Midway down the trunk, he also added a few tomatoes that he had plucked from Mama's garden and that were all a bit too ripe – not good to eat, but perfect for shooting. As a special treat, he put one carton of milk – the little blue and white carton that you might get in a school cafeteria – in the middle of all the makeshift targets. He loved shooting these little cartons of milk. If you hit one right in the middle, it would spew out streams of thick, creamy milk in all directions.

"Okay, let's do it!" Winnie cried, nearly jumping up and down like a child.

Justin grinned at Bryan, who rolled his eyes.

"Alright," Bryan said. "Come here – but hey, you gotta listen, okay? Don't just start shooting things."

Winnie nodded at Bryan with an exaggerated expression of seriousness on her face. She glanced at Justin and grinned.

Bryan moved beside Winnie and showed her how the gun worked. She already knew the basics and was anxious to start shooting, but she tried to be patient and let him tell her all that he needed in order to move on with the process. Finally, Bryan had her load the gun.

Bryan helped Winnie raise, position, and aim the gun at the targets resting on the fallen tree.

"Okay," he said. "Whenever you're ready, just squeeze the trigger. Just keep in mind it's gonna kick back a little."

Winnie looked at Bryan, then she looked through the gun's sights at the targets, gritted her teeth so that she would not bite her tongue when the gun kicked, and pulled the trigger. The sound of the gun reverberated through the surrounding trees and dissipated in the fields. One of the cans flew into the air and landed on the ground a few yards away, its side torn open where the bullet had struck it.

Winnie strained to see, then, seeing her success with the can, she yelled a note of excitement and turned around quickly, swinging the gun widely as she did so. Bryan and Justin both dropped to the ground as she turned. Bryan cursed loudly, and Justin started shaking with laughter.

"Winnie!" Bryan said harshly. "Point that down – not at us!" His sharp tone caught her off guard, and her face froze, her eyes reddening and glistening with moisture. One hand went to her mouth, and she quickly pointed the gun toward the ground.

"It's fine," Justin said, laughing. "It's no big thing. Nice shooting, though." He stood up and grinned at her, and she beamed back at him.

They spent the rest of the afternoon shooting. Among them, Justin turned out to be the best shot, which was not particularly surprising, given how few times Bryan had actually shot a gun in his life. They saved the carton of milk for Winnie, and she was finally able to hit it, spewing milk outward in all directions like some cloudy fountain.

After a few hours, they packed up and started to head in. Winnie walked ahead, with Wilbur trotting along beside her. Boomer trailed further behind. She had a slight bounce to her step and was clearly delighted by the afternoon excitement.

Bryan smiled as he watched her. "We should do this again," he said to Justin.

Justin nodded. "I'm game whenever you are. I've got all the time in the world." He grinned, then had a thought. He looked back at Bryan, slightly more serious now, and said, "So, are you still thinking you'll just stay at the farm till the end of the summer?"

Bryan looked up, considered for a moment, then nodded slowly.

"Yeah, man," he said. "I gotta get out of there. I hate it, and I suck at it. I'm not like you –" Bryan paused for a moment, wondering how his last sentence had sounded to Justin's ears. Justin was looking down.

"What I mean is," Bryan continued, "is that I can't just push through, you know? I gotta get out of there before I lose my sanity. It's just, it's just not for me." He looked at Justin, who was scratching his head and looking down. He waited for a response.

Justin sighed, frowning. "Yeah, I mean, I get it." He shrugged, "Sucks, though."

Bryan looked at him for a moment. "You know, you could leave, too." Justin looked up, and Bryan clung to the idea. "Yeah, yeah, pack up, head to the coast, get a job fishing or whatever you want. Just get out of here."

Justin said nothing. His mind seemed to be wandering, and Bryan was not sure if he was listening.

"You could do better than that farm, Justin," Bryan said softly, looking at Justin expectantly.

Justin was looking away. "Oh I will, man," he said. He shrugged and added, "I'm just waiting for the timing to be right."

Bryan narrowed his eyes at him but said nothing. The three went back to the Bradfords' house and sat on the porch for a while. Mama brought out sweet tea and little cheese biscuits, which Justin immediately gulped down with a grin. Mama ruffled his hair and brought out more.

They remained on the porch, laughing and eating, until the sun sank down behind the horizon, and the heat of the day started to be replaced by the cool evening air. The high-pitched songs of the birds were switched out for the low murmuring sounds of cicadas and the occasional hooting of a barred owl. When the first stars started to shine through the evening sky, and the moon shone brightly among them, Justin finally rose, wiped tears of laughter from the corners of his eyes, and told them goodnight.

As Justin left, he lingered a moment at the bottom of the porch steps. Bryan and Winnie both invited him to stay longer, but he said that he needed to get back home, as he was watching Conner again in the morning. He gave them a final grin, turned quickly, and headed home.

* * *

Justin came in quietly, releasing the door handle slowly to allow the bolt to slide back into place with a nearly silent click. He was facing the door when he heard footsteps behind him.

"'Bout time you got back, little brother," Amanda said.

Justin gave her the hesitant smile she hated and nodded. "Yeah," he said, without explanation. "Hank out?" Justin asked absentmindedly. He opened the fridge and looked inside for a minute, trying to find something that piqued his appetite.

"Actually no," Amanda said, slowly. "I think he wants to talk to you."

Justin glanced at Amanda. She was looking down and picking at the skin on her arm.

"Oh yeah?" Justin said, moving a carton of milk out of the way in the fridge, hoping to find something more appetizing behind it. "About what?"

"I think," Amanda said, slower than before, "I think about the pig."

Justin stopped rummaging through the fridge. He closed the door slowly and looked at his sister. "Amanda?" he said, questioningly.

She flicked her eyes up to his. She frowned and cocked her head. "Oh come on, little brother, you couldn't expect me to keep that from him forever, could you?"

Justin's eyes widened as he looked at her. He cursed himself for ever having mentioned Wilbur to Amanda. He hesitated, then he decisively started toward the door.

"Justin, wait," Amanda said, somewhat loudly.

Justin ignored her and pulled the door open, only to find Hank coming up the steps of the front porch. Justin stopped where he was and waited.

"Going somewhere?" Hank asked, as he neared the door. He did not slow down as he approached, and Justin had to move backward to let him enter. As he came in, he shut the door behind him.

"Just out for a bit," Justin said, taking a step back slowly. He smelled the sour smell of alcohol on Hank, and he could tell from the slight slur in his voice and the heavy way he walked that he had had more than a little to drink.

Hank eyed him for a minute, tilting his head slightly. Then he nodded and gave a cold smile. "Going to hang out with the Bradford clan, huh? Seems like you spend most of your time over there now. Why is that? You got something going on with that boy's sister?"

Justin moved to put the table between Hank and himself. He felt his forehead crease with lines. "No," he said, shaking his head. "No, she's only fifteen."

Hank laughed a humorless laugh. "Well, shit, boy, that's nothing."

Justin watched Hank but said nothing. He was suddenly aware that Amanda was still present, still picking at the skin on her arm, looking up occasionally with a pleased expression on her face.

"Anyway, I'm gonna go," Justin said, inching toward the door. "I'll be back in a bit."

Hank was holding his head down and leaning heavily on a kitchen chair. Justin made a quick move to the door, but Hank suddenly revived from his stupor and moved quickly toward Justin, cutting him off and putting his thick coarse hand on his shoulder. He tightened his grip and held Justin there.

"Listen, boy, you can go when I say you can go, but first I want you to tell me about this fucking pig." Hank leaned in closer to Justin.

Justin tried to shift away, but Hank held him firmly. He felt sweat beading up on his forehead and neck. He shook his head slightly.

Hank narrowed his eyes. "Now don't play with me. I heard these Bradfords have a pig, and I'm guessing it's mine."

Justin shot a glance at Amanda, who returned a slight, innocent-looking shrug.

"I don't know, Hank." Justin began, shaking his head, "I don't –"

Without another word, Hank released his hand from Justin's shoulder and moved it to the back of his neck. He pulled him forward and slammed him down onto the kitchen counter. Justin cried out more in surprise than pain. Hank kept his right hand pressed down on the back of Justin's neck, holding him down on the hard countertop. He then grabbed his left arm, twisting it behind Justin's back. Justin gritted his teeth and cried again, this time from the shock of pain that ran through his body. He tried to move, but, even in his drunken state, Hank was as strong as an ox, and he had Justin effectively immobilized.

Justin heard Amanda gasp softly, but she said nothing. He winced with pain but tried to keep from emitting any more cries. *I won't give him that fucking satisfaction.* He felt the cold counter under the left side of his head, and as he was held eye level with the countertop, he saw small crumbs sprinkled on it like ash from a crumbling building. *We need to clean better*, he thought, and he almost laughed out loud at the thought, given his current situation.

His attention snapped back as Hank twisted his arm further behind him, causing what felt like electric jolts to shoot through his body. He groaned slightly and inhaled a quick burst of air, realizing that he had been holding his breath.

Hank moved his mouth close to Justin's ear. "You better think real hard, boy," he growled. "Is that my fucking pig?"

Justin closed his eyes, focused on his response, then attempted, unsuccessfully, to shake his head. "I don't know," he gasped out. "I don't think so."

Hank held him for a moment, saying nothing. He looked at Amanda. "Sweetheart," he said. "Is that what you heard? Amanda?"

God damn fucking Amanda, Justin thought. *Of course she told him. Can't keep her fucking mouth shut.*

Amanda had started to retreat to her room, but she stopped at the sound of her name. She looked at Hank innocently, then she nodded. "Yeah, Daddy, that's what I heard."

Hank smiled. "Well there you go. So how is it that Amanda knows but not you, Justin? Doesn't that seem odd? Makes me feel like you're lying to me."

Justin said nothing. He felt his heartrate increasing as each word Hank spoke sounded more slurred than the last.

Hank laughed, "You know, I really don't like being lied to in my own house. I guess when you finally decide to stop being a God damn leech and move out, you can do whatever the hell you want, but you're in my house now. My house, my rules."

Hank waited but Justin still said nothing. His breaths were shallow, as Hank, swaying slightly, was starting to lean heavily on the back of his neck.

Whatever good humor was left in Hank seemed to now dissipate. He looked at the boy for a moment, then, without a word, he slid him along the countertop. He gave the back of his neck another hard push into the countertop, then he released his neck, still holding his left arm tight behind him and using it to keep him pushed down. Hank reached into a drawer beside Justin and rifled momentarily, finally pulling out a pair of pliers. The inside of the pliers was a dull blade for cutting wire. Hank twisted Justin's arm higher behind him, causing him to gasp with pain, then he opened the pliers and wedged his left index finger inside.

At the feel of the cold metal and blade against his skin, Justin's stomach turned, and he struggled in a mad panic. Hank tightened his grip and twisted his arm harder. Justin felt something snap in his shoulder, and pain surged through his body. He stopped moving.

"Hank, Hank please," he mumbled, tears squeezing out of his eyes.

Hank pressed the pliers' blade into Justin's skin, until blood started to seep out.

"Let's try this again," Hank said in a thick, low voice. "Is that my fucking pig?"

Justin's mind raced. He did not know how to get out of this one. He opened his mouth and started to speak, but his mind instantly brought up an image of Winnie with the pig. He saw her soft smile as she patted the pig's coarse fur and listened to its rhythmic grunts. He hesitated, and as he did so, he felt Hank squeezing the pliers tighter, cutting deeper into his finger.

Justin closed his eyes and answered. "Yes, God damn it. It's yours." He kept his eyes closed and waited. Hank stopped moving but did not release his grip on either Justin or the pliers. Justin wondered if he might just continue with cutting his finger off for good measure. He breathed slowly, holding his breath every few seconds to try to calm his panic. After what seemed like an eternity, he felt Hank pull the pliers away and release his arm.

Justin pulled his aching left arm in front of him and surveyed the damage to his finger, which showed ripples of exposed flesh and the meat beneath, with blood spewing up from it. He turned around, clutching his left hand to his chest with his right, and raised his eyes to Hank, who was still standing close to him.

Hank had a sneer on his face, and he seemed repulsed by Justin as he looked him. He wrinkled his nose. "You're so fucking weak," he said, glaring. "Just like your fucking mother."

For the first time, a burst of anger ran through Justin. He felt pure hatred for Hank. He dropped his left arm and swung out with his right, punching Hank squarely in the face.

Hank staggered back and bumped into the dining table. He lost his balance, groped for one of the chairs and missed, and tumbled to the floor.

Justin hesitated, then he bolted for the front door. He reached it and started to pull it open, but before he could get out, Hank grabbed him from behind and shoved him forward with all his strength. Justin's head slammed into the door with a sickening crack, and his body crumpled, falling to the floor.

Hank, breathing heavily, turned to Amanda, who had her hands clasped over her mouth. "You better have him out of the way in the morning, Amanda. I'll be leaving early."

Hank wiped a trace of blood off his lip, looked at the crimson droplet on his sleeve, then spat on Justin's unconscious body. He pulled out his phone and dialed a number, then he walked off swiftly, leaving Justin where he lay and Amanda where she stood, dazed and confused.

CHAPTER XXI

The following morning, Mama got up early, made a quick breakfast, and then headed in to work. It was Sunday, but she sometimes had to go into work for emergencies on the weekends, and this was one of those days.

"Animals still get sick on the weekends," she said smiling whenever Pa complained.

Of course, Pa had not complained in quite some time, as he knew that realistically, complaining to Maggie did no good. She was going to do what she was going to do, and complaining only wasted his energy.

Bryan finally emerged from his room and made his way to the breakfast table.

Winnie, already up and throwing bits of biscuit to Wilbur, grinned at Bryan.

"Well look who's finally up," she said in sing-song voice.

Bryan squinted his eyes at her, then he downed the glass of orange juice she handed him.

"So what are your plans for today, big brother?" Winnie asked.

Bryan shook his head. "I don't really have any."

"You could mow," Pa said from behind a newspaper at the end of the table. "That grass don't cut itself."

Winnie laughed, and Bryan frowned. Bryan was about to say something about how he did in fact have something to do, and that that something certainly did not involve mowing, when they heard a car pull into the driveway.

Winnie went to the window and looked out. She furrowed her brow.

"It's a sheriff's car," she said, "and a truck pulled in after that."

Pa put down his newspaper and went to the door. Bryan got up and looked out the window. He saw a tall balding man with a round belly climb out of the sheriff's car. He knew from pictures he had seen before that it was Sheriff Frank Johnson. The middle-aged man's gut stuck out noticeably in the brown uniform and hung in a flap over his belt. Once out of the car, he reached back in and pulled out a sheriff's hat, which he proceeded to plop over his shining scalp and few remaining whips of hair.

From the passenger side of the patrol car, a younger, slightly thinner – although far from lean – man emerged from the car. The man, apparently a deputy, frowned and spat. His greasy black hair shimmered in the sunlight. He hoisted his pants up and went around the car to where the sheriff was standing.

Bryan looked at the truck that had pulled in behind the sheriff's car, and for a moment he stopped breathing. It was Hank's truck. Hank lumbered out of the truck and came over to the sheriff. He said something, then he pointed at the house.

Beside him, Winnie noticed the change in Bryan's breathing. "Bryan?" she said, looking at him nervously.

"It's Hank," he responded.

Winnie's face froze in a look of fear. Bryan, watching her, had the sudden thought of telling her to run and hide Wilbur. He opened his mouth to speak, but Pa suddenly broke in.

"Bryan," Pa said sharply. "Let's go see what this is about."

Bryan hesitated, quickly told Winnie to put Wilbur in her room, then followed Pa outside.

Hank, Sheriff Johnson, and the deputy approached and met Bryan and Pa in the yard.

"Mr. Bradford," the sheriff said, tipping his hat.

"Sheriff," Pa said, as pleasantly as he could. "What can I do for you?"

"Mr. Bradford, I'm sorry to have to come out here, but it seems that you may have some stolen property in your home." The sheriff looked at Bryan as he spoke.

"What do you mean, sir?" Pa's firm voice responded.

Hank stepped up. "Your son took one of my pigs while he was working at my farm. That's my pig. He stole it, and we're here to get it back."

Bryan, his heartbeat increasing, looked at Pa. Pa's face was expressionless, and Bryan knew that his mind was turning over his options.

The sheriff, clearly annoyed that Hank had spoken, stepped forward and waved Hank off dismissively.

"Just hold on, Hank," the sheriff said in an irritated tone. "I have to speak with him first."

The sheriff, readjusting his hat on his wide head, turned back to Pa. Winnie had appeared on the porch and was watching quietly. The sheriff glanced at her, nodded, and continued.

"Yes, Mr. Bradford. Mr. Brewer had the sum of it. Apparently your boy – what's his name? Bryan? – yes, your boy, Bryan, took a pig from Mr. Brewer's farm. We have sworn testimony from Mr. Brewer's son attesting to that fact."

At that, Bryan felt a cold hatred run through him. He gritted his teeth. Beside him, Pa reached out and put a strong hand on his arm. Bryan, knowing Pa meant to steady him, relaxed his jaw, but the hatred he felt remained.

The sheriff, getting no comment from Pa, cleared his throat and went on. "The fact is, Mr. Bradford, normally we would just arrest a suspect when we have such evidence." He glanced at Bryan. "We're here, though, to give your boy a chance to make it right. All Mr. Brewer wants is his pig. He's already got a truck here for transport."

The sheriff motioned behind him. Bryan looked past him and saw for the first time that a tractor trailer was parked at the end of the driveway. The truck had the split metal railing that he knew was for transporting livestock. Bryan shook his head and turned toward Pa. "Pa?" he said softly.

Pa sighed heavily. "I think," Pa started, glancing at Bryan, "I think we probably need to speak with a lawyer. I don't like all these accusations against my son, and I don't feel equipped to speak to them. We need to consult with a lawyer before this goes any further."

Bryan, standing near Pa, heard his heavy breathing and knew he was nervous.

The sheriff nodded. "Now that's all fine, Mr. Bradford. That's fine. But, if you don't want to give the pig back now, we're gonna have to proceed with arresting your boy. You can talk to a lawyer, that's fine – and you should really, that's your right. Us being here was just to avoid all that. Like I said, we got sworn testimony about the pig, so we really are in a pickle if we don't make things right, one way or another."

The sheriff turned to look at his deputy, who had been, rather indiscreetly, attempting to pick his nose.

"Deputy," the sheriff said with annoyance. "Go ahead and arrest the Bradford boy, if you would."

The deputy, suddenly aware that all eyes were on him, quickly snorted, wiped his hand on his pants, and moved toward Bryan. Bryan, feeling a slight panic rise in him, stepped back. Pa, still with his hand on his arm, held him firmly.

"Don't," Pa said in a low husky voice, not looking at Bryan.

"Hank," Pa said. "Let me pay you for the pig. I think this is all a misunderstanding, but I'm willing to pay whatever you're out. Will that work?"

The deputy, who had reached Bryan, paused to look at Hank.

Hank shook his head. "No, James, I don't want your money. I just want my pig."

Pa frowned. "Oh come on, Hank, what's the difference? I'll pay you whatever you want to make it right."

Hank shook his head again. "There's a difference. Your boy took my pig, and that's what I want back."

The deputy, sensing no resolution to the current conflict, firmly grabbed Bryan's arm and started to pull him toward the patrol car. "Come on," he said. "Let's go."

Bryan, starting to panic, pulled back, and the deputy quickly moved after him. The deputy put one hand on his gun without drawing it.

"Son," he said, "you need to stop right there."

Bryan stopped, and he stood as the deputy moved to him, pulled his arms roughly behind him, and handcuffed him. The deputy then hastily pulled him toward the patrol car.

Pa was breathing heavily now and starting to show his distress. "God damn it, Hank," he cursed. He looked at the porch and saw Winnie watching with her hands over her mouth. She looked like she was about to burst into tears and was struggling to hold her composure. He saw that Bryan, who was now being pushed into the patrol car, was tense and pale.

God, I wish Maggie were here, Pa thought. He ran his large right hand over his face, and, as the sheriff was starting to turn away, he said, "Fine, take the God damn pig. Just leave my family alone."

A cry came from the porch, and Winnie ran down the steps and up to Pa. She clutched at his shirt.

"Pa, no," she said, shaking her head violently. "No, no, no."

Pa held her face in his hands. "Honey, they're gonna arrest your brother."

Winnie, eyes red and wide, shook her head. "We can get a lawyer. We can fight it, but don't give them Wilbur." Her words were becoming jumbled as she started to cry.

Pa held her close and let her cry into him. Then, looking over her, he said to the sheriff, "The pig is probably in her room. You can go in and get him."

Winnie, on hearing this, attempted to tear away, but Pa held her tightly. She screamed and struggled, but she was unable to budge from his grasp.

Bryan, sitting in the patrol car with the door still open, quickly stood up and tried to move past the deputy.

"Hold it, son," the deputy said. He grabbed Bryan, and, when Bryan struggled, he pushed him to the ground, holding him down with a knee on his back and a hand on the back of his neck.

The sheriff nodded at Pa, and he and Hank went up on the porch and entered the house. After what felt to Bryan like an unbearable amount of time, they emerged, holding Wilbur upside down by the legs as he squealed out piercing screams and jerked wildly in the men's hands.

Winnie, on seeing the pig, became nearly frantic. She screamed and thrashed, and Pa, big as he was, stumbled a bit as he held her.

"Stop, Winnie, stop," he whispered in hushed tones to her.

Winnie did not or could not listen. She could only see Wilbur, in a state of terror and panic, kicking and struggling and screaming in the hands of the strangers.

The sheriff, struggling to hold two of the pig's legs, puffed along beside Hank, dripping sweat and wondering how he had come to spend his Sunday carrying a screaming pig as a child cried in the background. *Not your best day, Sheriff Johnson.*

As the sheriff and Hank came off the last step on the porch, the sheriff stumbled forward and released the pig's hind legs so that he could reach out and catch his considerable weight as he fell. As the pig's newly freed hind legs fell downward,

Hank, seeing what was happening, tightened his hold on Wilbur's front legs.

Wilbur, feeling the release of two of his legs, struggled harder, until he finally jerked one leg loose from Hank. Hank cursed and jerked the remaining leg back with all his might. A loud crack was heard as the bone in the leg snapped. Wilbur felt a shocking pain in the leg, and he emitted a louder scream than ever.

Winnie, hearing this, jerked loose from Pa and started to run, but Pa caught her again quickly. Unable to control her thrashing, he sat on the ground and pulled her down with him, wrapping his strong arms around her and using all his strength to hold her still.

"Come on, Winnie girl," he said. "Please stop. There's nothing we can do."

Bryan, still held down by the deputy, was able to see Pa and Winnie ahead of him. He saw, for perhaps the first time in his life, tears running down Pa's face as he held his daughter.

The sheriff, regaining his balance, righted himself and reached out again for the pig's two legs. Wilbur was weakening from pain and exhaustion, so Sheriff Johnson was able to hold his hind legs with less effort now, while Hank clung to the front legs.

The two men unceremoniously carried the pig past Winnie and Pa, then past Bryan and the deputy, down the driveway to where the tractor trailer was waiting. A driver hopped down from the cab and helped them open the back. They were out of view of Winnie at this point, and Bryan was glad of that, as he saw them swing and then toss the squealing Wilbur onto the hard floor of the truck.

A sense of extreme helplessness overcame Bryan. He had seen Winnie upset so many times in his life, but never had he seen her thrashing and screaming and clawing with the intensity of someone insane, someone overcome by pure emotion. The truck was starting to pull away, and there was nothing he could do.

Bryan felt the deputy ease off of him and pull him to a sitting position. The deputy moved in front of him.

"Okay, son, are you calm? If you're calm, I'm gonna let you go, but I need to know you're not gonna act crazy when I do." The deputy watched him for a response.

Bryan nodded.

"Okay, then," the deputy said. He released the handcuffs, and Bryan made a concentrated effort to move slowly, rather than run, to Winnie and Pa.

Hank had returned to his truck. "There's no need for you to return to work," he said to Bryan, spitting on the ground. He climbed into his truck, backed it out of the driveway, and was gone.

The sheriff, still wiping sweat from his forehead with his chubby arm, lingered for a moment. He looked uncomfortably at the scene he had created.

"Mr. Bradford, are you okay here? Do you need some help?" he asked awkwardly.

Winnie's screams had diminished, and Pa was holding her closely and rocking her where he held her.

"It's okay, Winnie girl," he whispered over and over.

Pa's eyes were closed, but he opened them to shoot a look of hatred at the sheriff – a look that Bryan thought he had never seen from his mild-mannered father. Pa shook his head slowly, then he closed his eyes again.

The sheriff frowned and looked uncomfortably at the deputy, who shrugged. Then, with a nod toward Bryan, the sheriff got into the patrol car, along with the deputy, and the two men reversed out of the driveway.

Bryan reached Pa and Winnie and stroked Winnie's hair. She was whimpering softly and seemed almost catatonic. Bryan looked over her at Pa, and Pa stared back at him.

"You okay?" Pa asked.

Bryan, brow furrowed, nodded at him.

They sat on the ground for close to an hour as Winnie continued her soft whimpers. Finally, when it seemed like she was asleep, Pa picked her up and carried her to the house. Bryan followed them inside.

When Pa laid Winnie on her bed, she suddenly seemed to wake again. A look of fear spread over her face, and she cried and jumped up. She bolted for the door of her room, but Pa caught her.

"Winnie, please don't do this again," Pa pleaded.

Winnie turned and looked at Pa with such hatred that Pa withdrew slightly, although he still held her.

"Get away from me," she said in a low tone.

Pa's eyes reddened, and Bryan, watching from the doorway, came in.

"I'll stay with her," Bryan said, gently easing Winnie away from Pa.

Pa stood for a moment, looking hurt and confused. He watched as Winnie melted against Bryan, and Bryan pulled her back to the bed. She leaned into him and sobbed again, and he stroked her hair and hushed her.

Bryan glanced up at Pa and gave him a weak smile to let him know he was not needed. Pa slowly turned and left the room.

Bryan stayed with Winnie for another hour. When he thought she was truly asleep, he laid her down, waited a few moments to ensure she did not rise, then left the room. He saw that Pa had gone to the back porch and was sitting, watching Boomer as he made his rounds through the yard.

Bryan sighed, ran his hands through his hair, then pulled out his phone. He saw that he had a missed call from Justin. He stared at the phone for a moment, a feeling of rage rising within him. He looked at Pa again, who now had his head buried in his hands, then he went to the door, got his keys, and left.

CHAPTER XXII

On the truck, Wilbur struggled to stand as the truck bumped over the uneven ground. His broken leg was aching, and a small sliver of pearl-like bone was just protruding through his skin. He attempted to hold the leg up, but the jostling of the truck forced him to place it down again and again to keep his balance.

The truck was dark and dank, and dozens of other pigs, much larger than Wilbur, crowded around him. A smell of fear and ammonia permeated throughout the truck, and Wilbur felt an intense terror take hold of him.

He had been dragged from his home by strangers, and in the process he had felt the intense pain of the leg break. To add to the confusion and fear created by this event, he had seen his human, Winnie, screaming and crying, which had amplified the distress he already felt.

Now, crowded among the softly grunting pigs, he tried to hide himself in a corner. He bumped into several other pigs, one of whom reached out and bit his tail. Wilbur screamed and pulled away, ripping large chunks of the skin off his tail and leaving them dangling in the mouth of the attacking pig. He scurried away but ran into other pigs, who snorted and squealed. Another pig clamped down on his ear, and Wilbur again jerked and screamed, ripping his ear and leaving a trail of blood as he limped away.

The interminable ride continued in much the same manner. Wilbur would bump into a pig, more often than not be bitten, and then he would scuttle away, only to run into another pig and start the process all over. Before long he had several cuts, tears, and bruises covering his body. His coarse fur, which Winnie had often bathed and brushed, was covered in dirt, blood, and feces.

The air in the truck was thick, hot, and putrid. As the heat increased, Wilbur saw a couple of the pigs fall, convulse momentarily on the ground, and then lie still. These scenes increased his fear, and he quivered both from the shaking of the truck and from the anxiety that ran through him.

After an extended length of time, when Wilbur felt himself growing faint, the truck stopped. Wilbur heard humans talking outside the truck. They were strangers, and this made his nervous. The back doors on the truck creaked and opened, allowing bright sunlight to spill onto the pigs huddled inside. Wilbur's eyes stung at the touch of the light, and he closed them momentarily, then he blinked rapidly to try to see what was happening.

Loud voices came from the sides of the truck, along with banging, and several of the pigs started down a ramp at the back of the truck. Wilbur, although terrified of his current location, was even more petrified of going down the ramp to whatever was below. He pushed against the wave of oncoming pigs and ran to the back of the truck, as the majority of the pigs around him squealed and grunted and filed out and down the ramp.

When there were only about a dozen pigs left on the truck, including Wilbur, the silhouette of a tall, broad man appeared at the top of the ramp. The man held some sort of stick in his right hand, and he yelled and swatted at the remaining pigs with the stick, herding them toward the ramp. Most of the pigs left, but Wilbur pressed further into the back corner of the truck.

When the man approached him, Wilbur squealed but stayed put. The man swatted at him with the stick, but he merely ran to the opposite corner at the back of the truck. The man repeated the process, and Wilbur returned to the first corner. He understood that the man was agitated or angry, and he attempted to keep his distance from him.

After a fourth run back and forth between the two corners, the man reached down and did something to the stick he was carrying. It suddenly came alive with a loud crackling noise. The man touched the stick to Wilbur, and a hot wave of pain shot through his body. Wilbur shrieked and ran blindly around the truck. He ran into the side of the truck and bounced back, but the man was close behind him and again touched the stick to his side, sending jolting pain through his body. Wilbur was near the open doors of the truck now, and the man was closing in near him, so he finally turned and ran out of the truck and down the ramp.

The ramp funneled Wilbur downward and into a narrow corridor that led into a building. The building was dimly lit and filled with the echoes of pigs murmuring and hooves clattering on the concrete flooring. Several feet into the building, Wilbur was overcome with a thick, overpowering metallic smell.

The smell, new to Wilbur, scared him, and he froze. Behind him, he heard voices, and he saw the man with the stick coming toward him. Wilbur squealed and moved forward again, running into the mass of other pigs at the end of the corridor. Wilbur huddled into the other pigs as best he could, risking a bite over the shock of the stick the man carried.

In front of him, pigs were thinning out, and he was moving forward. He heard squeals ahead that sent a chill of terror through him, but he was unable to see anything beyond the pigs ahead of him.

As the pigs quickly decreased in number, he found himself nearing a narrow ramp. Beside the corridor, a new man, who also held one of the painful sticks, was reaching over the side of the corridor and guiding pigs up the ramp. Wilbur backed away, but he immediately felt the shock and burn of one of the sticks as it touched his lower back. He squealed and ran forward, scurrying up the narrow ramp.

At the top of the ramp, Wilbur entered a narrow wooden box with an open top. A door shut behind him, locking him into this area. As small as he was, he had room to turn around, and he turned and rammed his head into the closed door, trying to get back down the ramp.

A man stood at the end of the box opposite the ramp. He held another stick in his hand, although this one looked slightly different than the ones Wilbur had previously seen. Wilbur pushed madly against the closed door as the man approached him with the stick, but the door did not budge. A moment later, he felt the man touch the stick to his head, and an extreme burst of pain shocked his body. He squealed briefly, then he fell on his side, unable to rise and shaking uncontrollably.

Wilbur's vision became hazy, and his body felt heavy. He could not move; all he could do was wait and watch. He numbly felt something wrap around one of his hind legs, and he felt himself being dragged first backward, and then off of the ground and into the air. He hung upside down, feeling drowsy and clinging to consciousness.

As he hung, he thought of Winnie. He thought of her gentle touch and her warm body next to his. He thought of rocking in the swing with her as she stroked his back. He thought of her soft lips that she liked to gently plant on his snout and then pull away. He thought of all these images in a flash, until a sharp blade cut into his throat, and his blood drained out. The girl's image slipped from his mind, and darkness overcame the pig.

CHAPTER XXIII

When Justin woke up, he was lying on his back on the living room floor. He heard a bird chirping in a high-pitched trill outside. He thought that the bird sounded almost frantic, as if there were a snake or fox approaching the bird's eggs.

As more alertness came into Justin, he realized that his entire body was aching. As the pain intensified, he closed his eyes for a moment to focus on what he needed to do. First off, he thought, he needed to get up.

He was on a pile of blankets, which he figured Amanda had put out for him. What he could not understand was why he was here at all. *Had he not been about to leave? What had happened?* He felt a dull throbbing in his head, and he raised his hand to his forehead. His fingers gingerly traced trails of hardened blood, and he thought that Hank must have hit him with something.

Remembering what he could of the night, he thought of his nearly severed finger and held his left hand up in front of his face. He saw a messy bandage covering the wound. Blood had soaked through the bandage and had covered his hand in a thick red crust. *Well, at least she tried*, he thought, assuming Amanda had attempted the bandage.

As he lay on his back, trying to gain the energy to push himself up, a small face came into view over him, startling him.

"Uncle Jus?" a small voice asked.

Justin grinned. "Hey, little man. What are you doing up?"

Conner looked at Justin for a moment with a somewhat confused expression, then he smiled. "I was waiting on you," he said, grinning. "Mama said to wait till you got up."

Justin furrowed his brow. "Is she not here?"

Conner shook his head. "No, she and Papa went out this morning. She said to wait on you."

A sick feeling started to sink into Justin. "How long ago was that?" he asked.

Conner shrugged, and Justin remembered that he had no sense of time at his age. With a considerable amount of effort, Justin pushed himself up onto one arm, then he rolled over onto his stomach. His head was now throbbing with intensity.

"You okay, Uncle Jus?" Conner asked, watching him closely.

Justin closed his eyes for a moment, but the pounding in his head did not let up. He inhaled a deep breath, grasped the couch, and pulled himself up to a sitting position, leaning back against the couch. He tried again to gather his thoughts. *I need to call Bryan.*

As Conner carefully watched him, Justin fumbled through his pockets. Not finding his phone, he looked around on the floor.

"Conner, buddy, have you seen my phone?"

Conner nodded. "Mama has it."

Justin stared at Conner. The sick feeling he was starting to get had worsened, and now a tinge of fear was settling in.

"Buddy, why does she have it?" Justin asked slowly.

Conner shrugged. "I don't know. I just saw her take it before she left."

Justin breathed out heavily. "Is there any phone here, buddy?"

Conner shook his head, then he shrugged as if he were not sure. Conner understood the importance of phones, as his mama was nearly always looking at hers, but he did not have a great grasp of how many phones were in the home, or why exactly it even mattered.

"Okay, that's fine," Justin said. He pushed back against the couch and slowly stood up. His head was spinning, and he had to close his eyes momentarily to steady himself. "That's fine," he repeated. "Can you take a ride with me?"

Conner nodded and said happily, "Okay!" He headed toward the door.

Justin searched his pockets for his keys. Not finding them, he turned back to Conner. "Buddy, does your mama have my keys?"

Conner nodded.

Justin went to the key holder next to the front door. Normally, he would find a spare key to his truck, as well as the keys to an old Ford F150 of Hank's. Now, however, not a single key was present.

"Fuck," Justin said, then he quickly looked at Conner. "Sorry, little man, don't say that."

Justin thought about his options. He could go to a neighbor's house and use their phone, but he had absolutely no idea what Bryan's number was. Why did he need to? It was in his phone. He cursed again. Would it be in the phone book? He did not think cell phones were listed in phone books, and, in any case, did anyone even still have a phone book? He did not think so.

Justin, dread overcoming him, ran his hands through his hair. His fingers met with thick, hardened blood when he touched his head, and he winced with the pain that his own touch caused.

"Uncle Jus," Conner said, looking at him.

Justin snapped his attention back to the boy. "Yeah, buddy?"

"Uncle Jus, I'm hungry. Can you give me some food? Mama said you would make me some food when you got up, but you've been asleep a long time."

Justin looked at him. "Yeah, buddy, of course. Do you want breakfast or lunch?"

"Breakfast," Conner said, happily. He pulled a chair out from the kitchen table and climbed into it.

"Okay," Justin said, nodding. He looked blankly toward the door but realized that, at least for the time being, he was not going to be able to go anywhere or call anyone. He felt a pain in the left side of his chest at this realization, but he pushed it aside and went into the kitchen to scramble some eggs.

* * *

A couple of hours later, Amanda pulled into the driveway. She sat in her car for a moment, looking at the house. She saw the sage green mold covering the siding, and she saw a scattering of paint on the ground that had chipped off of one of the dark blue shutters.

Hank had told her to take Justin's keys and phone and leave for three hours. She had done so without question, seeing Hank's anger bubbling just under the surface of his calm exterior. She had not wanted to push him. Unsure of what to do, she had driven to the high school and sat in the parking lot, staring at the empty football field.

She thought about Amber and Nicole and wondered what they were doing. Amber, she knew, was in college. She knew this from Facebook, as she had not spoken with Amber in years. Amber had received numerous acceptances and several scholarships, and she had decided on one of the most expensive private universities in the state. From her posts, which Amanda followed fairly religiously, it looked like she was planning to be a pediatrician. *Maybe she can see Conner*, Amanda thought bitterly.

Nicole, on the other hand, had worked in her parents' liquor store for about a year after graduation. Amanda had seen her a few times when she had gone in to buy vodka for herself or gin for Hank. Nicole did not care much for school and had no interest in college. After a year of working at the store and being robbed four times, twice at gunpoint, she had left the store and joined the military. Her parents had not been thrilled, not in small part because they had lost their best source of cheap, reliable labor. Nicole's Facebook posts had become less frequent after that, and Amanda knew that the last time she had posted, she was stationed somewhere in Afghanistan. In one of her last posted photos, she had on military fatigues and had her hair pulled up tightly in a bun. She had looked happier than Amanda had ever seen her.

Amanda had sat in the parking lot until a school resource officer had rapped on her window, asking if she needed help. She said no, apologized, and left. She had driven to a strip mall nearby. It was one that she, Amber, and Nicole had frequented when she was younger, gossiping and clutching each other's arms. Now, the mall appeared small and empty. One store had its windows covered and all of its signage removed, leaving bare, light-colored spots where the lettering had been on the face of the building. Another store had a large *Going Out of Business* sign on it, with neon signs scattered about the front windows. Amanda, having lost her interest in going inside, leaned back in her seat and slept. When she awoke, it had been nearly four hours since she had left the house, so she headed home.

Now, sitting in the driveway, she heard the screen door slam and saw Justin come out on the porch. She sighed and got out of the car, just as Justin reached her.

"What the fuck, Amanda?" he said angrily, pushing her back against the car. "Give me my God damn keys and phone."

Amanda looked at him hesitantly. She had rarely seen him this angry, and she was not sure that she had ever seen him this angry with her. She looked at him without moving or responding.

"Come on, Amanda," he fumed. "I swear to God –"

Amanda's eyes flicked past Justin to the porch. Justin turned in the direction she was looking and saw Conner watching them. Justin furrowed his brow and looked down.

"Just give me my stuff, Amanda," he said quietly.

Amanda, finally seeming to wake up, rifled through her purse and pulled out first Justin's keys and then his phone. She handed both items to Justin, who snatched them back as if he wanted no contact with her. He looked down at the phone, which was dead. He sighed.

"I think you're probably too late, Justin," Amanda said.

He looked up at her. His forehead creased. "Why did you help him? I mean, really, why did you do that to me? I'm your brother, Amanda."

Amanda stared at him. He looked terrible. He had dried blood crusted into his hair and pasted onto his forehead. He looked tired and worried, with dark circles under his eyes. Why had she helped Hank? She thought about it. She loved Justin. She did. Of course she did, but she also hated him sometimes. She hated the way he seemed to just push through life, more or less content, when she constantly felt stuck. He had a shit job and did not seem to mind. But she minded. She hated her two crappy jobs with her two crappy bosses, one of whom was always hinting that she could make more money if she would just give him a little off-the-clock action. She hated that she was tied down with a son and could never live her own life, while Justin could come and go as he pleased.

She closed her eyes. That was not it, though. More than anything, she hated Bryan and his sister. She hated that Bryan rejected her. He seemed to think he was better than her. He was not better than her. He was not even close to better than her. And his sister? She had never even met Winnie, but she hated her. She had heard Justin talk about her, about how sweet she was and how pretty she was, and how she was going to have no trouble getting into a great college. She knew that Justin liked her, and not even in a romantic way. Maybe that would have made it better. He liked her almost like you would like a sister. He wanted to help her and protect her, and that made her nearly insane with bitter jealousy.

All these thoughts went in a flash through Amanda's mind, but she simply opened her eyes, met Justin's stare, and shook her head. She said nothing, but she pushed past him and moved toward the house. Justin watched her go, running his hands through his hair.

Justin started to leave, but he heard Conner call him. "Uncle Jus, are you leaving?"

Justin turned back and saw Conner staring at him through the railing on the porch. He forced a smile. "Yeah, little man, I'm gonna go see my friend Bryan real quick. I'll be back soon. You okay?"

Conner looked at Justin without response. Amanda had already gone into the house, not having spoken to Conner.

"Uncle Jus, will you stay with me for a little bit?" Conner asked in his small voice.

Justin hesitated. "Buddy, I –" Justin stopped, just as Conner squeezed his eyes closed and emitted a wail that turned into sobbing.

"Conner, stop that!" Amanda called from inside the house.

Conner, however, did not stop but only increased his cries.

"Okay, okay, little man," Justin said. "I don't have to go right now." He rushed back onto the porch and picked up Conner, who clung to him.

"Let me go plug my phone in, then we can play for a bit, okay?"

Conner nodded, still sobbing.

Justin carried him inside and plugged in his phone. As soon as it came on, he called Bryan. Bryan's phone rang and then went to voicemail.

"Hey man, call me as soon as you get this," Justin left on the voicemail, then he hung up the phone.

Conner had finally started to settle and was quietly leaning into Justin. Justin pulled him back to look at him.

"There we go, little man," Justin grinned at him. "Now what do you want to play with?"

Conner, as expected, chose Legos. Justin played with Conner for what seemed like hours, although in reality it was only about forty-five minutes. Amanda, closed up in her room, never came out, and Justin did not bother calling for her, as he knew she hated it when Conner cried, which would just make him all the more upset.

About an hour into the Legos, when Conner and Justin had managed to build a small city, complete with a fire station, a fire truck, and, somewhat oddly, a windmill, the front door opened and Hank came in. Hank stared at Justin for a long moment, his lips pressed tightly together.

Justin returned the stare. As he did so, he felt the throbbing not only in his head but also in his left hand.

"What did you do?" Justin asked, narrowing his eyes at Hank.

Hank snorted, then he smiled coldly. "I got my pig."

Justin's eyes widened. "What? Where is it?"

Hank's smile spread across his face. "Long gone. Turning into bacon right about now. It wasn't quite market weight but that don't really matter. I got it on the morning transport and sent it straight to Buckhorn's." Hank looked at his watch. "It would have arrived a few minutes ago I'd guess."

Justin stared open mouthed at Hank. "You're lying."

Hank laughed. "No, boy, I'm not. I know you're all crazy about these Bradfords and the girl, but at the end of the day, no one is gonna take something from me. Not them, not you, no one. You'll learn that one way or another."

Justin's eyes were red, and he was looking at Hank in a daze. "You're fucking crazy," he said.

Hank narrowed his eyes and stepped toward Justin, who did not move. As he moved away from the door and came around the kitchen table, he noticed Conner, who was sitting next to Justin and watching Hank intently. He held a Lego loosely in one hand, and his other hand was clutching the bottom edge of Justin's shirt.

Hank stopped and frowned. He looked back and forth between Justin and Conner. Finally, with an animal-like grunt, he turned and went into his room.

Justin looked at Conner and realized that he had become visibly tense when Hank arrived. His eyes were slightly red, and his lip was quivering.

"Hey, hey, it's okay, buddy. What's wrong?" Justin moved to rub his back.

Conner said nothing but started crying again. Justin heard Amanda groan with annoyance in her room, and he rubbed Conner to try to calm him. When the crying spell had passed, they continued on with their Lego city. The city continued to grow, until Justin, hearing a car pull up outside, left Conner to go see who it was.

CHAPTER XXIV

Bryan spun into the driveway leading to Justin's home, spewing dirt and rock into the air. He threw the truck into park, jumped out of the driver's seat, and slammed the door in a single motion. He moved toward the house in a fog, unable to think clearly or see anything other than Winnie's face, strained and tear stained, her eyes closed and spilling out uncontrollable tears.

Justin appeared on the porch. He gave a hesitant smile that quickly faded as he watched Bryan approach. He glanced behind him, back at the house, then he swiftly moved off the porch and toward Bryan, raising a hand slightly.

"Bryan, man," Justin started, but the words came to an immediate stop as Bryan swung out with all his strength. His right arm connected with Justin's left jaw with an audible cracking sound. Justin stumbled backward, dazed, and fell on the ground. Blood streamed from his mouth. He quickly pulled himself to a sitting position and started to rise, but Bryan was on top of him.

"You son of a bitch," Bryan spat, knocking him back down with another blow to the head. Justin gasped and spat blood. He opened his mouth in an apparent attempt to respond, but Bryan met him with a rain of blows. Justin held up his hands to protect his face but did not attempt to hit back. It would not have mattered. Bryan had nearly half a foot in height and some 40 pounds on Justin. He was built for physical confrontation and now, as he pictured Winnie and heard her cries mixed with the pig's screaming, he held nothing back. Anger pulsed through him and powered each blow to Justin. At some point he became aware of the thick, warm blood pouring from Justin's face, but even then he was unable to stop. He continued hitting even as he felt himself tiring and his muscles aching.

Bryan felt an iron grip on his shoulders as he was pulled off of Justin and slung backward. He turned and saw Hank in front of him, glaring down, and the anger he had felt intensified. He rushed at Hank, fists raised, but before he reached him he saw a blur of movement and felt a blow to the side of his head. There was an immediate rush of pain and a loud ringing in his ears. He furrowed his brow in pain and confusion. Bryan stumbled and fell to his knees. Hank stepped closer and delivered another blow, knocking Bryan to the ground. His vision became momentarily blurry, and he fumbled in the dirt in search of help. Hank moved forward again, expressionless, and kicked him hard in the side, breaking, he later learned, two of his ribs. Pain surged through Bryan, making him retch with nausea.

Hank moved forward, spitting. "All for a stupid fucking pig," he growled. The words sent another rush of anger through Bryan, and he pulled himself up, attempting to rise and unleash his anger on Hank. He made it to his knees, tried to stop his head from spinning, and stumbled to his feet. He took an unsteady step toward Hank, fists raised. The dry smile that crossed Hank's face made him shudder and replaced some of the intense anger he felt with a feeling of sick dread, but he took another step forward.

He raised an unsteady arm but felt himself pushed down from behind. Bryan fell forward onto his hands and knees. Blood dropped onto the dirt beneath him. "Stop," a voice hissed in his ear. "Stop or he'll kill you." Bryan turned to see Justin, his face split open and oozing blood. He immediately felt an intense feeling of regret. *Had he done that? Did he really do that? Holy shit.*

Justin's words were mumbled, but he stepped in front of Bryan toward Hank. "He's done," he said to Hank. "Leave him alone. He's done."

Hank considered Justin for a moment. Bryan raised his eyes to Hank and saw the sunlight glint off of a piece of metal in Hank's right hand. He squinted and saw that Hank was holding a piece of rebar.

Hank looked from Bryan to Justin a few times, then he spat on the ground and started toward the house. "Get yourself cleaned up," he said to Justin as he passed. "You're embarrassing. And get him the fuck off my property." Hank pushed past Justin and went into the house, letting the door slam behind him.

Justin pulled Bryan to his feet. Bryan felt sick looking at his bloodied, bluish face. His lips were busted in several places and fresh blood was still running from his nose and mouth. Justin saw the look on Bryan's face and gave a small grin, wincing with the pain when he did. Even as the guilt flooded into Bryan, he could not replace the hatred he felt. He felt his face tighten, and he saw the smile fade from Justin's face. He turned to go back to his truck, stumbled, and fell.

Justin tried to help him up, but Bryan pushed him back roughly. "Stay the hell away from me, and stay the fuck away from my sister." He looked at Justin, whose bloodied face was frozen in a strained expression.

"Bryan, please, it's not –" Justin began, but he stopped talking as Bryan stood quickly and approached him, clearly angry. Justin looked down, face tight, but stood his ground.

Bryan's hands were shaking and balled into fists as he neared Justin, getting close enough to hear his ragged breathing. He paused for a moment, waiting for Justin to look up at him. When he did not, Bryan leaned in close to him and, trembling with anger, said, "Stay away from my family."

Justin finally looked up, brow furrowed, but said nothing. Bryan turned and made his way back to his truck. He fell twice along the way, but he quickly got up and did not turn to see if Justin was watching.

Bryan pulled himself into his truck and turned it on. He moved the gear shift to reverse, but just before he moved, he saw Pa's rusted Ford truck pull into the driveway, with Winnie in the driver's seat.

Bryan narrowed his eyes. Winnie had her learner's permit, but she did not have a driver's license. He turned his truck off and lumbered out of the seat, going toward the truck and meeting Winnie just as she opened the door.

"What are you doing?" Bryan said with slight exasperation. He was feeling fatigue starting to take over, and he had been hoping to go home and be done with this day.

Winnie looked at him. Her green eyes were glossy and bright from crying, and her face was tear stained and smudged with dirt.

Bryan could not chastise her for driving in her current condition. He leaned into her and held her close, waiting for her to respond.

At Bryan's touch, Winnie began sobbing again. Her sobs were deep and caused her entire body to convulse, but she was quiet, making hardly a sound as she stood and shook with grief.

Justin, at seeing Winnie, had drawn closer, and now Bryan looked over Winnie at Justin, glaring at him and readying himself to lunge if he came any closer. Justin saw Bryan's face and hesitated.

Winnie pulled back from Bryan, tried to find her words, and broke into sobs again. After another minute she gained control of her body and said, "I needed to see him." She tilted her head backward to indicate Justin, who she knew was not far behind her.

Bryan's eyes narrowed, and he shook his head, but Winnie, lifting a hand to his face, said, "Give me a minute, big brother."

Bryan regarded her a moment longer and then nodded. Winnie gave a small strained smile that disappeared as she turned toward Justin. She took a few steps toward him, and Justin, seeing this as an invitation, moved closer to her.

She winced when she was close enough to see his face, and she turned to look back at Bryan, questioningly. Bryan said nothing but simply looked down at the ground, kicking at a clump of dirt. Winnie turned back to Justin and looked at him. He started to speak but she held up a hand, causing him to instantly stop.

"I really love him," she said. "I know maybe you don't get that, but I do." Justin held her gaze with a pained expression.

"I just want to know if there's any chance he's alive." Winnie continued. "I mean, do they hold them anywhere for a day or so? Is there anywhere we could go to have a chance of getting him back?"

Justin's eyes had widened slightly as she spoke. He knew the answer, without a doubt, but he did not want to say it. Winnie's eyes were bright and pleading. She wanted hope. She wanted a chance. He could not give it to her, and he did not want to tell her that. He looked past Winnie and saw Bryan, fists clenched and white with anger.

Justin met Winnie's eyes and slowly shook his head. "No. I'm so sorry, but no."

Winnie's eyes immediately filled with tears again, and Justin instinctively reached for her. She drew back, and at the same time Bryan moved forward to block Justin. He stood face to face with him, his teeth grinding and his body trembling with anger. "Don't you fucking touch her," he growled.

Justin did not want to go against Bryan again, but he was starting to feel a near mania at the idea of what he was losing. He reached out and grabbed Bryan's arm, speaking quickly. "Bryan, man, it wasn't my fault. I swear. Please. I slipped up when I was talking to Amanda. I never meant for this –"

Bryan thrust Justin off of him with such force that he stumbled backward and fell. He got up quickly to avoid any possible further attack and watched Bryan carefully.

"What the fuck do you mean it wasn't your fault?" Bryan growled. "Whose fucking fault would it be?" In anger, Bryan moved toward Justin. Justin immediately moved back, raising his hands defensively.

Winnie quickly went after Bryan and grabbed his arm. He turned to her with so much anger in his expression that she instinctively released her hold and froze. His face relaxed as he looked at her, then he turned to leave, grabbing her by the hand and pulling her back to Pa's truck.

After he got Winnie back into the truck, Bryan moved to the driver's side of his own truck. He pulled open the door, then he paused. He turned to look at Justin, who was standing in the same place.

"I don't care what excuse you have," Bryan said through clenched teeth. "I really don't. You and your whole family are fucking insane. If you ever come around us again I swear to God you'll regret it." Bryan stared at Justin long enough to see a look of intense pain come over him, then he turned, got into his truck, and reversed out of the driveway, spinning up gravel as he went.

He paused at the end of the driveway to wait for Winnie to follow. Winnie, sitting in Pa's truck, stared out the window at Justin. He stared back at her, but he did not approach, knowing that Bryan could easily see him and would likely run him over if he neared Winnie.

After another moment, she stopped crying, gave him a final stare, and reversed the truck. She pulled out of the driveway after Bryan, and Justin slumped to the ground, running his hands through his hair and staring blankly at the settling dust in the driveway.

CHAPTER XXV

Winnie spent nearly the entirety of the next two weeks in her room. A great deal of the time she was sobbing, as Bryan could hear from his own room. He went in to see her several times. When she was not sobbing, she would lie completely motionless, except for the slight rise and fall of her chest. She did not want to talk, but she would give him a weak smile from where she lay on the bed, and he would stroke her hair.

When Mama came home the day that Wilbur was taken, she found the house eerily quiet. Pa had been sitting on the back porch staring blankly into the yard. Mama had known something was wrong, but she was not fully aware until Bryan arrived home, followed by Winnie. Mama narrowed her eyes and initially sprang from the front porch to demand why Winnie was driving when she had no license. On seeing Bryan, however, with blood smeared into his hair and dry, crusted blood flaking off the side of his face, she stopped short. She looked harder at Winnie and saw the tear stains dried onto her face. Winnie struggled to lift her red, exhausted eyes to meet Mama's face, and, as soon as she did, the emotion inside of Mama exploded. She wrapped her children around her and let them cry.

Mama checked on Winnie frequently, bringing her food and occasionally pushing her to eat. Winnie might have laid there and never gotten up again, but Mama kept a close watch on her, and she urged Bryan to stay near her when she was not available – although, realistically, Bryan needed no urging. He felt a heavy weight of guilt for what had happened. He had brought Justin into their lives, just as he had brought the pig into their lives. He spent his spare time thinking over the chain of events that had led up to this moment, thinking of ways it might have all been avoided – if he had not agreed to go fishing with Justin, if he had not brought the pig home, if he had not taken the damn job in the first place. His mind constantly considered a number of paths that might have been taken that would not have resulted in his sister crying in her room day after day.

The crying was not the worst of it, though. Bryan saw that Winnie wanted nothing to do with Pa. All of her life she had been close to him. She would run to him for comfort, tease him when she was being playful, sit close to him – nearly on his lap really –

when they were all watching movies together. But now, as she lay grief stricken in her room, she had begun to display a deep loathing of Pa. Bryan realized that the reason likely came down to Pa's allowing Wilbur to be taken, but he hoped that with time, Winnie would open herself back up to Pa. Part of him knew, though, as much as he did not want to admit or accept it, that this would never be the case. While Winnie might and likely would get past what she was feeling, a wall had emerged between her and Pa. A rift had opened up that Bryan thought could probably never be filled.

It was hard for Bryan to see Winnie's narrowing eyes and cold stares when Pa came near her, but it was worse to see Pa. It was worse to see his blank, confused face when she looked at him like she hated him. He would start into her room, see her expression, and freeze, not sure of what to do. As big as he was, both in reality and in Bryan's mind, he was overcome by his daughter's deep disgust for him. On receiving one of her distasteful expressions, he would stop and move backward, as if being pulled back by an invisible force. He would linger in the doorway, then he would move past it and on to somewhere else. After about a week of this, he stopped going into her room at all and only paused slightly at the threshold of the room to glance in, hardly daring to make eye contact with his daughter.

Twice during this time, Justin came to the Bradford home. The first time, he knocked gingerly on the front door, and Mama answered. She looked at him with an expression of great pity, and he dropped his eyes, shuffling slightly on the porch. He looked pale, and large bruises covered his face. He had several healing cuts around his mouth and eyes, and Mama, suspecting that her son was responsible for his appearance, felt a great sickness come over her as she looked at him.

"I was hoping to maybe see, to maybe talk to Bryan or Winnie," he said, not looking up.

Mama sighed. "Justin, honey," she started, but then she stopped. She looked at him, and he finally raised his eyes. Deep lines of age, stress, and worry crossed her forehead. He looked at her expectantly, and she shook her head, sighing again.

"I'm sorry, Justin," Mama said. She started to say more, but she found she had no more words. She stepped forward, hugged him lightly, and then, stepping back inside, she closed the door on him.

The second time Justin came, Pa met him at his truck as soon as he got out. Pa came at him fairly quickly, causing Justin to take a step back toward the truck.

"Mr. Bradford," Justin started, but Pa held up a hand, cutting him off.

"Son, you need to get out of here, and you need to stay away from here for a while." Pa's voice was not unkind, but he was firm, and he seemed slightly distressed by Justin's presence.

Justin looked at him for a moment, and he noticed that he seemed to have a deep-set look of worry that Justin had not previously seen. He felt a sharp pain in his chest as he thought that this look was a direct result of his presence in the Bradford family's lives. Justin furrowed his brow, started to say something, but not knowing what to say, he simply nodded, climbed back into his truck, and left.

Another week passed, and Winnie started to leave her room – at least at times. She was weak from her decreased food intake, and she had nearly a constant headache from the amount of crying she had done. Everywhere she looked in the home reminded her of Wilbur, and she broke into heavy sobs several times each day. She did, however, start to sit on the porch, sometimes reading, sometimes simply staring off into the fields behind the house. In any case, Mama, Pa, and Bryan were all glad to see her beyond the confines of her room.

During the following week, on a humid summer evening, Winnie found herself swinging slowly back and forth in the porch swing on the back porch. She was holding *Wuthering Heights* and attempting to read it, but she had been on the same page for nearly an hour. She stared at the words on the page before her, which seemed to swim lazily in front of her eyes the longer she looked. The cool air of the evening felt refreshing as it mixed with the day's remaining heat, and the cicadas cried loudly in the otherwise silent night.

Boomer lay still at her feet, breathing in and out heavily. With a grunt, he raised his head, looked around lazily, and gave a low, muffled bark. His ears perked slightly, and his nose rose a bit as he sniffed the air. Winnie looked up and initially saw nothing. Her eyes returned to the same paragraph that she had started to read at least ten times, but the snap of a twig near the porch made her quickly look up.

Immediately behind the porch, she saw someone approaching in the dark. She sucked in a quick breath as fear initially overcame her. An instant later, she realized that the dark-shrouded figure was Justin. Her face turned from surprised to angry in a second, and she stood and started to open her mouth.

"Wait, Winnie, please – please don't yell," Justin said, quickly approaching the edge of the porch and raising his hands slightly. "Please don't," he said again, shaking his head. "Just give me a minute, please."

Winnie paused, looking at him. He looked wide eyed and desperate, and some of her resolve started to fade away.

Before she had time to decide, she heard footsteps and saw the screen door leading to the porch starting to swing open. Justin, seeing it as well, immediately dropped below the edge of the porch. He crouched low to the ground and waited.

Bryan came out onto the porch. "You okay?" he asked, looking at Winnie.

He thought that she looked slightly pale, and he glanced around for a moment. He saw nothing, and he reminded himself that she had looked pale for some time now. *It will pass*, he thought to himself. *She just needs some time, and then it will pass*.

Winnie hesitated. She looked at Bryan, wanting to tell him everything, but she knew he was unlikely to stay level headed if he saw Justin again. She thought of Justin's anxious look as he had approached her, and she knew that he was listening to her now.

She slowly nodded. "I'm good," she said quietly. "Just needed to stand for a minute."

Bryan smiled. "You staying up a bit?"

Winnie nodded. "You?"

Bryan shrugged. "Maybe a little? I just came to check on you. You sure you're good?"

Winnie nodded, and Bryan, seeing the strain on her face, moved to her and pulled her to him in an embrace. He rubbed her back as he held her close, then he gently released her, smiled at her, and turned to go.

"Just let me know if you need me, okay?"

Winnie nodded, and Justin heard the door open with a groan and then slam shut a moment later. He stayed where he was, crouched down, and he heard Winnie slowly approach. She sat down on the stairs to the porch, directly beside him, but said nothing.

Justin, hesitating, stood up slowly and glanced back toward the porch, half wondering if the sounds had just been a trick, and thinking that Bryan would suddenly jump out, knock him to the ground, and finish pounding the shit out of him.

Seeing no one on the porch, Justin moved over to Winnie and sat down on the stairs next to her at her left side. He gave her a couple of feet of space between them.

"Thanks," Justin said. "I don't think I can handle Bryan again right now." He gave her a light grin.

Winnie kept looking down, but she finally turned to him and gave him such a look of contempt that the grin slid off of his face like melting butter.

"I don't like lying to my brother, Justin," she said, narrowing her eyes. "But, I don't want him to jump on you again. I'm not cruel."

She emphasized the last word, and she gave him a harsh look that made him wince back as if she had struck him.

"Winnie," he started, looking down and fumbling with his keys. "Winnie, it's not –" Justin shook his head, attempting to find the right words. "I never would have hurt you on purpose," he said in a slightly pleading tone. "I didn't want the pig to get killed." He looked back up at her, and she was glaring.

"That pig had a name, Justin. His name was Wilbur." She spat the words out angrily.

Justin cursed himself, nodding. "I'm sorry, Winnie. I didn't –"

Winnie suddenly stood up. "Why are you here, Justin? Haven't you done enough to my family?"

Justin flinched back from her anger and looked down. "I just needed to tell you," he started. "It wasn't, it wasn't like you think. I didn't tell anyone on purpose. I didn't mean for this to happen."

Winnie's face relaxed somewhat. She paused, then she sat back down next to Justin. "Okay," she said. "Then tell me."

Justin did. He told her everything from the moment he had slipped up and told Amanda about Wilbur. He looked down as he spoke, and at times Winnie noticed sweat beading up on his forehead as he recounted his interactions with Hank. He stumbled through several parts, dropping his speech to a low murmur that, coupled with his reddening face, suggested to Winnie that he was deeply ashamed. She felt a flush of embarrassment for him as he spoke. When he had finished, he kept looking down, waiting for Winnie to speak.

Winnie simply looked at him for several minutes. She was overcome with an intense, almost overwhelming feeling of pity that made her nearly sick. She looked again at the healing cuts and bruises on his face, most of which she knew Bryan had inflicted, not knowing the entire story. She glanced down at his left hand and saw a deep indention around his index finger, where the skin would never fully return to its former shape. She saw a bluish hue on his right arm where she imagined Hank had recently grabbed him, and she wondered how many other bruises were not visible to her.

Winnie sighed, searched for words, and found none. She reached out her left hand and held his right. He felt hot and sweaty in the thick summer air, and she suddenly thought that he looked much younger than he was, younger than her even, with the unsure expression that young people often wear.

He glanced up at her tentatively, and, seeing that she was no longer glaring at him, he attempted to smile again. He squeezed her hand lightly, and she returned his smile. He thought that she looked exhausted and pale, but she no longer looked angry.

Winnie released his hand and sighed heavily. "So what are you doing now? How can you stay with Hank after what he did – I don't just mean to Wilbur, but to you?"

Justin furrowed his brow and looked directly at Winnie. "I'm leaving." He tilted his head backward, apparently in the direction of his truck, and added, "I've already got all my stuff packed and in the truck. I'm leaving tonight."

Winnie looked at him with wide eyes. Despite not having spoken to Justin in over a month, she felt a twinge of sadness at losing him. But she heard just a touch of excitement in his voice, and she knew that for once, he was making the right decision for himself.

She suddenly thought about something and frowned. "What about Conner?" she asked.

The fleeting smile quickly fell from Justin's face, and he looked down again. "I mean, Conner's not mine, you know? I do the best I can for him, but I can't make decisions about him, and Amanda's not really – she's not interested in talking about options."

He breathed out a heavy sigh and continued. "I'm gonna try to get a job fishing, maybe with some big commercial operation. Then, you know, if I can save some money, then maybe I can get Amanda to move out, you know? Maybe she and Conner can get their own place and get out of there. I know" – he ran his hands through his hair – "I know it's not a good, not a *safe* place for him. I know that. I just can't fix that right now."

Winnie saw the stress on his face. Not knowing what to add, she simply nodded.

"So you're leaving tonight?" Winnie asked.

Justin nodded. "Yeah, as soon as I leave here."

"Does Hank know?"

Justin shook his head.

Winnie laughed lightly, and Justin looked up.

"I'd like to see the look on his face when he finds out," she said, smiling.

Justin grinned a little. "Yeah," he laughed. "He'll be pissed as hell."

Winnie glanced back over her shoulder, and she noticed Justin tense beside her.

"Do you, do you want to see Bryan?" she asked. "I mean, I can go talk to him first."

Justin looked down for a second, then he slowly shook his head. "No, I don't think so."

Winnie felt a bit of pain in her chest. "You know he was just trying to protect me, right? You get that, don't you?"

Justin smiled and nodded. "Yeah, Winnie, I definitely do. It's no big thing."

They sat for a few more minutes in silence, until Winnie heard the slight buzzing of Justin's phone. He pulled it out of his pocket, looked down at it, frowned, and then, after a moment of hesitation, pressed a button to silence it.

"Hank looking for you already?" Winnie asked in a slightly teasing tone.

"No," Justin said. "It's an alarm at the farm. We get automated alerts whenever one goes off. It's probably nothing," he said, shaking his head.

A moment later, his phone buzzed again, and, before he could look at it, it buzzed a third time.

Justin stared down at the phone and furrowed his brow.

"What's wrong?" Winnie asked, seeing his face.

He shook his head. "It's, it's all the alarms. They're all going off." He looked up, sighed, and stood up.

"So are you not leaving now?" Winnie asked.

"No, I am, but, I mean, I'll just go by and check. One more time won't kill me." Justin scratched his head and looked at Winnie.

"I'm really glad you talked to me, Winnie."

Winnie nodded. "Me too." She paused, looked again toward the house, and said, "You sure you don't wanna see Bryan? I'm afraid," she spoke slowly and carefully. "I'm afraid he's going to regret things when he understands the full story."

Justin considered a moment, then he shook his head again. "He'll be okay. And, I'll be back at some point, you know? It's just not good timing right now. Too many, too many emotions."

Winnie nodded. She stood up, looked up at Justin, then gave him a strong hug. She felt him accept her embrace then raise his arms to squeeze her tightly. A moment later, he loosened his hold and pulled back.

He grinned and said, "Thanks again, Winnie."

She nodded, smiled, and watched as he headed back through the yard in the direction of the road. He turned as he was just fading into the darkness, and, as a final goodbye, he gave a slightly awkward wave.

CHAPTER XXVI

When he was still at least half a mile away, Justin saw the flames rising up from the farm. Confusion settled over him, as he wondered how the hell there could be so many flames in so many places. He accelerated his truck, feeling an overpowering urge to get to the farm as quickly as possible.

As he pulled his truck up to the pig buildings, he saw that all four of the buildings appeared to be on fire. Red hot flames streamed upward at the end of the buildings, lighting up the entire front of the farm. The heat was already palpable, and Justin was taken back by it when he first exited his truck. Squeals, more like screams, rose up from the buildings, and a constant murmuring of grunts and snorts sounded like a train speeding toward the farm.

Justin hesitated a moment, unsure of the best course of action. There had been a small fire, once, due to a shorted-out fan, but that had been easy enough to contain. He had been much younger, not yet working on the farm, and Hank had gotten the text that the alarm was going off. Hank had taken him to the farm, and he had seen the fire.

What Justin remembered most about the last fire was that the pigs had refused to move. While Hank was trying to extinguish the fire, Justin had thought he would open the pens and get the pigs out. He had run inside the blazing building, barely able to open his eyes against the intense heat, and he had started opening the pig pens. To his surprise, none of the pigs had moved. They simply milled about in their pens, looking at him with wide eyes and grunting incessantly. He had yelled at them to move, but not one had. He would have started pulling them out, but Hank, realizing what he had done, had come in, shaken him, and told him to get the damn pens shut up and get the hell out of the building.

Now, looking at the sight before him, Justin realized that there was no point in attempting to get the pigs out. Instead, he needed to get the fire out.

He pulled out his phone and quickly called 911 to relay the information. As he was on the phone, he moved between the buildings to get a better view of the fires. He hung up the phone just as he rounded a corner at a slight jog and ran directly into someone.

Justin hissed out a breath as the wind was knocked out of him, and he tumbled backward onto the ground. He scrambled up quickly and peered in front of him.

The stranger had stumbled at the impact, but that was all. He stood solid in front of Justin, and he took a step forward as Justin stared at him, moving his face slightly into the reddish glow from the fire.

"Darren?" Justin said, confused.

Darren looked at Justin for a minute without saying anything. His eyes were wide and intense, giving Justin a slight feeling of unease. Before he said a word, Jenna appeared, somewhat breathless, at his side.

"Justin," she said in surprise, stopping short. She looked at Darren, but Darren was too focused on Justin to return her stare.

Justin tilted his head at them in confusion. "What are you doing here?" he asked, shaking his head, as if that might sort out everything for him.

Darren said nothing, but Jenna took a step forward. "We saw the flames," she said. She tilted her head in one direction, apparently toward her parents' home. "We were both home, and we saw the flames. We figured you'd need help."

Justin slowly nodded, looking from Darren to Jenna and back again.

"Okay," he said. "I called 911, but we're so far out it'll take a while. We gotta work on getting the fire out." Justin, trying to push away his questions about Darren and Jenna, tried to get his mind back on task.

"There's some hoses at the end of each building. I'll show you. Maybe we can make a dent in the fire or at least slow it down," Justin said.

Jenna nodded and pulled on Darren's arm. They both followed Justin, as he nearly ran to the first building. He went to the end of the building, where a hose was wrapped tightly around a hose reel. He turned on the spigot and started to unwind the hose, as Jenna and Darren stood behind him, watching.

In his haste, Justin stumbled backward as he unrolled the hose, and he fell hard on the ground. Darren reached out and pulled him up. Justin grinned a quick thanks, but then, as he was standing within inches of Darren, he felt his face freeze. He momentarily held his breath as he recognized a strong odor on Darren – gasoline.

Justin furrowed his brow and looked up at Darren, who stood a solid foot taller than him.

"What the fuck –" Justin breathed out in a low, harsh whisper. He tried to step back, but Darren held his arm where he had pulled him up.

"I'm sorry, Justin," Darren said, and the pained look in his eyes suggested that his words actually had some truth to them.

"You did this," Justin said more than asked. He heard sirens faintly approaching in the distance, and he felt some relief.

Jenna, who had been a few feet back, moved forward. She put a hand on Darren's arm, where he still clung to Justin. After he shared a quick glance with his sister, Darren released Justin. Justin moved a step back and stood there, facing them.

Justin shook his head and ran his hands through his hair. "Why would you do this, Jenna? You have your God damn court case – why do this? Do you know how insane this is? Do you know you're probably going to fucking prison?"

Justin glared at Jenna angrily. She returned his stare. Her eyes were wide, suggesting just a touch of fear, but she held her head up as she spoke.

"There was no other choice, Justin. This case will drag on for years. We both know that. And really, it doesn't matter how good our lawyer is. Agriculture always wins in this state." She sneered. "And all the while, all the while the lawyers fight this out, and we fork out thousands or even tens of thousands to keep the fight going, all the while my parents are sitting in their pig shit-covered house, hardly able to breathe through the fucking stink, getting sicker every day." She was salivating heavily, and spit spurted out as she spoke.

Justin was shaking his head vigorously with his eyes closed. "This is so crazy," he said, opening his eyes to look at Jenna. "I don't have time for this, Jenna. I have to put the fire out."

Justin started to move away, but out of the corner of his eye he saw Darren make a move toward him. He side stepped him and moved back, but he froze as he saw Darren take out a small pistol and raise it toward him.

Well fuck, he thought, lifting his hands slightly. *Why the hell didn't I just leave?*

"Darren," Jenna said sharply, her tone suggesting she was not aware that Darren had brought a gun.

"We'll go to prison for this, Jenna," Darren said slowly, regurgitating Justin's words. He spoke to Jenna but kept his eyes fixed on Justin, who was starting to breathe heavily.

Jenna shook her head. "He's not going to tell, Darren." She looked at Justin.

Justin looked back at her with a confused expression. *Wasn't he?* He considered this for the first time.

Darren frowned. "Of course he is, Jenna. What are you talking about? Why the hell wouldn't he tell?"

Jenna moved closer to Darren. He readjusted his grip on the gun.

"He won't," Jenna said. "Darren, I've hated Justin for a long time." She shot a glance at Justin, and he looked down. "But, I know him – we both know him. He won't tell."

Darren, for the first time, took his eyes off of Justin and looked at Jenna. He considered her, then he looked back at Justin, who was looking down and taking in deep breaths and releasing them slowly.

"Are you gonna tell?" Darren asked.

Justin looked up. He looked first at Darren, then at Jenna, then back to Darren again. He shook his head. "Honestly, Darren, I don't know. I just want to get the God damn fire out."

The sirens had increased in volume, but Justin suspected it would still be a few minutes before they arrived – plenty of time to shoot someone and let them bleed out on the ground. He swallowed and waited.

Darren sighed, looked at Jenna again, and finally lowered the gun. Justin breathed out heavily, visibly relaxed, and reached down for the hose. He lifted it awkwardly, realizing that the release of tension from the last few minutes had made him weak and shaky. He gave Darren and Jenna another look, and then he moved away from them and toward the fire. He somewhat expected to feel the piercing pain of a bullet in his back as he moved toward the fire, but he felt nothing, and, when he turned back, Darren and Jenna were gone.

Justin turned the hose toward the fire, which was now rising at least two stories into the air. The water sizzled as it hit the flames, but it did very little to actually quell the blaze. Justin cursed repeatedly to himself as he waved the impotent water over the fire, unable to reduce the flames. He remembered that Hank had once looked at installing a sprinkler system in the buildings, after a neighboring farm had lost around 12,000 pigs following a large fire during a summer drought. The sprinklers were expensive, and Hank had said that they cost more than the pigs were worth.

This thought made Justin grin an ugly, spiteful grin. *Well, Hank, here it is. No sprinklers, no pigs. That's pretty much the gist of it.*

The heat seemed to be increasing as Justin stood fighting the fire. It now felt like a nearly tangible wall, pushing him backward, away from the building. Sweat was dripping down his face, and he heard the murmur of the pigs rising into an unbearable roar.

He took a step back and blinked his eyes, which were leaking tears from the heat and dry air. He wiped his brow with his sleeve, took a breath, and prepared to make another attack on the fire.

He could tell that the fire trucks were nearly at the end of the driveway now.

Justin heard the crunch of gravel and looked up to see Hank barreling toward him. Hank looked insane in the red light of the fire, with his face twisted into a look of anger so sinister that he resembled a cartoon character. *No, not a cartoon,* Justin thought. You would not put such a crazed person into a child's television show. That would leave countless children with nightmares for weeks. No, he looked more like some desperate character you would see at a roadside circus – something slightly inhuman and dangerous.

Justin dropped the hose and took a step back as Hank moved toward him.

"What the hell is going on, Justin?" Hank demanded, nearly knocking Justin over in his hasty approach.

"The buildings are on fire," Justin said flatly. "The fire department should be here soon."

Hank looked around, pressing his lips together tightly.

"And how," Hank started, growling out the words, "how the hell did these fires get started?" He glared at Justin. "I know these were set," he said, accusation dripping from his words.

Justin looked at him, then he shrugged.

Hank glared at him angrily, but Justin simply looked back steadily and said nothing. He heard what sounded like a large truck pulling up in the front of the farm. He turned to pick the hose back up, and he felt Hank grab him by the shoulder. Hank slung him around to face him, and Justin gritted his teeth as he turned, anticipating a blow to the face.

Hank lowered his face close to Justin's. "I know you packed your shit up, boy. I know you think you're too good for all this and you're leaving." Hank sneered. "Did you set these? Is this a little goodbye gift from you?" Hank gave Justin a sharp shake as he as questioned him, causing his head to snap forward.

Justin felt exhausted – exhausted not only from trying to get the fire out but even more exhausted from the mental strain of dealing with Jenna and Darren. He looked wearily at Hank.

"I didn't set the fires, Hank," he said. "But, yeah, I'm going. I'm done with this. Good luck to you."

Justin pulled back from Hank and started to walk away.

"God damn it, Justin," Hank yelled. "If you didn't set the fires, you sure as shit know who did. You better fucking tell me right now."

Justin, who had taken a few steps away from Hank, now paused. He looked down and furrowed his brow. He considered what Hank had said, and then, without looking at him, he kept walking.

"God damn it, Justin. Don't you walk away from me!" he heard Hank bellow.

Justin paused again and looked at the fires tearing into the long pig buildings. He heard the screaming of the pigs, smelled the sickening scent of burning flesh, and saw the dark, toxic air billowing up in clouds and covering up any visible stars in the night sky. He thought for a moment how pointless this all seemed and how preventable this had all been. He shook his head, gave a light chuckle, and took a step in the direction of his truck.

Justin heard a slight whirring noise as the metal bar cut through the air and smashed against the side of his head. He had no time to react, but instead he simply blinked, gave a soft groan, and fell to the ground. Blood began to slowly leak from his broken head and pool around him. His eyes slowly closed as he lay on the ground.

Hank, breathing heavily, took a step away from Justin. The rebar fell from his hand, and he looked at his unconscious son with palpable disgust. He started to move away but was thrown to the ground by someone stronger than himself.

"Jenkins!" a voice cried out behind him. "Jesus, Jenkins!"

Hank felt a heavy weight on his back and found himself unable to stand. Beside him, he heard the clatter of apparatus clinking and clanging as a fireman came around the corner of the building. The fireman, breathless, leaned over with his hands on his knees.

"Jesus," he said, looking around.

"Jenkins!" The voice came from behind Hank. "Jenkins, check on the kid. He hit him pretty hard. And radio that we need an ambulance now."

Jenkins, looking wide-eyed at an unseen speaker behind Hank, moved over to Justin. He reached down, pulled back a hand that was soaked in blood, and looked back at the speaker, his eyes widening to a degree that would not have seemed possible.

"Walsh, Walsh, it's not good," Jenkins said slowly.

Walsh nodded. "Okay, we need that ambulance, and we need some deputies."

Hank had started to struggle, but Walsh centered his weight on his back, making it impossible for him to rise.

"You need to stay there, you son of a bitch," Walsh said. "Wait for the cops to get here."

Walsh looked up and saw that Jenkins was still standing motionless over Justin, with his eyes wide and a confused expression on his face.

"Jenkins," Walsh said slowly. "Jenkins, buddy, look at me."

Jenkins, still frozen, managed to raise his eyes to look at Walsh.

"Jenkins, I want you to go get Anders, okay? Tell him we need the first aid kit, okay? Tell him to see about an ambulance and then to come here. Got it?" Walsh waited for Jenkins to nod.

"Then, I want you to make sure the deputies are coming, and then you can tend to the fires, okay?"

Jenkins nodded slowly, then he moved back toward the front of the farm.

Once Jenkins had gone, Hank again attempted to get up, but Walsh was easily able to keep him down.

"Get the fuck off me," Hank growled. "This is my fucking property, and that's my fucking son. You've got no business here."

Walsh looked at Justin as he lay on the ground. He was still, except for a slow rise and fall of his chest as he breathed.

Walsh considered the scene for a moment. Until Hank's most recent statement, he had not realized that the man he was holding down, who he had seen bash in the head of the boy bleeding out on the ground, was the boy's father. Walsh had three boys himself, and what he had just seen, coupled with the information that it was the boy's father who had given the blow, made his stomach turn with nausea.

He thought of his oldest boy, Turner, who had just turned seventeen. When Turner was younger, the boy had, in a fit of anger over something most likely trivial, kicked their dog, Cheyenne. Cheyenne had yelped, and Walsh, in reaction, had knocked the boy to the ground with the back of his hand. He knew that the blow had not really hurt, and that he had knocked Turner off balance and caused him to fall, but Walsh distinctly remembered Turner's face. The boy had laid on the ground and looked up at him, eyes wide and reddening with forced back tears. He had looked both hurt and betrayed, and Walsh had felt a sick feeling as he saw his son's expression. He had reached down to pull him to his feet, and Turner had flinched back, causing Walsh to feel a deep and sickening regret. He had never again raised a hand to Turner or either of his other sons.

Now, looking at the boy on the ground, he imagined what he must have felt to have been knocked down by his own father. He hoped that the boy did not know who hit him. That would be best.

Walsh heard the jingling of keys and saw Anders approaching.

"Anders," he called. "Take a look at the kid. His head's busted."

Anders, a tall, thin, dark-headed man with small round glasses that covered his small beady eyes, nodded at Walsh and then moved to Justin. He looked at him for a moment, took in a breath slowly, then started tending to his bleeding head. After a few minutes, he had a bandage wrapped around Justin's head to stop the bleeding. Nearly as soon as that was done, Walsh heard the sound of the ambulance pulling in.

"Over here," Walsh yelled. Two men rushed over, looked around quickly, then, after Walsh waved them in the direction of Justin, they focused on the boy with the smashed head. One of the men disappeared and returned with a stretcher, onto which they loaded Justin and carried him to the ambulance.

A few moments later, Jenkins returned with a deputy by his side. The deputy was young and dark-headed. Walsh thought that he hardly looked older than his oldest son. Unlike most deputies that Walsh ran into on these fire calls, this deputy was still slim and healthy. He had no gut sticking over the top of his pants but rather fit well into his uniform. His skin had a tanned, toned appearance, unlike the pale, loose skin present on the majority of the sheriff's deputies.

The deputy furrowed his brow when he saw Walsh and the man on the ground.

"He's the one who assaulted the boy?" the young deputy asked, nodding toward Hank.

Walsh nodded. "That's right. He's apparently the boy's father."

The deputy raised his eyebrows at that information. "Okay, thank you. I'll take it from here."

Walsh hesitated, then he slowly got up off of Hank. Hank quickly stood up. He glared at Walsh and then took a few steps toward the deputy.

The deputy put up his left hand for Hank to stop, and his right hand lowered to his gun. "Woah, woah," the deputy said. "Hold up right there, partner."

Hank, obviously infuriated by the instructions, stopped, but he visibly gritted his teeth. His hands were clenched in tight fists that opened and closed as he stood in the glow of the fire.

"This is my property," Hank growled.

The deputy nodded. "That may be, but we're gonna have to get a statement down at the station. I'm gonna need you to come with me."

The deputy reached out and put a hand on Hank's shoulder, and Hank jerked back with a grimace.

The deputy sighed and frowned. "Come on, then," he said, coaxing Hank. "Let's go get in the car."

Hank seemed to be almost growling. He turned back to Walsh and, for a moment, looked as if he might lunge at him. Instead, he exhaled deeply, then he turned and followed the young deputy to his patrol car.

With Hank gone, Walsh turned to the fire. To say it was out of control would have been an understatement. The fire was really a multitude of fires. Four buildings had separate fires, but the flames rose and seemed to intertwine in a blistering furnace. Despite the late hour, he could see almost clearly around him from the flames. He saw several other firefighters, including Jenkins, attempting to control the flames, which danced wildly against the night sky.

Jenkins was advancing on the fire like a soldier going into battle. His face was set, his teeth clenched, and his eyes focused on the task ahead. Walsh gave a short laugh. Jenkins could never handle the people on these fire calls. Yes, tonight had been a bit worse than usual as far as the people element goes, but even a distressed wife or a crying child would be too much for him. He would freeze up, stumble over his words, and look around awkwardly until Walsh or someone else came to rescue him. Walsh knew that people often thought that Jenkins had no brains at all, but really, he was probably the best fireman on the team. He just dealt better with fire than people, which, to some degree, Walsh could understand.

Walsh checked on his team members, then he made a quick trip to the front of the farm to see if any new firefighters had arrived. He saw that the deputy had Mr. Father-of-the-Year in the back of his patrol car, and the ambulance was nowhere in sight.

Good, Walsh thought. *Maybe the kid has a chance.*

Walsh turned to go join the rest of his team, but he hesitated as he heard another vehicle pull up. He heard a door slam and turned to see a boy who appeared to be in his late teens or early twenties standing by a pickup truck and looking around wide eyed at the blazing buildings.

Walsh glanced at the deputy, who was sitting in his car and typing something on his laptop. He obviously had no intention of getting out and handling this newcomer to the scene. Walsh sighed and walked over to the boy.

"Son," Walsh said. "We've got a fire here. You need to get out of here."

The boy looked at him and seemed about to speak, but no words came.

Walsh frowned. He did not have time for this.

"Son," Walsh said, but the boy was looking away from him, toward the fires.

"Son," Walsh said louder. He reached out and grasped the boy's shoulder, causing him to startle and look at him.

"Son, what's your name?"

The boy stared at him for a moment, then he managed to say, "Bryan."

"Okay, Bryan, why are you here?" Walsh asked, speaking slowly.

"I'm, I'm looking for someone. Justin. This is his father's farm." Bryan kept scanning the farm for signs of Justin.

Walsh breathed out heavily. He nodded toward the patrol car. "Is that the father?" he asked.

Bryan turned his head and saw Hank glaring at him from the back of the patrol car. Pure hatred seethed out of Hank's eyes as he looked at Bryan.

Bryan's confused expression contorted into one of anger and disgust. His upper lip lifted into a sneer. "That's him," he breathed.

"Okay," Walsh said, nodding and looking down. He gave Bryan's shoulder a light squeeze to pull his attention back. "Your friend is at the hospital. You need to go there."

Bryan's attention shot back to Walsh. "What? Why? What's wrong?"

Walsh shook his head. Better to not get involved, he thought. But the pained look on Bryan's face was more than he could stomach.

"The father," he said, choosing his words carefully. "The father – *his* father – hit him pretty hard in the head. He was," Walsh sighed, "he was bleeding a lot."

Walsh saw a look of sick dread come over Bryan's face.

"You need to go on to the hospital if you want to see him, okay?" Walsh said, gently guiding Bryan back toward his truck.

Bryan nodded but still seemed dazed. Walsh got him to his truck, waited a moment while he climbed into the driver's seat, and then watched as the boy pulled out and turned in the direction of the hospital.

Walsh sighed, scratched his head, and then turned and headed back toward the fires.

CHAPTER XXVII

Bryan spent the majority of the next two weeks in the hospital. The evening of the fire, after Justin had left the Bradford home, Winnie had gone to Bryan. Bryan cringed when he thought of his immediate reaction on hearing that Justin had been there. He had stood up and nearly flown to the back porch, completely ignoring Winnie's protestations and ready to attack if he caught sight of Justin.

When he was satisfied that Justin was no longer there, he had finally stopped to listen to Winnie, who was becoming angry herself. As she spoke, his anger started to cool, and by the time she had finished, his feeling of rage was completely replaced with a feeling of regret.

"Shit," Bryan said, staring at Winnie. "I didn't know." A pained expression came over his face, and he started to shake his head.

"Neither did I," Winnie said quietly. "But maybe, maybe we should have."

Bryan looked at her, struggling to resist the urge to lean over the side of the porch and vomit.

"You said he went to the farm?" Bryan asked.

Winnie nodded. "Yeah, he said all the alarms were going off."

Bryan looked down, considered this, then started moving toward the front of the house and his truck.

"Are you going there?" Winnie asked.

Bryan nodded. "Yeah. Yeah. I've got to talk to him before he leaves."

Bryan had left after that, gone to the farm, and found the chaos there.

That was two weeks ago, and since then, he had been in the hospital day and night, sitting in Justin's room, waiting for him to wake up.

Bryan did not understand anything about the machines hooked to Justin, other than the fact that they were keeping him alive. He had been unconscious for two weeks, and through it all those machines had hummed and clicked, keeping him breathing and his heart beating.

Winnie had been with Bryan most of the time, but Mama and Pa had insisted that she go home each night. If Bryan stayed at the hospital, which he did more than half of the time, she would return in the morning with breakfast and coffee for him.

Bryan knew from the local news that the destruction to the farm had been substantial. It had taken the firefighters over four hours to finally calm the flames. By that point, most of the pigs – somewhere between six and eight thousand of them – were dead. Many of those remaining had to be "put down," according to one article. The same article noted that the farm owner had "lost his mind" and attempted to kill his son and that he was now in jail and awaiting trial.

At least one good thing came of all this, Bryan thought, considering Hank.

Amanda had come to see Justin twice during the two weeks. Bryan, uncomfortable in her presence, had left the room when she came in. She had simply sat down next to Justin's bed and stared at him blankly. If she was feeling something, Bryan could not tell it.

Another week passed, and Amanda returned for another visit. This time she had Conner. Bryan stood to leave, and she held out a hand to stop him. Winnie was also present, and she stood up next to Bryan, eyeing Amanda carefully.

"Wait," Amanda said. "I need to tell you something." She looked down and sighed. When she looked back up, her eyes were red and moist.

"They're asking me to make a decision." She glanced at Justin, then back at Bryan. "They say it's unlikely he will wake up." She paused for a moment. When Bryan said nothing but rather continued staring at her, she continued.

"They want to know when I think they should cut the machines," she said flatly.

Bryan's eyes widened, and Winnie's mouth fell open.

"You can't let them do that," Winnie said, with a touch of accusation.

Amanda pressed her lips together tightly and looked at Winnie. A trace of hatred still remained. Bryan saw it and stepped slightly in front of Winnie.

"Why not wait a little longer, Amanda? Something could change," he said.

Amanda shook her head. "It's not going to change, Bryan." She looked up at him, continuing to shake her head. "It's not."

Bryan felt a bit of panic rising in him. He furrowed his brow and reached out to touch Amanda's arm.

"Amanda, please, wait just a bit longer. He'll wake up. You'll see. He will." Bryan tried to make eye contact, but Amanda was looking down.

Amanda's eyes locked on the cold tile floor. After a moment, she took in a deep, deliberate breath, then she looked up squarely at Bryan. "I've brought Conner to say goodbye," she said. "You should do the same. I'm giving them the okay to turn the machines off tonight."

Bryan looked at Amanda with a blank expression. He shook his head slightly back and forth. He opened his mouth, but he said nothing.

Beside him, Winnie's hands went to her mouth, and a small strangled cry escaped her lips. She clamped her hands over her mouth, and nothing further came out. Her eyes were narrowing, and tears were starting to trickle out the sides. Bryan put an arm around her and pulled her close to him. She buried her face in his shirt and started sobbing. Her shoulders shook furiously, and Bryan's shirt was soon damp with her tears.

As Bryan held Winnie close to him, he noticed Conner. Conner had approached Justin and was watching him, flicking his eyes back and forth between the motionless body on the bed and the rhythmically beeping machines beside him.

Conner put both of his small hands on one of Justin's somewhat cold and still hands. He laced his fingers through Justin's and looked up at him.

"Uncle Jus?" he asked shyly, looking hopeful, but no response came. His face fell, and he let his eyes fall back to Justin's hand.

Amanda looked away from Bryan and to Conner, with some slight annoyance.

"Conner," she started, somewhat coldly, "Uncle Justin can't hear you. He's asleep, and the doctors here say he's gonna keep sleeping for a while. You go ahead and tell him goodbye, okay?"

Conner looked at his mother without full understanding but apparently comprehending that something significant – and bad – was happening. His eyes filled up with tears, and his face reddened. He threw back his head, opened his mouth, and started wailing.

"Conner!" Amanda said sharply, moving toward the boy. "There's no point in squawking like that. Say goodbye and let's go."

The boy kept crying. Bryan stood looking at Amanda, and Winnie, still sobbing herself, finally removed her face from her brother's shirt and took a step over to the small child. She put her hand gently on his back and rubbed it in small circles. The boy stopped his screeching, but his eyes still flowed with tears.

Bryan took a step toward Amanda, who was staring at Winnie and Conner with a dull look of hatred. Her upper lip was pulled up in a sneer.

"Amanda," Bryan said. "Please don't do this. Give it a bit longer. Please."

Amanda turned and stared at Bryan. She pulled her mouth into a slight smile – not a friendly smile, but a cold, ironic smile. She shook her head.

"I'm sorry, Bryan," she said. "But I've made my decision."

Amanda turned, brushed quickly past Winnie, and took Conner's hand. She glanced down at Justin, pressed her lips together tightly, then started pulling Conner away.

Conner screamed and clung to Justin's hand. He held fast as Amanda cursed and pulled him away, causing Justin to be pulled slightly to one side of the bed.

"God damn it, Conner," Amanda cursed. "Come on."

Amanda reached back and pried Conner's fingers off of Justin's. She scooped the boy up as he screamed and kicked, and, without another word, she carried him out of the room. Winnie and Bryan could still hear him screaming for "Uncle Jus" as he disappeared down the hallway.

Winnie looked at Bryan for a moment, then she ran to him and started sobbing again. They spent the next few hours in this manner, with Winnie sobbing in sporadic spurts and Bryan looking blank and helpless.

Toward the late afternoon, when the sun was getting low in the sky, Jeffrey and Mama J entered the room. Jeffrey grinned goofily at Bryan, then he went over and sat down next to Justin. Mama J gave Bryan a hard stare at first, then she relaxed, opened her arms, and moved over to him for a long, steady embrace.

As Bryan hugged her, the smell of mothballs, ammonia, and stale coffee washed over him. She pulled back, held him by the shoulders, and looked at him. She kept her face just inches away from his, and he could see her yellow-stained, crooked teeth.

"I'm glad you're here," she said, patting Bryan on the shoulder. "It would mean a lot to him."

Bryan flushed, and Mama J smiled, released him, and sat down beside Jeffrey.

Mama J and Jeffrey stayed a while, talking to Justin, holding his hand, and pushing his somewhat shaggy bangs out of his closed eyes. Finally, as the last of the daylight was dimming, two hospital staff appeared. Both were in scrubs, and one had on a white coat, suggesting to Bryan that he was a doctor.

The doctor gave a nod and a barely perceptible smile, then, as if he suddenly remembered what was about to happen, he quickly removed the smile and looked slightly embarrassed. Mama J was giving him a disgusted look with her brow furrowed.

"You here to do the deed?" Mama J asked flatly.

The doctor raised his eyebrows and stammered, apparently taken off guard by Mama J's abrupt question.

"Oh, yeah, yes, I'm here to, to cut life support for Mr. Brewer." The doctor looked down, then he glanced back up and quickly added, "Per the wishes of his sister."

Jeffrey seemed unaware of any of the statements being made. He was simply looking at Justin and seemed to have been talking to him in a low voice. Winnie started crying again; although, this time she did so quietly, looking down with large teardrops leaking from her eyes and falling to the floor. Mama J kept her eyes leveled on the doctor, a look of contempt building on her face.

Bryan stared at the doctor blankly. He was struggling to understand how this was possible – how it could be legal to take away someone's life support, as the doctor put it, and just let them lie there and die.

The doctor looked awkwardly at the nurse, who smiled pleasantly back at him. He sighed and took a step over to the main machine hooked up to Justin, the one that kept beep, beep, beeping and flashing a bright red light at intervals.

The doctor looked over some paperwork that the nurse held, then he nodded, put a hand on the machine, and looked back at Bryan, Winnie, Mama J, and Jeffrey.

"I'm very sorry," he said, and his tone suggested that he meant it. He started to change the settings on the machine, but Bryan suddenly jumped up and moved toward the doctor. Bryan put his hand on the doctor's to stop him from making any further moves.

The doctor, who appeared to be just a few years older than Bryan, with slick, dark hair brushed to one side, flinched back and looked wide eyed at Bryan. Bryan suddenly wondered if the doctor often dealt with irate family members in these sorts of situations.

Bryan saw the nurse silently move to press a call button, and he quickly removed his hand from the doctor's, fearing that he would be thrown out of the room in a matter of seconds. He remained standing near him, though, unwilling to move away.

"Please," Bryan said. "Can't you wait a bit? See if he wakes up? I mean he has to wake up at some point. Or maybe there's something else you can try?"

The doctor watched Bryan carefully, his brow furrowing. His eyes flicked past Bryan to the door, and without turning Bryan knew that more staff had arrived, most likely there to remove Bryan if he tried to interfere again.

The doctor, looking a bit more comfortable, returned his gaze to Bryan. He shook his head slowly.

"No," he said. "No, there's nothing more we can do, and these are his family's wishes." The doctor glanced around the room. "Is there anyone from the family here?"

Mama J scoffed, and Jeffrey continued looking around as if he had just been told a somewhat confusing joke. Winnie just looked up with bloodshot eyes and a tired expression.

The doctor, looking a bit surprised, frowned and looked at Bryan again.

"We're not blood," Bryan said, "but I guess we're the closest thing he has to family."

The doctor nodded. He sighed again, then he put a hand on Bryan's shoulder.

"I have to continue," he said carefully. He waited for Bryan's response.

Bryan opened his mouth, but he could find no words. He looked at Winnie, and her head was down. She was shaking quietly, and he knew she was crying again. He then glanced at Mama J, who gave him a stern look and a slow nod. He turned back to the doctor, who was still watching him. He felt desperate, but he could think of no options. He looked down, nodded, and then took a step back, away from the doctor.

The doctor watched him a moment, then he sighed and pushed several of the buttons on the machine. The electric whir of the machine slowed and then stopped. The beeping associated with Justin's heartbeat continued and seemed louder now that the other noises had stopped.

Bryan saw Justin's chest rise and fall for several minutes. He half thought that at any second Justin would sit up in the bed and grin at him, chuckling and saying, "Got you, man." He looked at his face, which was now fairly free of the bruises he had inflicted. He saw a small white scar that stood out on his upper lip against his otherwise tanned skin, and Bryan immediately felt sick, knowing that the scar was a remnant of where he had punched him, knocking his lip into his teeth and splitting it open. He remembered that the last time he had seen Justin awake had been right after this moment, when he had told Justin that his whole family was fucking insane and that he had better stay away from him. He vividly remembered the hurt look on his face, and, with a sickening dread that spread over his entire body, he realized that that look would be imprinted on his mind for the rest of his life.

Bryan looked up as the beeping following Justin's heartrate sped up. He felt a moment of hopefulness and glanced up at the doctor. The doctor was looking at Justin with the same flat expression that he had carried earlier. The hope faded from Bryan, and the beeping, seeming to hit a peak in its frequency, suddenly stopped and turned into one single, endless tone. Bryan watched Justin for a moment and found that he could no longer see his chest rising and falling. He felt his legs go weak, and, as he crumpled to the cold, hard floor, he felt Winnie's arms wrap around him and hold him tightly.

EPILOGUE

A decade later, as Bryan drove down the worn, dusty road to his homeplace, he looked out at the fields of unruly cotton. He could not help but smile, as the small tufts of white fluff on the tangled plants were brilliant under the bright summer sky. As his "forest green" Toyota Tacoma cut through the thick heat of early August, whisps of cotton were swept up by the motion of the truck and followed behind it momentarily.

A pointed pain struck through the left side of Bryan's chest as he thought of Mama and how she loved that little piece of cotton she kept on the mantle. She had been gone for two years, and not a day went by that Bryan did not think of her. She had a way of lighting up the room when she came in, and so many rooms had remained dark since she passed.

The cancer had come for her quickly, and really Bryan thought that was a blessing. She had spent very little time being sick, and even that short amount of time had nearly crushed Pa. It had been only three months from when she first felt a bit sick to when she finally collapsed on the kitchen floor, unable to get up, passing two days later in the hospital. During that time, she had lost a significant portion of her body weight. She had worn her clothes loosely, so it had been hard to tell, but the skin on her face had become slack and gaunt, and dark circles had been perpetually present under her eyes. Her good humor had remained until the end, and, when she was resting in her hospital bed on the last day of her life, she had winked weakly at Pa and said, "Guess I get to go first, slow poke."

Bryan and Winnie had come home more during those three months than they had been home during the previous six years. Following Justin's death, Bryan had wanted to be alone. He had spent four months backpacking along the Appalachian trail, covering a significant distance, until he finally woke one morning to the sharp trill of a sparrow, looked up at the serenely blue sky, and decided that it was time to go home.

At home, he had enrolled in the local community college, working part-time jobs – one at a hardware store and the other at a sandwich shop – to cover the costs. After two years, by the time Winnie was graduating and preparing to start at State, Bryan was ready to transfer there as well. They started at State the same year, sharing a cheap apartment off campus.

There were a significant number of conflicts in the beginning, as Bryan's overly protective nature interfered with Winnie's desire to make the most of being away from home for the first time in her life. When she brought home a pot-smoking musician with lazy eyes, Bryan had roughly thrown him out of the apartment, threatening to do worse if he ever returned. Winnie had glared at Bryan and slammed her bedroom door in his face. The next day, she had gone out looking for another apartment. She had found one the following day, but before she had a chance to complete the paperwork, Bryan had come to her with an apology, asking her to stay.

"You're not Pa, and you're sure as hell not Mama – you get that?" she had asked sharply, with a hand on one hip.

Bryan had looked down and frowned. He shuffled momentarily, then, hearing her sigh and worried that she might lose patience at any moment, he had nodded.

"I'm sorry, Winnie. I really am," he looked up at her. "You know you're so much better than guys like that, though, so it's just really hard." He saw that she was frowning, and he quickly added, "I'll try to give you space."

Winnie had hesitated, then she hugged his neck and said, "And I'll try not to make bad decisions, big brother."

The first year at college, Winnie had only gone home for Thanksgiving and Christmas. Bryan had pushed her to go more often, as he made the two-hour drive at least once each month, but she would just smile, flick her hair, and say that she would go next time. Bryan knew, or at least suspected, that the break in her relationship with Pa was the main reason for her refusal to visit home. She spoke on the phone with Mama constantly, but whenever Mama asked her to hold so that Pa might speak with her, she would say that she had to get back to her studies or get off the phone so that she would not be late to a meeting.

When Bryan would visit home, Pa would ask, somewhat hesitantly, about Winnie, and Bryan would fill him in on the latest news. Bryan saw the anxious way that Pa waited for the news and how he eagerly listened to hear what was going on with his daughter. Bryan felt a deep pain in his chest as he watched, seeing the strain and age growing on Pa's face. He knew that

Winnie had forgiven Justin for his involvement in Wilbur's death, but she was unable to get past the role Pa had played.

Winnie had been focused on journalism since starting college, and she stayed during the summers, working internships at various local papers. While Bryan had planned to go home during the summer, he realized that Winnie would not be able to afford the small apartment on her own, so he had stayed as well, working at the university to help keep up with the apartment's scant rent.

After her first year, Winnie only went home for Christmas, and by the time Mama passed a few years later, Winnie had stopped going home at all. Upon graduation, Winnie got a job at a local newspaper where she had previously interned. She was ecstatic. She wrote countless stories over the next several years and built her reputation as a journalist.

Bryan had more trouble finding his calling. He had to focus fairly hard to get through his base classes, and beyond that, he had no idea what he should take. Winnie suggested that he do some volunteer work to see what he liked, and he did. He volunteered at a local animal shelter, at the downtown soup kitchen, with a student group focused on conservation that helped build and maintain the trails around campus, and with several other student groups committed to saving the world in various ways.

He had nearly given up and decided to call it quits when he volunteered with an afterschool program for "troubled" youth, as the director put it. This one had been Winnie's idea, and he had frowned when she suggested it.

"Just give it a try," she said smiling. "I think you might like it more than you think."

She was right. Bryan had enjoyed working with the kids, talking to them about their lives, and trying his best to displace the surly looks on their faces with actual smiles. After a week of this, he had officially changed his major from sports education to sociology, and he had completed it with a minor in childhood psychology.

After graduation, he had worked at a local nonprofit committed to helping at-risk teens. Bryan found the work incredibly stressful, time-consuming, and generally draining, but he kept at it, unable to pull himself away. He was still sharing an apartment with Winnie, and, with her also working at all hours to finish her stories, the two managed fairly well.

A few years into the job, Bryan called Winnie one night and told her that he was at the emergency room. He asked her to not panic – which of course only increased her panic – and told her that he just needed a ride home. One of the teens he had been working with on a daily basis had decided that he had had enough of Mr. Bryan's prodding and had stabbed him with a well-sharpened pencil. The pencil had gone into his left shoulder and had hurt worse than anything Bryan could remember, but it had avoided hitting anything important, as the doctor, attempting some humor, had put it.

Winnie had arrived at the hospital looking whiter than the unruly whisps of cotton. She had broken into sobs when she saw Bryan, and she had hugged him so tightly that pain from the wound shot through his body, causing him to inhale quickly as he forced down a scream.

"I think it's time for you to find a new job," Winnie had said through broken cries.

"And miss all this excitement?" Bryan had said, teasingly.

Since that night, Winnie had been on the lookout for another job for Bryan. Two months ago, she had found one.

"Hey, you remember Miranda?" she asked as soon as he arrived home one evening.

Bryan looked at her blankly.

"You know," Winnie said with slight annoyance. "She was on the school paper with me? Dark hair, blue eyes? She came over pretty often actually." Winnie looked at him expectantly.

"Um, maybe?" Bryan answered, shrugging.

Winnie rolled her eyes and put a hand on her hip. "You're impossible," she said, with a touch of Mama's playfulness. "Anyway, she's been working with kids since she got out of school, and she just started up this place in Ashfield for teenagers with attitude issues. It's all boys. I think it's basically like an orphanage, 'cause the kids live there, but they all have one issue or another, so they go there rather than a normal group home or foster home or whatnot."

Bryan had made his way to the refrigerator and was looking inside. Winnie sighed and narrowed her eyes at him.

"Well Miranda," Winnie said more loudly, "is looking for a program coordinator for her place. She wants somebody to help with the daily programming for these kids, to come up with things for them to do to help with their attitudes or whatever."

Winnie stopped talking and waited until Bryan, noticing the silence, looked up at her.

"*And*," she said loudly and slowly when he looked up, "I recommended you to her."

Bryan frowned. "Oh come on, Winnie. I'm fine where I am."

Winnie frowned herself and threw her hands up. "Bryan, no you're not. You need to get out of there. Plus," she hesitated, looking down, "plus, you know, it would be good for Pa to have one of us near him, now that Mama's gone." She hesitated and looked down. "And, and it can't be me."

At this, Bryan looked at her squarely. He said nothing, but she could tell that her words were sinking into him.

"Look," Winnie said. "Just talk to Miranda. See what you think."

Bryan continued staring at her, his brow starting to furrow, then he slowly nodded.

"Okay," he said. "I'll talk to her."

Winnie beamed. "Good," she smiled. "I've already told her you would call."

Bryan frowned, but not unkindly.

"And," Winnie added, grinning, "she always had a huge crush on you, so, you know, heads up." She laughed, and Bryan watched her as she turned and left the kitchen.

As usual, Winnie had been right. Bryan talked to Miranda and found that her organization, Hopewell House, was just what he had been looking for. He would have the chance to work with kids in true need, who had no parents present for one reason or another. These were kids who absolutely needed some guidance and positive influences in their lives, and he was ready to provide it.

If Bryan were honest to himself, Miranda was part of the attraction for the job, as well. He remembered her when he saw her. She had wavy black hair that curled around her ears, and her eyes were a bright blue that lit up when she talked. What he remembered most about her was that she had a surprisingly

241

hearty laugh for a girl. Years ago, on lazy Sunday afternoons when she would be hanging out in Winnie's room, painting her nails a dark shade of plum and sharing the latest high school hallway gossip, Bryan could hear her deep belly laughs all the way outside, and she still had that way of laughing now.

He moved back home, deciding that it would not hurt to stay with Pa for a while. Pa was clearly happy to have him back, as, since Mama had passed, he had struggled daily to find the motivation to keep moving forward. He smiled when Bryan proposed moving back in, and Bryan saw the pain and desperation that constantly haunted his face start to lighten, for the moment at least.

Now, as Bryan left behind the cotton fields and drove further into town, he thought about the day ahead. He was two weeks into the job and already knew this was the right fit for him. He had met most, but not all, of Hopewell House's residents over the past two weeks, and his goal was to meet the remaining kids by the end of the week.

After checking his calls and emails, he started making rounds through the building, talking with a few kids he had already met, and introducing himself to a few whose faces were new to him. Some of the kids would look at him shyly, sometimes refusing or unable to make eye contact, while others would roll their eyes and mumble under their breath. Bryan did not particularly mind one way or the other.

Today, before going back to his office, he stepped outside into a sunlit courtyard. He saw a few boys milling about by one of the picnic tables. They glanced up as he came out, watched him a moment with cautious expressions, then turned back to one another to continue their conversation in a low murmur.

Bryan glanced around the courtyard and saw another boy at the far end of the yard. He was fair haired, and he was sitting cross-legged on the ground, peering over a book that, based on its fairly large size and breadth, appeared to be a textbook.

Bryan did not recognize the boy, so he headed in his direction. When he was within a few yards, the boy looked up and started. His pale blue eyes locked onto Bryan's for a moment, then he quickly dropped his gaze and tensed, remaining where he was.

Bryan slowed and stopped a few feet from him. He dropped to one knee to reach eye level with the boy.

"Hey, friend," Bryan said, smiling.

The boy glanced up briefly, furrowed his brow, then looked down again. He gave a mumbled "hey" and kept his eyes locked on his book.

Bryan, used to this kind of reluctance and wondering how long it would take the boy to open up, said, "I'm Bryan. I'm the program coordinator here. I pretty much just started. What's your name?"

The boy fidgeted slightly with his hands before looking up. When he looked up this time, he held Bryan's gaze for a moment, and, on seeing the blue eyes and furrowed brow, a hint of recognition came over Bryan. He stared harder at the boy, trying to remember where he had seen him.

The boy, apparently seeing the confusion in Bryan's face, returned an uncertain stare. He shifted uneasily, and his eyes darted around the yard.

"Hey," Bryan said, raising one hand, "it's okay. You're fine. What's your name?"

The boy eyed Bryan nervously, then he said, in a quiet voice, "Conner."

Bryan raised his eyebrows as his eyes widened. He felt his heart thumping against his chest.

"Conner what?" he asked, trying to keep his voice steady.

He must have been unsuccessful, as Conner was starting to inch backward, away from Bryan. Bryan felt a strong urge to grab him, to keep him from running, but he knew that doing so would wipe out any chance he had at breaking through to the boy.

Bryan leaned back, to give the boy space, and held up a hand, again repeating, "It's okay. You're safe here. What's your last name?"

The boy hesitated, again looked around, then said, "Conner Brewer."

Bryan exhaled slowly and shakily. As he stared at Conner, a flood of memory washed over him, contorting his face into a pained expression.

Conner, clearly uneasy, stood up slowly without taking his eyes off of Bryan. He glanced quickly behind him, but he saw that he was near the end of the courtyard, with only a brick wall behind him marking the edge of the yard. He swallowed and ran his right hand through his somewhat shaggy hair.

Bryan realized the effect his behavior was having on Conner, so he shook his head to clear his thoughts, ran his hand over his face, and stood up.

"I'm sorry," Bryan said. "I'm sorry, Conner. I'm not trying to upset you. I just, I knew your uncle."

The boy, who had been looking past Bryan and considering making a run for it, suddenly flicked his eyes up to Bryan's.

"Justin?" he asked.

Bryan nodded. "Yes, yeah, Justin. We worked –" Bryan paused. "We were friends. I met him the summer before –" Bryan trailed off and did not finish.

The tension in Conner's face had relaxed somewhat, and he was looking at Bryan with curiosity now.

"I met you, too," Bryan added, giving a slight smile. "And your mama. How is she?"

Conner frowned and looked down, and Bryan suddenly realized that if she were well, then Conner would likely not be here talking to him.

Conner shook his head but said nothing.

"I'm very sorry," Bryan said. Then, not feeling that it was particularly true, but not knowing what else to say, he added, "She always seemed to love you very much."

Conner tilted his head at Bryan.

Bryan then gave a half grin and added, "Your uncle Justin was crazy about you."

Conner brightened. "Yeah, I know, I can remember a little." After a moment, Conner said, "Can you tell me more about him? I don't remember that much."

Bryan smiled. "Yes, I definitely can. And, I'd like to get to know you a little better, too. Is that okay? I see a lot of him in you."

Bryan grinned at Conner, and Conner, finally mostly at ease, grinned back.

Conner nodded, "Yeah, that sounds good."

* * *

On the way home, Bryan drove past the fields where the Brewer farm had once been located. When he arrived, he had to check his GPS to make sure the location was correct, as it looked nothing like it had looked so many summers ago.

There was no sign of a building anywhere in sight. Instead, there was some sort of bright green, leafy plant covering the fields as far as he could see. The leaves swayed lazily in the warm summer breeze, and there was no sound other than the rustle of the plants and the calls of a few crows.

Bryan pulled over onto the side of the road and remained parked for a few minutes, simply taking in the change in scenery. He heard a low rumble approaching, and he turned to see a young, blonde-headed boy in a light blue pickup truck pulling into the long drive that led to the center of the fields.

The boy slowed as he neared Bryan and then put the truck in park beside him.

"You need some help?" the boy yelled from his truck, smiling.

Bryan shook his head. "No, sorry, I'll get off your land."

The boy eyed him with interest.

Bryan, before starting his truck, said, "I just spent a summer working here a long time ago. It was a pig farm then, though."

"No shit," the boy said, surprised. "I didn't know it was a pig farm."

"What are those crops?" Bryan asked, motioning to the fields.

"Soybeans," the boy said, grinning. "Pig food," he added, laughing.

Bryan grinned but could not quite get to a laugh. "Ah," he said nodding. "Well, it sure has changed a lot." He looked back at the fields one more time, then he nodded and gave a quick wave to the boy in the truck. He backed up and pulled back onto the road.

Dust billowed into dirty brown clouds as the pickup rambled down the two-lane road.